Dear Reader,

She's your one-person ~~support~~ ~~team~~ advocate. Your voice ~~of~~ ~~reason~~ ~~and~~ comfort~~er~~. She always knows how to make you ~~feel~~ ~~better~~ ~~when~~ it just isn't your day. She's your mom. And one day of thanks just doesn't seem enough. This Mother's Day, don't forget to let Mom know how truly one-of-a-kind she is—make her queen for the day. And if you're a mother yourself, you know firsthand that motherhood is the toughest—and most important—job you'll ever love. So don't forget to treat yourself to your favorite indulgence!

In celebration of moms everywhere, we've put together this collection of classic stories featuring reader favorites Diana Palmer, Candace Camp and Elizabeth Bevarly. This charming anthology features some very special moms as they meet and fall in love with some very special heroes.

A "Calamity Mom" is all Faulkner Scott's young son wants. The boy is determined to appoint Shelly Astor his new mom after she saves his life. Looks as if there's another accident in the works—Faulkner and Shelly may *fall* head over heels!

Beth Sutton's "Tabloid Baby" might not be famous producer Jackson Prescott's love child, but there may indeed be some cupid wings hidden beneath the newborn's receiving blanket. Who better than a baby to bring two soul mates together?

"A Daddy for Her Daughters" is what Naomi Carmichael gets when she finds herself doing parent duty with *über*-hunk Sloan Sullivan. Now, if Naomi could just figure out how to get the sexy bachelor to say "I do," she'd be one happy mama!

We hope you enjoy this must-have springtime collection by three of the best-loved authors in romance!

The Editors,
HQN Books

Rave reviews for Diana Palmer

"Nobody does it better."
—Award-winning author Linda Howard

"Palmer knows how
to make the sparks fly…heartwarming."
—*Publishers Weekly* on *Renegade*

"Nobody tops Diana Palmer when it comes to delivering
pure, undiluted romance. I love her stories."
—*New York Times* bestselling author Jayne Ann Krentz

Praise for the novels of Candace Camp

"This one has it all: smooth writing, an intelligent story,
engaging characters, and sexual tension that positively
sizzles."—*All About Romance* on *Swept Away*

"I loved this wonderful story! Camp is so-o-o-o good."
—*Romance Reviews* on *Impulse*

"Readers who are fond of Amanda Quick…
will like this one."
—Mrs. Giggles on *Mesmerized*

Romance fans love Elizabeth Bevarly

"[Readers] will be rewarded by Lucy's convincing
transformation from ditzy daughter into capable wife."
—*Publishers Weekly* on *The Ring on Her Finger*

"Elizabeth Bevarly knows how
to show readers a good time."
—*Oakland Press*

"Elizabeth Bevarly writes with irresistible style and wit."
—*New York Times* bestselling author Teresa Medeiros

motherhood

Diana Palmer
Candace Camp
Elizabeth Bevarly

HQN™

ISBN 0-373-77083-9

MOTHERHOOD

Copyright © 2005 by Harlequin Books S.A.

The publisher acknowledges the copyright holders of the individual works as follows:

CALAMITY MOM
Copyright © 1993 by Diana Palmer

TABLOID BABY
Copyright © 1998 by Candace Camp

A DADDY FOR HER DAUGHTERS
Copyright © 2002 by Elizabeth Bevarly

This edition published by arrangement with Harlequin Books S.A.

® and TM are trademarks of the publisher. Trademarks indicated with ® are registered in the United States Patent and Trademark Office, the Canadian Trade Marks Office and in other countries.

www.HQNBooks.com

Printed in U.S.A.

CONTENTS

CALAMITY MOM
Diana Palmer

Chapter One

THE BEACH WAS CROWDED. A group of college students on spring break were gathered around a ghetto blaster, happily unaware of the vicious looks they were getting from older sunbathers.

"Turn it down," Shelly Astor suggested, grinning as she nodded toward two glowering faces behind them on the beach. "You're creating enemies for us."

"Don't be a wet blanket," the boy chided. "We're young, it's spring break, no more biology and English and algebra for a solid, sweet week!"

"Yeah, right," another student muttered. "I might as well drown myself. I flunked my first exam in prealgebra!"

"Less fun, more pencil-to-paper contact," another suggested.

"Right, Mr. Egghead," came the reply and a glare. "Edwin here blew the curve in biology 101," he added, jerking his thumb at the tall, thin, redheaded boy. "He made 100."

"Dr. Flannery says I'm the best student he's ever had. Can I help it if I'm brilliant?" Edwin sighed.

"You're not brilliant in trig," Pete murmured to him, then said to the others, "I had to tutor him or he'd never have passed Bragg's exam."

"Can't you turn that damned thing down?" An exasperated bellow broke the silence.

"Have a heart, man!" Pete wailed, facing his attacker. "We just survived eight weeks of hell, not to mention trigonometry!"

"And one of us failed it!" Edwin yelled, pointing at Mark.

"We're all on the cutting edge here," Pete agreed, shaking his head. "If we don't get a music fix, God only knows what we might do to the world at large!"

The irate man began to laugh and threw up his hands. He made a dismissive gesture and lay back, closing his eyes in defeat.

Shelly grinned at her friends. "Pete's a sociology major," she whispered to Nan, who was her best friend. "Minoring in psych. Isn't he great?"

"A true credit to his alma mater," Nan agreed. She got up and went to dive into the surf, with Shelly at her side.

"Isn't it wonderful here?" Nan sighed. "And you weren't going to come!"

"I had to fight to get to go to college, much less come to Florida with the group for spring break," Shelly said quietly. She pushed back her windblown blond hair, and her soft blue eyes echoed the smile on her full lips. "My parents wanted me to go to finishing school and then join the young women's social club back home in Washington, D.C. Can you imagine?"

"You haven't told them that you want to become a caseworker for family and children's services, I guess?" Nan fished.

"My father would have a nervous breakdown," she mused. "They're sweet people, my parents, but they want to give me a life of luxury and serenity. I want to change the world." She glanced at dark-eyed Nan with a mischievous smile. "They think I'm demented. They have a nice husband picked out for me: Ivy League school, old family name, plenty of money." She shrugged her slender shoulders. "That's not what I want at all, but they won't take no for an answer. I had to threaten to get a job and go on the work/study program to get my father to pay my tuition."

"I wonder if all parents want to live through their children?" Nan asked. "Honestly my mother has pushed me toward nursing school since I was in grammar school, just because she got married and couldn't finish nurses' training. I get sick at the sight of blood, for Pete's sake!"

"Did someone mention my name?" Pete asked, surfacing beside them with a grin.

Nan sent a spray of water at him with a sweep of her palm, and all the serious discussions were drenched in horseplay.

BUT LATER, WHEN they went to the motel to change before supper, Shelly couldn't help wondering if she was ungrateful. Her father, a wealthy investment counselor, had given her every advantage during her youth. Her mother was a socialite and her brother was an eminent scientist. She had an impeccable background. But she had no desire to drift from luncheon to cocktail party, or even to do superficial charity work. She wanted to help people in trouble. She wanted to see the world as it was, out of her protected environment. Her parents couldn't, or wouldn't, understand that she had to feel useful, to know that her life had a purpose of some sort beyond learning the correct social graces.

She enjoyed school. She attended Thorn College, a small community college in Washington, D.C., where she was just one of the student body and accepted without hassle, despite her background. It was the kind of atmosphere that was friendly and warm without being invasive. She loved it.

Living off campus did limit some of her participation in social activities, but she didn't mind that. She'd always thought in her own mind that she was rather a cold woman—at least where men were concerned. She dated, and boys kissed her from time to time, but she felt nothing beyond surface pleasure at the contact of warm lips on her own. She had no desire to risk her life for the sake of curiosity, experimentation or for fear of ridicule. She was strong enough not to flinch at the condescending remarks from one of the more permissive girls. Someday, she thought, she would be glad that she hadn't followed the crowd. She stared at her reflection and smiled. "You-stick-in-the-mud," she told herself.

There was a quick knock on the door followed by Nan's entrance. "Aren't you ready *yet?*" she grumbled. She glared at Shelly's very conservative voile dress, yellow on black, with sandals and her long hair in a French braid. "You're not going like that?" she added, groaning. "Don't you have any idea what the current style is?"

"Sure. Spandex skirts or tights and funny smock blouses. But they're not me. This is."

"Wouldn't catch me dead in that." Nan sighed. Her curly hair sported a yellow-and-white bow, and her white tights were topped off by a multicolored short dress.

"You look super," Shelly said approvingly.

Nan struck a pose. "Call *Ebony* magazine and tell them I'm available for covers." She chuckled.

"You could do covers," came the serious reply. Nan really was lovely. Her skin had a soft café au lait demureness. Combined with her liquid black eyes and jet black hair and elegant facial structure, she would have been a knockout on the cover of any magazine. She looked like an Egyptian wall painting. "I've seen gorgeous movie stars who were uglier than you are," she added.

Nan chuckled. "You devil, you."

"I'm not kidding. Why haven't you ever thought of modeling?"

Nan shrugged. "I have a good brain," she said simply. "I don't want it to get lost in the shuffle. I'm going to be an archaeologist."

Shelly groaned. "Don't remind me that I have two more exams to go in introductory anthropology or I'll scream!"

"I'll coach you. You'll do fine."

"I won't! I barely passed biology! We've still got fossil forms of man and kinship systems and subsistence patterns to go...!"

"Piece of cake." Nan dismissed it. "Besides, you got Dr. Tabitha Harvey, and she's the best. Oops, I mean Dr. Tabitha Reed. Can you imagine her getting married? And to such a dish!" She shook her head. "But to get back to the subject, don't you realize that anthropology is *part* of sociology? How can you understand the way we are as a culture today without understanding how we came to be a culture in the first place?"

"Here you go again."

"I love it. You would, too, if you'd let yourself. I've taken every anthropology course Thorn College offers. I loved them all!"

"This stuff is hard."

"Life," Nan reminded her, "is hard. You can't appreciate a good grade in anthropology until you've had to dig for it." She looked surprised. "I made a funny!"

"On that note, we're leaving," Shelly murmured, dragging her friend out the door.

THEY HAD SUPPER IN THE SAME restaurant each night. It was their one extravagance, and mainly because Nan had a crush on one of the other diners, a student from Kenya whom she'd met on the beach.

Shelly looked forward to the evening ritual because of another patron who frequented the restaurant. She ran into him everywhere, accidentally. He nodded politely and never stopped to talk, but she watched him with open fascination, to the amusement of her friends. In fact, her fascination was a ruse to keep her friends from trying to pair her off with Pete. She liked Pete, but her attitudes weren't casual enough to suit him. By pretending infatuation for a stranger, she elicited not only sympathy for her unrequited love, but also avoided well-meaning matchmakers among the group she'd accompanied on spring break.

Her unwilling object of affection was beginning to notice, and be irritated by her, though. It had become a challenge to see how far she could push him before he exploded. The thought was oddly exciting for a woman who almost never took chances. In fact, in all her twenty-four years, he was the first man she'd ever pursued, even in fun. It was unlike her, but he wouldn't know that. Her flirting seemed to disturb and irritate him.

To complicate matters, he had a son, about twelve or so, and the son spent considerable time staring at Shelly. She was afraid he was developing a crush on her and she worried about trying to head it off while keeping up her facade of being infatuated with his father. Showing up here for dinner every night wasn't helping her situation, even if it did seem to be doing wonders for Nan's social life and give Shelly the opportunity to stare longingly at the man she'd singled out for public adoration.

As if she'd conjured him up in her thoughts, a movement caught Shelly's eye, and she saw him. He was tall and elegant, a striking man somewhere in his middle or late thirties with thick dark hair and pale silvery eyes. He had his son with him. The boy was a younger and much more amiable version of him. Shelly found herself wondering what the man did for a living. He was very handsome, but he didn't look the male-model type. He was probably someone who carried a gun, she thought. Maybe a secret agent, or a hired assassin. That thought amused her and she smiled mischievously. Before she could erase the smile, the man turned his head and saw it, and his glare was thunderous.

How could someone that handsome look so vicious and unfriendly? she wondered vaguely. And those silver eyes looked like cold steel in his unsmiling face. An ugly man might have an excuse for that black scowl, but this man looked like every hero she'd ever dreamed of. She put her chin in her hands and stared at him with a wistful smile. She was always so friendly that it was hard to accept that anyone could hate her on sight for no reason.

He looked taken aback by her refusal to be intimidated. But even if the scowl fell away, he didn't smile back. He turned his attention to a movement of white silk beside the table and abruptly stood up to seat a thin brunette. The boy with him glowered and made some reluctant remark, which prompted an angry look from his father. Undercurrents, Shelly thought, and began to analyze them. She felt a wave of sadness. She'd overheard a tidbit of gossip about him in the restaurant the night before—that he was a widower. She'd known that a man so handsome would have women hanging from both arms, but she had hoped he was unattached. It was her fate to be forever getting interested in the wrong man. She sighed wistfully.

"Stop staring at him," Nan chided, hitting her forearm with her napkin as she put it into her lap. "He'll get conceited."

"Sorry. He fascinates me. Isn't he dreamy?"

"He's years too old for you," Nan said firmly. "And that's probably his fiancée. They suit each other. He has a half-grown son, and you are a lowly college student, age notwithstanding. In point of fact, you are barely higher on the food chain than a bottom feeder, since you aren't even a sophomore yet."

"I'll be a sophomore after summer semester."

"Picky, picky. Eat your salad."

"Yes, Mama," she muttered, glaring at the younger woman, who only grinned.

THE NEXT DAY IT SEEMED to Shelly that providence was determined to throw her into the path of trouble. She always got up early in the mornings, before Nan stirred, and went down to the beach to enjoy the brief solitude at the ocean before the tourists obliterated the beach completely. She threw on her one-piece yellow bathing suit with a patterned chiffon shirt over it and laced up her sandals. For once she left her blond hair loose down her back. She liked the feel of the breeze in it.

This morning, she didn't find the beach empty. A lone figure stood looking seaward. He was tall, and had thick black hair. He was wearing white shorts that left his powerful, darkly tanned legs bare and a blue-and-white checked shirt, open over a broad, hair-roughened chest. He was watching the ocean with eyes that didn't seem to see it, a deep scowl carved into his handsome face.

Shelly gave him a wistful glance and took off down the beach in the opposite direction. She didn't want to infringe on his privacy. Since he was obviously attached, it would do her no good to go on mooning over him, for appearances or not. She was giving him up, she thought nobly, for his own good. That being settled, she strolled aimlessly down the beach, drinking in the sea air.

The stillness was seductive. The only sounds to be heard were the cries of the sea gulls and the watery growl of the ocean. Surf curled in foamy patterns up onto the damp beach, and tiny white sand crabs went scurrying for cover. They amused her and she laughed, a soft, breathy sound that seemed to carry.

"What can you find to laugh about at this hour of the morning?" came a rough, half-irritated deep voice from over her shoulder. "The damned coffee shop isn't even open yet. How do they expect people to survive daybreak without a dose of caffeine?"

With the vestiges of her amusement at the crabs still on her face, Shelly turned. And there he was, as handsome as a dark angel, his hands deep in the pockets of his white shorts.

He was devastating enough at long range. Close, like this, he was dynamite. She could hardly get her breath at all. Some sensual aroma exuded from him, like spice. He smelled and looked clean and fastidious, and she had to force herself not to stare at the physical perfection of his body. Hollywood would have loved him.

"I like coffee, too," she murmured shyly. She smiled at him, pushing back her pale, windblown hair. "But the sea air is almost as good."

"What were you laughing at?" he persisted.

"Them." She turned back to the crabs, one of which was busily digging himself a hole. He dived into it like a madman. "Don't they remind you of people running for trains in the subway?" She glanced at him wickedly. "And people who can't get their coffee early enough to suit them?"

He smiled unexpectedly, and her heart fell at his feet. She'd never seen anything so appealing as that handsome face with its chiseled mouth tugged up and those gray eyes that took on the sheen of mercury.

"Are your friends still in bed?"

She nodded. "Most of us have eight o'clock classes during the semester, so there isn't much opportunity to sleep late. Even if it's just for a week, this is a nice change."

She started walking again and he fell into step beside her. He was very tall. The top of her head came just to his shoulder.

"What's your major?" he asked.

"Sociology," she said. She flushed a little. "Sorry I was staring at you last night. I tend to carry people-watching to extremes," she said to excuse her blatant flirting.

He glanced at her cynically, and he didn't smile. "My son finds you fascinating."

"Yes," she said. "I'm afraid so."

"He's almost thirteen and a late bloomer. He hasn't paid much attention to girls until now."

She laughed. "I'm a bit old to be called a girl."

"You're still in college, aren't you?" he mused, obviously mistaking her for someone not much older than his son.

"Well, yes, I suppose I am." She didn't add that she'd only started last year, at the age of twenty-three. She'd always looked young for her age, and it was fun to pretend that she was still a teen. She stopped to pick up a seashell and study it. "I love shells. Nan chides me for it, but you should try to walk across tilled soil with her. She's down on her hands and knees at the first opportunity, wherever she sees disturbed dirt. Once she actually climbed down into a hole where men were digging out a water line! I'm glad they had a sense of humor."

"She's an archaeology student?"

"Other people are merely archaeology students—Nan is a *certifiable* archaeology student!"

He laughed. "Well, that's dedication, I suppose."

She stared out at the ocean. "They say there are probably Paleo-Indian sites out there." She nodded. "Buried when ocean levels rose with the melting of the glaciers in the late Pleistocene."

"I thought your friend was the archaeology student."

"When you spend a lot of time with them, it rubs off," she apologized. "I know more than I want to about fluted points and ancient stone tools."

"I can't say I've ever been exposed to that sort of prehistory. I majored in business and minored in economics."

She glanced up at him. "You're in business, then?"

He nodded. "I'm a banker."

"Does your son want to follow in your footsteps?"

His firm lips tugged down. "He does not. He thinks business is responsible for all the ecological upheaval on the planet. He wants to be an artist."

"You must be proud of him."

"Proud? I graduated from the Harvard school of business," he said, glaring at her. "What's good enough for me is good enough for him. He's being enrolled in a private school with R.O.T.C. When he graduates, he'll go to Harvard, as I did, and my father did."

She stopped. Here was someone else trying to live his child's life. "Shouldn't that be his decision?" she asked curiously.

He didn't bat an eyelash. "Aren't you young to question your elders?" he taunted.

"Listen, just because you've got a few years on me…!"

"More than fifteen, by the look of you."

She studied his face closely. It had some deep lines, and not many of them were around the corners of his eyes. He wasn't a smiling man. But perhaps he wasn't quite as young as she'd suspected, either. Then she realized that he was counting from what he thought her age was.

"I'm thirty-four. But that still makes me an old man compared to you," he murmured. "You don't look much older than Ben."

Her heart leaped. He was closer to her age than she'd realized, and much closer than he knew. "You seem very mature."

"Do I?" His eyes glittered as he studied her. "You're a beauty," he said unexpectedly, his silver gaze lingering on her flawless complexion and big pale blue eyes and wavy, long blond hair. "I was attracted to you the first time I saw you. But," he added with world-weary cynicism, "I was tired of buying sex with expensive gifts."

She felt her face go hot. He had entirely the wrong idea. "I'm…" she began, wanting to explain.

He held up a lean hand. "I'm still tired of it," he said. He studied her without smiling, and the look he gave her made her knees go weak, despite its faint arrogance. "Do your parents know that you're making blatant passes at total strangers? Do you really think they'd approve of your behavior?"

She almost gasped. "What my parents think is none of your business!"

"It certainly is, when I'm the man you're trying to seduce." He glared at her. "So let me set you straight. I don't take college girls to bed, and I don't appreciate being stalked by one. Play with children your own age from now on."

His statement left her blustering. "My goodness, just because I smiled at you a time or two…!"

"You did more than smile. You positively leered," he corrected.

"Will you stop saying that?" she cried. "For heaven's sake, I was only looking at you! And even if I was after that kind of…of thing, why would I pick a man with a son? Some father you are! Does he know that his father wanders all over the beach accusing people of propositioning him? And you must be attached—"

He was oddly watchful, not at all angry. He was studying her face with keen, faintly amused interest. "My, my, and you're not even redheaded," he murmured, watching the color come and go on that exquisite complexion. "My son is too smitten with you to consider my place in your thoughts, and I don't have a wife. She died some years ago. I do have a fiancée—almost," he added half under his breath.

"The poor woman!"

"She's quite well-to-do, in fact," he said, deliberately misunderstanding her. "So am I. Another reason to avoid college students, who are notoriously without means."

She wanted to tell him what her means were, but she was too angry to get the words out. She flushed furiously at being misjudged and insulted. She decided then and there not to tell him about her background. He'd have to get to know her for herself, not her "means."

"Thinking up appropriate replies?" he asked helpfully. "Something along the lines of feeding me to the sharks?"

"They'd have to draw straws so the loser could eat you!" she blurted out.

She turned and set off back down the beach, hot all over from her surge of fury.

She ran along the beach in her haste to get away from him. She'd been playing mind games with herself. She hadn't realized that he mistook her rapt regard for serious flirting. She'd certainly be more careful in future to keep her fantasies to herself! Never again would she so much as glance at that man!

It was a pity she didn't look back. He was standing where she left him with a peculiarly predatory look in his pale eyes, and he was laughing.

SHELLY AND NAN STUCK to the beach and the shops for the rest of the day, and that evening she persuaded Nan to go to a fast-food joint with some of the other students instead of the restaurant. She didn't dare tell anyone why, or confess the result of her stupid behavior. If Nan suspected, she was kind enough not to say anything.

Two good things had come out of the experience, Shelly thought as she now walked by herself along the beach. It had been two days since she'd run into the man. She'd managed to avoid the worshipful glances of Mr. Sexy's son, and she'd learned a painful lesson about obvious flirting. He was a banker. Wasn't he supposed to be dignified and faintly reticent and withdrawn? Her father was an investment counselor, and he was like that. Of course, he had inherited wealth, too, and that made him faintly arrogant. Mr. Sexy almost cornered the market on arrogance, of course, and conceit. She had to add conceit to the list, since he thought she couldn't wait to jump into bed with him!

I might have known, she told herself, *that no man could be that perfect to look at without having a few buried ugly flaws. Conceit, stupidity, arrogance…*

As she thought, she walked. There was a long pier that ran down from the hotel, and usually at the end of it were fishermen. But this particular day the pier was deserted. A sound was coming from it. A series of sharp cries.

Curious, Shelly walked onto it and started out toward the bay. The sounds grew louder. As she quickened her pace to reach the end of the pier, she heard splashing.

She stopped and peered over the edge.

"Help!" a young voice sputtered, and long, thin arms splashed for dear life. She knew that voice, and that face. It was the teenage son of Mr. Sexy, the one she'd been dodging for two days. Talk about fate!

She didn't stop to think. She tugged off her sandals and dived in after him, shoes, cutoffs, sleeveless white blouse and all. She'd taken a Red Cross lifesaving course and she knew what to do.

"Don't panic," she cautioned as she got behind him and caught him under the chin to protect herself. Drowning swimmers very often pulled their rescuers down with them, causing two deaths instead of one. "Stop flailing around and listen to me!" she said, moving her legs to keep afloat. "That's better. I'm going to tow you to shore. Try to relax. Let your body relax."

"I'll drown!" came the choking reply.

"No, you won't. Trust me."

There was a pause and a very exaggerated bout of breathing. "Okay."

"Good fellow. Here we go."

She struck out for shore, carrying the victim she'd appropriated along with her.

It wasn't that far to shore, but she was out of practice towing another person. By the time they reached shallow water, she was panting for breath along with the boy.

They flopped onto the beach and he coughed up water for several seconds.

"I thought I was a goner." He choked. "If you hadn't come along, I'd have drowned!" He looked at her and then grinned. "I'm sure you've heard the old axiom about saving a life."

She frowned. Her brain wasn't working. "What axiom?"

His grin grew even wider. "Why, that when you save a life, you're responsible for it as long as you live!" He threw his arms wide. "I'm yours!"

Chapter Two

"THANKS," SHE SAID. "But you can have your life back."

"Sorry, it doesn't work that way. You're stuck with me. Where are we going to live?"

She knew her expression was as perplexed as her thoughts. "Look, you're a nice boy…"

"I'm twelve and a half," he said. "I have all my own teeth, I'm in good health, I can do dishes and make beds. I don't mind cooking occasionally. You can trust me to feed and water whatever pets you possess," he concluded. "Oh, and I'm an Eagle Scout." He raised three fingers.

She glared at him. "Two fingers, not three fingers! Three fingers mean you're a Girl Scout!"

He snapped his fingers. "Darn." He looked at her. "Does that mean I have to give back the green dress?"

She burst into laughter. After the shock of seeing him almost drown, and the strain of rescue, her sense of humor came back in full force. She fell back onto the beach and laughed until her stomach hurt.

"I can't stand it," she choked.

He grinned down at her. "Great. Let's go and feed me. I do eat a lot, but I can get a part-time job to help out with groceries."

"Your father is not going to give you to me," she told him somberly, and flushed when she remembered what his father had said to her two days ago, and what she'd said back. She'd been lucky, because she'd managed to avoid him ever since.

"Why not? He doesn't want me. He's trying to give me to a school with an R.O.T.C. and after I get out of there, he's going to sell my soul to Harvard."

"Don't knock college fees," she told him firmly. "I've had to fight every step of the way for mine."

"Yeah, Dad and I saw you with the other college students," he agreed. "Dad was right. You really *are* pretty," he added critically, watching her look of surprise. "Do you like chess and can you play computer games? Oh, you have to like dogs, because I've got one."

She looked around to make sure he was talking to her.

"Well?" he persisted.

"I can play chess," she said. "I like cats, but my dad has two golden retrievers and I get along with them. I don't know about computer games…"

"That's okay. I can teach you."

"What am I auditioning for?"

"My mother, of course," he said. "Dad's business partner has this daughter, and she's done everything but move in with us trying to get Dad to marry her! She looks like two-day-old whitefish, she eats carrot sticks and health food and she takes aerobics. She hates me," he added curtly. "She's the one who thinks I belong in a school—a faraway school."

"And you don't want to go."

"I hate guns and stuff," he said heavily. They were both beginning to dry out in the sun. His hair was dark brown, a little lighter than his father's. He had those same silver-gray eyes.

"I know what you mean. My parents didn't want me to go to college." She leaned toward him. "My dad's an investment counselor. All he knows are numbers and accounting."

"Sounds just like my dad." He scowled. "Listen, you won't hold that against him? I mean, he's real handsome and he has good manners. He's a little bad-tempered," he confessed, "and he leaves his clothes laying all over the bedroom so that Jennie—she's our maid—fusses. But he's got a kind heart."

"That makes up for a lot," she said, thinking privately that his father hadn't been particularly kind to her.

"He likes animals, too."

"You're very nice to offer me your life, and your father, to boot," she said pleasantly, "but I've got at least three more years of college to go, and I can't think about a family for a long time. I want to be a social worker."

"My dad's real social," he remarked. "You can work on him."

"God forbid," she said under her breath.

"He'll grow on you," he persisted. "He's rich."

She knew about being rich. She came from old money herself. His father seemed to think that she was after his. That was almost laughable.

"Money can't buy a lot of things," she reminded him.

"Name three."

"Love. Happiness. Peace of mind."

He threw up his hands. "I give up!"

"Try to give up swimming alone," she advised. "It's dangerous."

"Actually," he confessed, "I didn't just jump in on purpose as much as I tripped over a bucket and fell in. But I would have been just as dead."

"Indeed you would. Keep your mind on what you are doing," she admonished.

He saluted her. "Roger, wilco."

"You might like R.O.T.C.," she said.

He shrugged. "I like to paint birds."

"Oh, boy."

"See what I mean? My dad hunts ducks. He wants me to. I hate it!"

This boy had a real problem. She didn't know what to tell him. His father was obviously rock-headed and intractable.

"Have you been without your mother for a long time?" she asked gently.

"All my life. She died just after I was born. Dad and I get along all right, but we aren't close. He spends so much time at work, and out of the country on business, that I almost never see him. It's just Jennie and Mrs. Brady and me most of the time. They're good to me. We had a wonderful Christmas together…."

"Where was your father?" she exclaimed.

"He had to fly to Paris. *She* found out and got on the plane when he wasn't looking. Since he couldn't send her home, she went with him," he muttered.

"She?"

"Marie Dumaris," he said curtly.

"Maybe he loves her," she suggested.

"Ha! She comes from an uptown family and he's known her since Mom died. She was a cousin or something. She's always around. I guess he was too busy to notice other women, and she decided to acquire him. From the way she acts lately, she has."

Shelly could have debated that, about his father being too busy to notice women. From what little he'd said to her, she gathered that he was no stranger to brief liaisons. He'd even thought she was angling for one. The brunette's skinny form flashed into her mind and she wondered absently how a man could find pleasure in caressing ribs and bones with skin stretched over them.

"If he marries her, I'll run away," the boy said quietly. "It's bad enough that I don't get to say what I want to do with my life, or where I want to go to school. I can't stand having her for a stepmother as well." He looked up at Shelly. "We'll have to work fast, since you're only here for a week."

"I'm sorry to disappoint you, but I really don't want your father," she said.

"That leaves me," he said worriedly. "Look, I'm only twelve. I can't get married for years yet, and I'm too short for you. My dad's a much better bet."

"I don't want to get married," she said kindly. "Couldn't you settle for being friends?"

"That won't save me," he moaned. "What am I going to do? My whole life's an ongoing calamity!"

She knew how it felt to be young and helpless. She still had to fight her own well-meaning father to live her own life.

"Have you talked to your father? I mean, have you really talked to him, told him how you felt?"

He shrugged. "He thinks I'm just a kid. He doesn't talk *to* me, he talks *at* me. He tells me what I'm going to do and then he walks out."

"Just like my dad," she mused.

"Aren't fathers the pits?"

She chuckled. "Well, from time to time they are." She studied his wet profile. "Are you sure you're all right?"

"I'm fine. Are you?"

She nodded. "Just wet. And I think it would be a good idea if we both went and got dried off."

"Okay. I'll be back to see you later," he promised. "My name's Ben. Ben Scott. My dad's first name is Faulkner."

She shook the hand he offered. "I'm Shelly Astor."

"Nice to meet you. Shelly Scott would have a nice ring to it, don't you think?"

"Listen…"

"A life for a life," he reminded her. "Mine belongs to you, and you're responsible for it."

"I didn't do anything except pull you out of the ocean!"

"No. You saved me from a calamity," he said. "But we have several calamities to go. Calamity Mom—that's *you*," he added with a grin.

She glared at him. "I'm not a mother."

"Yes, you are."

"No!"

"Are so, are so, are so!" he called, and ran away, laughing.

She threw up her hands in frustrated impotence. Now what was she going to do? And how was she going to explain what had happened if his father came gunning for her after he was told that his son now had a mother? She didn't know where they came from, or anything about them.

She almost wished she'd never agreed to come with the other students on the trip. But it was too late now. She'd jumped into the ocean, and into the frying pan—so to speak.

THAT EVENING, SHE AND Nan walked through the lobby of their motel and came face-to-face with a haughty Marie Dumaris, with Faulkner Scott at her side, and a subdued Ben trailing behind.

The boy brightened at the sight of Shelly. "Hi, Mom!" he said brightly. Faulkner's eyebrows shot up and Marie bristled.

"She is *not* your mother!" Marie snapped.

"She is so," Ben told her belligerently.

Shelly colored, and Nan patted her on the shoulder. "I'll meet you at John's Burger Stand, okay?" she asked quickly, and retreated.

Shelly would have a few things to tell her later about desertion under fire, she thought wickedly. She didn't look at Faulkner. She was barely composed and painfully aware of her shabby attire. She and Nan had decided to have a casual supper, so she hadn't bothered over her appearance. She wasn't even wearing makeup. Marie had on a green silk pantsuit with designer shoes and bag. Last year's style, Shelly thought with gentle spite, but trendy enough. Shelly herself was wearing faded jeans and a worn blue-striped top with a button missing at the top.

"She says you shouldn't send me to military school." Ben set the cat among the pigeons, grinning as he retreated toward the television on one wall.

"I did not!" Shelly gasped.

"You have no right to comment on Faulkner's decisions about his son," Marie said with cool hauteur and a speaking look at Shelly's attire. "Really, I can't imagine that Ben's education is of any concern to a tacky little college girl." Her cold green eyes measured Shelly and found her lacking in every respect.

Shelly's eyebrows rose. Tacky college student? This social climbing carrot-eater was looking down her nose at Shelly? She could have burst out laughing, but it was hardly a matter for amusement.

Faulkner wasn't saying anything. He was watching Shelly with those devil's eyes, smiling faintly.

Shelly glared at him with bitter memories on her face. "Ben is my friend," she said, turning her eyes to Marie. "I have a vested interest in his future. Or so he says," she added under her breath. "He hates military school and he doesn't want to shoot things."

"Don't be absurd, they don't have to shoot anything! Besides," Marie added, "people have hunted since time began."

"They hunted when they had to eat," Shelly agreed. "That was before supermarkets and meat lockers."

"Faulkner enjoys hunting," Marie countered, smiling up at him. "He's very good at it."

Shelly nodded, staring at him. "Oh, I don't doubt it for a second," she agreed readily. "Drawing blood seems to be a specialty of his. You don't have any vampires in your family lineage…?"

Faulkner was trying not to smile, and Marie was about to explode, when Ben came running back up blowing a huge bubble.

"Throw that stupid bubble gum away," Marie told him icily. "And stop slouching. Must you dress and act like a street person?" She glanced haughtily at Shelly, beside whom Ben was standing. "It must be the influence."

How dare that woman talk about Ben that way, and in public! The youngster went scarlet and looked as if he wanted to go through the floor. That was the last straw. Shelly glared at her, her eyes deliberately noting Marie's silk jacket. "That particular jacket was on sale last fall, wasn't it? You do know that it's out of style this season?" She smiled deliberately, having delivered an insult calculated to turn the other woman's face white. It did, too.

Marie took an indignant breath. "My wardrobe is no concern of yours. Speaking of which…!"

"Ben, I want to know what's going on between you and Ms. Astor," Faulkner drawled, leaving Shelly stunned because she hadn't realized he knew her name.

"Nothing is going on. Ben and I are friends," Shelly said firmly.

"I don't want Ben associating with her," Marie said coldly.

"I hardly think that's your decision to make, Marie," Faulkner interrupted. "Ben told me what you did this afternoon," he added quietly, searching Shelly's eyes. "I'm in your debt. You're no shrinking violet when the chips are down, are you?"

"No guts, no glory," she quipped. He was making her nervous. The way he was watching her made her knees week. She had to get away. "Sorry, but I have friends waiting. See you, Ben."

Ben waved, but he looked miserable. And that haughty brunette treating him like a pet animal…! Shelly's blood boiled.

BEN GROUND HIS TEETH TOGETHER. He'd wanted to drag Shelly into his family circle, but Marie was spoiling everything!

"That was terrible of you, to involve your father with a haughty, ill-bred little tramp like that," Marie scolded Ben. "How could you…?"

"She saved my life," Ben told her curtly, his voice firm and authoritative, amazingly similar to his father's.

"She did what?" Marie asked, taken aback. They hadn't told her.

Ben sighed. "I fell off the pier. She jumped in and pulled me out."

Faulkner studied his son with new eyes. He'd done a lot of thinking since Shelly had exploded into their lives. Now he was regretting what he'd said to her. Her comments the other day had helped him to realize that he had a son he didn't even know. He'd spent years making money, traveling, letting business occupy every waking hour of his life. And in the process, Ben had become a stranger.

"Can we go and eat now?" Marie asked petulantly. "I'm hungry. We can have salads and spring water."

"I'm not having a salad and spring water," Ben told her belligerently. "I'm having a steak and a soda."

"Don't you talk that way to me!" Marie shot back. "And you're not having red meat…!"

"He can have a steak if he wants one," Faulkner told her coldly. "In fact, I'm having one myself. Let's go."

Ben and Marie wore equally shocked looks. Faulkner moved ahead of them toward the restaurant. He spared a sad, regretful glance toward the door where Shelly had vanished. He supposed he was going to have to apologize to her. He wasn't looking forward to it.

A LITTLE WHILE LATER, Shelly had worn out her meager supply of bad language on Marie's behavior and was catching her breath when Pete came up to join the two women at the burger place.

"There's a beach party tonight, dancing and beer. You two coming?" he asked.

"Sure," Nan said. "How can we resist dancing?"

Pete glared at her. "Well, there's me, too."

"I can resist you," Nan said, smiling.

"I can't," Shelly said with a theatrical sigh. "You make me swoon!"

Pete grinned. "Do I, really? What a treat! That's radical!"

"She's acting," Nan whispered loudly. "She's already promised to an investment broker back home."

Pete stared at Shelly blankly. "Are you?"

"My father keeps trying," Shelly said ruefully. "He wants to see me settled and secure." She laughed. "Well, I've got long legs and I can run fast. Not to worry. I'll escape."

"Make sure you escape by way of the beach," Pete made her promise. "We're going to have a ball."

"The last time he said that, six of us spent the night in the holding tank down at Fort Lauderdale."

"I gave you an intimate look at life in the raw," Pete said, wounded. "You learned incredible things about people."

"Three hookers, two drunks and a man accused of murder were in there with us," Nan translated. "The drunks were sick at the time," she added pointedly. "One threw up on me."

"Oh, my," Shelly mused.

"No police this time," Pete promised. "No drugs, no trouble. Drugs are stupid, anyway. We'll just drink beer and eat pizza and dance. Okay?"

"In that case, I'll come," Nan said.

"Me, too, I guess," Shelly said. "I don't have much of a social life these days."

Nan was looking past Shelly's shoulder. "I wouldn't say that."

Shelly followed the wide-eyed stare. Mr. Sexy was walking toward her, resplendent in his white slacks and electric blue silk shirt and white jacket. He looked very sophisticated, and women up and down the strip of developments were openly staring at him.

"Wow," Nan sighed softly.

Shelly had time to wonder what he'd done with Marie and Ben before he stopped in front of her.

"I'd like to speak to you. Alone," he added with a meaningful stare toward Nan and Pete.

"I'm a memory already," Pete said quickly.

"Same here." Nan followed him, leaving Shelly alone at the table with Faulkner.

He sat down, giving his surroundings a cold appraisal. His silver eyes settled on Shelly's face in its frame of wind-blown, wavy blond hair. Her complexion was perfect, softly pink, and her blue eyes were like pools at midnight. He studied her in reluctant silence, drinking in her beauty.

"Ben told me that you saved his life. I want to apologize for the things I said to you."

"Don't apologize for your bad manners, Mr. Scott," she said gently. "It would ruin your image."

He grimaced. "Is that how I sounded?"

"Despite what your woman friend thinks, I am neither a street person nor a lady of the evening," she said quietly. "As for Ben, I pulled him out of the water and we talked for a few minutes. That is the extent of our acquaintance. I have no desire to become his mother, despite the impression he may have given you."

"I appreciate what you did for Ben," he said quietly. "You may not think so, but he's very important to me."

"Is he?" she asked with faint sarcasm, and a ruddy flush ran over his high cheekbones.

"Yes, he is," he returned curtly. "I can do without any more insults from you."

"Isn't turnabout fair play? You've done nothing but insult me since the first time you spoke to me. All right, I shouldn't have flirted with you. I made eyes at you and pretended unrequited love to get my friends off my back, and it was wrong. But you had no right whatsoever to assume that because I smiled at you, I was eager and willing to warm your bed!"

"No, I didn't," he agreed surprisingly. "Perhaps I'm more jaded than I realized. You're very lovely. It's been my experience that most women with looks find a market for them."

"Perhaps you've known the wrong kind of women," she said. "And while we're on the subject, whether or not she's your fiancée, that woman has no right to talk to Ben as if he's a pet dog!"

His dark eyebrows arched and he smiled. "My, my."

"He's a fine boy. Better than you deserve, and a walking miracle considering the lack of guidance he's had."

He sighed slowly, watching her through narrowed eyes. He toyed with a plastic fork on the table and muscles rippled in his broad chest, dark hair visible through the thinness of his shirt as they moved.

"I've been busy supporting us," he said.

"Your son will be away from home for good in about six years," she reminded him. "Will he want to come back for visits then?"

He scowled. "What do you mean?"

"Ben doesn't want to be a military man. He doesn't want to go to a school with rigid discipline or become a hunter. He wants to be an artist. Is it really fair of you to try to relive your life through him?"

He looked shocked. "I wasn't."

"Ben doesn't see it that way." She grimaced. "Neither do I," she said honestly. "My father is just like you. I've had to fight him constantly to get to do anything my own way. He's got a husband all picked out for me. College, you see, is a waste of time for a woman."

He lifted an eyebrow and didn't reply.

"You think that way, too, I gather. A woman's place is in the bedroom and the kitchen—"

"I wouldn't know," he said curtly. "My mother was a corporate executive. She was never home."

She stared at him warily.

"Surprised?" he asked mockingly. "My father worked himself to death before he was fifty. Mother inherited the company. In order to keep it going, she decided that I was expendable. She stuck me in a private school and devoted the rest of her short life to high finance. She died when I was in my final year of college. She dropped dead of a heart attack in the middle of a heated board meeting."

She was shocked. "I see."

"No, you don't see anything. My father thought my mother was a home-loving woman who would want to give him children and love and care for them until they were old enough to live alone. But she never wanted children in the first place. God knows, she said so often enough when I was growing up!"

"Oh, you poor man," she said softly, and with genuine sympathy. "I'm so sorry!"

He glowered at her. "I don't need pity!"

"Some women aren't suited to domestic life," she said gently. "Surely you know that by now?"

"Then they shouldn't marry."

She searched his hard face. A lot of things were clearing up in her mind. He was raising his son as he'd been raised, in the only way he knew.

"There are other ways to make a boy self-sufficient and independent," she said. "You don't have to banish him to make him strong. He thinks you don't want him."

He got to his feet, towering over her. "I can manage my own private life."

"Heavens, what kind of life is it?" she asked, searching

his silver eyes. "You aren't happy. Neither is Ben. Haven't you learned that business isn't enough?"

Her assessment of his life hurt. He'd already had enough of Marie's criticism that he was too soft with Ben, and here was Shelly telling him he was too hard. He reacted more violently than he meant to. "What is enough?" he asked abruptly. "To turn out a penniless, scruffy little college student like you?"

Probably if his assumption about her had been right, his attitude would have hurt. But it didn't. She smiled mockingly. "I wouldn't presume to think so," she said. "Marie's just your style. But I feel sorry for Ben. He's sensitive, despite his brashness. She'll destroy him if you let her."

He gave her a speaking glare and strode off with anger evident in every line of his hard body.

SHE DRANK TOO MUCH that night. She hadn't eaten right, she'd been too annoyed at Mr. Sexy, and before she knew it, she'd had much too much beer. Three cans of it, when she hardly ever had more than a sip of white wine. If Nan hadn't been there to look after her, her carelessness could have had terrible repercussions. Pete, who'd had four cans of beer on his own, was more than willing to take advantage of her condition. But Nan warded him off, parceled up Shelly and herded her back to the motel.

"Idiot," she muttered as she helped a swaying Shelly into the lobby. "What on earth would you do without me?"

"I'm not drunk, Nan," Shelly said, and smiled vacantly.

"Of course not! Come on, hang on to me."

She got into the elevator with her heavy burden and was about to select the proper floor number when Faulkner and his ladylove joined them.

"Of all the disgusting things I've ever seen," Marie said with a haughty glare. "You college girls have no morals at all, have you?"

Nan stared at the other woman without speaking, her liquid black eyes full of muffled insults. Marie flushed and looked away, but Nan didn't stop staring.

"Hello, Miss Ribs," Shelly said, smiling at the thin brunette. "If you had a little meat on those bird bones, you'd be much more attractive. I expect Mr. Sexy over there bruises his fingers every time he touches you."

"How dare you!" Marie exploded.

"Here's our floor. Out you go, my dear," Nan mumbled, helping Shelly out of the elevator.

"I'll see you tomorrow, Marie. Go on up." Faulkner got off the elevator and, without breaking stride, lifted Shelly in his arms. "Lead the way."

The elevator closed on Marie's startled gasp, and Nan hesitated only a minute before she started off down the hall toward their ocean-facing room.

Shelly looked into Faulkner's hard, dark face with dazed curiosity. "I'm sorry you don't like me."

He smiled gently. "Don't I?" he asked. "Hold tight, little one. I wouldn't want to drop you."

He pulled her very close and eased her hot face into the curve of his neck, enveloping her in his warm strength and the seductive scent of his cologne. She felt like heaven in his arms. He had to stifle a groan.

Shelly was barely aware of his reaction, but she was feeling something similar. Smiling, she sighed and drifted into a warm, wonderful sleep.

Chapter Three

SHELLY WOKE THE NEXT MORNING with a frightful headache and vague memories of being carried to bed in a man's hard arms.

Nan held out a bottle of aspirin and a cup of black coffee the minute Shelly walked into the living room. "Here," she said curtly. "And next time you pull a silly stunt like that, you'll be sharing a single room at this motel, all alone, by yourself."

"Don't yell," Shelly groaned.

"I'm whispering, *can't you tell?*"

"Oh!" Shelly put her hands over her ears. "You're horrible!"

"One of us is, that's for sure."

"I dreamed that I was being carried," she murmured, holding her aching head.

"That wasn't a dream."

She stared blankly at Nan. "Oh, no."

"Oh, yes. Your nemesis carried you in here and put you to bed. He was pretty nice, considering what you said to his fiancée."

Shelly groaned aloud. "I don't want to know, but what did I say?"

"You're right. You don't want to know. Sit down and drink your coffee."

Shelly sat down and held out her cup. "Have you got any hemlock?"

Nan only shook her head.

BEN WAS LYING IN WAIT FOR Shelly when she came out onto the beach much later, wearing dark glasses and feeling vaguely sick. Nan had promised her that some sea air would cure her. So while Nan was having a shower, Shelly slipped into her yellow one-piece bathing suit and her terry cover-up and oozed down to the beach.

"Marie's really mad at you," Ben said, and grinned. "I knew you'd make a great mother!" He scowled. "You look terrible. What's the matter with you?"

"Excess," she said.

"Excess what?"

"Beer." She found a single bare spot between tourists and sat down gently on the sand. She groaned at the blazing sunlight, which hurt her eyes even through the dark glasses. "It's your father's fault."

"My dad made you drink beer?" he asked hesitantly.

"He drove me to it. He's a terrible man!"

"Well, he isn't, really. I exaggerated a little because I was mad at him," Ben said pleasantly. "But he's rethinking sending me to that school. Thanks, Mom!" He grinned at her.

"Think nothing of it. Is there a facility near here? I think I have to throw up."

"Why don't you lie down?" Ben suggested. "It might help. Where did your friends go?"

"They are going sailing." She took off the robe and stretched out on a towel, grimacing as her head contacted the ground. "I feel awful."

"I can imagine. I'm glad I don't drink," he observed. "Neither does Dad, except for a glass of wine occasionally."

"Delighted to hear it. I'm sure your future stepmother doesn't approve of wine."

"She only hates things that taste good," he agreed. "I hate wine."

"Haven't you got something to do?"

"Sure. I have to look after you. Poor old Mom."

"I'm not your mother," she croaked.

"Yet."

"Ever!" She let out a pained sigh.

"How about something cold to drink?"

"Anything, as long as it isn't beer!" She dug into her pocket for change and handed him some.

"That's too much."

"Get yourself something, too."

"Gee, thanks!"

He darted off. She lay quietly on the sand, trying to breathe, and a dark shadow loomed over her.

"Nan?" Shelly said.

"Not Nan," came a familiar deep voice. He dropped beside her on the sand. "How do you feel?"

"Sick."

"Serves you right. If you can't hold your liquor, don't drink. You could have ended up in severe circumstances last night, except for Nan."

"Rub it in," she muttered.

"I intend to. Nan's had a go at you already, I'm sure."

"Several. My head hurts."

"No wonder." He smoothed back her windblown hair. His hand was big and warm and surprisingly gentle. She opened her eyes and looked up. She wished she hadn't. He was wearing white swimming trunks and nothing else, and he looked better than the sexiest suntan commercial she'd ever seen. He was beautiful, just beautiful, and she was glad she had on dark glasses so that he couldn't see her appreciation.

"Where's your shadow?" she muttered, closing her eyes again. "Or does she sunbathe? It must be disconcerting to have men screaming 'put your clothes back on!'"

"Not nice," he said firmly. "Being thin is fashionable in our circles."

"It is not," she said, forgetting that he didn't know she frequented the same circles he did. "Thin is fashionable only with models and—" she sat up, taking off her sunglasses to glare at him "—your ladylove."

He shrugged, powerful muscles rippling in his chest and arms. "Some men like well-endowed women, I suppose. I never have."

She was too aware of her full hips and generous bosom. She glared at him. "Then don't waste your time sitting here talking to me."

He laughed mirthlessly. "I have a vested interest in you, and kindly don't take this as a sign of sexual intent. Even if you appealed to me, which you do not physically," he added pointedly, "the fact is, you're still in school."

She started once again to correct his assumption about her age, and stopped. Plenty of time for confidences later, if he stuck around. Otherwise, pretending a lesser age than she owned might not be a bad form of protection. He was obviously pretty experienced, if the look he was giving her body was any indication. He wasn't blatant, but he had seductive eyes and a voice that was more than a little persuasive. His words denied any interest or intent, but his eyes belied that. She wondered if he even realized it.

"I'm back…!" Ben hesitated before he sat down beside his father and Shelly. "Oh. Hi, Dad. Where's Marie?"

"Sleeping late, I suppose." He watched as Ben handed Shelly a soft drink.

"Delicious," she whispered, holding the icy can to her temples.

"Are you assimilating it through osmosis?" Ben asked. "We studied that in biology."

"You don't know what biology is until you've had to study DNA, enzymes, proteins and genetics in college."

Ben blinked. "What happened to animals?"

"You study them in zoology."

"You study enzymes in biology?" Ben muttered.

"That's right. And if you really want to understand biology, taking chemistry helps. I haven't yet." She grinned. "I'm a sociology major. I only have to take biology. Since I passed it, I don't have to take chemistry."

"How far along are you?" Faulkner asked.

"Oh, I'm still a freshman."

He didn't reply. His face grew thoughtful, and he turned his attention seaward.

"Where are you from?" Ben asked her suddenly.

"Washington."

"State?" he persisted.

"D.C."

"So are we!" Ben said excitedly, and Shelly was aware of his father's interested gaze. "Where do you go to school?"

"Thorn College," she replied. "It's very small, but nice."

Faulkner knew the college and the area in which it was located. A nice, middle-class community. Nothing fancy. Older homes on small lots near the interchange.

"Oh," Ben said. "We live several miles away from there. Some of our neighbors are senators."

"Are you on vacation?" she asked hesitantly.

"No," Faulkner replied. "There's a convention here this week—bankers."

"Dad's the keynote speaker," Ben said proudly. "Shelly, didn't you say your dad was good at numbers and accounting?"

He certainly was. He was on the board of directors of two banks. She hoped Faulkner's wasn't one of them. "Sort of," she said.

"What does he do?" Ben persisted.

"Actually very little," she said, feeling her way.

"I see," Faulkner said quietly, and his tone indicated that he was developing an impression of Shelly's father that classed Mr. Astor as a street person. Shelly had to bite her lip to keep from laughing at the picture that came to mind. Her father contributed to several charities that helped street people, but he was far from being homeless.

"What are you going to do with your degree when you get it?" Faulkner asked with genuine curiosity.

"I'd like to be a social worker," she said. "There are plenty of people in the world who could use a helping hand."

"No doubt about that," he replied.

"Well, I want to be a wildlife illustrator," Ben said firmly.

"He wants to do his duck shooting with a camera," Faulkner said with a sigh.

"Good for him. I think it's atrocious the way people treat our living natural resources."

Ben grinned from ear to ear. "You tell him, Mom!"

"I am *not* your mother," she said shortly, and then groaned and held her head.

"She's much too young to be anyone's mother," Faulkner agreed, and there was, just briefly, a wistful look about him. He quickly erased it and got to his feet. "I've got to go and collect Marie. We have a luncheon engagement. Ben..."

"I can stay with Mom. Can't I?"

"I'm not—!"

"—your mother! I know, I know!" Ben said chuckling. "Can I stay with you?"

"She's not able to look after you," Faulkner said.

"I want to look after her," Ben replied solemnly. "She certainly needs looking after, and her friends are going sailing. I don't think she can go sailing, do you?"

Shelly swallowed and made a moaning sound.

"Good point. Is it all right?" Faulkner asked Shelly.

"Just as long as he doesn't talk too loud," she agreed.

"Don't give her any trouble," Faulkner cautioned the boy.

"Isn't Marie going back home today?" Ben asked with glee.

"She's leaving with her father. If he goes today, so will she, I imagine."

So they weren't sharing a room, Shelly thought. She was surprised that a woman of Marie's age would travel with her father, especially when she was apparently all but engaged to Faulkner.

"Marie's father is one of the bankers at the convention," Ben explained. "We flew down together."

"None of that is of any interest to Ms. Astor, I'm sure," Faulkner said. "Stay out of trouble. We should be back around three o'clock."

"Okay, Dad."

Faulkner wandered off, absently thinking that he'd much rather be on the beach with Ben and Shelly than sitting around talking business. But that was part of his job.

SHELLY AND BEN LEFT the beach half an hour later and after two pain tablets and another icy drink, Shelly felt well enough to go fishing off the pier with Ben.

"Isn't this fun?" she asked on a sigh, lying back on the boards with her eyes closed and the fishing pole held loosely in her hand. "I'll bet that fishing concession makes a fortune without selling a single worm."

"Your hook isn't baited," Ben muttered. "That's not fair."

"I don't want to catch a fish, for heaven's sake! I just want to lie here and drink in the smell of sea air."

"Well, I want to catch something. Not that I expect to," he said miserably when he pulled up his hook and it was bare, again. The minnows under the pier kept taking the bait in tiny nibbles and missing the hook.

"Don't fall in," she said firmly.

"Okay."

The sound of footsteps didn't bother her, because there were plenty of other tourists dropping lines off the pier. But these came close. She looked up and there was Ben's father, in jeans, a gray knit designer shirt and sneakers. He didn't even look like the same man.

"Catch anything?" he asked.

"Some sleep," Shelly remarked.

"I'm catching cold," Ben grumbled as he baited his hook for the fourth time.

Faulkner's narrow silver eyes slid over Shelly's trim figure in tight white jeans and a pink sleeveless blouse tied at the midriff. Her glorious hair was tamed into a French braid and even without makeup, her face was lovely. He couldn't stop looking at her.

She flushed a little and sat up. That level stare was making her self-conscious. "Since you're back, I'll leave Ben with you. I have to try to find Nan and the others."

"I thought they went sailing."

"They did," she agreed. "But Nan's a much worse sailor than I am. I expect she's lost breakfast and lunch by now, and is praying for land."

He reached down a big, strong hand and helped her up. Oddly his fingers were callused; her fingers lingered against the tough pads on his and she looked up at him with kindled interest.

"Your hands are callused," she remarked.

He smiled slowly, closing his fingers around her own. "I have a sailboat," he remarked. "I love sailing."

"Oh."

"And you don't like the sea," he murmured dryly.

"My stomach doesn't like the sea," she corrected.

He searched her soft eyes and she didn't look away. Currents of electricity seemed to run into her body from the intensity of that stare, until her breathing changed and her heartbeat doubled. He still had her hand in his and unexpectedly, he brought the soft palm up to his lips and pressed them hard into its moist warmth.

She felt the color run into her face. "I, uh, really have to go." She laughed nervously and extracted her hand from his.

He smiled at her, without rancor or mockery. "Thanks for taking care of Ben."

"He sort of took care of me," she replied. Her eyes searched his, and there was a little fear in them.

His smile was indulgent, faintly surprised. "It's all right," he said softly, his voice deeper than ever, his eyes narrowed and intent.

She gnawed on her lower lip, understanding his response in her subconscious even if it sounded odd to her conscious mind. She turned away. "See you, Ben!"

"Sure. Thanks!"

She almost ran the length of the pier. She dated, and boys liked her. But she'd never liked them. Now, in the space of a few days, a man who thought she was much too young for him had blazed a path to her most secret self, and she didn't know how to chase him out again. There were plenty of reasons she should keep her distance from him, and she wanted to. But Ben was making it impossible.

She walked into the motel, almost colliding with a very irritated Marie Dumaris.

"You again," the older woman said curtly. "Stay away from Faulkner. I don't know what you think he'd see in a ragamuffin like you, but I don't like the way you've attached yourself to him and Ben."

The attack was staggering. Shelly stared at her blankly. "I beg your pardon?"

"If you don't leave Faulkner alone, I'll make you sorry. My

people are well-to-do and I have influence. I can have you kicked out of school if I feel like it." She smiled haughtily at Shelly's expression. "Faulkner told me that you go to Thorn College. So watch your step. You don't know who you're dealing with."

Shelly looked her in the eye, and she didn't smile. "Neither do you," she said with quiet dignity.

Marie started to say something else, but Shelly turned and kept walking. She couldn't imagine why Marie would warn her away from Faulkner, who wasn't interested in her that way at all. Besides, she was only going to be here for four more days. That was hardly enough time to capture a man's heart. She overlooked the fact that hers was slowly being chained already....

THAT EVENING, AFTER THEY'D eaten fish and chips, she and Nan were startled by a knock at the door.

Shelly went to open the door and found Faulkner. He smiled gently at her surprise. She was still wearing her jeans and pink blouse, but he'd changed into white slacks and a patterned shirt.

"Do you like Latin music?" he asked.

She was flustered, and looked it. "Yes."

"Come on. There's a live band down the way. Nan?" he added, looking past Shelly. "Want to come with us?"

"I'd love to, but there's a PBS special on about a dig in Egypt," Nan said apologetically. "I *love* classical archaeology."

"Indulge yourself, you stick-in-the-mud," Shelly grumbled. "I will. Have fun!"

Faulkner waited while Shelly tied a pink knit sweater loosely around her neck in case it got cooler, and found her purse.

She waited until they were in the elevator headed down to the ground floor before she spoke. "Isn't this sudden?" she queried. "And where's Ben?"

"He's staying with some friends of mine for a few hours."

She lifted both eyebrows.

He chuckled. "You know how I feel about May-December relationships. I've already said so. I don't have anything indiscreet in mind. I thought you might like the impromptu Latin concert on the beach, so I came to get you."

"Am I substituting?"

He tilted her face up to his and shook his head, holding her eyes. "Oh, no," he said quietly. "Not you."

She smiled gently. "That was nice."

"I am nice," he replied, letting go of her chin. "It takes some people longer than others to notice it, of course."

She laughed. "Conceit, yet."

"I am not conceited. In fact, my modesty often shocks people."

"I'll let you know if I feel in danger of being shocked."

His silver eyes twinkled. "You do that."

"You aren't what you seem," she said with faint curiosity. "I thought bankers were staid and businesslike."

His powerful shoulders rose and fell. "I am, when I'm in the office." He glanced down at her. "I'm not in the office tonight, so look out."

She chuckled. "I can hardly wait."

The music got louder the closer they got to the beach. A boom box was blasting Latin rhythms and food and beer were being passed around while couples danced in the sand. A crowd of merrymakers had gathered to watch, including some of the students Shelly was travelling with. One of them, unfortunately, was Pete.

"So this is where you went to!" he said impatiently, glancing warily at Faulkner. "Want to join us?"

Faulkner slid a possessive arm around her waist, and smiled at Pete. It wasn't a pleasant smile. "She's with me," he said quietly.

"Yes, I am," Shelly added. "Thanks for the invitation anyway."

Pete didn't say another word. He stalked back off to the other group.

"He's been drinking again," she said. "Ordinarily he's very nice."

"Nan told me that she was barely able to peel him off you last night," he said curtly. "I don't like that. A man who'll take advantage of an intoxicated woman is no man at all."

She stared at him. "Which means that you wouldn't seduce me if I got drunk?"

"Of course not. Besides, even cold sober, a college freshman is a little green on the tree for a man my age," he added, and his voice was unusually soft.

She should have been glad that her subterfuge had been successful. But instead, she was miserable that he thought she was too young for him.

"Will you relax and enjoy the music?" he chided.

"Sorry." She smiled. "I'm glad you asked me. I love music."

"So do I."

"Elevator music and classic rock and roll?" she teased.

He cocked a thick eyebrow. "Axl Rose and Aerosmith," he shot back.

She chuckled. "Mr. Scott, you are nothing like your image."

"Thank God for that."

The music got louder and couples moved into the circle to dance. Because her parents were ballroom dancing fans, she'd grown up knowing how to dance the mambo and tango. Faulkner seemed surprised that someone of her tender years would know how to do a sophisticated tango, but after he gauged her style, they seemed to flow together to the passionate refrain.

The music was wild. What she felt with every sensual brush of his body against hers was wilder. Her heart ran away with her. There was no tomorrow—only tonight. She began to act as if the moment was all that existed, deliberately tempting him with the brush of her breasts against his broad chest, the soft glide of her thighs beside his, the intoxicating fencing of her steps with his.

She hung beneath his narrowing gaze, feeling the effect she was having on him in his quickened breath, the tightening of his hands on her waist and then, sliding lower, on her hips as he brushed her body against him.

It was arousing and she was too hungry to hide her reaction to him. As the music built to a climax, her eyes found his and held them. By the time it wound down, she was clinging to him, like a life preserver.

They finished the dance with a trembling Shelly draped over one powerful arm. Faulkner's mouth poised scant inches above her own. The whole crowd applauded, but they were so lost in each other, in the intoxicating magic of aroused awareness, that they barely noticed.

"Oh, for a few seconds of privacy," he murmured huskily, searching her eyes as he slowly drew her back up again, the sensual brush of his hard body against her soft one arousing her suddenly and violently.

The dance had been sensual. She could feel her heart, and his, pounding in rhythm. "What would you do?" she challenged.

"I think that you're not quite that naive," he said, and his silver eyes fell to her soft mouth, lingering there until her lips parted and a tiny, frustrated moan escaped them.

His breathing was suddenly audible. "Shelly, stop it!"

She wanted to, she really did. But for the first time in her life, she wasn't quite in control. The feel of his chest against her soft breasts made them swell and she felt a sweet trembling all through her body. She was young and untried and hungry for her first taste of physical ravishment. All that was in the eyes she lifted bravely to his.

His jaw clenched. He swallowed. "All right. But not here," he said roughly.

He took her hand in his and drew her along with him. Her head was spinning; he'd read her thoughts as surely as if she'd spoken them. She'd never before experienced that kind of communication. It was frightening, similar to the headlong rush into passion that made her legs tremble.

"People. Damn people!" he muttered under his breath as he searched for a single uncrowded place. There wasn't one. He looked toward the beach, where the sea oats and sand dunes gave at least the illusion of privacy.

If he'd been thinking rationally, he'd have taken her straight back to the hotel and left her with Nan while there was still time. But she was wearing some sort of tangy perfume that made his senses whirl, and the thought of her softly rounded body in his arms made him reckless.

He led her along the dunes and then helped her down to the level of the beach with him, holding her so that, for an instant, her eyes were even with the aroused glitter of his.

He let her slide gently against his muscular body until her feet touched the sand. Behind him was the roar of the surf with moonlight glistening like diamonds along the waves that ran into the beach. But louder even than that was the frantic beat of her heart as he drew her to him with a self-mocking smile and bent his head.

"Every man is entitled to make a fool of himself once," he whispered into her mouth as he took it.

Chapter Four

SHELLY WASN'T MODEL-LOVELY, but her wealth had guaranteed that she'd had suitors in the past. None of them, not one, had made her mouth ache for his kisses, her body plead to be touched and caressed. But Faulkner did. Her response to him was instant and alarming.

Once, she tried to draw back, but his big hands slid to her hips and pushed them hard into the changing contours of his body while his lips teased around her trembling mouth.

He felt her instinctive withdrawal and checked it expertly. His nose brushed against hers and there was no urgency, no brutality in the touch of his mouth on her face. He was remarkably tender for the level of arousal he'd already reached.

"Don't be afraid of me," he whispered, his voice gentle, indulgent. "You can stop me whenever you like. Force is for bullies."

The calm tone pacified her. For just an instant she'd counted her folly in coming out alone with him, when she hardly knew him. There was a very real danger in being secluded with a strange man. The papers were full of tragedies that a little common sense, caution and wise counsel could have prevented.

"I read too many newspapers, I guess," she said unsteadily.

"Some women should read more," he replied flatly. He pushed the hair back from her flushed cheeks and stared down at her in the faint light. "You're quite safe with me. I wouldn't advise you to come out here with your friend Pete, though."

She smiled at the dry tone. "I know that already, thanks." The smile faded as she studied his broad, rugged face. It had lines that an artist would have loved. She reached up hesitantly, and stroked his thick eyebrows. He had big, deep-set eyes that seemed to see right through people. His nose was a little large, not oversize, and very straight. She traced it down to the wide, sexy line of his mouth, to the chiseled lips that had teased her into reckless response.

"This isn't wise," he said quietly, a little regretful. "You taste of green apples, young Shelly."

She reached up and caught his full lower lip gently in her teeth, acting on pure instinct. His big frame shuddered a little. "Teach me," she whispered unsteadily.

His hand tightened on her waist. "Teach you what?" he asked roughly.

Her lips opened and brushed against his. "How to…make love."

"That would be dangerous," was all he could get out. His body was burning; his heartbeat shook him.

"Yes." Her hands went to the front of his shirt. Holding his eyes, she gently undid the top button. He didn't say a word. Encouraged, she opened the next, and the next, and the next, until she'd bared his hair-covered chest to her fascinated gaze.

"Oh, my!" she whispered. She pressed both hands into the thickness of the hair and felt the hard, warm muscle through it. He was strong. She could feel it. He indulged her, letting her explore him, until the needs she kindled became unmanageable.

"That's enough," he said softly, stilling her hands against him.

"Why?"

"Because I'll want equal time."

Her eyes met his; her gaze was curious, a little shy. "I haven't let anyone see me like that. Not yet."

His eyes fell to her pink blouse and he saw the hardness of her nipples through it.

"I didn't have time to put on anything under it," she whispered softly.

"Oh, my God!" He ground out the words.

That deep groan, she decided, was pure frustration. As she thought it, he looked around to make sure they were still isolated. Then, with a total disregard for sanity, he dropped her sweater to the beach and began to unfasten her blouse.

His lips parted, as if he was finding it hard to breathe while he worked the tiny pearl buttons. So was she. But she wanted his gaze on her so badly that she banished common sense. When he pulled the edges of the blouse apart and looked at her, it seemed that she wasn't the only one with that terrible need. His eyes were narrow and hot with admiration as he savored the firm, beautiful curve of her pink breasts.

"You said you liked...small women," she whispered unsteadily.

"Did I? I must have been out of my mind! Shelly," he whispered. "Oh, Shelly...!"

She didn't know what she'd expected, but it wasn't the sudden descent of his dark head and the warm moistness of his open mouth on her breast. His tongue pressed against her while she cried out in a strangled voice and clutched his head closer. Her whole body throbbed, ached, shook with an avalanche of uncontrollable need. She whispered to him, pleaded with him for more, more, her eyes closed, her body in anguish.

Vaguely she felt the cool sand at her back and the weight of Faulkner's body as he lifted his head to find her mouth. He kissed her with open passion, his tongue pushing deep inside her mouth while his hair-roughened chest rubbed over her bare breasts and made the ache intolerable.

Her hands found his hips and pulled him to her, trembling as she pleaded for something she'd never experienced. As far gone as she, he indulged her for one brief ecstatic second, levering down between her soft thighs to press himself hard against the very core of her hunger. She cried out and shifted to accommodate him, and the stars seemed to crash down on her.

But he groaned and threw himself over onto his back, shuddering, openly vulnerable to her hungry, fascinated eyes.

She looked at him as if he belonged to her already, sketching him with eyes that adored the power and sensuality of his aroused body. He seemed to be in agony and she wished she were more sophisticated, that she knew what to do for him.

She sat up, hugging her knees to her bare breasts. Probably she should fasten her blouse, she thought dazedly, but everything seemed a bit unreal now.

He sat up beside her and glanced sideways, noticing the open blouse. "Put your knees down," he said quietly. "I want to look at you."

She obeyed him, watching his eyes stroke her with pure pleasure, feeling sensations that made her tingle.

"You make my head spin," he said, leaning close to put his lips softly over her breast. "Do you like this?" he whispered, teasing the nipple with his tongue. "Or is it better for you...like this?" His mouth opened and suckled her with tender ferocity.

"Faulkner." She lay back on the sand, her arms spread, her eyes welcoming, her body completely open to him. She wanted him so badly that nothing else mattered for the moment.

He studied her with banked-down hunger for a long time while he fought his better judgment and lost. "It would be the first time, wouldn't it, Shelly?"

"Yes."

"If you've said no to men before—and I must assume that you have—why are you saying yes to me?"

She didn't want to think about that. She felt uncertain, when she'd been out of her mind with need of him only seconds before. Embarrassed now, she sat up and tugged the edges of her blouse together, buttoning them up in an excruciating silence.

She had to say something. Words were difficult in the cold sanity of the aftermath. "Listen, I want you to know…I don't go around doing things like this…" She faltered. "I'm sorry. I feel…rather ashamed."

He turned her face toward his and searched her eyes with a somber, intense scrutiny. "You did nothing to make either of us ashamed or embarrassed. We both know I'm too old for you. That doesn't make me regret what happened just now." He traced her lips slowly with his hand, and there was a faint unsteadiness in his fingers. "I'll dream of you as you were tonight for the rest of my life," he said through his teeth. "God, Shelly, why do you have to be so young…?" He caught her to him and his mouth burned into hers for endless moments while he fed an impossible hunger. He forced himself to lift his head. She lay against him, her lips swollen, her eyes wide and soft and willing. He groaned audibly. "You'd let me, wouldn't you?" he asked in a hoarse, agonized tone. "You'd lie here in the moonlight and let me undress you. You'd open your arms and lie under my body and envelop me in your softness…"

She blushed at the images he was creating in her mind, shivering as she pictured his muscular, hair-roughened body pushing hers into the sand while he possessed her. She moaned.

"Shelly!" His cheek lay against her soft breasts and he shivered in her arms. "Shelly, I want you so badly, honey!"

"I would let you," she whispered brokenly. "I would, I would…!"

His arm contracted and he rocked her against him with rough compassion, his face lifting to nestle against her throat, in the scented softness of her hair, while the wind blew around them and the surf crashed.

"I'm years too old for you," he said quietly, looking past her at the ocean. "And while my son wants a mother, I do not want another wife."

"Then why are you marrying *her?*" she asked.

"I'm not. And she knows it. She likes to pretend that things will change, and so does her father, who owes me money and thinks that my marriage to his daughter would negate his debt."

"I see."

His cheek nuzzled her hair. "I'm in my middle thirties and you're a college freshman. We're a generation apart. I come from a social set that you couldn't begin to cope with," he added when she was tempted to speak and deny what he was saying. "I come from money. Plenty of it." He laughed bitterly. "You'd have to organize and plan luncheons, dinner, business gatherings. You'd have to know how to dress, how to defend yourself at social functions, because I have enemies and former lovers who would savage you." His chest rose and fell heavily. "Marriage is out of the question, and I can't offer you an affair because my conscience would beat me to death."

"I see."

"Will you stop saying that?" He lifted his head and searched her eyes, looking for secrets that they wouldn't yield. She looked odd. Faintly amused and bitter, all at once.

"You want to make love to me, but that's all it is." She summed up what he'd told her.

"Basically that's about it." He couldn't tell her what he was beginning to feel for her. The cost was too dear. She'd forget him and he'd forget her, because they had no future together. Let her think it was only physical with him. It might make it easier for her to get over him.

She smiled with controlled dignity. "In that case, we'd better break this up and go back to the motel, hadn't we?" She got up, brushing off her jeans. She retrieved her sweater, shook the sand out of it and slipped it on. She was suddenly chilled.

He got up, too. "I'll walk you back to your room," he said formally.

"Thank you."

They didn't touch. She felt betrayed. He thought she was several years younger than she really was, and that she was beneath him socially. She could have told him the truth, but if he couldn't accept her as he thought she was, then he obviously didn't care about anything except her body. In fact, he'd said so. Thank God he was too much a gentleman to take advantage. She'd been crazy for him. It was embarrassing to remember how wanton she'd been. The memory was going to hurt for a long time.

She couldn't love him, of course. It was impossible to think that when she'd only been around him briefly. It was physical infatuation, surely, and she'd get over it.

They were at her door all too soon. "Thanks for the music," she said, without quite meeting his eyes. She even smiled. "Tell Ben good-night for me. Nan and I have plans, so I don't imagine I'll see much of him until we leave for home."

He frowned. Until now, he hadn't remembered how close Ben was getting to her. "You don't have to jettison Ben because of what happened tonight," he said curtly.

"I'm not."

He tipped her face up to his, scowling at the way she avoided his eyes. "Look at me, damn you!" he said sharply.

The anger shocked her into meeting his eyes, and she wished she hadn't. They were blazing.

"I didn't want to hurt you," he said shortly. "I never meant to do more than kiss you. You deliberately baited me until I made love to you, so don't put all the blame on me!"

She went scarlet. She was too sick with embarrassment and too flustered to even answer him. Jerking away from him, she fumbled the door open and went through it, locking it nervously behind her.

Faulkner stood staring at the closed door with shocked self-contempt. He couldn't believe he'd made a remark like that to her, when she'd been so generous and uninhibited with him. He hadn't meant to make her ashamed of such a sweet giving, but the look on her face had hurt him. He cared deeply for her, even if he didn't want to. He had no right to wound her, to scar her young emotions by taunting her with her responsiveness.

"Shelly," he said quietly, one big hand against the door. "I'm sorry."

He didn't know if she'd heard him, but he hoped she had. He turned and walked away, aching with regrets.

Shelly went to bed, pleading a headache from the music. She figured that Nan wasn't fooled, but she couldn't face questions now. She'd moved away from the door so quickly that she hadn't heard Faulkner's apology. She climbed under the covers, and her pillow was wet when she finally slept.

SHE MEANT TO AVOID BEN, so that she could avoid his father, but the boy was waiting for her in the restaurant the next morning. He stood up, beaming, when she and Nan came in.

"I've already ordered coffee for both of you," he said with a flourish. "Do sit down."

Shelly and Nan chuckled involuntarily as they took their seats.

"What am I going to do with you?" Shelly asked softly.

"Adopt me," he said. "She saved my life," he told Nan. "Now she has to take care of me for as long as I live." He frowned. "She's sort of reluctant, but I'm working on her. I really do need a mother, you know. And don't say I'll have one when Dad marries Marie," he added gruffly when Shelly started to speak.

"Where's your dad?" Nan asked, because she knew Shelly wouldn't. Something had happened the night before, and it must have been something major for Shelly to be so tight-lipped about it.

"Dad's gone to a meeting," Ben said. "He sure was upset. He didn't even want breakfast. I guess he's missing *her*," he added miserably. "He said something about us going home earlier than expected."

Shelly felt her pulse leap. So he was that anxious to be rid of her. Did he think she'd make trouble? Embarrass him with confessions of undying love? He needn't have worried. She wasn't that sort.

"I'll miss you, Ben," she replied, smiling. "But life goes on."

"You look sick," Ben remarked. "Are you okay?"

"I'm just fine. No more hangovers," she promised.

BUT SHE WASN'T FINE. She went through the motions of having a good time, joining in a volleyball game on the beach and sunbathing and swimming. But her heart wasn't in it. Nan had paired off with a nice student from New York she'd met on the sailing trip, and Shelly wished she had someone, if only to keep Pete at bay.

"We could go back to my room and have a drink or two," he suggested. "Come on, Shelly, loosen up!"

She looked straight at him. Courtesy wasn't working. Perhaps stark honesty would. "I don't want to have sex with you."

He actually flushed. "Shelly!"

"That's what you're after," she said flatly. "Well, it isn't what I'm after. I came down here to have a good time. I'm managing it, barely, *in spite of you!*"

He got up, looking embarrassed, and shrugged. "Okay. You don't have to get upset. No hard feelings." He walked off, and very soon he was talking up another girl. Thank goodness, she thought. One complication resolved.

She felt tired and drowsy, and she began to doze. A sudden sharp movement brought her awake.

"This is stupid," Faulkner said roughly. "You're baking yourself. Haven't you put on any sunscreen at all?"

"Of course I have."

"Not on your back."

"Well, I can't reach it, can I?" she asked angrily. She sat up. "And don't offer to do it for me, because I don't want you touching me. Go away."

He searched her eyes slowly. "I apologized, but you didn't hear me, did you?"

Her eyes dropped. She didn't like looking at him in swimming trunks. He was disturbing enough fully clothed.

"I have to go back to the room," she said stiffly. "Nan and I are going shopping with some other—Faulkner!"

He had her up in his big arms and he was carrying her lazily down the beach to the water.

"Listen, you…!"

He put his mouth softly over hers, closing the words inside it, while he waded far out into the ocean until they were up to their shoulders in it. Only then did he release her, just enough so that he could bring her body completely against his and deepen the long, slow kiss that locked them into intimacy.

"Oh, don't," she pleaded, but her arms were already holding him, her mouth searching for his.

He gave it to her. His big hands slid down to her hips and

his fingers teased under the brief yellow bikini bottom as he pulled her to the hard outline of his body and moved her against him.

He nibbled her lower lip while he positioned her in an intimacy that made her gasp and shiver.

"I can't get you out of my mind," he whispered into her mouth, groaning. "You torment me."

"Faulkner...!"

"I want you so, Shelly!" He kissed her hungrily. His hands released her hips and slid up to untie her top. It fell to her waist and his hands caressed her while his mouth teased and tormented hers. She felt his fingers teasing her nipples into even harder arousal, and she moaned sharply.

"Come here."

He caught her against him, rubbing his chest against her breasts in a soft, sweet abrasion that made her cry out. His arms enfolded her and he buried his face in her wet neck, holding her, rocking her in an intimacy she'd shared with no one else.

"You feel of silk and it excites me when I touch you and you make those sharp little noises deep in your throat. Shelly, you want my mouth on your breasts, don't you?" he whispered, letting his cheek slide down hers until he could reach her mouth.

The thought of it made her body ache. "Yes," she moaned. "But we can't!"

"I know. I'd have to lift you out of the water to get to you, and we'd be seen. Shelly...!"

His mouth fastened onto hers and his hands slid down her back, under the bikini briefs. He touched her with slow, deft intimacy. He held her like that, feeling her shiver and moan against his mouth as the intimacy took away all her inhibitions.

But he was too hungry for her. He had to pull back while

he still could. An unwanted pregnancy was a terrible cost for a few minutes of pleasure.

For her, he thought as he restored her bathing suit to belated decency, it probably wouldn't be very pleasant at all, after the foreplay. Because she was virginal. Virginal. His head spun wildly at the thought of initiating her into sex, teaching her how to feel and give the ultimate sensual pleasure. But she was young. Too young, and too far away socially and economically.

"Why did you do that?" she asked miserably when he was holding her, soothing her in the heated aftermath.

"For the same reason you didn't stop me," he replied quietly. "Because I needed to touch you. Just as you needed to be touched by me."

"I'm too young and I don't know anything and there's Marie…!"

He bent and brushed his mouth softly, softly, over hers. "Open your mouth," he whispered tenderly. "You know already that I like to touch the inside of it with my tongue while we kiss."

She moaned. He could have thrown her down on the beach and made love to her in full view of the population and she didn't think she'd have a protest in her.

He drew back with evident difficulty. His face was drawn and wan as he looked down at her. "There are just too many obstacles," he said, thinking aloud.

She knew it. Standing in his arms, with her whole body screaming to belong to him, she realized that after the pleasure would come regret, shame, hurt. "Far too many," she agreed sadly.

He sighed heavily. "You deserve more than a man's lust."

She swallowed. "Are you…sure…that's all it is, Faulkner?" she asked miserably.

His face closed up. He let go of her. "Yes," he said flatly, ignoring the denial building deep inside him. "An uncontrollable, feverish lust that makes me ashamed. I'm sorry. I genuinely meant to apologize, not to compound the problem."

"I know."

"I go mad the instant I touch you." He laughed coldly. "It's a quirk of nature. Fate mocking both of us." He grimaced. "This can't happen again."

"I know. It won't. I was trying to avoid you," she confessed.

"So was I," he agreed ruefully. "And you can see where it got us both."

She flushed, averting her eyes as she remembered with unwanted vividness exactly how intimate they'd become in the water.

"I'll try to think of it as a reality-based exercise in sex education," she said bitterly.

He turned her face up with a long sigh. "Oh, no," he said. "It wasn't that." His eyes dropped to her soft lips. "It's been years since I've enjoyed a woman's body, since I've indulged the need to touch and stroke and arouse. You make me want to find out how gentle I could be, Shelly." He stopped, looking puzzled and irritated and even a little vulnerable.

Shelly searched his face with sad, quiet eyes. "Do I?"

He touched her face with something like wonder. "In the very beginning, I loved Ben's mother. I felt such tenderness for her, such aching need. But she wanted what I could give her in a material sense. For her it was a business deal, and Ben was my price." He winced. "She never loved me. She died in the arms of another man, and I hated her and loved her and mourned her for years afterward. Since then, women have been nothing more than an amusement. I've used them," he confessed, lifting his eyes to hers. He searched her face slowly. "But, I couldn't use you. And that being the case, I think it's better for both of us if we forget everything that's happened."

Chapter Five

SHELLY LOWERED HER EYES to his chest and tried not to appear as devastated as she felt. She was already looking ahead to a time when she wouldn't see him again. He wanted her, but wanting was not going to be enough. She knew that and so did he. His mind was clouded by the desire he felt. Once he satisfied it, the clouds would vanish and he'd hate them both. Even if she were tempted, and she was, it wouldn't be wise to let things go any further.

"You mean we shouldn't see each other again," she said miserably.

"That's about it." He moved away from her, pushing the wet hair from his damp face. "We won't be here much longer," he added. "We'll muddle through." He searched her face quietly. "Somehow."

She forced a smile. "What about Ben?" she asked.

"He's crazy about you. Don't deny him your company."

"I hadn't planned to."

He touched her soft cheek gently. "Shelly," he said huskily, "you know it wouldn't work. Even if I took a chance on your age, our social backgrounds are too far apart."

"And that would never do," she agreed, averting her eyes.

"I'm a banker. I have a position that requires discretion." He shrugged. "I've never cared much for convention, but when the jobs of other people depend on it, I can give the image I need to give. Besides," he added bitterly, "it isn't as if marriage would ever enter into any relationship I had. Do you understand?"

She lifted her eyes to his hard face, seeing the resignation and stubborn determination there. "You don't trust women. Is that why you let Marie get such a hold on you? She was safe?"

"I know all about Marie," he said, without taking offense. "She's devious and snappy, and selfish to a fault. She has grown up around wealth. She enjoys throwing her weight around."

"So I noticed," Shelly said.

"Ben thinks you're very special," he said, his voice deep and soft. "So do I, Shelly. I'm sorry. I wish…I really wish things had been different. We seem to have a lot in common. We might discover even more."

"So we might. But taking risks isn't your specialty, is it?"

He shook his head. "I only bet on a sure thing. This isn't." He touched her mouth and slowly drew back. "I'm sorry."

"So am I. But," she added, drawing in a steady breath as she struggled for something light, "whatever happens, we'll always have Paris."

It took a minute for that to sink in. By the time he started to laugh, she was already halfway to the beach.

FAULKNER, TRUE TO HIS WORD, didn't come near her again. Ben did. He haunted her.

"Can't you find something else to do?" she wailed.

He grinned and shook his head, because he knew she

liked him. Her face was an open book. "You can't banish your only child."

"But you're not!" she cried.

"How do you know?" He looked very serious. "I mean, you could have had me and forgotten about it. You might have advanced amnesia."

"I couldn't have become a mother when I was twelve," she muttered. "And besides that, I'd remember having had a child. It isn't something anybody forgets."

Ben didn't say a word, but he could add. His father thought Shelly was in her teens, but she'd just subtracted his age from hers and come up with twelve. That made her twenty-four. He pursed his lips.

"How old are you?" he persisted.

"How old do you think I am?" she asked foxily.

"Twenty-four."

She glared at him. "How in the world…"

He told her how in the world, and she let out a long, slow breath.

"I won't tell Dad. But why don't you want him to know?" he asked.

She couldn't explain that without giving herself away. "I have my reasons," she said. "So it's our secret. Okay?"

"Okay. After all, a boy can't afford to argue with his own little mother."

She opened her mouth to protest, groaned and closed it again. Arguing did no good.

The night before they were to leave for home, Ben maneuvered Nan and Shelly into a leisurely supper with him and his father. It was a less than sparkling evening, with Shelly and Faulkner trying to ignore each other and act normally. They failed miserably. Finally Nan and Ben went in search of souvenirs at the shop next door to the motel office, leaving them alone.

"This wasn't my idea," he said gruffly.

"I know." She stared into her coffee cup with eyes that barely saw it. She was leaving and so was he. They'd never see each other again.

"Damn it, you know it's for the best," he said through his teeth. "Will you look at me?"

She lifted her eyes and winced at the temper in his. "Yes, I know it's for the best!" she muttered.

His lips parted on a rough breath. His silver eyes searched hers until she flushed. "I want you," he said unsteadily.

She glared at him. "That's it, reduce it to the most common terms you can!"

"What else is there besides lust?" he demanded. "That's all we really have in common. And we wouldn't have that if you hadn't spent your entire holiday here coming on to me!"

"That's right, blame it on me," she raged. "Tell the world I tried to seduce you!"

"Tell me you didn't," he shot right back. His hand curled around his wineglass and tightened until the stem threatened to snap. "Every time I turned around you were making eyes at me."

"I told you why…"

"You lied," he said flatly, his smile world-weary and full of cynicism. "Don't you think I know when a woman finds me attractive? I'm rich. I've spent my adult life fending off willing women."

"Including Marie?" she asked sweetly, with blazing pale eyes.

"I don't need to fend off Marie," he returned. "She has status of her own."

"You mean, her parents do," she shot back.

"It's the same thing."

"No, it isn't," she replied seriously. "Life is about making choices on your own, taking your own chances, making your own way. A life-style should be earned, not inherited."

"Ahhh," he murmured sarcastically. "A budding socialist."

"Hardly." She glared at him. "Haven't you been listening? I think people should earn what they get."

"Marie earns it," he said, his tone faintly suggestive.

She remembered how it felt to be in his arms, and she flushed, averting her eyes.

"I keep forgetting how young you are when you bait me," he said angrily. He drained his wineglass.

"I'm not so young that I don't know what you were insinuating about your relationship with Marie," she said shortly. "If she's what you really want, why were you kissing me on the beach?"

He searched her eyes. The memories were darkening his. "Maybe I wanted to see how far you'd go."

She felt her cheeks becoming even ruddier. "As you said, I'm young," she muttered. "A pushover for any experienced man," she added pointedly.

He wanted to believe that, but he couldn't. He toyed with the empty wineglass, watching the light from the chandelier reflected in the faceted crystal. "No," he replied. "It was much more than that, for both of us." He lifted his eyes back to hers and felt the heat shoot through him like fire as he saw his own hunger reflected in her soft, sad eyes.

His breathing roughened; quickened. "I want to make love to you, one last time."

Her lips parted. "Faulkner…"

He signaled the waiter and paid the bill. Scant minutes later, he'd asked Nan to take a delighted Ben back to the girls' motel room, and he and Shelly were walking down the dark, deserted beach.

Shelly was much too aware of the brevity of the strappy little green sundress she was wearing with high-heeled sandals. She felt vulnerable as she thought about his strong, callused hands on her bare skin. But she had no pride left and she couldn't pretend that she didn't want this. It would be their last time together.

He turned to her when they were along a sheltered bit of beach, elegant in his white dinner jacket and dark slacks. He seemed bigger somehow, towering over her, unsmiling.

"You came with me," he reminded her. "I didn't drag you here by the hand."

"I know." Her voice was almost drowned out by the crashing of the surf. She searched his dark eyes in the faint light. "I'm not taking anything," she said abruptly.

He drew in a long breath. "Shelly, we can't make love to each other here. And I can't take you to my room because Ben might decide to come back on his own, without Nan." He caught her shoulders in his lean, warm hands and drew her to him. "You're a virgin," he whispered softly, drowning her in his strength and the drugging, delicious scent of masculine cologne as he moved closer. "I'm not quite that much of a rogue…"

His mouth opened as it touched hers, teasing her lips apart. He felt them tremble softly as he began to increase the pressure of his mouth. She moaned, pressing against him, and he felt his body react sharply to her proximity.

She tensed and started to draw back, but his hand swept down to the base of her spine, gently preventing the withdrawal.

"You're safe," he whispered into her mouth. "This feels good. Don't ask me to stop."

It felt good to her, too, but it was embarrassing. She tried to tell him, but his mouth became slowly invasive, and she clung to him as the intimacy of the kiss grew suddenly and exploded into something approximating possession.

He felt her nails through the thick fabric of his jacket. He wanted to feel them his skin.

With a rough sound, his hand moved between them, his knuckles brushing over the tops of her breasts as he worked at fastenings. Seconds later, he coaxed her hands into the thick mat of hair that covered him and let her caress him.

"Oh, God, it isn't enough," he whispered shakily, his mouth harder now, hungrier. "Shelly!"

His mouth covered hers again. He moved the thin straps of her dress away from her shoulders and abruptly stripped her to the waist with deft, economic movements of his hands. Before she could utter a protest, he had her against him, inside the folds of his shirt and jacket, her breasts rubbing with exciting abrasion against his bare skin.

His thumbs caressed her breasts while he kissed her, his teeth nibbling, his tongue probing deeply. She was trembling and so was he, and the surf was hardly louder than their erratic heartbeats.

"Please!" she sobbed against his mouth.

He barely heard her. His body throbbed where hers touched it. His hands were possessing her, exploring her exquisite softness in a silence that was total and overwhelming. None of the differences between them mattered when they were this close. He'd never felt this way. Not even with his late wife when he was in the throes of first love.

He lifted his head a few inches and looked into her rapt, vulnerable face.

"If you were on the pill," he said roughly. "Would you let me?"

"I don't know." She rested her forehead on his chest, shivering with reaction. "It's a big step. I've always believed that it belongs in marriage, between two people who are committed to each other for life." She lifted her eyes to his. "Is that unrealistic, in a world where love is nothing more than a euphemism for sex?"

"What a profound question." He smiled, but a little bleakly. "I'm not the one to ask. Anyway," he added with a forced note of humor, "where would we make love? This is hardly a deserted place, and Nan and my son are in your room. If we went to mine..." He sighed heavily. "I couldn't. I want to, and if you were even faintly experienced, I would. But this isn't for you, Shelly. As I've already told you, I have nothing else to offer."

She pressed her cheek against the warm, heavily throbbing flesh of his chest. The thick hairs tickled her nose as they stood together in the semidarkness, unspeaking.

"If I were older," she began. "Richer…"

"You'd still be a virgin," he replied simply. "And I've had all I want of marriage." He tilted her chin up to his eyes. "I'll regret this night until I die."

"That you kissed me?"

He shook his head. "Oh, no. That I couldn't strip you down to your silky skin and ease you under me, here in the sand," he whispered, tracing her soft, swollen lips. "As intensely as we want each other, I don't think I'd ever hurt you."

She nibbled on his thin upper lip, her fingers stabbing into the hair that covered him. "It would take a long time, wouldn't it?" she whispered. "For me, I mean."

"Yes." He kissed her back, lazily, tenderly. His hands found her soft breasts and caressed them in a warm silence.

"They feel good."

"What?"

"Your hands on my skin," she said at his lips. "Do it…harder."

"I can't."

"Why?"

He teased around her mouth with the tip of his tongue. "You know why. Your breasts are very delicate, and I'm no sadist. I don't want to hurt you."

She smiled. "It wouldn't hurt. I meant like this."

She guided his thumb and forefinger to the hard, dusky tip and showed him what she wanted. She gasped as it sent a wave of heat through her body.

"Shelly," he whispered roughly, "does it make you hot all over when I do that?" he asked at her lips. He asked something else, something very intimate and explicit. "Does it?" he persisted huskily.

"Yes," she confessed shyly.

It wasn't wise. He knew it, even as he bent his head and took the nipple between his teeth. But the sensations she was describing very closely resembled those of fulfillment. It excited him to think he could give her complete ecstasy with such a small demonstration of love play. He had to know…

When he felt her convulse and cry out in his arms, he groaned and kissed her with slow anguish. He'd never been able to do that to another woman. Was it because she was a virgin that she reacted so violently to his ardor? Or was it something more?

He lifted his head and she hung in his arms, her body trembling, her face flushed with embarrassed shame.

He held her up, slowly replacing her bodice and refastening the soft straps. His hands were a little unsteady. He was still blatantly aroused.

"You shouldn't have…!" she managed to say, flustered.

"I think I should." He tilted her eyes up to his quiet, wise ones. "You do understand what happened?"

She flushed and averted her eyes. "Well, yes…"

"It's nothing to be ashamed of. You're one in a million," he said, his voice deep and slow and tender. "Most men would kill for a woman as passionate as you."

"It's embarrassing!" she groaned.

"That you should reach fulfillment because I suckled your breast?" he asked, his voice explicit but somehow comforting. "Shelly, I feel ten feet tall. I've never felt so much a man."

She looked up, slowly. "You don't think I'm odd?"

"I think you're dynamite." He smoothed back her disheveled hair with hands that weren't quite steady even now, although he was less tormented. "I'm flattered that you want me that much."

She lowered her eyes to his chest. "But this is all there is."

"That's right." He held her close for a long time, savoring the scent and feel of her in his arms. "Shelly?"

"Yes?"

He kissed her hair. "We'll always have Paris."

Despite her sorrow, she smiled.

THEY WENT HOME the next day. Shelly hadn't seen Faulkner again, and she hadn't tried to. She'd said her goodbyes to Ben when they'd returned to her motel room, a little tearfully. Ben had wanted to keep in touch, but Shelly didn't dare do that. She couldn't risk having them find out the truth about her background, about her parents. Washington was a big city, and despite her father's wealth and influence, he was one of many wealthy investment bankers in the city. She didn't remember her father ever mentioning Faulkner Scott, so it was unlikely that they knew each other. For the sake of her sanity, she had to keep it that way. After all, Faulkner had admitted that the main problem was his inability to make a commitment. He wanted an affair and she wanted forever. It wasn't easy to compromise on two such wide viewpoints.

She was going to miss him. And Ben. She'd lived her whole life without knowing either one of the Scotts, but she knew she'd live the rest of it without forgetting them.

Nan had noticed her friend's pallor and unusual quietness, but she hadn't remarked on it.

They boarded the plane and with adjoining seats, had time to talk, away from the rest of the students they traveled with.

"I'm sorry it didn't work out for you," Nan told her. "Really sorry. He was a dish, and the boy was special."

"Thanks. I'm sorry, too." She leaned back, closing her eyes. "Nan, if only I were liberated."

"You are."

"You know what I mean."

"Liberated as in sharing one night of explosive passion and spending the rest of your life living on it?"

Shelly glared at her. "Stop confusing me."

"You don't live the rest of your life on one night, no matter how explosive it is," Nan said firmly. "And in that one night, you could catch a disease that would kill you or make you untouchable. You could sacrifice all your principles and have nothing left except the certainty that the man you worshiped felt justified to treat you like a fast-food plate."

"A fast-food plate?"

"Something you use to feed yourself from and then throw away."

"Nan!"

"Well, it's true," the black girl said firmly. "You won't catch me risking my life or my health for the sake of a romantic one-night stand. Not me. I'm saving it all up for one lucky man who's going to thank God daily, on his knees, that I waited just for him." She leaned close. "*That's* romantic."

Shelly grimaced. "You have this nasty way of making me feel like pond scum."

Nan frowned. "Speaking of pond scum, where's Pete?"

"He got on the plane just behind you," Shelly said, chuckling. "Shame on you for calling him that."

"But he is pond scum," the other woman said seriously. "He seduced one of the freshman girls and then wouldn't have a thing to do with her the next day."

"You're right. He is pond scum!" Shelly exclaimed.

"So are a lot of other men, whispering sweet nothings so that they can have their way."

"Not all of them," Shelly said miserably. "There are men who feel protective toward women with no sense of self-preservation."

"So that's why he looked like that last night," Nan mused dryly.

"How did he look?"

"Frustrated. Confused. Puzzled. Delighted," she added softly. "The way he looked at you when you didn't see him!"

She sighed. "Oh, Shelly. If you'd had another week together, there would have been wedding bells."

"I'm afraid not. He doesn't want to get married."

"What man does?"

Shelly closed her eyes. "Well, it doesn't matter, does it? Spring break is over and I'll never see him again."

"He knows that you go to Thorn College," Nan remarked. "And he lives in D.C., too."

"It won't matter." Shelly said it with conviction, but deep inside, she hoped she was wrong....

THE SEMESTER WAS FINALLY OVER, and Shelly went home to sweat out her grades until the registrar notified her on what they were. She felt pretty confident about her subjects, but she always worried.

"Darling, must you wear *that* dress?" her mother muttered. "It's perfectly respectable..."

"It's so old-fashioned, Shelly," Mrs. Astor replied, glaring at the deep blue velvet gown that covered Shelly from neck to toes, except where it dipped seductively in the back.

Tonia Astor wore a black silk dress that flattered her still-youthful body, helping the contrast between her naturally black hair and its streak of pure silver. She looked elegant and chic, which she was. Shelly despaired of ever having her mother's unshakable poise at society gatherings.

The Astors were giving a gala party tonight in honor of a new president at one of the banks where Bart Astor was a member of the board of directors. Shelly had been persuaded into helping her mother hostess. She had no excuse, because she wasn't going to attend summer semester at the school.

"You've just been on holiday," her mother reminded her. "This is just a small get-together, darling. You'll enjoy yourself. It's time you stopped this silly college idea and got married. Charles is a delightful man, very settled and influential."

"Charles is a bore. He likes to quote stock averages to me."

"He's settled," her mother repeated.

"He should be, he lives with his mother."

"Shelly, really! Oh, there's Ted."

Her mother moved away, dragging Shelly with her across the crowded room where a full orchestra was playing. With her upswept salon coiffure and discreet but expensive sapphire choker and matching bracelet, Shelly's subdued elegance matched the tone of the party.

"Ted Dumaris," Tonia exclaimed, taking both his hands in hers. "So nice to see you again!" she added, totally unaware of Shelly's shocked expression and sudden panic as a tall, dark-haired man with a familiar thin brunette in tow made their way through the crowd to Antonia Astor and Shelly. "And is this the daughter you were telling me about?" she exclaimed with enthusiasm.

"Yes, this is my Marie and her…*our*…friend, Faulkner Scott. This is Antonia Astor."

Faulkner's expression was faintly curious. He hadn't seen Shelly, standing just to the side and behind her mother. He was obviously connecting the name.

"How lovely of you to have invited us," Marie was gushing to Antonia. "I adore your home. So impressive!"

Shelly wasn't impressed. Marie's fawning made her nauseous. And seeing Faulkner again wasn't helping.

"Where's Shelly? Oh, there you are, darling, do come and be introduced. She's a college freshman, you know, at twenty-four! We were absolutely horrified…!"

Her mother rambled on, but Shelly wasn't listening to the explanations or introductions. She was lost in Faulkner's glittering silver eyes. He stared at her with shock and dawning realization, barely aware of her mother or his surroundings.

"Twenty-four?" he asked gruffly.

"Yes, isn't she ancient to be starting college?" Tonia laughed. "But she has a high grade point average and we're very proud. What do you do, Ms. Dumaris?" she asked Marie.

"When she isn't looking down her nose at other people, I expect she goes to parties, don't you, Ms. Dumaris?" Shelly, diverted, fixed her cold blue gaze on the shaken older woman. "Ms. Dumaris mentioned just recently that she could use her influence to have me booted out of college."

"Shelly," Tonia began uncertainly, because she'd never seen her daughter lose her temper.

Marie swallowed, blushing and back-stepping. "I never meant it that way!" She laughed nervously, chattering. "I'm sure you must have misunderstood me!"

"I didn't misunderstand a single word, unfortunately for you."

She turned her back on Marie and her eyes found Charles. She motioned to him, ignoring Faulkner and Marie's almost pitiable attempts to smooth over her vicious attitude in Daytona Beach with Shelly's mother.

Shelly caught tall blond Charles by the hand and turned to face the others. Her face was pale but she was as composed as she'd ever been.

"I'd like you all to meet Charles Barington," she said with a forced, dazzling smile. "He's my fiancé!"

Chapter Six

"I can't believe you're finally willing to marry me," Charles blurted out when they were out of earshot of the others. "Shelly, what a surprise!"

"I hope you aren't going to be upset, Charles, but I really didn't mean it," she said gently. "I'm sorry, but I was in a very tight spot. I'll explain later."

He looked torn between disappointment and relief. His eyes glanced toward a young woman named Betsy, for whom he was slowly developing deep feelings. "What will everyone say?" he asked.

"Nothing at all," she assured him. "And I'll simply say that I wasn't quite enough for you, if anyone asks why we got unengaged."

"That's very nice of you," he said, surprised.

"Not really, and I'm sorry I had to involve you. But we've been friends for a long time, and I hoped you wouldn't mind."

"Of course I don't."

"I'm glad." She smiled, watching him blush. He was a

sweet man, in his way, but he had no imagination and no stomach for a fight. Shelly knew instinctively that she'd spend her life walking on him if they got married. And that wouldn't suit either of them, especially Charles. She noticed a familiar younger woman watching him with covetous eyes and an idea was born. "Do go and have something to drink, Charles, and we'll talk later. Oh, there's Betsy, remember her? She's looking very lonely. Wouldn't it be nice if you asked her to dance?"

"Yes, of course," he said eagerly.

"Why don't you, then? She's a dear girl."

Charles nodded. He'd never understand Shelly. But Betsy was sweet, and she seemed to like him very much. She only danced with him at parties. He smiled as he approached her and she blushed. He wondered if he hadn't been turning his interest in the wrong direction all along as he took a radiant Betsy into his arms on the dance floor.

Shelly, meanwhile, went to the drinks table and poured herself a large brandy. She made a face as she sipped it.

A big, lean hand shot past her, took the glass and put it down on the table. "You can't hold your liquor. Leave it alone."

She whirled, her eyes angry. "Don't tell me what to do. I don't like it."

His eyebrows arched. "My, how you've changed. A young, virginal, college freshman with no money—isn't that how the story went?"

"All lies," she said, smiling up at him. "I had fun. Didn't you?"

"Not all lies," he replied, reading fear through the bravado. Her eyelids fell quickly. "I may not be able to tell a poor student from a socialite, but I damned sure know a virgin when I make love to one."

"We didn't," she said sharply.

"Make love? No, we didn't," he replied quietly. "You're

twenty-four and wealthy. There are no barriers, isn't that what you expect me to say?"

She lifted her eyes. "I still believe in forever after, and you don't want to get married." He looked stunned. She laughed coldly. "I don't believe in fairy tales. You told me yourself that commitment was the real obstacle, not my background. Or, rather, what you thought was my background." She smiled cynically. "I'm much sought after, you know. Men love my father's money."

"So that's why."

"Why what?"

"Why you went back to school without letting anyone know who you were."

"It beats being on the appetizer list."

He searched her flushed face. "Your fiancé is dancing with another woman. Much too close," he added with a glance at Charles and Betsy. "Don't you mind?"

"I would if I planned to marry him. He thinks I do. So does my father, who arranged it. My father wants me to be Mrs. Charles Barington. With all due respect," she added softly, "I hardly think a banker would be high on his list of son-in-law prospects. Unless, of course, you owned all the assets in your bank."

He glared down at her. "You know nothing about me, financially or otherwise. And if I wanted to marry you, the only opinion I'd give a damn about would be yours."

"My father has taken down bigger men than you. I fought him to get to go to college." She glanced towards Charles with sad resignation. "I don't feel like fighting him anymore. You were right. There's no such thing as love and happily ever after. I've been dreaming."

He caught her arm. It hurt to find her like this, so cynical and self-effacing and sad. He'd been lonely, but she looked as if the weeks they'd been apart had hurt her even more.

"Shelly," he said softly.

She pushed his hand away and smiled that social smile that never reached her eyes. "So nice that you could come tonight, Mr. Scott," she said. "If you'll excuse me, I have to circulate."

She took Charles away from Betsy with a murmured apology. "Do you mind being engaged to me for the rest of the evening? I'll square it with Betsy."

"No, of—of course not," he faltered.

She laid her cheek on his chest and closed her eyes. "Then dance, Charles. Just dance."

THE NEXT DAY, she went to Nassau and checked into a hotel and casino complex overlooking Cable Beach, with its blistering white sand and incredibly clear turquoise waters. She'd told Betsy about the masquerade before she left and hoped that Charles would have enough sense to notice that the young woman was crazy about him.

Shelly herself had no interest in Charles or marriage. Seeing Faulkner again had destroyed her serenity. Now she had to find it again, and she didn't know how she was going to manage. What she'd felt for him hadn't vanished. It had grown stronger.

The yellow bikini was all too brief, but everyone else was wearing things just as skimpy. She closed her eyes with a sigh and let the sun warm her back.

The sudden sprinkle of icy water on her spine made her lift up. "Hey!" she said angrily.

A pair of gray eyes in a young face met hers—laughing eyes. "Hi, Mom!" Ben said chuckling. His hair, and the rest of him, were wet. He was wearing bathing trunks and carrying a towel. "Fancy meeting you here!"

"Oh, God," she groaned, laying her head on her forearms.

"Not quite," came a deep, gravelly voice from overhead.

She didn't look up. She didn't have to. She knew who it was. "What are you doing here?"

"Taking a vacation. Marie and her father have flown to

England on business and I had some time off due. Ben's just out of school. We like the Bahamas, don't we, son?"

"There are seven hundred islands down here in the Bahamas chain," she mentioned. "Couldn't you like another one?"

"This is great," he said. "There's even a casino. Do you gamble?"

"I don't gamble. I lose. That's all I do." She lifted her head and glared at him. "Lately it's getting to be an affliction!"

"Not nice," he chided, sliding closer to her. He looked as relaxed as his son. He was wearing dark bathing trunks with white stripes down the side, his magnificent chest bare and rippling with muscle and thick black hair. He watched her watching him and chuckled. "Throw me that towel, Ben," he said, and sat down beside her. "Nice hotel. I'm glad you picked one close to the water."

"All of them are close to the water."

"Not really. Ben and I once stayed in a hotel high on a hill overlooking the bay. Very nice. Swimming pool and five-star food. But no ocean."

"That's right. This is a nice hotel, Mom. Dad had to call half the hotels in Nassau to find you...."

"Don't you want to go and swim, Ben?" he was asked.

"Oh. Oh, sure!" He chuckled. "See you later, Mom!"

Shelly groaned, giving up all hope of denying that she was. Nobody listened anyway.

Faulkner lay back and stretched hugely, his powerful legs crossing. "Your mother said to tell you that Charles has asked Betsy for a date. Your father is livid."

"Poor old Daddy," she said unenthusiastically.

"He only wants you to be happy."

"If he did, he'd let me live my own life."

"Parents sometimes take a little convincing that children are capable of making their own decisions. I did," he reminded her. "You'll be glad to know that Ben and I are getting along very well these days. He's hardly the same boy he used to be."

"I hope he gets to stay that way," she said stiffly. "Your Marie strikes me as a woman who wants to reshape everyone around her in her own image."

"She didn't used to be quite so bad," he replied. "You set her on her heels. It did her good. She'll think twice before she acts in an offensive way to strangers again."

"When's the wedding?" she asked, trying to sound casual when her heart was breaking.

"I don't know." He rolled over onto his stomach and looked down at her. "When do you want it to be?"

She swallowed. "Don't make jokes."

"I'm not." He lifted his hand and just the tip of his forefinger began to work its way slowly down the strap of her bikini, teasing the soft bare skin of her shoulder down to the slope of her breast.

"Don't!" she whispered.

"Why not, little one?" He caught her eyes and held them, and still that maddening finger moved, traced, teased. The nipple beyond it grew visibly hard and she bit her lip to keep from crying out as he increased her sensual anguish.

"Faulkner, don't," she pleaded brokenly.

"I wouldn't if you didn't enjoy it so much." He smiled, spreading the radius of his touch until she flinched. "That's nice," he murmured huskily. "I like the way you look when I touch you."

"There are people everywhere, didn't you notice?" Her voice sounded high-pitched, squeaky.

"Yes, but they're sunbathing and swimming. No one's watching us. Not even Ben." He moved, shifting just slightly so that his body was between her and the other sunbathers. "Which means," he breathed, "that I can do this…"

His whole hand slid gently beneath the yellow triangle and over her soft breast. He watched her shiver, felt her nails biting into his arm. He smiled through his own excitement. She was very sensual, and he loved the way she felt under his hand.

"Faulkner, no!" she whispered.

His thumb and forefinger gently caressed the taut nipple and she pushed at him, frightened of the sensations slicing through her body.

She wasn't the only one who was becoming aroused. As he watched her reactions, he felt his own body growing tense.

With a groan, he moved away from her and lay on his belly, trying to breathe normally.

"Are you all right?" she asked when she could speak again.

"Isn't that my line?" He took a slow breath and glanced at her with a rueful, self-mocking smile. "Would you like to make a guess at why I'm lying on my stomach instead of my back right now?"

"Not really," she murmured, averting her eyes.

"Coward."

"You should be ashamed of yourself, trying to seduce innocent women on crowded beaches," she muttered.

"Not women. *Woman*. Only you."

"Still…"

"But the first time should be on a beach, don't you think?" he mused, lifting his head to watch her. "In the moonlight. Just the two of us, our bodies fitting together as perfectly as two puzzle pieces."

"You're driving me crazy!" she said through her teeth.

"I ache in very unpleasant ways," he remarked. "There's a Jacuzzi in my room. Ben has a room of his own. You could come upstairs with me while he's swimming and we could make love in the whirlpool bath."

"Faulkner!"

"It was just a desperate thought." He shifted his attention to the sand. "A white wedding is going to be horrific. I dread the thought of it. Between us, we know far too many people. That will mean just the right clothes, the right caterer, reception at the country club…"

"Then why don't you and Marie elope?" she asked, trying to hide her misery.

"I'm not marrying Marie and you know it. You knew the night we almost went too far on the beach," he said quietly. "I think I knew, too, but I couldn't quite accept it then. I've had time to get my priorities straight. You and Ben come first with me."

The earth was spinning around her. She was sure of it. She forced her gaze up to his and her eyes widened. "What are you saying?" she whispered.

"Don't you know?" He moved closer and kissed her. His lips were soft, and slow, and tender. "I love you," he whispered. "Say yes and put me out of my misery."

"But…but Marie, and Charles…!"

"Shut up!" he breathed into her mouth, and dragged her close while he deepened the kiss to madness.

Something wet was dripping on them. She opened her eyes and looked up a little blankly.

"Well?" Ben asked impatiently.

"She said yes," Faulkner managed huskily, pulling her back to him.

"Whoopee!" Ben yelled. He turned around and told everyone on the beach that he was going to have a brand-new mother. Everyone laughed and cheered him on. Everyone, that was, except the couple on the beach, who were oblivious to everything except each other.

THE WEDDING WAS HELD a month later in the big Presbyterian Church near where Shelly and her parents lived. Her family had belonged to this church for three generations, so it was like home. The minister who'd baptized Shelly at the age of three months officiated at the ceremony, and Ben was his father's best man. Nan, of course, was maid of honor.

It had been the longest four weeks of Shelly's life, and she was certain that Faulkner felt the same way. They'd been incredibly circumspect during the strained engagement. It wasn't Shelly's idea. She'd tried repeatedly to tempt him into her bed, going so far as to remind him that even the Puritans didn't condemn premarital sex between engaged couples. But it didn't work. He was determined that they were going to have a white wedding and a wedding night.

The big day had arrived. Shelly was almost shaking with nerves, and her new husband didn't seem much calmer. They were off to Jamaica on their honeymoon, and Shelly thought to herself that it was going to feel like years before they finally had any time to themselves.

"Take deep breaths," he whispered when they were half-way through the reception. "We'll get through it."

"I hope so." She glanced at him. "You didn't kiss me at the altar."

He searched her soft eyes. He'd lifted her veil, but he hadn't kissed her. He'd kissed the palms of both her hands and given her a look that would have fried tomatoes.

"The way I want to kiss you would be almost indecent in a church," he said quietly. "That's why I'm saving it."

Her lips parted. She searched his hard, lean face hungrily. "I want you," she said unsteadily.

"I want you, too." He traced her mouth with a long finger. "It won't be much longer."

"I know."

Her parents came up to congratulate them again. Her father was more enthusiastic about the match than she'd imagined he would be. Even her mother raved about Faulkner and young Ben. There had been nothing but congratulations and praise from the morning they announced the engagement. It was a little surprising, but Shelly hadn't questioned it.

They were wished well by the others when they drove

away in the nicely decorated car, courtesy of a beaming Ben, who was to stay with his new mother's parents for the duration of the honeymoon, and then Nan and some other college classmates. As they were driven to the airport by Faulkner's chauffeur, Shelly kept staring with wonder in her whole expression at the wide gold band Faulkner had slid onto her finger.

It was a long, tiring trip. By the time they got to their hotel in Montego Bay and got checked in, it was time to eat something. Shelly had little appetite, but she sat with her new husband in the dining room and nibbled on seafood while he ate a rare steak.

They walked along the beach on the way back, staring out over the ocean as the sun set. Then he turned her and led her back into their room.

There was a balcony overlooking the bay—a very private balcony, high up and concealed. Faulkner led her onto it, where a big chaise longue was already spread with a beach towel.

Gently he undressed her and laid her on it, standing over her to savor every soft line of her with eyes that shone like beacons with love.

"Do you want me to make you pregnant, or do you want to wait a few months?"

Her lips parted on a shocked breath. This was something they hadn't discussed. She was embarrassed by the heat that accompanied the softly spoken words, by the thought of allowing him to give her a child. She shivered, her eyes lost in his.

"You want it, don't you?" he asked huskily.

"I'm sorry," she whispered. "Yes...I do!"

"There's nothing to be sorry about," he said, his voice deep and slow. "I want it as much as you do."

"Will Ben mind?"

He smiled. "No. He won't mind."

His hand went to his shirt. He stripped very slowly, letting her watch him. His breathing changed when the last of the fabric came off and she could see the altered contours of his powerful body. Her eyes lingered there, fascinated.

"How does it feel to look at me like this?"

She caught her breath. "Intimate," she whispered, forcing her eyes up to his. "Very, very intimate. And very exciting. I feel hot all over."

"I can take care of that," he said, smiling gently.

He eased down onto the chaise with her, and began to kiss her. At first the kisses were lazy and soft and undemanding. But then he touched her, and with each soft exploration of his fingers, her body shivered even more, until she sought the full length of him with a need as violent as a summer storm.

He indulged her, his mouth as slowly invasive as the fingers that traced her and teased her and discovered her most intimate secrets. When she was ready, he slid her over onto her back and moved his body gently to fit hers.

He kissed her tenderly while he moved between her soft thighs and eased down. She jerked a little, but a few seconds later, she relaxed and shifted to make it easier for him.

"You flinched then," he whispered, lifting his dark head to look directly into her eyes. "Do you want me to arouse you a little more before I take you?"

She flushed at the explicit question. "But you already are…!"

"No." He kissed her eyelids closed and moved forward. As he did, she felt the sting and began to stiffen. "It's going to be difficult," he whispered at her lips. "You need more time. It's all right," he added when she looked set to protest, because he was shivering with a need of his own. "I can wait. Here, Shelly…"

True to his word, he started all over again, his mouth and his hands so tender, so thorough, that he very quickly brought her to a stormy peak of tension. Far from trying to push him away, she went crazy with the need for him. She sobbed against his mouth and pushed up with her hips, completing his possession even before he realized what she meant to do.

He shuddered and suddenly there was a rhythm, a fierce urgency that blotted out the sea and the sky and the night. She heard his voice against her mouth, but she was climbing, climbing, climbing…

There was a sharp explosion of heat that caught her unawares. She clung and stiffened, aware of desperate motion, a harsh cry and the convulsive shuddering of the body so intimately joined to her own. And then, slowly, the world came back into focus.

She lay beneath him, exhausted with pleasure, too shaken to move, fighting to get her breath.

"As first times go," she managed to say unsteadily, "and on a scale of ten, that was at least a twenty."

"Even as experience goes, that was a twenty," he breathed at her ear. "Are you all right? It isn't too bad?"

"It isn't bad at all." She moved against him, glorying in his nudity and her own, at the feel of him so close. "Are you going to roll over and go to sleep now?"

"Yes, and so are you." He chuckled.

He got up, lifting her, and carried her to bed. He slid her under the covers, pulled her gently into his arms and turned off the light. "Try to get some rest," he whispered. "You're going to need it in the morning."

She laughed delightedly, resting her cheek on his chest with exquisite delight.

"Shelly."

"Hmmmm?"

"You haven't said you love me."

"Yes, I have," she murmured drowsily. "I've said it a hundred times, but you haven't heard it. I love you madly. I always will."

He smiled and brushed his lips against her forehead. "I'm glad. Because you're my life now."

She sighed, stretching as she snuggled closer. "Faulkner."

"Hmmmm?"

"We'll always have Paris."

He chuckled. Just before he closed his eyes, he felt a twinge of sorrow for that fictional character who'd walked away with only a gendarme for consolation. He had something much, much sweeter. He had Shelly…and Ben…and a future full of love.

* * * * *

Turn the page for a preview of
New York Times *Bestselling author*

Diana Palmer's

newest hardcover for HQN Books

BEFORE SUNRISE

Available this July at your favorite book outlet.

Chapter One

THE CROWD WAS DENSE, but he stood out. He was taller than most of the other spectators and looked elegant in his expensive, tailored gray-vested suit. He had a lean, dark face, faintly scarred, with large, almond-shaped black eyes and short eyelashes. His mouth was wide and thin-lipped, his chin stubbornly jutted. His thick, jet-black hair was gathered into a neat ponytail that fell almost to his waist in back. Several other men in the stands wore their hair that way. But they were white. Cortez was Comanche. He had the background to wear the unconventional hairstyle. On him, it looked sensual and wild and even a little dangerous.

Another ponytailed man, a redhead with a receding hairline and thick glasses, grinned and gave him the victory sign. Cortez shrugged, unimpressed, and turned his attention toward the graduation ceremonies. He was here against his will and the last thing he felt like was being friendly. If he'd followed his instincts, he'd still be in Washington going over a backlog of federal cases he was due to prosecute in court.

The dean of the university was announcing the names of the graduates. He'd reached the K's, and on the program, Phoebe Margaret Keller was the second name under that heading.

It was a beautiful spring day at the University of Tennessee at Knoxville, so the commencement ceremony was being held outside. Phoebe was recognizable by the long platinum blond braid trailing the back of her dark gown as she accepted her diploma with one hand and shook hands with the dean with the other. She moved past the podium and switched her tassel to the other side of her cap. Cortez could see the grin from where he was standing.

He'd met Phoebe a year earlier, while he was investigating some environmental sabotage in Charleston, South Carolina. Phoebe, an anthropology major, had helped him track down a toxic waste site. He'd found her more than attractive, despite her tomboyish appearance, but time and work pressure had been against them. He'd promised to come and see her graduate, and here he was. But the age difference was still pretty formidable, because he was thirty-six and she was twenty-three. He did know Phoebe's aunt Derrie, from having worked with her during the Kane Lombard pollution case. If he needed a reason for showing up at the graduation, Phoebe was Derrie's late brother's child and he was almost a friend of the family.

The dean's voice droned on, and graduate after graduate accepted a diploma. In no time at all, the exercises were over and whoops of joy and congratulations rang in the clear Tennessee air.

No longer drawing attention as the exuberant crowd moved toward the graduates, Cortez hung back, watching. His black eyes narrowed as a thought occurred to him. Phoebe wasn't one for crowds. Like himself, she was a loner.

If she was going to work her way around the people to find her aunt Derrie, she'd do it away from the crowd. So he started looking for alternate routes from the stadium to the parking lot. Minutes later, he found her, easing around the side of the building, almost losing her balance as she struggled with the too-long gown, muttering to herself about people who couldn't measure people properly for gowns.

"Still talking to yourself, I see," he mused, leaning against the wall with his arms folded across his chest.

She looked up and saw him. With no time to prepare, her delight swept over her even features with a radiance that took his breath. Her pale blue eyes sparkled and her mouth, devoid of lipstick, opened on a sharply indrawn breath.

"Cortez!" she exclaimed.

She looked as if she'd run straight into his arms with the least invitation, and he smiled indulgently as he gave it to her. He levered away from the wall and opened his arms.

She went into them without any hesitation whatsoever, nestling close as he enfolded her tightly.

"You came," she murmured happily into his shoulder.

"I said I would," he reminded her. He chuckled at her unbridled enthusiasm. One lean hand tilted up her chin so that he could search her eyes. "Four years of hard work paid off, I see."

"So it did. I'm a graduate," she said, grinning.

"Certifiable," he agreed. His gaze fell to her soft pink mouth and darkened. He wanted to bend those few inches and kiss her, but there were too many reasons why he shouldn't. His hand was on her upper arm and, because he was fighting his instincts so hard, his grip began to tighten.

She tugged against his hold. "You're crushing me," she protested gently.

"Sorry." He let her go with an apologetic smile. "That training at Quantico dies hard," he added on a light note, alluding to his service with the FBI.

"No kiss, huh?" she chided with a loud sigh, searching his dark eyes.

One eye narrowed amusedly. "You're an anthropology major. Tell me why I won't kiss you," he challenged.

"Native Americans," she began smugly, "especially Native American men, rarely show their feelings in public. Kissing me in a crowd would be as distasteful to you as undressing in front of it."

His eyes softened as they searched her face. "Whoever taught you anthropology did a very good job."

She sighed. "Too good. What am I going to use it for in Charleston? I'll end up teaching…"

"No, you won't," he corrected. "One of the reasons I came was to tell you about a job opportunity."

Her eyes widened, brightened. "A job?!"

"In D.C.," he added. "Interested?"

"Am I ever!" A movement caught her eye. "Oh, there's Aunt Derrie!" she said, and called to her aunt. "Aunt Derrie! Look, I graduated, I have proof!" She held up her diploma as she ran to hug her aunt and then shake hands with U.S. Senator Clayton Seymour, who'd been her aunt's boss for years before they became engaged.

"We're both very happy for you," Derrie said warmly. "Hi, Cortez!" she beamed. "You know Clayton, don't you?"

"Not directly," Cortez said, but he shook hands anyway.

Clayton's firm lips tugged into a smile. "I've heard a lot about you from my brother-in-law, Kane Lombard. He and my sister Nikki wanted to come today, but their twins were sick. If you're going to be in town tonight, we'd love to have you join us for supper," he told Cortez. "We're taking Phoebe out for a graduation celebration."

"I wish I had time," he said quietly. "I have to go back tonight."

"Of course. Then we'll see you again sometime, in D.C.,"

Derrie said, puzzled by the strong vibes she sensed between her niece and Cortez.

"I've got something to discuss with Phoebe," he said, turning to Derrie and Clayton. "I need to borrow her for an hour or so."

"Go right ahead," Derrie said. "We'll go back to the hotel and have coffee and pie and rest until about six. Then we'll pick you up for supper, Phoebe."

"Thanks," she said. "Oh, my cap and gown...!" She stripped it off, along with her hat, and handed them to Derrie.

"Wait, Phoebe, weren't the honor graduates invited to a luncheon at the dean's house?" Derrie protested suddenly.

Phoebe didn't hesitate. "They'll never miss me," she said, and waved as she joined Cortez.

"An honor graduate, too," he mused as they walked back through the crowd toward his rental car. "Why doesn't that surprise me?"

"Anthropology is my life," she said simply, pausing to exchange congratulations with one of her friends on the way. She was so happy that she was walking on air.

"Nice touch, Phoebe," the girl's companion murmured with a dry glance at Cortez as they moved along, "bringing your anthropology homework along to graduation."

"Bill!" the girl cried, hitting him.

Phoebe had to stifle a giggle. Cortez wasn't smiling. On the other hand, he didn't explode, either. He gave Phoebe a stern look.

"Sorry," she murmured. "It's sort of a squirrelly day."

He shrugged. "No need to apologize. I remember what it's like on graduation day."

"Your degree would be in law, right?"

He nodded.

"Did your family come to your graduation?" she asked curiously.

He didn't answer her. It was a deliberate snub, and it should have made her uncomfortable, but she never held back with him.

"Another case of instant foot-in-mouth disease," she said immediately. "And I thought I was cured!"

He chuckled reluctantly. "You're as incorrigible as I remember you."

"I'm amazed that you did remember me, or that you took the trouble to find out when and where I was graduating so that you could be here," she said. "I couldn't send you an invitation," she added sheepishly, "because I didn't have your address. I didn't really expect you, either. We only spent an hour or two together last year."

"They were memorable ones. I don't like women very much," he said as they reached the unobtrusive rental car, a gray American-made car of recent vintage. He turned and looked down at her solemnly. "In fact," he added evenly, "I don't like being in public display very much."

She lifted both eyebrows. "Then why are you here?"

He stuck his hands deep into his pockets. "Because I like you," he said. His dark eyes narrowed. "And I don't want to."

"Thanks a lot!" she said, exasperated.

He stared at her. "I like honesty in a relationship."

"Are we having one?" she asked innocently. "I didn't notice."

His mouth pulled down at one corner. "If we were, you'd know," he said softly. "But I came because I promised that I would. And the offer of the job opportunity is genuine. Although," he added, "it's rather an unorthodox one."

"I'm not being asked to take over the archives at the Smithsonian, then? What a disappointment!"

Laughter bubbled out of his throat. "Funny girl." He opened the passenger door with exaggerated patience and smiled faintly. "You bubble, don't you?" he remarked. "I've never known anyone so animated."

"Yes, well, that's because you're suffering from sensory deprivation resulting from too much time spent with your long nose stuck in law books. Dull, dry, boring things."

"The law is not boring," he returned.

"It depends which side you're sitting on." She frowned. "This job you're telling me about wouldn't have to do with anything legal, would it? Because I only had one course in government and a few hours of history, but…"

"I don't need a law clerk," he returned.

"Then what do you need?"

"You wouldn't be working for me," he corrected. "I have ties to a group that fights for sovereignty for the Native American tribes. They have a staff of attorneys. I thought you might fit in very well, with your background in anthropology. I've pulled some strings to get you an interview."

She didn't speak for a minute. "I think you're forgetting something. My major is anthropology. Most of it is forensic anthropology. Bones."

He glanced at her. "You wouldn't be doing that for them."

"What would I be doing?"

"It's a desk job," he admitted. "But a good one."

"I appreciate your thinking of me," she said carefully. "But I can't give up fieldwork. That's why I've applied at the Smithsonian for a position with the anthropology section."

He was quiet for a long moment. "Do you know how indigenous people feel about archaeology? We don't like having people dig up our sacred sites and our relatives, however old they are."

"I just graduated," she reminded him. "Of course I do. But there's a lot more to archaeology than digging up skeletons!"

His eyes were cold. "And it doesn't stop you from wanting to get a job doing something that resembles grave-digging?"

She gasped. "It is not grave-digging! For heaven's sake…"

He held up a hand. "We can agree to disagree, Phoebe," he told her. "You won't change my mind any more than I'll change yours. I'm sorry about the job, though. You'd have been an asset to them."

She unbent a little. "Thanks for recommending me, but I don't want a desk job. Besides, I may go on to graduate school after I've had a few months to get over the past four years. They've been pretty hectic."

"Yes, I remember."

"Why did you recommend me for that job? There must be a line of people who'd love to have it—people better qualified than I am."

He turned his head and looked directly into her eyes. There was something that he wasn't telling her, something deep inside him.

"Maybe I'm lonely," he said shortly. "There aren't many people who aren't afraid to come close to me these days."

"Does that matter? You don't like people close," she said.

She searched his arrogant profile. There were new lines in that lean face, lines she hadn't seen last year, despite the solemnity of the time they'd spent together. "Something's upset you," she said out of the blue. "Or you're worried about something."

Both dark eyebrows went up. "I beg your pardon?" he asked curtly.

The hauteur went right over her head. "Not something to do with work, either," she continued, reasoning aloud. "It's something very personal…"

"Stop right there," he said shortly. "I invited you out to talk about a job, not about my private life."

"Ah. A closed door. Intriguing." She stared at him. "Not a woman?"

"You're the only woman in my life."

She laughed unexpectedly. "That's a good one."

"I'm not kidding. I don't have affairs or relationships." He glanced at her as he merged into traffic again and turned at the next corner. "I might make an exception for you, but don't get your hopes up. A man has his reputation to consider."

She grinned. "I'll remember that you said that."

TABLOID BABY
Candace Camp

Chapter One

It was not supposed to happen like this.

BETH SUTTON SCANNED THE HORIZON, fighting down panic. It stretched limitlessly all around her, the flat West Texas landscape, dotted with low mesquite bushes and prickly pear cacti. The road beside which she stood bisected the empty landscape, disappearing into the distance like a gray ribbon. She had been standing here for ten minutes, and there hadn't been a car yet.

Another pain gripped her, and she leaned against her crippled car, trying to breathe as she had learned in Lamaze class. *Why hadn't they taught her what she really needed to know now: what to do when you're having labor pains and are stranded in the middle of nowhere?*

The worst of it was, she knew that it was all her own fault. She had been utterly, hopelessly stupid. She had felt two pains this morning, about thirty minutes apart, but after that there had been nothing. She had assumed it was like last week, when she had had a few false labor pains one day and nothing else had happened. Of course, she realized now that it had been foolish to assume it was false labor— and even more foolish to decide to drive into town to get the eggs that she needed for muffins. She understood now— too late—that her sudden burst of energy and the urge to start cleaning and baking were part of the nesting instinct the Lamaze teacher had told them about.

She should have stayed home, should have waited to see if the pains began again. Instead she had driven into town, but as she was returning to the ranch house, a sudden pain had struck her, so much sharper and more severe than the others that when it hit, her hands had jerked on the wheel and the car had wound up in the ditch. So now here she was, miles from anywhere, with her car half in the ditch and one tire blown. Not only that, her water had broken during the accident, soaking her dress. Only a few minutes later, she had had a second pain.

Tears battered at the backs of her eyes. Beth blinked them away. *She had to be strong.* She was all alone, but she told herself that she was used to that. She had always been an independent woman. It was, after all, why she had moved away from the ranch when she was nineteen. She had felt as if she was being smothered by the small town, where everyone knew everything everyone else did, and by her father and three doting older brothers, who were convinced it was their duty to protect her from all life's little bumps and scrapes. She had been living alone in Dallas and taking care of herself for ten years now, and even if she had come back to her dad's ranch for help when she found out she was pregnant, it had been a purely practical move. It did not mean that she was any less capable of taking care of herself.

She drew a calming breath and made herself think. She obviously could not stand there dithering beside an inoperative car and wishing she had brought the cell phone with her. The fact was that she didn't have it; Dad and Cory had taken it when they went out to work on the other side of the ranch today, so that she would be able to get hold of them if she had an emergency. Another fact was that no one had come down this road in almost twenty minutes, and she could easily stand here for another hour before someone did, since it was only a side road.

She took her purse from the car and slung it over her shoulder. Then she set off down the road in the direction in which she had just come. Though it was a good deal farther to the town of Angel Eye than it was to the ranch house—ten miles instead of five—at least in another mile or so she would reach the main highway. While it was not exactly heavily traveled, her chances would be much better of flagging down a ride. She trudged along, refusing to think about the horror tales she had heard about hitching rides. She also tried not to think about how hot the sun was or how thirsty she had become or how far a mile was when one was heavily pregnant and being blasted by pains every ten minutes.

Suddenly there was the sound of a car behind her. It was so faint, and she was concentrating so hard on walking, that for a moment she did not recognize the sound. When it finally dawned on her that she was hearing the purr of an engine in the distance, she whirled and looked behind her, shading her eyes. Sure enough, there was a dark shape on the road. Relief flooded her, leaving her knees so shaky she almost sank onto the ground. She hadn't realized until that moment how tensely she had been holding herself.

As the car drew closer, she could see that it was a large, dark, expensive car, a Mercedes, in fact. In one way, that was reassuring; a Mercedes seemed like the car of a solid citizen, not a psycho serial killer who preyed on hitchhikers. On the other hand, it also meant that it was not anyone she knew. She could not think of a soul in or around Angel Eye who drove a Mercedes. Just then another pain hit her, and she almost doubled over with it.

The car screeched to a stop beside her, and she heard the car door open and the sound of running feet. She could not look up, could not even open her eyes. It was difficult enough just remembering to breathe right.

"Ma'am? What's the matter?" It was a man's voice, deep and with the faintest tinge of the South in it.

She could see his feet. They halted a few feet from her, then came forward more slowly. "Ma'am?" he repeated, and now, as the pain began to blessedly recede, she could hear the wariness in his tone. "Do you need some help?"

He was close to her now, and the pain was beginning to be almost bearable. She uncoiled from her defensive posture, and for the first time she looked up at him—and found herself staring into the most beautiful blue eyes she had ever seen.

She knew she must look like a fool staring at him, but she could not help it. This was a man who did not belong in Angel Eye, Texas. He wore loafers, off-white linen trousers and a collarless shirt of the same color. It was the sort of casual outfit she had seen on male models in GQ, and the clothes suited him to a T. His hair was black, thick, excellently cut and just a fraction too long, giving him a hint of the rebel. His lips were modeled and firm, his jaw strong and his nose straight. A slash of a scar, about an inch long, cut through one of his dark eyebrows and saved his face from perfection.

"Who in the world are you?" she blurted out.

His brows went up at her words, and he replied coolly, "The man who stopped because you looked as if you were in a great deal of pain."

"I'm sorry. That was rude. I was…just so surprised. I—yes, I was in pain, and I'm extremely glad you stopped." Her hand went instinctively to her swollen stomach. "My car broke down back there."

She turned and pointed and was surprised to see how short a distance she had walked from her automobile. It had seemed like forever. She looked back at him. Those cool blue eyes were still on her assessingly, and Beth realized, embarrassed, how awful she must look: sweating and dusty, her curling red hair, never tame, now blown in every direction by the wind, her stomach huge and pressing against the cloth of her dress.

"I'm sorry. I know this must seem bizarre. But I—you probably guessed. I seem to have gone into labor. Could you possibly take me into town?"

"Of course." He took her arm and guided her toward the car. Beth decided that she must have been wrong in thinking he had been wary a moment earlier. No doubt it had merely been the surprise of finding a woman in this situation.

"Thank you," she said, as he opened the passenger door for her. "This is very kind of you."

He came around and got in on the driver's side. The car started with a smooth purr, and he took off. He glanced toward her and said, "My name is Jackson Prescott."

"I'm Beth Sutton. It's nice to meet you," Beth responded

politely. His name sounded faintly familiar, and she wondered if he was someone she was supposed to know. "Have
you moved into the area recently?"

His eyes lit up with amusement, and he let out a bark of
laughter. "No. That is, well, I was just looking around.
Checking the place out."

"I see." She didn't, really. She supposed he must be considering moving here, and she had the uneasy feeling that
his face was one she had seen before. Perhaps he was some
politician or well-known businessman or something, someone she should have recognized. It was obvious from the
clothes and the car that he was wealthy. A trial lawyer? She
supposed he might even be a sports figure—he was tall and
well-built, although he didn't have the thickly muscled
frame she associated with football. Tennis, perhaps? A
swimmer?

At that moment another pain seized her, and she forgot
all about Jackson Prescott. Fingers digging into her palm,
eyes closed, she concentrated on her breathing.

Prescott glanced over at her. She was in obvious pain and
struggling not to show it. There was strength in every taut
line of her body. *Beauty and strength.* They were the hall-
marks of a Prescott heroine. Indeed, it had become a cap-
sule description in Hollywood to call a gutsy, intelligent
female character a "Prescott woman." Looking at her, Jackson felt certain that this woman would someday, someway,
work her way into one of his productions.

Her head was back against the seat, and her eyes were
closed. Her skin was translucent in the way of some redheads, pale and luminous, with just a sprinkling of light
brown freckles across her cheeks. Her mouth was wide,
with a full lower lip. Her nose was straight and a trifle short;

he suspected that at better moments the combination of the snub nose and freckles gave her face a gamin look, particularly when she smiled. Her hair was a mass of red curls, tied in the back by a ribbon, but a great deal of it had gotten loose and tangled around her face.

Though he could not see them now, he knew that her eyes were mahogany. He had taken in the detail just as he had taken in all the other details about her. It was part of what made him good, that attention to detail. Another of his assets was his calm, the unruffled attitude that was capable of seeing him through a continual series of crises, and that soothed the frazzled nerves of studio executives and insecure stars alike. It was rare that anyone saw him lose his temper on the set or give way to the gut-gnawing anxiety that dogged every director at one time or another.

But that calm was certainly being tested at this moment. Prescott was accustomed to daily film crises. He was not accustomed to crises being of the life-and-death variety.

He pressed down a little harder on the accelerator, and the speedometer moved up to eighty. It made him feel a trifle queasy to think that he had been tempted not to stop when he first saw Beth Sutton. Fifteen years of living in L.A. had taught him to be wary. Fame had made him even more so.

Of course, he had not driven past her. He could not have ignored the vision of helplessness and pain she had presented, even if it had been on the carjacking streets of L.A. instead of a deserted road in West Texas. However, as he had walked over to her, there had been a niggling suspicion at the back of his mind that this was some sort of setup, a stunt by a would-be actress to meet him, or even one of those bizarre celebrity practical jokes that had been popular on TV a few years back. Then he had seen the panic in her eyes, the remnants of pain on her face, and all such thoughts had fled his mind, replaced only by the instinctive need to help.

He reached the intersection of the highway and turned right, assuming that the sign pointing toward Angel Eye, 8 Miles was the correct direction. They sped down the road.

"I'm sorry." Beth spoke and Jackson glanced over at his passenger. Her eyes were open again and tinged with the aftermath of pain. Her skin and the hair around her face were damp with sweat.

He raised his brows. "For what?"

She shrugged. "Stopping you. Forcing you to have to deal with this." She fluttered her hand in a vague way.

He smiled faintly. "Don't worry. Don't apologize to me. You're the one who's having to go through this. I'm just driving the car."

Even in the backwash of fatigue that followed her pain, Beth had to smile back at him. There was something quite calming about him, she thought—a sort of sureness, an inner strength that reached out and enveloped her. She could count on him, she sensed, and the thought made her feel stronger.

She sat up straighter. It would be a few more minutes, she reassured herself, before she had to go through that again. "You can drop me off at the sheriff's office in town," she told him.

Her brother Quinn would not be there, of course. He was over in Hammond today, testifying in a district court case. But any of the deputies would take her, sirens blasting, over to the hospital in Hammond. She was, after all, the sheriff's sister, and besides, she had known most of them all her life. But she hated to do it. She didn't like asking favors of anyone, even one of her brother's deputies, and she particularly did not like the thought of having to ride all the way to Hammond with Darryl Hawkes, who apparently had never gotten over his high school crush on her and who, with her luck, would be the very deputy chosen to take her.

But there was little other choice. Cater was out of town, and it would take too long to phone her father and Cory to come in from the ranch and take her to Hammond. Her oldest brother, Daniel, lived just as far out of town. She knew time was of the essence. Already she was beginning to feel the first little twinges that she now knew presaged another contraction.

"The sheriff's office?" her driver repeated, puzzled. "Don't you think you ought to go to the hospital?"

"The hospital isn't in Angel Eye." She frowned and began to do her breathing in preparation for the pang. "It's in Hammond."

"Hammond?" His voice rose a little. "Is that another town? Is that where you're going?"

She nodded and gasped out, "Thirty miles from here." She pointed vaguely east as she tried to stay above the pain.

"Then that's where I'll take you."

Beth nodded again, in too much pain to argue. It would be faster than stopping at the sheriff's office and explaining. Besides, she realized that she would rather have this calm stranger with her than Darryl Hawkes, who would probably drive her to distraction with his chatter as he tried to take her mind off her labor.

"We'd better call ahead—" He reached automatically for his cell phone, then remembered. "Damn! I didn't bring it with me."

He had wanted to be by himself today, away from the

people and the distractions. That was why he had insisted on coming to look at the West Texas locations himself, not bringing the assistant director or even his personal assistant. He had been feeling stifled and restless, and he had wanted a day or two of complete peace and silence. So he had left his cell phone lying in his briefcase and set out with only a minimum of clothes, a pad of paper and Kyle's memo about the possible locations for the desert scenes that he had scouted.

"I'm sorry," he said, looking over at her. But her eyes were closed and she was in the midst of her battle with pain.

The contraction subsided before they reached Angel Eye. Beth glanced at her watch to time the next contraction. "Turn left at the stoplight and keep driving till you get to Hammond," she said when they reached the outskirts of the small town of Angel Eye. "The hospital's on the edge of town—on this side, fortunately."

"Will do." His voice was as cool as if they were out for a Sunday drive, but Prescott glanced at Beth anxiously. He didn't know much about labor, but it seemed to him that there had been very little time between her contractions.

He made the turn carefully, not wanting to jar her. "Odd name for a town, Angel Eye."

"Yeah." Beth wiped away the sweat from her forehead with the back of her hand. "Comes from the name the Spanish explorers gave it—Los Ojos de Los Angeles."

"The Eyes of the Angels. Poetic. Referring to the stars, I presume."

"Yeah. They're so bright out here. 'Course, the gringos weren't about to have to say a mouthful like that. They worked the name down to Angel Eye. *Mmmph.*" She let out a muffled noise as the pain started again and glanced at her watch. "Damn! Five minutes."

They were out on a flat, deserted highway again, and Prescott floored it, nerves beginning to dance in his stomach. Five minutes apart sounded way too close to him, particularly when the hospital was thirty miles away.

The contraction left Beth panting, her dress drenched in sweat. She thought with longing of the ice chips that the Lamaze instructor had said the nurse would give them to chew on in labor. She noticed out of the corner of her eye that Prescott reached over and turned the temperature lower.

"I'm sorry," she said. "You're probably freezing in here."

"No problem." He gave her a slow, reassuring smile. "I've been colder. So tell me, how'd you get stuck in this situation?"

She gave him a wry glance. "The usual way."

A corner of his mouth lifted at her small attempt at humor. *Gutsy.* He liked this lady. "I meant going into labor by the side of the road."

"Stupidity. I was driving back home when I got a contraction, and I went off the road. Got a flat tire. I think I might have hurt the axle, too. The wheel was at a funny angle."

"Is there someone I should notify when we get to the hospital?"

"Yes, if you want to go to the trouble." She looked grateful. "My father. I can write down his number." She glanced around vaguely, and Prescott reached up to his visor, tearing off a piece of paper from a pad there and handing it to her, along with a pen.

Beth wrote down her father's name and the numbers of both the ranch house and the cell phone. Prescott plucked the paper from her fingers and tucked it into his shirt pocket.

"What about your husband?"

"No husband."

"Oh. Well, uh, the father, then. Don't you want—"

Beth let out a harsh laugh. "No, I don't want. He's in Chicago and he doesn't know a thing about it. And he wouldn't care if he did."

"Oh."

Her breathing was beginning to sound as if another pain was coming. She put her hand on her stomach and winced. He could see her whole body grow taut. "Damn!"

Prescott knew it hadn't been even five minutes this time. More like three. Surely things weren't supposed to develop this quickly. She groaned, panting. He had never felt so helpless in his life. He was used to controlling things, to making the worlds and people he created move in the direction he wanted. But here, he had absolutely no control over anything.

"I hope Dad and Cory don't come home and go looking for me," she gasped as the wave of pain gripped her.

"Don't worry about them right now. You've got enough on your mind." He looked across at her. Her hands were balled into fists.

He reached out, the only thing he could think of to help, and took her hand. She gripped it gratefully, squeezing it hard as she rode out the pain. When the contraction ended, her hand relaxed in his, but she didn't let go. It felt too good, strong and reassuring, and at the moment she needed those qualities badly.

"Cater was supposed to be my coach," she panted. "But he's gone on a book tour. We thought…we thought it would be all right. I wasn't due for another week. He'll be back the day after tomorrow."

"Your brother's an author?"

She nodded. "Mysteries. Cater Sutton."

"I think I've heard of him." *Hadn't he once optioned a Cater Sutton book? If so, nothing had come of it.*

"Damn! Why did it have to come early?" Beth was seized with panic at the thought of going into the delivery room by herself. She had counted on having Cater's strong presence by her side. "Cater's the calmest, you see. Quinn—well, he's so easy to fire up. He'll always fight your battles for you, but you can't rely on him to keep everything under control. Daniel's reliable, of course, but everyone knows he can't stand to see a woman in pain, especially his baby sister. Dad's the same, only worse, and Cory's only nineteen." Beth realized that she was babbling, but she couldn't seem to stop.

"It'll be okay." Prescott squeezed her hand comfortingly, feeling inadequate to the occasion. He watched as another contraction gripped her. Her fingers dug into his hand, and he felt her struggle.

"Go ahead. Scream if you want to." It hurt, somehow, to watch her fight her pain.

"I…refuse…to…scream," she panted out, as if it were somehow part of the battle she was waging.

"It's happening so fast," she went on when the pain subsided. "The contractions are coming so close together. I thought I would have more time in between. You know, to sort of gather up my strength for the next one. They kept talking about it taking hours and hours. Now…God, I'm hoping we can make it to Hammond."

Prescott was, too. He was driving too fast for safety. *Where were all the cops?* He would have welcomed seeing flashing red-and-blue lights in his rearview mirror right now. He could feel Beth's rising panic, and it was infectious, but he made himself push down his own uneasiness and keep his voice calm and free of stress.

It was the longest twenty minutes of his life. Beth continued to gabble between contractions, stopping abruptly when the pain seized her and gripping his hand so tightly that her nails dug into his flesh. Jackson held on, trying to impart strength and calm to her; it was all he could do to help. His own nerves were becoming increasingly jangled. It was obvious that her contractions were growing closer together at an alarming rate, until he thought there was no more than a minute between them.

The number of cars on the road increased. There were more billboards, even a building or two. Hope rose in him that they were nearing the town of Hammond. Then, blessedly, right on the edge of town, as she had said, rose a blocky, modernistic white building with the unmistakable look of a hospital.

"Here we are," he told Beth encouragingly. "Just a minute more now."

Beth opened her eyes and looked, and a sob caught in her throat. "Thank God!"

Prescott felt like sending up a few hallelujahs himself. He whipped into the driveway and surged up the long driveway to the emergency entrance. He came to a screeching halt and jumped out, running around to open Beth's door. She was leaning back in the seat, breathing hard, her eyes closed and her face shiny with sweat.

"We're here." He leaned in and unfastened her seat belt, then slid his hands behind her back and beneath her legs and gently pulled her out of the car.

She opened her eyes, murmuring a faint protest as he lifted her up.

"Shh," he said softly, smiling. "Don't spoil my big scene."

Beth gave in gratefully, leaning her head on his shoulder. He hurried toward the automatic doors, which whooshed open before him. Inside, there were three people in the small waiting room, looking bored, and they glanced up with interest at Prescott's entrance. A woman behind a raised, horseshoe-shaped counter looked up, also.

"Can I help you, sir?"

"I need a doctor!" he barked back. "Are you blind?"

"Of course, sir." She pushed a button. "A nurse will be right out. Are you admitting this patient to the hospital?"

"She's having a baby!" His voice escalated to the roar that, though rarely used, sent underlings running.

Fortunately, at that moment, a nurse hurried toward them, pushing a gurney, and he turned toward her. Gently he laid Beth down on the rolling table. The nurse began to take Beth's pulse, asking her questions in a soothing voice. "Now, honey, how far apart are your contractions?"

"If you're admitting your wife to the hospital," the receptionist went on doggedly in her flat voice, "you'll need to fill out some paperwork." She picked up a clipboard stuffed with forms and held it out to him.

"I can't fill that out! Can't it wait? She needs help immediately!"

Beth listened to the bickering, awash in pain and feeling as if she might burst into tears at any moment. She missed Prescott's large, warm hand in hers.

"And she's getting it, sir." The receptionist nodded toward the nurse, who was starting to wheel Beth toward one of the small examining rooms. Then she picked up a pen with an air of resigned patience and held it poised over the top form. "Now, if you would just give me your name, Mr.—"

"Why the hell do you care what my name is?"

"Elizabeth Anne Sutton!" Beth shrieked from the gurney as she disappeared into the examining room. "I'm preregistered, dammit!"

"Oh." The stiff-haired receptionist gave Jackson an exasperated look. "Well, it would have been much easier, Mr. Sutton, if you had simply told me that to begin with. Let's see." She began to type on the keyboard of her computer. "Yes, you are." She pushed another button, and the printer began to click away. Tearing off the sheet of paper, she handed it to him with a practiced smile. "There you go, Mr. Sutton."

"Thank you," he responded with awful politeness. "Now, could you please call this number?" He handed her the slip of paper on which Beth had written her father's numbers. "It's her father. He needs to know that she's here."

"I'm afraid that I can't use the hospital line for—" the woman began officiously.

"Lady." Jackson leaned forward, fixing her with an icy-blue stare that had been known to frighten powerful stars and even studio executives into submission. "You have been a pain in the butt from the minute we walked in. Now, if you don't want everyone in the administration of this hospital, from the top down to your supervisor, not to mention the local press and my attorneys, to be told in great detail of your uncooperative, insensitive, bullheaded, downright inhumane attitude—then I suggest you call this number and very nicely explain to this gentleman that his daughter is here having a baby. Understood?"

The woman nodded mutely. Jackson straightened, taking the hospital printout, and strode away to the admitting room.

He found Beth with a sheet draped over her and a doctor examining her. The nurse had just turned away from a phone on the wall and was saying, "I've called your doctor, honey, and he'll be here in fifteen minutes."

Beth groaned. "I don't think I can make it that long," she growled. The pains were continuous now. She could hardly tell when one ended and the next one began. And now there was this force building in her, this thing that shoved down through her abdomen, demanding release.

She sensed Prescott's presence beside her, and she reached out for him. He slid his hand into hers, and she grasped it as if it were a lifeline. She was scared. She had never thought she would be this scared.

"Just remember to breathe." The nurse began to demonstrate.

The doctor cut in. "She's fully dilated. Get her up to obstetrics. Stat."

The nurse called for an orderly as she shoved the gurney from the room. An orderly appeared and began to roll the cart down the hall toward the elevators. The nurse rushed to push the button for the elevator. Prescott strode beside the gurney, still holding Beth's hand, his heart pounding.

The elevator seemed to take forever to come. Beth squeezed Jackson's hand, letting out a groan, and jackknifed her legs, bracing her feet against the gurney.

"She's bearing down," the orderly commented.

"Don't push," the nurse instructed as the elevator doors opened and they rolled her inside.

"I can't stop!" Beth snapped back.

When the doors opened, they got off the elevator in a rush. Another nurse came toward them, holding out a pile of green clothing with a mask on top. "Here, you'll have to get into your surgicals quick," she said cheerfully to Jackson, "or you'll miss the show."

"What?" He stared at her blankly.

"You have to change," the nurse said patiently, obviously used to dealing with distraught fathers-to-be. "You have to wear scrubs in the delivery room. So hurry and change."

"But I'm not—"

Beth squeezed his hand tightly, and he looked down at her. "Please…" she said hoarsely. Her eyes were wide and panic-stricken.

"All right," he said and took the clothes. Apparently, he was going to attend a birth today.

Chapter Two

BETH CLOSED HER EYES TO SHUT out the sickening movement of the ceiling above her head as the attendants wheeled her down the hall at a trot. Doors banged open, and then they were in a chilled room, bright with lights. There were people and noise around her. Everyone wore green surgical scrubs and masks. They lifted her onto a different table, this one with a back that slanted her up to a half-sitting, half-reclining position. Someone began to put an IV into her arm. A man stopped beside her, looking down at her with kindly brown eyes.

"I'm Dr. Hauser," he told her. "Sorry. Your doctor isn't here yet, but I'm afraid we're going to have to go ahead. You seem to have an eager one there."

"That's fine." Beth was in the grip of the fierce pain again, the force that seemed to be tearing her apart. "I don't care…who delivers it…as long as you do it *now!*"

He smiled, unperturbed, and moved away. "Let's see what we have here."

Beth bore down, the pain ripping through her, panting and almost sobbing. *Where had Jackson gone?* She wished desperately that he was there. She didn't want to go through this alone. "Jackson!"

"Right here." His calm voice came from behind her head, and then he was beside her, taking her hand. A silly-looking surgical cap covered his hair, and a green mask hid most of his face, but she could still see his eyes, as blue as a lake, calm and smiling, and that made her feel much better. "It took me a while to get into these things. How are you doing?"

"I'm about ready to kill somebody." She let out a sigh, relaxing as the intense pain went away. "I'm just not sure who to start with." She took another gulp of air. "I think I'm in delivery now."

The pain was vastly different. Much better, she thought. At least for these few moments of breathing space, the pain was gone. It was not the constant, unbearable contractions that had plagued her earlier. And the pain, when it came, had a purpose; it was making her *do* something.

A nurse moved around her, handing things to the doctor and reminding her to breathe. "Bear down," she said when the pain slammed through Beth again. "Bear down."

Beth didn't need the instruction. Bearing down was all she *could* do. She clung to Jackson's hand. He murmured encouragingly to her, wiping the sweat from her face with a cool, wet rag. She couldn't really make sense of his words, but the tone was comforting, something to focus on in the haze of pain.

"All right, come on, you're doing great," the doctor was saying. "Just one more push. We're almost there."

It slammed through her again, and then suddenly there was a blessed release. Beth let out a gasping sob.

"It's a boy!" the doctor announced gleefully, and the thin wail of a newborn filled the delivery room.

"You did it!" Jackson Prescott beamed down at her, his eyes sparkling with excitement. He pulled down his mask and bent to plant a kiss on her lips. "Congratulations."

"Thank you." Beth was still holding on to his hand, half crying, half laughing in the blessed aftermath of the pain. She gave his hand a squeeze. "Thank you so much."

"Are you kidding? You did all the work."

There was another pain, which the doctor encouragingly told her was the afterbirth. By the time it was over, the nurse was on the other side of her, laying a little bundle, wrapped in a thin blanket, on her chest. Beth's arms went instinctively around the baby, cradling it to her, and she bent her head to it, murmuring gently. The baby was tightened up into a ball, legs hunched up and arms waving around. His face was scrunched up, eyes closed and mouth wide-open. When Beth cuddled him closer, murmuring to him, his tight little body relaxed, and the crying ceased.

"Look. He knows you already." Prescott leaned over them, beaming. He felt almost high with excitement and wonder.

The baby was deep red and wrinkled, wet dark hair plastered across his head, and his eyes were swollen, with bluish patches.

"Looks like he's gone a few rounds," Jackson commented, and Beth chuckled waterily.

"Isn't he beautiful?" she asked, and Jackson agreed.

"Just like his mother."

"Yeah, right." Beth made a face.

But Jackson meant what he had said. It didn't matter that she was sweaty and pale with exhaustion. Beth *was* beautiful, her face glowing as she gazed down at her child.

A nurse stepped in and scooped up the baby, saying, "Now, now, don't worry. We'll bring him back soon. There are just a few things we have to check, and you have a little more to do here." She turned toward Jackson, smiling. "You want to hold him for a minute, Dad?"

"What? Oh. Uh…" The little bundle seemed impossibly small and fragile, and Jackson felt clumsy taking it in his arms. But the urge to do so was far greater than his fear. The baby nestled naturally in the crook of his arm, he found, and he stood for a moment, gazing down into the little red, wrinkled face as if he were viewing the eighth wonder of the world.

Finally, with a smile, the nurse reached for the baby, and with some reluctance, Jackson let her take it. They wheeled Beth first to Recovery and then, since she had been given no anesthetic and was obviously healthy and alert, after only a few minutes they whisked her down to her room. Jackson stayed with her the whole time. They talked and laughed, giddy in the aftermath of the adrenaline-charged experience. They rehashed the events of the morning, chuckling now over the skirmish with the receptionist and the headlong dash to the delivery room. Jackson wondered idly what had happened to his car, left, door open, in front of the emergency room, and they giggled over that, too.

Everything seemed rosy to Beth. Problems did not exist. Even the lingering ache she felt was a minor annoyance, easily borne as she floated on a cloud of euphoria.

It was bizarre, perhaps, for this man was an utter

stranger, but at the moment Jackson Prescott was the person closest to her in the world. He had been with her through the most important and intimate event of her life; he had been her rock in the haze of pain. He had shared with her that wondrous moment when they had laid her baby in her arms. It seemed only natural that he stayed with her now.

A nurse brought the baby in, swaddled tightly in a thin blue blanket, and settled him in Beth's waiting arms. The two adults gazed down at the child in awe.

"Look at him," Beth breathed. "Isn't he absolutely perfect?"

"Absolutely."

She pulled the sides of the blanket away, exposing his waving arms and legs. Tenderly she ran her hand down one little arm and tucked a finger into his hand, holding it up to examine each astounding tiny finger and minuscule nail. Jackson bent over the bed, watching with the same kind of wonder as she inspected each finger and toe.

The baby's arms and legs moved ever more frantically. His face started to screw up; then a wail issued forth. Beth looked at him anxiously. Guiltily she decided that he was cold, and she quickly wrapped him back up in the blanket, but that did not stop his cries. She turned to Jackson as if he might have the answer, but he simply stared back at her in consternation. For a moment Beth was swamped with uncertainty. She didn't have a clue what was wrong, and it occurred to her that she was going to be a horrible mother.

Then she felt a sort of tingling in her breasts, a fullness that was not quite pain, and suddenly, she realized what was wrong. "He's hungry."

"Oh." It sank in on Jackson that she needed to breast-feed the baby. "Oh!" He could feel a flush of embarrassment rising in his throat. He almost laughed; he had thought himself incapable any longer of actually blushing. "I—I guess I'll leave now."

Beth felt a little lost. She didn't want him to go. It was awkward. He was a stranger, and yet for the last two hours they had been incredibly close. She wanted to ask him to come back, yet she knew that she had no hold on him. "I—thank you so much. I don't know what to say." Tears shimmered suddenly in her eyes. "You were my lifesaver."

Jackson shrugged. "I didn't do anything special. I should thank you for letting me be a part of it." He reached out and ran a gentle finger down the baby's soft cheek. "I've never experienced anything like it."

It was the truth. None of the fancy premieres of his movies could even begin to compare to this. He knew studio heads and world-famous actors and actresses on a first-name basis. He had met the wealthy and the famous, politicians and rock stars and businessmen. But none of those people, none of those experiences, had ever filled him with the sense of awe that he had felt holding Beth's hand while she gave birth. Nothing had ever seemed as wondrous as this tiny scrap of flesh in her arms.

The baby made himself known with an even heartier cry, and Jackson stepped back. "I'd better go."

"Will you come back?"

"Of course!" He smiled. "You couldn't keep me away."

"Good." Beth smiled back.

He turned away and walked out the door.

A few feet down from Beth's door, the hallway was blocked by a crowd of enormous men. Jackson stopped, intrigued.

There were only four of them, actually, but as tall and broad-shouldered as they were, they seemed to fill the hall. They were all glaring balefully down at one short, squat nurse, who stood, arms akimbo, facing them.

"Now, blast it!" the oldest of the men said, slapping a stained, creased Stetson against his leg. "That's my daughter, and I am going in to see her!"

"Not while she and the father are spending their first time with the baby. We will take the baby out in thirty minutes, when it's visiting hours. You may go in at that time. Until then, you can sit in the waiting room." She pointed toward a small room down the hall.

None of the men even glanced in the direction she pointed.

"The father!" one of them repeated in shocked tones.

"Yes, the father," the nurse repeated, as if they were rather dense. She glanced back over her shoulder and spotted Jackson. "Why, there he is!" Her voice was tinged with relief. "Gentlemen, you can talk to him. He will tell you all about the birth."

With that, she shouldered through the line of men and strode off down the hall. The men all focused on Jackson. They were an imposing group. Their faces were hard, their dark eyes cold and narrowed with emotions ranging from contempt to fury as they looked at Prescott. All of them were dressed in casual Western garb—boots, jeans and sweat-stained shirts—except for the one who was dressed in khaki, with a sheriff's badge pinned to his chest. Jackson was not a short man, standing about six foot one, but all of these men topped him by at least two or three inches. With the heels of their cowboy boots adding to their height, they loomed even taller. One, the youngest-looking, must have been at least six-five. They were, Jackson realized, Beth Sutton's family.

"The local basketball team?" Jackson asked lightly. "You're missing one."

"Cater's not here," the boy responded, as if it had been a serious statement.

"Don't be dense, Cory," the one in the sheriff's uniform snapped. "He's making a joke." He stepped forward, his hands clenching into fists. "No doubt he thinks this is all real funny. Don't you, you little scum-sucking, bottom-feeding, slimy son of a bitch?"

Jackson stared back at him in amazement. "I beg your pardon?"

The others moved forward, too, advancing on him like something out of *High Noon*. Jackson held up his hands in front of his chest, palms out, in a stopping gesture. "Hold on. Wait a minute, fellas. Let me explain."

"You think you can just get her pregnant and leave her stranded, then come waltzing back into her life when the baby arrives?" This came from the one with the gray-streaked hair and the most lines in his face.

"I take it you're Beth's father," Jackson began in his calmest voice.

"You're damn right about that. I am also the man who's going to shove that pretty-boy face of yours out the back of your head."

"I wouldn't—" Prescott began.

"Yeah, well, I would," said the fourth man, the only one who hadn't spoken yet, and with that he stepped forward and swung, his fist connecting smartly with Jackson's cheek.

Jackson, taken by surprise, stumbled back and crashed into the door of Beth's room. It swung back easily, and he tumbled inside, falling to the floor. Beth let out a shriek, and the baby began to cry. Jackson came up lithely to his feet as the man who had hit him headed toward him again.

"Daniel! Don't!" Beth shrieked.

Jackson punched the man with a short, hard jab in the ribs, surprising him, and followed up on the advantage by grabbing the man's arm and twisting it up behind his back. Hooking his leg across Daniel's shin, he knocked him off balance at the same time that he threw all his weight against him from behind. Daniel crashed into the wall beside the door, and Jackson pinned him there.

For a moment all the other men froze in shock. Then, with a curse, the khaki-clad one started forward. Behind Jackson, Beth scrambled off the bed, laying the baby down on it. "Quinn! Don't you dare! *Daddy!*"

She threw herself into the doorway between the men and Jackson. At that moment the squat nurse came charging down the hall and burst through the men as if she were a linebacker.

"What do you think you're doing?" she snapped. She gave Beth a quick glance and pointed a forefinger at her. "You! Get back in that bed right now. And you!" She turned to glare at Jackson. "Release that man."

Jackson did so, feeling rather like a third-grader who had been caught fighting on the playground.

"Gentlemen—and I use the term loosely—may I remind you that this is a hospital? This woman just had a baby, and I am sure the last thing she needs is to have her family brawling in the corridor like a bunch of yahoos."

"Yes, ma'am," Beth's father answered, and all the Sutton men seemed to find something highly interesting to look at on the floor.

"All right, then, any more outbursts like that and I will have to ask you all to leave."

She took the baby from Beth, cast a last admonitory look around the room and marched off down the hall, shoes squeaking, leaving a much chastened group behind her.

"All right," Beth said in a coldly furious voice. "You three get in here and close the door."

The men, looking disgruntled, shuffled into her room to join Daniel and Jackson. Jackson started to slip away, but Beth said, "No. You, too. I want you to meet my family the right way."

With a sigh, Prescott stayed. Beth folded her arms and gave each of her brothers and her father a hard stare in turn.

"I can't believe you. Attacking strangers in the hospital!"

"Ah, Beth…"

"What the hell are you doing protecting that sorry—" Quinn began.

"Shut up, Quinn." Beth shot him a look, and he subsided.

"Now." She took a long look around at her family. "I would like for all of you to meet the very kind *stranger* who stopped to help me when my car broke down and I was stranded by the side of the road. He drove me all the way into Hammond and stayed with me through the whole delivery, even though I had no claim on him whatsoever."

"You mean he's not the guy who—"

"No. He's not 'the guy who,'" Beth retorted pointedly.

"But the nurse said…" the youngest one protested.

"She was mistaken, Cory. They all assumed Mr. Prescott was the father of the baby because he brought me in. We didn't tell them any differently because I was scared and wanted him to stay with me during the birth. Which he very kindly did." She cast a significant look at Daniel.

"And he managed to hang in there and not faint, like some people I could mention when their son was born sixteen years ago."

Daniel blushed to the roots of his hair. "Ah, Beth…why'd you have to bring that up? I didn't faint. I just…"

"Had to leave the room," Quinn, the sheriff, put in, his brown eyes, so much like Beth's, dancing with unholy amusement.

"Shut up," Daniel told him without heat. "It's different seeing blood when it's *your* wife doing the bleeding. And screaming…damn! I'd rather take a shot to the jaw any day."

Beth cleared her throat ostentatiously. "Now, then, if you guys can conduct yourselves like adults, I would like to introduce you to Jackson Prescott. Jackson, this is my father, Marshall Sutton."

"Mr. Sutton." Jackson, suppressing his amusement at the other men's abashed expressions, reached out and shook the oldest man's hand.

"Mr. Prescott. I can't tell you how grateful I am or how sorry about that—that incident in the hall."

"It's perfectly understandable."

"And this is my oldest brother, Daniel."

Jackson nodded and shook the hand of the man who had hit him, a younger version of Beth's father. Both men were tall and lean, with an impressive set of shoulders and hands roughened from years of hard physical labor. But the resemblance went beyond the similarities of their dark brown hair and brown eyes. There was a kind of stillness, a quiet, in them that wasn't in the other two.

"I'm awfully sorry about that," Daniel said, gesturing vaguely toward Jackson's face and looking embarrassed. "I don't usually lose my temper."

"I know," the redhead added, grinning irrepressibly. "I was real impressed, Daniel."

"The sheriff here is Quinn." Beth cast a smile that was part exasperation, part affection at her quick-tempered brother.

"Sorry. Pleased to meet you." Quinn reached out and shook hands with him. "Thank you for helping my sister."

"I was happy to do it."

"And this—" Beth smiled at the teenage boy with special affection "—is my baby brother, Cory."

"Do you have to call me that?" he protested, but he stepped forward manfully and shook Jackson's hand. "Sorry, sir."

"No problem." Jackson looked up at the towering boy and wondered if he had stopped growing yet. He glanced around at the men. "I'm glad I met all of you. But now I think I'd better go and let you all talk with Beth."

With a nod, he slipped quietly out of the room. For a moment there was an awkward silence. Then Beth sighed and held out her arms. "Oh, you guys. Come here and give me a hug."

She could never stay mad at her family for long.

It had been devastating when her mother had died when she was a teenager, but Beth had managed to get through it with the love of these men. Hardworking, loyal, even a little rough-and-tumble, they had done their best to make sure their little girl had a good life. Their concern had sometimes made her want to scream such as when she was a sophomore in high school and had sat home alone every Friday and Saturday night because Quinn had threatened all the boys at school with the wrath of the Suttons if they tried anything with his sister. But she had never doubted that they loved her or that she could go to any one of them if she was in trouble. It was, after all, one of the reasons she had come home to the ranch when she learned she was pregnant. She had known they would take her in and wrap her around with their rock-hard love.

Finally, after all the hugging was done, her father said, "We called Cater."

"Boy, he was mad as fire about missing everything!" Cory added. "Said he was going to jump the tour and fly down on the first possible plane."

"He shouldn't do that," Beth protested. "He has two more days of it. Besides, it's already over. I'm fine."

"I know, but he's feeling bad because he wimped out and went on the tour," Cory said bluntly.

"Cory!" Beth looked at him reprovingly, but she could not keep the loving light from her eyes. She was close to all her brothers, but she knew that there was a special place in her heart for Cory. Ten years younger than she, he had been only three when their mother died. Beth, at thirteen, had been a little mother to him. The hardest thing about leaving home when she was nineteen had been leaving Cory. "I hope you didn't say anything like that to him!"

"No, but it's what he thinks. And he's right."

"For heaven's sake. He had to go. And we didn't figure it was going to happen this early." She waggled her finger at Cory. "You tell him to stay on that tour and finish it. The baby and I will barely be out of the hospital by the time he's through."

Her father shrugged. "You know Cater. He'll pretty well do what he pleases."

"Mmm." The corner of Beth's mouth quirked in amusement. "So unlike all the rest of you Sutton men."

"I hope you aren't including me in that," Quinn said, grinning. "We all know that *I* am a model of flexibility."

"Uh-huh. Right." Beth rolled her eyes. "Now, tell me. Have you seen the baby yet?"

"Nothing but a glimpse of him when that drill sergeant of a nurse whisked him out of here." Marshall Sutton frowned at the memory.

"Then you'd better get down to the nursery and look at him."

"It's a boy?"

"What else?" Beth answered. "I would probably have been drummed out of the family if my first hadn't been a boy."

At that moment the door burst open, and a sixteen-year-old boy entered excitedly. "Hey! Hi, Gramps. Hi, Dad. Hey, Cory. Quinn. Aunt Beth. How are you doing?"

"What are you doing here?" Daniel looked suspiciously at his watch. "School isn't out yet."

"They let me out early as soon as Coach Watkins heard about Aunt Beth having the baby."

Quinn shook his head in disgust. "Best spy system in the world," he said. "The CIA ought to come train in Angel Eye."

"It was on the scanner."

"Jimmy." Beth opened her arms, and the boy went to her for a hug. Daniel's son made up the last of her family of men. Daniel's wife had left when James was just a boy, and Daniel had raised James alone. Since Beth had moved back to the ranch, the boy had taken to hanging around their house, confiding in Beth about his teenage problems.

"Have you seen it?" James asked the other men, straightening up from the hug. "It's only about this big." He demonstrated with his hands. "And squalling! Hoo-wee! Raising hell already."

"It's a 'he,' not an 'it,'" Beth admonished, laughing.

"Why don't you take these guys to the nursery and show him to them?"

"Wait. First I want to hear the whole story about how you got here," Quinn said, folding his arms and fixing her with what she called his "cop stare." "Who is this Jackson Prescott guy? Don't get me wrong, I'm grateful to him for stopping to help you. But there was something weird about him."

"Dressed funny," Daniel concurred.

"Just because he doesn't wear cowboy boots and jeans…" Beth said disgustedly. "He dresses very nicely. He's a handsome, sophisticated, perfectly respectable—"

"Who did you say?" her nephew interrupted, an odd look on his face.

"Jackson Prescott. My car broke down, and I—"

"Jackson Prescott! You're joking, right?" James glanced around at the others.

"No. What's the matter? You act like you know him."

"Know him? Well, of course I know him. Everybody does."

"I don't," Daniel said, pointedly.

"Oh, Dad…not you. I mean, anyone who goes to the movies. Except it couldn't be him. What would he be doing in a jerkwater place like Angel Eye?"

"Oh, my God!" Beth exclaimed, her hands flying to her mouth. Her eyes grew wide. "I thought I knew that name! I thought there was something familiar about him!"

"You mean it *was* him?" James gaped at Beth.

"Him, who?" Beth's father interrupted impatiently. "What in the devil are you two talking about?"

"Jackson Prescott," Beth said numbly. She let out a groan and covered her face with her hands. "He must think I'm a complete idiot!"

"Oh, yeah!" Cory slapped his forehead. "That's the name

of the guy who made that movie you and I went to see last month, Jimmy."

"Right. *Flashpoint*. Also *The Fourth Day*. And *Pursuit*." James shook his head in despair at his family's ignorance. "Jackson Prescott is known all over the world. He's only one of the most famous, most important producers and directors in Hollywood."

WHEN HE LEFT BETH'S ROOM, Jackson strolled down the hall, trying to ignore the disapproving gaze of the nurse at the station. Apparently people who got involved in brawls in the hall were not popular here. He stopped in front of the nursery. Baby Boy Sutton lay in a clear crib in the center. He was awake again and obviously displeased. His little red face was screwed up, his mouth wide-open. Jackson couldn't keep the broad grin off his face.

After a moment he turned and walked down to the lobby. The same woman sat at the receptionist desk. It took a few minutes to wangle out of her the information about what had happened to his car, as well as the keys to the vehicle. He was so involved with the bureaucratic struggle that he did not notice that across the room a young woman was staring at him.

"Casey." She jabbed her boyfriend in the side with her elbow. "Casey, look at that man. Do you know who that is?"

The young man with her looked up disinterestedly. "No."

"It's Jackson Prescott."

"Who?"

"The director. *You know*...we went to see *Flashpoint*."

Casey turned his head and surveyed her with scorn. "Yeah. Right. A Hollywood director is here in the hospital in Hammond, Texas."

"Well, it could be," she replied defensively. "I just know it's him. Don't you remember those couple of teenage movies he was in before he became a director? I used to watch them on video." Jackson Prescott had, in fact, in his younger incarnation on video, been the focus of her adolescent dreams. *And this man—well, it hardly seemed possible, but it looked like him.*

The woman got up and moved closer, peering around a pillar at Jackson. Her boyfriend, curiosity aroused, followed her. Prescott turned, and she had a full view of his face. "That's got to be him!" she hissed.

Casey, taking in the expensive cut of the man's clothes and hair, was beginning to think that maybe Janine was right for once. This man definitely didn't look as if he came from around here.

Prescott walked out through the front doors. Casey strolled over to the information desk. "Say. Wasn't that Jackson Prescott who just left?"

"No," the woman behind the desk said coldly. "I don't know any Jackson Prescott. That man is Mr. Sutton. His wife just had a baby."

Casey made a noise of disgust and turned away. "See, Janine? It wasn't him."

Janine grimaced and followed him. "It was so. I've seen pictures of him in the papers and magazines."

Hurriedly she thumbed through the magazines on the small table beside her chair, then moved down to the next table. Finally, triumphantly, she returned, holding up an old issue of an entertainment publication. "Here he is. This is an article from last year, when *The Fourth Day* came out. Look."

She held open the magazine, pointing with one long, hot

pink nail to a photograph at the top of the article. Her boy-friend stared. "Holy—you're right. That *is* him. But what is he doing here? And why did that lady think his name's Sutton?"

"He's probably going incognito," Janine said knowledge-ably. "They do that a lot, you know, famous people."

"Is he married?" Casey asked suddenly.

"No way." She pointed to the article again. "See? 'Hol-lywood's most eligible bachelor, Jackson Prescott.'" She looked up into her companion's face. "Casey? What are you looking like that for?"

"Just had an idea, Jeeny. Those newspapers like you like, you know, like *Scandal*, they pay for stories, don't they?"

"Oh, yeah. Tons of money." She nodded solemnly. "So they can get an exclusive."

Casey's smile turned predatory. "You know, hon, I think I'm going to go home and get my camera."

"But why?"

"Well, if a man's 'wife' just had a baby, he's going to come back here to see it, isn't he?"

"Yeah. Ooh, Casey, that'd be great, to get his picture."

"Yeah. Great. Especially since I'll have an 'exclusive' about a big shot director who doesn't have a wife but whose girlfriend just had a baby."

Chapter Three

BETH LAY ON HER SIDE, contemplating the vase of twenty-four red roses that sat on her bedside table. The arrangement dominated the table, out of place in the plain little hospital room. Beth had never gotten anything quite like it. The roses were long-stemmed and utterly perfect, each a deep red, and they were set in an elegant crystal vase. Since it had arrived an hour ago, seven nurses and other hospital personnel had popped in to see it. Some of them hadn't even bothered with an excuse.

She turned over the simple, elegant small card that had come with it. It said only, "Jackson." She could not keep a smile from creeping over her lips again. Two dozen blood-red roses had a way of making one smile. Until they had arrived, her day had been less than joyous. The euphoria she had felt yesterday at giving birth had ebbed, leaving behind soreness, pain and a certain sadness. It had been wonderful, of course, when they brought in the baby. There was a kind of bliss in cradling her son in her arms as he nursed avidly that was like nothing she had ever felt before.

But in the middle of the night, when the nurse took the baby away after his feeding, Beth had lain awake, unable to return to sleep, thinking about the loneliness and fear of raising a child by herself. Only a few minutes ago, when she had shuffled down to the nursery, as the nurses kept telling her she needed to, and had stood looking in the window at her baby, she hadn't been able to suppress a pang of envy when she looked at a new mother and father who were looking at their child together.

Impatiently Beth shook her head. She was *not* going to give in to feeling sorry for herself. After all, there were lots of other women who were raising children on their own, and she knew that she was lucky in having the loving support of her family and friends around her. She looked at the roses again and reminded herself that even strangers had been exceedingly kind to her.

A tap on the door interrupted her thoughts, and Jackson Prescott stuck his head inside the room. Beth's spirits rose. "Jackson! Come in."

She gasped, and her hand flew to her mouth as she got a better look at him. There was a blue bruise high on his cheekbone where Daniel had popped him. "Oh, no! I'm so sorry."

He shrugged. "It's all right. I'll live."

"My family really isn't like that usually. It's just that they're so protective of me. I'm the only girl."

"I gather they're not too fond of the baby's father."

"They don't even know him. Obviously, since they thought you were it. All they know is that I'm raising the baby alone, and that's enough to make them hate him."

"I can see their point." He smiled and walked over to the bed.

There was an awkward pause. Beth gestured toward the flowers. "Look. Your flowers came. They're beautiful."

"You like them?" He had been carrying something behind his back, and now he brought his hand around and held out a fluffy white bear toward her. "I brought something for the baby, too. Figured I couldn't leave him out."

"It's beautiful." Smiling, she reached out and took the animal. It was incredibly soft, and she rubbed her cheek against its fur.

He nodded toward a chair in the corner of the room. "I see he's already starting a collection."

Beth chuckled. "Yes." She had had a steady stream of visitors since yesterday afternoon, and it seemed as if at least half of them had brought a little stuffed animal for the baby. "I foresee some serious spoiling going on here."

"He deserves it." Jackson looked down at her. "How about you? How are you doing?"

Beth shrugged. "Not as ecstatic as I was yesterday. I've discovered a few aches and pains I didn't notice then. But I'll be fine."

"A little blue?"

"How did you know?"

He shrugged. "Just guessed. Don't they always talk about postpartum blues?"

"Yeah. But I don't think this is enough to quality for that. I think it's more sleep deprivation. I had the hardest time sleeping last night, and it seemed like every time I'd finally doze off, a nurse would come in with the baby to feed or a pill to give me. Then they woke me up at the crack of dawn to feed me." She rolled her eyes. "I'll be glad to get home so I can get some sleep."

"Well, you're looking good."

"Bless you. I've looked in the mirror today, so I know you're lying, but it's very kind of you to say so."

"No. Just truthful." He smiled.

Beth shifted a little uncomfortably. There was something in his smile that started a strange flutter in her abdomen, a feeling she was sure was most inappropriate for a new mother still lying in the hospital.

Quickly she changed the subject. "Have you seen the baby?"

Jackson nodded. "Yeah. I went by the nursery as I came in. And I stopped by yesterday evening to look at him. I came to see you, too, but you were asleep."

Beth smiled. It pleased her that he had thought of her the evening before, too. "I wanted to ask you something."

"Sure."

"It's about the baby. If it had been a girl, I was going to name it after my mother. She died when I was thirteen. So now, I'm thinking I could name it after my dad, but I always hate to have two people with the same name in a family. Everybody would be calling him 'Little Marshall,' and that's not fair. So I was thinking I'd make Marshall his middle name."

"Sounds good."

"For his first name…well, you did so much for me. I don't know what would have happened to either of us if it hadn't been for you."

"Oh, no." He looked at her with horror. "Don't tell me you're thinking of naming him after me. You don't want to saddle the poor thing with Jackson. Trust me, it's awful. It's caused problems all my life. Everybody's always asking which is your first name and which is your last. This poor kid would have *three* last names—Jackson Marshall Sutton."

Beth giggled. "You're right. That would be awful. But I'd like to, I don't know, acknowledge what you did. Honor you somehow. What about your father's name? What was it? Would you mind if I used it?"

"It was Joseph."

"Joseph." Beth smiled, and Jackson found himself staring at the way her face glowed. "That's a good name. I like it. Joseph Marshall Sutton. It has a nice ring. Would it be okay with you? I won't use it if you don't want me to."

"I'd be honored. It's a wonderful name. If you're really sure that that's what you want to name him."

Beth nodded. "Yes. It's perfect. I've been worrying and wondering what to name him. And the lady from county records has been by twice asking me what I plan to name him. Joseph. Joey. Joe." She tried it out, savoring the name. "Joe Sutton."

Jackson grinned. "I'd say it's an improvement over Baby Boy Sutton." He hesitated, then said, "Thank you. I really mean it."

He could not explain precisely the bond he felt with this baby and this woman. For a brief moment in time he had been connected to them in a way he had never been connected to anyone else. His life had been filled largely with his career until now, and people had perforce taken a back seat. He had had relationships, of course, but he had never thought of marriage, let alone raising a family.

But when he had held Beth's hand during labor, feeling her fingernails scoring the back of his hand and hearing her struggling breaths, almost feeling the waves of pain that came from her, he had been close to her in a powerful and intimate way. When he had heard the baby's cry, it had shaken him. And when the nurse had laid Joseph in his arms, he had experienced a tenderness so profound, a connection so deep, that it had seemed as if the baby actually were his own.

It had been an emotional letdown later when he had realized that he really had no business staying with Beth in her hospital room. He was not connected to her or the baby in any real or important way, not even as close as the men who had crowded into Beth's room yesterday afternoon. He had known that there wasn't any reason for him to hang around today, either, even if he had used the excuse of checking out other locations in the area. He could have looked at them and driven on, he knew, rather than returning to Hammond to spend another night. But he had not been able to leave. He had been drawn back to the hospital and to the nursery, where he had stood gazing at the Sutton baby for at least twenty minutes last night. Nor was he really sure why he had felt the impulse to find a stuffed animal for the baby or to send the roses to Beth.

He had let his assistant in Austin take care of the details of getting the perfect roses delivered, but he had tried to find the stuffed animal on his own. It had been a shock to discover that his selection was pretty much limited to the local discount store. Once he returned to the city, he promised himself, he would find one of those huge lions or elephants or bears, the kind that stood thigh high and were as soft as rabbit fur.

"You stayed in Hammond today?" Beth asked, wondering why the thought pleased her so much. She'd had no interest in men, *any* men, not since that bastard Robert, and this was certainly not the time to start.

He nodded. "I had a few locations around here to check out."

She was aware of a certain disappointment that there was a practical reason for his staying. "Oh. For one of your movies?"

"Yeah. We begin shooting in Austin in two months. We have some 'barren land' scenes. That's why I'm out here."

"I see." She paused, then went on, "My nephew Jimmy told me who you were yesterday. I'm sorry. You must think that I'm an idiot for not recognizing your name."

He smiled, shaking his head. "Actually it was kind of enjoyable. It's good to get away from L.A., get a dose of reality. It's kind of fun to have someone relate to me as a person, not as 'a director.'"

"I have seen your movies, though," Beth went on. "When he told me, I remembered. And weren't you an actor first?"

He nodded. "For a couple of years. Two teenage movies that made a great deal more money than they had any right making. But I discovered that acting wasn't for me. I wanted to be running the show. Directing, producing."

"You're obviously quite good at it."

"What do you do? For a living, I mean. You said something about a ranch house. Is that what you do? Ranch?"

"That's what my father does. He and Cory work the family ranch. Daniel has a horse farm. He runs a few cattle, too, but it's a small operation. But I don't usually live here. I live in Dallas. And I make my living by painting portraits."

"Really?" He looked amazed.

She nodded. "Yes. You'd be surprised how many people

want their portraits painted—or their spouse's or their children's. I've even done a portrait of one lady's dog. It was beautiful, too."

"So you're good."

She chuckled. "Of course I am. I've been able to make a living at it for several years. It was a struggle at first, but I do all right now, and it will be a good career for raising a child. My studio's right there at my house. But when I got pregnant, I decided to take a break from it. I didn't think all the fumes I breathe in every day would be good for the baby. And all that standing would have gotten pretty tiring, too. So I moved back to the ranch."

"You'll return to Dallas?"

"Oh, yes. I rented out my house for a year. When that's up, Joseph and I will go back."

Jackson found himself wanting to ask about the father of the baby, but he managed to restrain himself. Beth had made it pretty clear the day before that she didn't want to talk about the man.

Soon afterward a hospital volunteer wheeled in the baby in its little rolling plastic cart. "Ready for a visit?"

"Yes." Beth held out her hands, her tired expression lightening perceptibly. She gazed at the baby for a long time, stroking his little cheek with her forefinger, letting him curl his hand around her finger, straightening the thin snap top that he wore. "I always have to check him out again," she explained sheepishly to Jackson. "Just to make sure he's still perfect."

"Understandable." He leaned closer over the bed.

"You want to hold him?"

"You wouldn't mind?"

"Of course not. I'll have plenty of opportunity to hold

him. They'll leave him here for at least an hour. He ought to be getting ready to eat soon."

"Okay." Jackson grinned and reached down to slide his hands under the baby. "I'm an easy sell."

"So I see."

Beth watched as he picked up the baby and cradled him against his chest. Jackson bent over Joseph, compelled, as Beth had been, to inspect every detail of his tiny face. He slipped his forefinger beneath the baby's palm and felt the miniature hand grasp his finger. Joe was frowning fiercely, his legs pumping beneath the light blanket in which he was wrapped, and his lips pursed and working as he looked all around in an unfocused way.

"What do you suppose he's thinking?" Jackson asked in an awestruck voice. "Do you suppose he thinks we're all idiots for grinning at him so fatuously?"

Beth chuckled. "I don't think they decide that until they're about twelve or thirteen."

"And nobody's grinning by that time."

Beth watched Jackson smile and talk to the baby. The baby was gazing back at him earnestly. It was a picture that made Beth's heart swell in her chest. *If only someone like this had been her baby's father!* She thought about Joseph growing up, never bonding with a father. She had thought her brothers and father would provide plenty of male role-modeling for the baby, but she could see now that it wasn't the same. There would not be a father who had shared the baby's birth, who would have the same sense of pride, awe and joy that she did.

She sighed. It was useless wishing for something she could not have, and she knew it. Robert Waring would never have been this kind of father, anyway. He was a cheating, sneaky bastard, and she had made the right decision.

Joseph's mouth began to work ever more furiously, and he flailed his arms and legs. By accident his fist landed on his lips, and he sucked it greedily.

"Time to eat, I think," Jackson said, turning and handing the baby back to Beth. "I, uh, I'll go now." No doubt she needed to breast-feed him, and the thought made Jackson feel uncomfortably warm. It was, he thought, peculiar to feel embarrassed at the thought, when he had seen plenty of actresses' bare breasts in any number of shots. Somehow, though, this was very different.

"All right. Goodbye. I'm glad you came back today."

"I have to go back to Austin now." He had stalled here as long as he reasonably could. "I'll be there for two or three more weeks, scouting locations before I go back to L.A. If you need anything, just get in touch with me. Will you do that? We're staying at the Four Seasons." He pulled out a pen and glanced around. Then he saw the small card from the flowers he had sent, and he picked it up and wrote a number on it. "This is my room number there. I'll put your name on the list of callers they should let through. If by chance they screw up and won't put you through, leave a message. I'll call you back. Okay?"

"Sure." Beth took the card, fighting back a giggle. There was something so silly about the idea of such security, as if he were the president or something.

He saw the amusement in her eyes and smiled. "Sure. Go ahead and laugh. You aren't the one who gets calls from every writer and actor anywhere in the vicinity any time you're on location—not to mention all the fans who just want to tell you what you ought to do for your next picture."

"I'm beginning to realize how lucky I was that you stopped."

"I'm always a sucker for a woman with a stomach out to here." He bent and planted a kiss on her forehead in a spontaneous gesture that surprised both of them.

He stepped back, feeling suddenly awkward. Joseph set up a howl.

"All right. I can see he won't wait any longer for his dinner." He turned away, strangely reluctant to leave. At the door he turned back for a last look. "Remember—call if you need anything."

She nodded. "Goodbye. Thank you for everything." She realized with some astonishment that she was hovering on the edge of tears.

He smiled and waved and was gone.

OF COURSE, BETH HAD NO intention of calling him. Jackson Prescott had done more than enough for her already. She was capable of doing things herself and, besides, she already had a father and four brothers who were eager to do everything for her.

The hospital sent her and Joseph home the next day, despite her father's protests that it was too soon. Cater, who had left his book tour a day early, was waiting to drive her home in his sparkling blue BMW.

"Cater!" Beth shrieked, momentarily startling the child in her arms into silence.

He bent to kiss her on the cheek, smiling, his dark green eyes warm with affection. "Sorry I missed the main event."

"Don't worry. I had an able substitute."

They talked all the rest of the way home, chuckling over the mad rush to the delivery room and the case of mistaken identity in the hospital corridor. The baby, ensconced in his car seat, promptly fell asleep.

However, he did not remain so. Cranky from the final shots he had received that morning in the hospital, he slept fitfully and cried often. During the next few days, Beth found herself spending most of her time rocking him, feeding him and coaxing him to burp or sleep. She gave her family credit for trying to help her, but they obviously could not feed him, and it seemed that he was already developing a preference for Beth's holding him. Besides, her father and Cory had to work during the day, and they needed their sleep at night. She blessed Cater for taking care of the cooking, cleaning and washing, as well as trying to relieve her of some of her burden with Joseph, but even so, she found herself run ragged.

They were awakened three times that first night by his cries, and though it got better as the days went by, Joseph was still crying to be fed every four hours. Beth had to catch her sleep as best she could in between his feedings. She wondered—panicked—what she would do when Cater went back home to Austin, as surely he was bound to someday.

ONE AFTERNOON THE DOORBELL RANG, and Cater went to answer it. He returned carrying a gray stuffed elephant that had to be at least three feet high. Beth stared at it, then began to laugh delightedly.

"Let me guess. Jackson Prescott."

Her brother looked at the card and nodded. "This thing's huge."

"I don't think Jackson thinks small. He told me he wanted a different stuffed animal for Joseph's room."

Beth went over and stroked the animal. It was plush and soft, even the two tusks. She ran her hands over it and picked it up, hugging it close. She wished suddenly that she could see Jackson. But she knew that was stupid. She hardly knew the man. He just took an interest in Joseph because of what had happened, and no doubt even that would fade with time.

That night Joseph got colic—or so her father pronounced knowledgeably. All Beth knew was that he cried and cried and almost nothing would shut him up. She fed him; she changed his diaper; she walked him; she bounced him; she rocked him. Cory, Cater and her father each tried his hand with him. Nothing seemed to do any good. Joseph occasionally nodded off, but as soon as she laid him down in his bed, he would start to scream again. Finally she gave up and just dozed in the rocking chair, the baby asleep on her chest, and didn't even try to put him to bed. Even that way, however, he slept only fitfully, no more than an hour at a time before his face would screw up and he would begin to wail.

Cory and Marshall went off to work. Cater made her breakfast and tried to take over rocking Joseph. But the baby sensed the change and would have none of it. Beth, bleary-eyed, took the baby back, grinding her teeth. She wondered what had happened to her much-vaunted patience. *Why had she ever thought she would make a good mother?* It was becoming clear to her now that she would in all likelihood go insane after a few more days of this and have to be locked up.

Then, miraculously, Joseph let out a little sigh, burrowed his face deeper against her chest and fell into a deep sleep. Beth sat in stunned amazement, unable to believe that his little body was actually limp in the deep relaxation of sleep. She waited a few more minutes, scared to believe it was real, then tiptoed into Joseph's room. Cautiously she laid him down in his bed, afraid that he would once more wake up and begin to scream, but he was out like a light, and he did no more than let out a shuddering breath and begin to make sucking motions with his mouth.

Beth left the room, closing the door softly behind her and leaned limply against the wall. If anyone wakened him, she thought, she would tear them limb from limb. She walked back into the kitchen, where Cater was rinsing out baby bottles and stacking them in the dishwasher.

Beth collapsed into a chair with a groan. "I'm going to go to bed and sleep for a year."

The telephone rang, and Cater pounced on it. Over the past few days they had turned off the ringers on all the phones except this one in the kitchen, since it was farthest away from the baby's room, and whenever it rang they all jumped on the nearest phone as if it might explode. The whole world now revolved around Joseph's sleeping habits.

Cater turned to Beth, his brows going up inquisitively. "It's for you. You want to take it?"

She sighed. "Yeah." Friends and neighbors kept calling to ask how she was doing, and she felt guilty for so often trying to get out of talking to them. All she wanted to do these days was sleep.

She took the receiver. "Hello?"

"Elizabeth Sutton?"

"Yes?" She regretted taking the call. It obviously wasn't anyone who knew her.

"This is Julie McCall, with *Scandal*." The speaker's voice went up a little at the end of the sentence, almost as if she were asking a question.

The words made little sense to Beth. What was *Scandal*? It sounded like a perfume.

"I understand that you're the proud new mother of a baby boy," the woman on the other end of the line went on cheerfully. "Congratulations!"

"Thank you." Beth realized that this must be a come-on for some baby product. But what baby product would be named *Scandal?* Maybe she had heard it wrong.

"I wanted you to know that we're very interested in what happened."

Beth could think of nothing to reply to that statement. *What was this woman talking about?* She wished she weren't so sleepy. Perhaps then this conversation would make sense.

"For instance, how did you meet Jackson Prescott?"

"On the road," Beth replied automatically. "I'm sorry. I'm a little confused. Why are you calling me?"

"We're very interested in your story, as I said before, Ms. Sutton. And I imagine that you would enjoy a little extra cash to help out with some of those baby bills, too—unless, of course, Mr. Prescott's taking care of those."

"What?" This whole conversation was surreal. Beth felt as if she were one of those characters in an absurdist play, where none of the conversations made sense. "Of course not. Why would—"

"Well, we here at *Scandal* are prepared to pay you 10,000 for your story."

"My story?" Beth was sure now that the woman was insane—or she herself was. "What in the world are you talking about?"

"Why, the story of you and Jackson Prescott, of course."

There was a long silence. Beth was too stunned to speak. Finally she managed to say, "Are you nuts?"

The woman on the other end of the line chuckled. "No,

Ms. Sutton. I'm not. And I'm not joking, either. We would like to publish your story."

"But there's nothing—" Beth shook her head as if to clear it. This whole conversation was making her vaguely uneasy. "No. No, thank you."

"Don't be too hasty. Perhaps I can persuade my editor to give you a little more money."

"I said, *no*." Beth hung up the phone.

"Who was that?" Cater turned to look at her.

"I don't know. Somebody name Julie Something-or-other from something called *Scandal*. Do you know what that is?"

"Sure. You really have been out of it lately," Cater teased. "It's a tabloid. You know, 'My baby is a 310-pound alien.' That kind of thing."

"She just offered me 10,000 to tell her my 'story.'"

Cater's straight black brows sailed upward. "What story? 'My baby is a crying alien with colic'?"

A giggle bubbled up out of Beth's throat. "No. I think that's too common. Apparently she wanted me to tell her about Jackson Prescott's rescuing me from the side of the road. Can you imagine?"

He shrugged. "I guess it'd make a fairly interesting story. The human side of a famous person and all that. But it sounds a little tame for a rag like that, I would think."

"But why do they think I would want the story of my delivery in some national scandal sheet?"

"Lots of people would."

Beth shrugged, dismissing the subject. "Well, I'm going to bed now. Don't wake me up unless the house is on fire."

To her astonishment, she was able to sleep for almost six hours before the baby awoke. The awful night of his colic seemed to have been a turning point, for after that, Joseph began to sleep for one good long stretch of six hours each day. At first he had his days and nights all turned around, sleeping during the day and staying awake during the night, but after a couple of days that straightened out. By Friday, two weeks after he'd been released from the hospital, he had awakened Beth only once during the night—about one o'clock—and she had been able to get an almost normal night's sleep. She thought she was beginning to feel almost human again.

She was feeling so chipper, in fact, that after her shower, she put on a bit of lipstick and mascara and tried on some of her prematernity clothes while Joseph lay waving his arms and legs on the bed. She was pleased to find two or three casual, loose-fitting old dresses that looked all right on her. Of course, she still had a few pounds to lose, but she was hopeful that the extra calories she expended daily on breast-feeding would help to take care of that, plus she had managed to fit in the exercises that the hospital had taught her every day—or almost every day.

Beth straightened and regarded herself from every angle in the mirror, smoothing her hand down over her abdomen. She sincerely hoped that little pouch was not here to stay. The worst-fitting part of her dresses, actually, was over her bustline. Her breasts, swollen with milk now, were at least a cup size larger.

The front door slammed, making both Beth and the baby jump. He gave out a little uncertain cry, and she swooped down and picked him up, cuddling him reassuringly. He stopped the beginnings of his wail and simply looked at her.

"Hi, darling." Beth smiled down at him and planted a kiss on his forehead.

"Beth!" came Quinn's roar from the living room. "Where are you?"

"I'm in here," Beth replied tartly, going into the hall. "Would you kindly stop shrieking like a banshee? You're upsetting the baby." She turned away and went into the baby's room to put him down in his crib. Then she walked down the hallway to the den, where Quinn was alternately standing and pacing, fairly vibrating with impatience.

Quinn's face was almost as red as his hair, and his brown eyes crackled with fury. In his hand he held a thin magazine, which he shook agitatedly as he came toward her. "Have you seen this?"

"No. What is it?"

"Lord, Quinn." Cater appeared in the doorway. "What are you yelling about? I could hear you all the way outside."

"Come see."

He thrust the magazine at Beth. She could see now that it was not a magazine but one of the tabloids sold at the checkout counters of grocery stores. Across the top of the front in bright red letters, it read, *Scandal*. Just below that was a headline in bold type: Director's Secret Love Child! Beneath it was a photograph of Jackson Prescott leaving the hospital in Hammond. Beside the photo it read: "Jackson keeps secret mistress and illegitimate son hidden in Texas."

Chapter Four

BETH STARED AT THE COVER, blood draining from her face. "Oh, my God."

"Yeah. I found my secretary reading it."

"What is it?" Cater had reached them by now, and Quinn plucked the tabloid from Beth's nerveless fingers and handed it to his brother.

"Holy—" Cater let out a whistle as he perused the cover. "Well, I guess *this* is the story that woman was trying to buy from you the other day."

The phone began to ring, and Quinn went to answer it. "Hello? Yeah, hi, Tina. No, Beth can't talk right now. She's, uh, lying down. Yeah, she saw it. Just now. What? No, of course it's not true! You know how those newspapers are."

He hung up, and almost immediately the phone rang again. "Everybody'll be driving you crazy now," he said and answered it. "Yeah? No, this is her brother. *Sheriff* Sutton. No, she doesn't have any statement to make." He put down the receiver, shaking his head. "Can you believe it? That was a TV station."

Cater opened the tabloid to the article inside and began to read aloud: "World famous director and producer Jackson Prescott is in Austin, Texas, today, following the birth of Joseph Marshall Sutton, in tiny Hammond, Texas. Local sources confirm that Prescott, going under the name of 'Mr. Sutton,' was present at the birth of the baby. Both baby and mother, Elizabeth Sutton, a statuesque redhead, are doing fine. Hollywood is all agog at the news. Apparently Prescott had kept the news of his Texas honey completely under wraps."

"Texas honey!" Beth let out a heartfelt groan. "Cater!"

"I didn't write it, darlin'. I'm just reading it." He continued, "Ms. Sutton told this newspaper that she met the renowned director while he was on a publicity tour for his blockbuster movie *Pursuit*."

"I never said that!" Beth protested.

Cater shrugged. "These guys are not known for their concern with accuracy. Didn't you say something to that lady about meeting him on the road?"

"Well, yeah. She asked me where we met, and I told her 'on the road.' I didn't say he was on a publicity tour."

"I guess they figured that was close enough."

"Where did they get this stuff?" Beth moaned. "How did they even hear about my having a baby? Or his being there?"

"Probably from him," Quinn said.

"Jackson? Don't be ridiculous! He wouldn't want something like this spread all over the tabloids."

Quinn made a noise of disgust. "He's from L.A. Those movie people will do anything for publicity. They don't care if it's good or bad, just so long as it gets their name in front of the public. Hell, they hire publicity guys just to make sure they *are* in the media."

"I don't believe it," Beth replied staunchly. "He was so nice."

Quinn pulled a cynical cop face. Beth turned toward Cater, who shrugged.

"I don't know," Cater admitted. "They got the news somehow. They certainly didn't get it from us. Who else knew that he was Jackson Prescott and that he was in Hammond with you?"

"Well, if it was him, surely they would at least have gotten the facts straight!" Beth said pointedly. "Maybe somebody recognized him at the hospital. After all, someone shot that picture of him. That had to be the day it happened or the next day."

"You think someone just happened to be hanging around the hospital with a camera who saw him, knew who he was and took a picture?" Quinn asked sarcastically.

"He certainly didn't take it himself!" Beth snapped.

"He could have called and gotten one of his guys down there from Austin to take the shot. That's probably why he hung around an extra day and came back to see you."

Quinn's words stung. Beth planted her hands on her hips pugnaciously. It had always been Quinn with whom she had the worst fights. Whenever they got into one of their flaming arguments, the others would turn away, saying, "The redheads are at it again."

"So you think that's the only reason a man would come visit me a second time?"

"I didn't say that." Quinn backtracked, realizing he was treading on dangerous ground. "But think about it, Beth.

You had a stomach out to here, and you were in labor. Do you really think he came back because of your looks?"

"Not *all* men are solely interested in a woman's looks. Just macho, chauvinistic—"

"Don't start in with me on that," Quinn warned. "You know that's not what I meant."

"Oh, yeah? Just what *did* you mean, then?"

Cater chuckled and folded his arms, waiting for Quinn's reply with an air of expectation. "Yeah, Quinn, I'd like to hear you get out of this one."

Quinn cursed. "Ah, hell, Bethie, you're just too nice. You believe everybody's good. I don't know that it was Prescott who leaked it. Maybe he *is* a wonderful guy who would never stoop to getting publicity like that. But it's the most obvious choice."

"He came back because he liked Joseph," Beth said stubbornly. "I don't fool myself that he fell for me. But he did fall for the baby. You didn't see him holding Joseph. I did."

"Okay. Okay." Quinn held up his hands in surrender. "The man's a saint."

"I didn't say that, either. Honestly, Quinn, you're as bad about twisting my words as that—that paper!"

Beth took the tabloid from Cater's hands and studied the article. There was little else there. It wasn't surprising, Beth thought, since they had so little to go on. She sighed and handed the newspaper back to Quinn.

"What should I do? Call them and demand a retraction? Threaten to sue?"

"Well...the article doesn't actually say that Joey is this Prescott guy's baby," Cater replied thoughtfully. "All it really says is that he was present at his birth, which is true. It calls you statuesque—no argument there—and says you met him on his publicity tour, which is false, but I'm not sure you want to even get tangled up in a telephone call with them over something as minor as that. There's no telling what else they might trick out of you and twist around for another story."

"But what about the front page? That says that Joseph is his. Doesn't it?"

Quinn and Cater studied the front. "It implies it, sure. It says director's love child right next to a picture of Prescott leaving the hospital. But it doesn't actually say that the director who has the love child is Prescott. I don't know. The thing is, they're used to being threatened all the time by pretty powerful people. They look on lawsuits as part of the cost of doing business. I don't think you're going to scare them with the threat of a suit. Are you willing to actually sue?" Cater asked.

Beth thought of the ordeal of a trial and all the attendant publicity. She shook her head reluctantly. "No. This is bad enough. It just makes me mad, though, to let them say stuff like this and not take any action."

"I know. I'll call them if you want me to," Quinn offered.

"I don't think a sheriff in Texas is going to scare these guys." Beth sighed. "I guess the best thing to do is just to keep quiet and let it all blow over."

DAYS LATER, BETH WOULD THINK back to her words and shake her head over her naiveté. The thing had not blown over at all. They had been deluged by phone calls from more tabloids and several members of the legitimate press, as well as from almost everyone they knew. Even friends of Beth's from Dallas called up to ask her if the story was true. Her father had finally had to give in and buy an answering machine, which he hated. But even worse was the fact that a reporter from one of the tabloids, *The Insider*, showed up at their front door one day.

He came back several times, until finally Beth's father met him at the door with a shotgun and a scowl and pointed out to him that he was trespassing on private property, and that the next time he did so, the sheriff would personally be out to escort him to jail. After that the obnoxious man took to sitting on the side of the road at the entrance to their land, waiting for Beth to come out. As a result, she stayed in the house until she could stand it no longer and finally decided she was going to go stir-crazy, so she set out for the grocery store. Within twenty minutes she was back, muttering imprecations on the man's head.

"I'm trapped!" she exclaimed, as she walked into the kitchen and slammed her purse down on the table. "Trapped! I can't go anywhere or do anything without that guy *stalking* me!"

She walked into the den, where Cory was sitting in the rocker, the baby in his lap gurgling and spitting. Cory was leaning over him, making faces and cooing. "Hi, Beth. I swear, I didn't wake him up. He just started hollering a few minutes ago."

Beth had accused Cory yesterday of tiptoeing into the baby's room to see if he was awake in order to wake him up so he could play with him. He wore a look now of such virtuous innocence that Beth had to smile. "It's okay. As long as you changed his diaper and didn't save it for me."

Cory assumed an even more saintly expression. "I certainly did. It was a stinker, too." He turned his attention back to the baby. "Wasn't it, Joey?" He bent down to rub his nose against the baby's, dissolving into baby talk.

Beth turned away, smiling at Cory's obvious infatuation with Joseph. Cater, sitting on the couch, feet propped up, smiled back at her. "Looks like you've got a permanent baby-sitter."

"At least until he goes back to college." She let out a sigh and plopped down on the couch beside him.

"Rough day?"

She nodded. "That *Insider* reporter followed me all the way to the grocery store, and when I got out in the parking lot, he came running after me, asking all these questions. I realized that if I went inside, everyone in the whole store would be staring at me, with this guy pursuing me. So I just got back into my car and left."

She did not add that she had been fighting a bluesy feeling for the past two or three days—or that she kept wondering why Jackson Prescott had not contacted her since the arrival of that stuffed animal ten days before. She supposed it was foolish to feel so bereft—after all, she hardly knew the man. Sure, he had been nice when he was caught up in the emotional aftermath of witnessing Joseph's birth. But it stood to reason that he would cool off after a few days. She had no real place in his life, and it was natural that he would more or less forget about her. Such reasoning, however, only served to make her feel even bluer.

"I'm afraid I'm not going to make you feel any better," Cater said, picking up a tabloid from the table beside him. He tossed it into her lap. "This is what you would have found if you *had* gotten inside the store."

It was yet another tabloid, this one emblazoned with the

words "Family Feud—Prescott And Suttons Brawl In Hospital!" Beneath was a fuzzy close-up of Jackson Prescott, a bruise clearly visible on his cheek.

"What!" Beth sat up with a shriek. She tore open the paper and began to read. It was an account of a major brawl in the corridor outside Elizabeth Sutton's hospital room. "Oh, my God, it makes it sound like you all jumped him and beat him to a pulp."

"Mmm."

"It even mentions Quinn by name and says he's the sheriff! Oh, no! He'll be furious!"

"Doesn't look too good for a county sheriff to be brawling," Cater agreed.

"I can't believe they wrote this! It's so untrue, so unfair. Oh! I'd like to get my hands on that Julie Whatsis… Where do they get this stuff? How did they find out?"

"Probably someone at the hospital. You've seen how willing the paper was to grease palms."

"But this isn't what happened. That nurse saw that Daniel just hit Jackson once, and then it was all over."

"It sounds more sensational this way."

"Yeah—it's a lot more sympathetic to Prescott, too," Cory added.

"You're saying it was Prescott who told them? You don't know that. It could have been anyone at the hospital."

Cory just looked at her, and Beth flushed. *Why was she clinging to the thought that Prescott had not let the story leak to the press?* She jumped up from her seat. "Okay. Let's just call him and see."

"Call who? Prescott?" Cater asked.

"Yeah, right," Cory said sarcastically. "Like you can just ring up his hotel and they'll put you through."

"He told me I should call him. He gave me the number. He said he would put my name on a list." She charged into the kitchen, opened her purse and pulled out the card Jackson had given her. Then she marched to the phone and rang the number.

When the hotel operator answered, Beth identified herself and asked for Jackson. There was a moment of silence. Then the operator said, "I'm sorry, ma'am, Mr. Prescott is not accepting phone calls."

Beth's stomach clenched. "He—he said he put my name on a list of approved callers. Did you check it?"

"Yes, ma'am. I'll check it again." She spelled Beth's last name questioningly and when Beth agreed that that was the spelling, she finished, "No, ma'am, I'm sorry, but I do not have your name on that list."

"Oh." Beth hung up the phone with suddenly nerveless fingers. *He had lied to her! He had told her that she could call him and acted as if he were concerned for her, and all the time it had just been an act.*

She stood for a moment staring at the kitchen wall, then slammed her fist down on the counter. "Damn him!"

She marched back into the den, her face pale and her eyes blazing. "I'm going to Austin."

"What? Why?" Cater and Cory stared at her.

"Because I'm going to find Jackson Prescott and tell him exactly what I think of him."

"Uh, Beth…" Cater rose to his feet. He had had some experience with his sister's hot temper. "Do you think that's a good idea?"

"Yes. I think it's a wonderful idea. It is exactly what I'd like to do."

"Are you sure you feel up to it?"

"I feel fine. It's been three weeks since I had Joseph. And having a baby doesn't exactly make you an invalid."

"No, but…what about the baby? You can't just leave him here while you run off to Austin. That's at least a six- or seven-hour round-trip."

Beth made a face. "Of course I'm not leaving him. I'll take him with me."

"You're going to cart the baby around with you while you track down a celebrity?" he asked skeptically.

"Fine. You come with me if you think I'm so incapable of managing on my own. Cory, too. You all can take Joseph back to your house while I locate Jackson Prescott."

"Beth…"

"What? Are you coming or not?"

Cater sighed. "Of course I'm coming."

Cory jumped up. "Me too." He grinned. "I wouldn't miss this for the world."

They left the ranch by the back road, then drove the three hours to Austin, going first to Cater's house in a quiet old section of Austin, where Beth fed the baby, then left him with Cory and Cater, adamantly refusing to take either one of them with her. "I am *not* taking one of my brothers with me, as if I can't handle it on my own."

She took Cater's car and drove to the Four Seasons hotel. She suspected that Cater had hoped that her anger would cool off on the drive over and that she would give up on her idea to confront Jackson Prescott, but it had not. She had spent the whole time fuming over what he had done, stoking her fury with memories of his kindness toward her and his apparent affection for Joseph, which made his betrayal all the worse.

She marched into the elegant hotel and asked at the

desk for Jackson Prescott. Predictably she was told he was not available. Beth had expected this, and she found a comfortable chair in the lobby from which she had a clear view of the front doors and sat down to wait for him.

She had been there almost two hours when Jackson walked through the front doors with two men and a woman, all of them dressed in typically casual Austin summer wear. Beth jumped to her feet, a ball of anger and anxiety swelling in her chest. She strode over to the group purposefully. They turned, sensing her approach. One of the men took a step forward, putting himself between her and Jackson.

"Hold it right there. We got a restraining order against you reporters. Remember?" he said flatly.

"Jackson." Beth stopped, her voice even but carrying. "Are you going to talk to me, or are you going to have your goon toss me out?"

It had taken Prescott a moment to recognize the tall, attractive redhead striding toward him. She was slender, and now that her features were no longer pale and drawn with pain, all the promise of her strong facial bones had come blazingly to life. Her hair curled riotously around her face, full of life and color. For an instant he had thought she was an actress or model hoping to talk her way into a part in his movie.

Despite the anger he had been harboring toward her since the *Scandal* article came out, he could not suppress the leap of instinctive physical appreciation inside him. Nor could he keep his lips from twitching with amusement at her words.

"He's not a goon, Beth. He's my assistant director. It's okay, Sam. I'll take care of this."

He moved around his AD, reminding himself why he was

angry with her. Beth, looking at his cold, set face, wondered why she had ever thought this man was warm and kind.

"I found out how much your word is worth," she began, pulling out the card he had given her and ripping it in two. "'Just call me if you need anything,'" she mimicked savagely.

"Sorry," he replied in a voice that made it clear he did not mean the word. "I figured you had already gotten plenty out of me."

His words slammed into her like a fist, hurting more than she would have thought possible. Beth blinked back the tears that started in her eyes. "Excuse me for taking up any of your precious time just because I was in labor."

He snorted. "Don't try to turn the tables here. I'm not talking about taking you to the hospital, and you know it. I am talking about your turning me ov—"

But Beth paid no attention to his words, sweeping on in her rage, "How could you do this to me? How could you be this low? To take my life and turn it into some sideshow so you could get a little extra publicity! Quinn tried to tell me, but I thought I knew you. I told him you would never be that cold or calculating, that you weren't the sort to sell someone out—"

"What in hell are you talking about!" Jackson snapped back. He had been disappointed and unexpectedly hurt when the story came out, but he had lived too long in Hollywood to be surprised or enraged that Beth had turned his helping her to her profit. But now, facing her and her anger, he found his own fury springing to life. "If you want to talk about selling someone out, what about what you did to me? Did you honestly expect me to take your calls after what you'd done? Were you hoping to find out a few more juicy tidbits to feed the press?"

"Uh, Jackson…" The AD sidled closer, glancing apprehensively around the lobby, where faces were turning to stare at Jackson and Beth, drawn by the loud, angry voices. "This is a little public…."

"What do you care?" Beth shot at him. "I figure the more public, the better for you guys. After all, it will mean more precious publicity for your movie."

Jackson, however, heeded the other man's warning. He clamped his hand around Beth's upper arm and started toward the elevators. "We'll finish this upstairs."

"I don't want to go upstairs with you!" Beth retorted.

"I realize that you prefer to make a public spectacle of yourself." Jackson jabbed the Up button of the elevator furiously. "But you are not going to use me to do it. If you want to talk, we will do it in private. If not, get out of the hotel."

Beth faced his level gaze and knew that he meant what he said. No doubt he would call security if she refused to go with him, and they would toss her out ignominiously. *That* would give those nasty tabloids a real field day.

In response, she jerked her arm out of his grasp and turned to face the elevator doors in silence. The silence continued between them after the doors opened and they got on. Upstairs, at his luxury suite, Jackson stuck his key card in the door and stepped back for Beth to pass into the room before him. He followed, snapping the door closed.

Beth marched across the spacious sitting room to the windows at the far end. She stood for a moment, staring out at the view of Town Lake. Jackson, who had struggled to bring his fury under control on the ride up, walked halfway across the room and stopped, arms folded across his chest.

"All right," he began tightly. "What are you here for? If

you expect me to pay you to stop the stories, you're dead wrong. I don't bow to extortion."

"Extortion!" Beth gaped at him, his words startling her out of her anger momentarily. "You're accusing me of extortion?" The idea was so absurd that she almost laughed. "Are you nuts?"

"No. And you can stop the histrionics, too. They're not going to convince me to pay you, either."

Her fury came flooding back at his words, so much so that she trembled under the force of it. Her hands itched to slap him. "How dare you! How dare you accuse me of asking you for money? After what you've done to me and my family? Do you honestly think you can scare me off with this talk of extortion?"

"I am not trying to scare you, Miss Sutton." Prescott struggled to keep his voice under control. He disliked this woman intensely, all the more so because he had liked her a great deal when he met her. It made him even angrier that seeing her now—her eyes bright and her cheeks flushed with rage, her body fairly vibrating—his body was responding to her in an unmistakable and very masculine way. He wanted to shake her, and at the same time, he wanted to kiss her, and that fact made him boil.

"I'm merely telling you the truth," he said carefully. "The money you got from the tabloids is all you're going to get."

"What are you talking about?" Beth took an involuntary step toward him. It required all her self-control not to rush at him, screaming and scratching. "What money? All I've gotten from the tabloids is grief, and you know it!"

"You mean you were foolish enough to talk to them without getting paid?" Prescott quirked an eyebrow in an infuriating way. "No wonder you're coming to me now."

"I am not here for money!" Beth shrieked. "What is your problem? Don't you understand English? I *do not want* any of your filthy money. I wouldn't take it if you offered it to me. You are a lying, treacherous, backstabbing son of a bitch, and I hope you choke on your money."

"Then why did you come here?" Jackson moved forward, his eyes bright with anger. His brain was filled with pictures of grabbing her by the shoulders and shaking her until she stopped her crazy, circuitous, infuriating talk—and immediately after that, kissing her until she melted against him, weak and repentant. Jackson pushed down the primitive need and asked curtly, "Did you expect me to welcome you with open arms?"

"I don't expect anything of you. Not anymore. I just wanted you to know what I think of you. I wanted to tell you what a snake you are."

Beth hated him. She hated his smug, handsome face, hated his calm control in the face of her own livid anger. She wanted to sink her hand into that thick dark hair and pull. And as she pictured that with great delight, she pictured him jerking her up hard against his body and bending down to kiss her. The rush of pure, unadulterated lust shocked her into silence.

"Dammit!" Jackson slammed his fist down on the long table beside him, making the lamp shake. "What the hell are you talking about? You went to the tabloids and told them that—that *dreck*, and now you're accusing *me* of being a snake? You have a lot of nerve. Or are you just insane?"

For a moment Beth could not speak. She stared at him, dumbfounded, as his words sank in. Finally she croaked, "Are you serious?"

Now it was his turn to stare. "What? Yes, of course I'm serious."

"You think—you honestly think that *I* went to the tabloids?"

"Well, of course. Who else? *I* certainly didn't run to them saying that I was the father of an illegitimate child by a woman I had kept secret in a little town in Texas!"

Beth pressed the palms of her hands against her temples. She wondered if she were in a madhouse. Jackson, watching her, felt his anger draining away. It occurred to him that perhaps she really *was* mentally unstable. Wasn't there some woman who had claimed postpartum insanity as a defense for killing someone?

"I did not tell the tabloids anything," Beth growled. "It had to have been *you*. You did it for the publicity."

Jackson let out a noise of disbelief. "After all the time I've spent avoiding those vultures, you're saying that I voluntarily told them this libelous stuff?"

"Well, *I* didn't!"

"Don't try to pull that on me," Jackson said in disgust. "*Scandal* called my publicist for verification of your story. That's the first I heard of it. My publicist denied it, of course. Then he called me and asked who the hell in Texas would have given *Scandal* a story about my having a baby in some backwater town there. He said they told him they had bought it from a woman in Texas, and that she had backed it up with pictures."

"It wasn't *me!*" Beth had a sick feeling in her stomach that she had been terribly wrong.

"That very first story quoted you as saying you met me when I was touring for *Pursuit*."

"I didn't say that!" Beth protested. "That Julie Whatever

called me and started asking questions. I didn't know who she was. She asked me how I met you, and I said, 'on the road.' She surprised me so much that I just answered automatically. But that's all I said. I didn't even know about your touring for *Pursuit*. Then she offered to pay me 10,000 for my story, and I hung up on her. The next thing I knew, there was this story about my giving birth to your son splashed all over the front page. Quinn said you had probably given them the story for the publicity, but I said, no, you wouldn't do that. Then that Carrigan guy—"

"Who?"

"The man from that other magazine, *The Insider*, the one who's been hounding me for the past three or four days! He told me that he had talked to you and wouldn't I like to give my side of the story? But I still thought they were lying, that you wouldn't do that to me. Then today Cater brought home another one of those tabloids, and it had an article about your fight with my brothers at the hospital. It had a picture of you with the bruise on your cheek, and it made it sound like they all jumped on you and beat you up. Well, it was pretty clear where they had gotten such a slanted story. But I still didn't want to believe it, so I called you to ask you about it, and I found out you hadn't put me on a list for my calls to be accepted, like you said you would. Naturally you wouldn't want to hear from me after you had done this to me."

Jackson stood for a long moment, looking at her. "I did nothing to you."

"It didn't look that way!" Beth snapped. "It looked like you had casually ruined my life—told the world I had an illegitimate child, held me up to public ridicule, sicced all those newspapers and magazines on me. How you could have believed that I would do that to myself! To my family!" She turned away, then swung back as a new thought hit her. "How could you have thought I would do that to you? After the way you helped me, if I had sold some tabloid that lie, I would have had to be the lowest, most despicable person ever! How could you think that of me?"

"Over the years, I have discovered that people are capable of almost anything, especially where money and fame are involved."

Beth shook her head. "I would hate to see the world the way you do."

She walked past him toward the door. Jackson turned, watching her, and as she opened the door, he said, "No, wait. Don't go."

Beth hesitated, then let the door close and turned back to him. He crossed the room until he stood directly in front of her, gazing down into her eyes. "I'm sorry. I—I didn't want to think badly of you. When David told me, my immediate reaction was that it couldn't have been you. I didn't want it to be you. But, you see, I knew it wasn't me or my people, and it made sense that it was you. And when they said they'd bought it from a woman in Texas…well, it seemed pretty obvious. I wasn't surprised. Nothing that anyone could do anymore would surprise me. A few years ago a woman claimed that I had fathered her child when I had never met her in my life. She was trying to get money from me, figuring I would buy her off rather than go to court. I had a business partner I trusted—he was a friend, as well—who embezzled money from our business for months. One of my friends was stalked by some guy for almost two years. He said that my friend had stolen a movie idea from him. He also thought that Nazis were hiding out in his attic. People are crazy. They're greedy. They seem to be willing to do almost anything just to get themselves in the news. I'm sorry, but it is easy for me to believe that someone would sell me out to a tabloid, even someone I liked."

He paused, then added, "And I did like you. But I've learned that trusting someone just because you like them is a good way to get burned."

"I understand. I guess it's easier not to be rich and famous." Still, she could not completely get rid of the little pang of hurt that came from realizing how despicable a person he had believed her to be.

He must have seen it in her eyes, for he reached out and took one of her hands between both of his own and said quietly, "I'm sorry."

"Then do you believe me now?"

"I suppose you could have made this whole thing up." Looking into her eyes, he knew he didn't believe that at all. "But I don't think so. I believe you."

He had not let go of her hand, and he raised it to his lips now and kissed her knuckles softly. Beth felt a quiver dart through her. Her hormones, she thought, were absolutely, utterly out of control. A few minutes earlier she had been consumed by rage; now she was getting all weak in the knees over the merest kiss.

"I apologize for doubting you," he went on. "And I apologize for blocking your call." He smiled.

Beth pulled her hand away from his. This man's smile had entirely too much effect on her.

"How about you?" he asked. "Still think I'm the one who gave the story to the tabloids?"

"No." She paused. "But how did they get the story? I mean, if neither of us told—and I'm positive that no one in my family would have—then who did?"

He shrugged. "Someone who saw me at the hospital and recognized me, I guess."

"But how did they come up with all that other stuff? About Joseph being yours?"

"Maybe the rag just made that up. Or they could have interviewed someone at the hospital…the nurses there thought I was the father. After all, that's where they must have gotten the story about the fight. No doubt gossip had amplified it, and the tabloid probably sensationalized it, too. Their version was wilder and more interesting than the truth—which, unfortunately, is why they print things like that instead of bothering to get the facts."

Beth stood for a moment. She didn't know what else to say, and there was really no reason to stay any longer. Yet she did not want to leave. "Well…" She glanced toward the door. "I better go now. Cater and Cory will be waiting to hear whether they have to bail me out of jail for attacking you."

Jackson smiled slightly and reached out a hand, taking her arm. "Don't go. Why don't you stay and have dinner with me?"

"I'd like to, but I have to be back to feed Joey in two hours." She smiled ruefully, realizing how very far away her world was from this man's. "I'm sorry. I'm afraid I don't live a very glamorous and exciting life."

"You would be surprised at how unglamorous and unexciting my life is," he responded. "We could eat now, if it's not too early for you. I didn't have any lunch, so I'm starving."

"Me either." She had been too consumed with getting to Austin and confronting Jackson to stop and eat. "That'd be great, if you want to." She hesitated. "Will there be a picture of us eating in the papers this week?"

"Surely that wouldn't rate high enough on the excitement scale. But if you want to, we can have it here in the suite. That's what I usually do." He smiled. "You can see exactly how exciting my life is."

"Mmm. Sounds like you're almost as much of a shut-in as I am. Today is the first time I've been off the ranch since Joey was born."

In the end, they decided to go downstairs and eat. Jackson's earlier companions were eating at another table in the hotel restaurant, and they cast surprised glances at Jackson when he walked in with Beth. He grinned at them and held Beth's chair for her.

"They'll be eaten up with curiosity," he told Beth, a mischievous glint in his eye. "I suspect that by now they've copped to who you are. Now they're wondering whether the story about Joseph is true, after all."

"You going to tell them?"

"I don't know. I may let them stew for a while. It will be interesting to watch them maneuvering to find out."

They spent most of the time talking about Joseph. Jackson wanted to hear the details of his progress in the past three weeks, and Beth was more than happy to supply them. She reflected that she would never have believed that she would be sitting here with a world-famous producer and director, telling him about her baby's smiles and weight gains. But it did not feel odd; Jackson was perhaps the easiest person to talk to that she had ever met—or, at least, easy for her. She felt, in a way, as if she had known him for years. On the other hand, she was also aware of a little sizzle of excitement in her gut that reminded her that she didn't know him at all, that he was drop-dead sexy, and the first man that she had felt the slightest interest in in eight months.

"What about you?" she said after a time, smiling sheepishly. "Here I've been going on and on talking about the baby. You haven't had a chance to get a word in edgewise."

"I like hearing about Joseph. And what about me? I have nothing exciting to relate. Just days of setting things up for filming, of looking at locations and talking to people, hiring people, signing contracts. It's the part I like least about a film. When we actually start shooting is when I begin to enjoy it." He did not add that he had not intended to stay in Austin this long, that he had lingered, overseeing things that his assistants usually handled, just because he had been restless and reluctant to return to L.A. Sitting here now, looking at Beth, he wondered if he hadn't been subconsciously hoping that she would show up.

"And when will that be?"

"I go to L.A. the day after tomorrow. Then we'll be back in Austin in six weeks to begin shooting. After a couple of weeks here, we move out close to you for the barren land scenes. That's to accommodate one of the actor's schedules. After that, we return to Austin for another month or so."

"Close to us? Really?" Beth could not stop the pleased smile that spread across her face.

"Yeah. The location I was scouting the day I met you." Another thing that Jackson had chosen not to examine too closely were his reasons for deciding that the locations thirty and forty miles from Angel Eye were much better than the ones Sam had found two hours away from the town.

"That will be nice. Will you come by and see us? Maybe *The Insider* won't be camped on our doorstep by then."

"Yeah. I'll come see you. I'll even brave *The Insider* to do it."

"Wow. I *am* impressed."

When dinner was over, Jackson walked her out to her car. He found that he did not want to say goodbye to Beth in the full public view of the restaurant or the hotel lobby. She unlocked the door of her car, and they stood for an uncomfortable moment. He felt like a high school kid again, he thought, not wanting to say goodbye to his date and not knowing how to keep her there. He could not deny the sexual feelings that had been stirring in him the whole afternoon with her. Yet he felt odd feeling that way about Joseph's mother, as if he were breaking some sort of taboo. She was, after all, a new *mother*; doubtless the last thing on her mind was sex, and she would probably be appalled if she knew that the whole time they had been arguing this afternoon, he had been thinking about kissing her.

"Well, goodbye," she said, opening the car door.

"Goodbye." He held the door open for her as she stepped into the wedge between the car and door.

They stood for an awkward moment, neither of them willing to take the last step away. He bent, meaning to kiss her on the cheek, but at the last instant, his lips went to her lips instead. Their mouths touched as soft as velvet, and clung. Jackson braced his hands on the car door on one side of her and the roof of the car on the other, holding back from touching her. Beth felt enveloped by his warmth and scent, but she ached for more. She wanted to feel his arms around her, wanted to step into him, to wrap her arms around him and hold on for dear life. Yet she could not let herself do that, as if it would make the moment too real, too scary and fraught with problems. So only their mouths touched, tasting and exploring. Her hands dug into the material of her dress; his clenched upon the metal of the car.

When at last Jackson pulled back, both of them were

breathing heavily. He gazed down at her flushed face, her eyes glittering like stars, and he wanted to jerk her against him and kiss her again. Instead he drew a deep breath and stepped back. Beth swallowed and managed a trembling smile, then quickly ducked into the car.

He walked away, not looking back. Beth went limp, crossing her forearms on the steering wheel and leaning against them, waiting for the trembling in her limbs to stop and her breathing to return to normal. *What was going on here?* She had come here breathing fire, furious with him and wanting only to slice him to ribbons. Now all she wanted was to be in his arms again—preferably naked and in a bed.

It was just the aftermath of pregnancy, she told herself—a flood of hormones that pulled her in strange directions. It was something she should have expected. It was no portent of the future. It had nothing to do with Jackson Prescott himself, other than that he was there—and quite handsome, of course—and potently male.

She drew a shaky breath. Who was she kidding? It had everything to do with Jackson Prescott and that sexy smile of his, those luscious blue eyes, the sharp angles of cheekbones and jaw. He was, in fact, devastating to her senses and, she was honest enough to admit, devastating to her emotions, as well. If she was smart, Beth thought, she would stay far away from him. He would not fit into the simple and uncomplicated life she had envisioned for herself and her baby, a life free of things like reporters hounding her and having her name splashed all over the tabloids—or having her heart broken again by another man far more worldly than she.

But then, Beth had never been one for playing it safe.

And she knew that if Jackson Prescott did show up in Angel
Eye two months from now, she would gladly open the door
and let him in.

Chapter Five

THE FUROR IN THE TABLOIDS gradually died down. After a few more fruitless days, the reporter from The Insider disappeared. There was another article or two, but they were mere rehashings of old stories, and after another week, Beth was pleased to find that she had slipped quietly back into anonymity. The reporters stopped calling, as did curious acquaintances. Beth's life returned to normal—or as normal as life could be with a new baby.

But even that was settling into an easier routine. Joseph began to sleep through the night, supplemented with a short nap in the morning and a long one in the afternoon. All the redness and discolorations of birth had faded, and he was turning into a beautiful plump baby with a mop of dark hair.

Cater had returned to his house in Austin, so it was just Beth, Cory and her father at the ranch, and even Cory would be returning to college in Austin soon. But Beth was now able to manage both the baby and the house without feeling as if she had been run over by a truck. Sometimes, when the baby was asleep, she even tried sketching again. She did not yet start to work again in oils, but she was beginning to feel restless and a little eager to get back to her work—something she had wondered about ever happening again when she was in the heavy lassitude of her pregnancy.

She drew pencil and pen-and-ink sketches of her father or Cory or scenes around the house. She even found herself a few times trying to draw a picture of Jackson Prescott from memory, though she never could seem to get it right. She was not, she thought, familiar enough with his face— though it seemed to her that she thought about him so often that she should be.

He called her a few times from L.A.—short unimportant conversations that were mostly about Joseph and his new accomplishments or the business that was keeping Jackson occupied in Los Angeles. But Beth always got a knot of excitement in her stomach whenever she picked up the phone and heard his voice on the other end of the line.

He was returning to Austin soon, and only two weeks after that he would start shooting near Angel Eye. Beth would have been aware of that fact even if Jackson had not told her, for the entire town of Hammond was gearing up for the coming of the movie crew. They were staying in a motel in Hammond, which had the closest motel to the desolate area where they would be filming. Hammond had not had this much excitement for years. The weekly newspaper kept up a "movie watch," and locals were excited about being extras in the film.

Still, Beth was astonished when the doorbell rang late one afternoon, and she opened the door to find Jackson

Prescott standing on her doorstep. "Jackson!" she cried, before she could stop herself.

Her hand flew up to her chest, and she felt suddenly hot, then cold. Her stomach started to dance. "What are you doing here?"

"Filming a movie, hadn't you heard?" He smiled, taking off his sunglasses. "You going to let me in?"

"Of course. I—I'm just so surprised to see you." Beth stepped back to let him enter the foyer, resisting an impulse to check her hair. She was sinkingly aware of the fact that she was wearing much-worn denim shorts and an old tank top, rather too stretched by her larger breasts. "Uh, I, how did you find our house?"

"Everyone in Angel Eye knows where you live. Didn't you know that? I stopped at a convenience store and asked, and they were quite happy to tell me. Guess you don't worry much about security here."

Beth chuckled. "Not really."

"I took the road the kid told me, checked the mailboxes, and voilà! Here I am. I was afraid you might have a gate or something. What *was* that thing I drove across when I turned into your road? It felt like I was driving on a washboard."

"That's a cattle guard, city boy." Beth smiled. His casual way had allowed her nerves to vanish, and now she led him to the den, where Joseph was lying on his back in his playpen, moving his arms and legs and batting at the activity toys dangling from the webbed strap strung across the top of the playpen. "You want to see Joseph?"

"Of course." Jackson's eyes went to the backs of Beth's legs as she bent over the playpen and picked up the baby. She had certainly gotten her figure back, he noticed. Her legs were shapely and looked a mile long, and she filled out the skimpy top admirably.

Beth turned, baby in arms, and Jackson pulled his gaze back to her face. "Look at that!" he exclaimed, staring at the baby in wonder. "He's so big!"

Beth beamed. "Well, you have to remember, he's almost three months old now. You want to hold him?"

"Sure." He took him with the exaggerated care of one not used to infants and held him, looking down at Joseph long and carefully. "He's beautiful. Or shouldn't one say that about a baby boy?"

"Why not? He is."

Jackson caressed the baby's cheek and traced one eyebrow. The baby stared back at him gravely, pacifier firmly in place, and arms and legs pumping. Suddenly Joseph grinned hugely around his pacifier, as if he and Prescott shared some secret and hilarious joke. Jackson let out a delighted chuckle.

"Did you see that! He smiled at me."

"Uh-huh. Maybe he recognizes you."

"After three months?"

"You were one of the first people who ever held him. That's got to make an impression."

Jackson put his finger against the baby's hand, and Joseph curled his little hand around it firmly. Jackson bent his head closer, staring into his face and talking, trying to win more smiles. He was rewarded with a coo and a frenzy of kicks.

Beth, watching the two of them, felt a lump rising in her throat. She realized that this was the way she would like to draw Jackson, him standing there holding the baby, so large in comparison, bent over in awe and affection, held captive by the little creature.

They spent the evening in the den, playing with the baby and talking. Beth's father came in and joined them, and they wound up watching an old movie on television. Beth was rather amazed. The last thing she would have expected of a hotshot Hollywood director was to spend a family evening playing with a baby and looking at the tube with her dad.

He did not stay late. "Have to get up in the morning early to start filming," he explained as Beth walked with him to the door.

"How early?"

"Five or so."

"Five?" she repeated, stunned.

"Yeah. Glamorous, huh? People always think movie people stay up late partying and then sleep till noon. Well, usually I do stay up late, watching the dailies. But I never sleep late. We have to get everything set up, take advantage of the light. Every day is money gone, so you have to make the most of each one."

They had reached the front door. He laced his fingers through hers and led her outside. They strolled over to his car. "It's hectic. I probably won't be able to get over here much."

"I understand." Her heart began to beat a little faster. His words must mean that he wanted to see her more. *Or was it just the baby that brought him here?*

He turned to face her, leaning against his car. "Would you come visit the set?"

"Really?" Beth smiled. "Would it be okay?"

"Sure. I'll put your name on the list. They'll let you in and tell you where to go."

"When?"

"Tomorrow. Or whenever you'd like. I'll approve you for every day. That way you can come whenever you get the chance."

"That's very nice of you."

He grinned. "Nothing's too good for the mother of my 'secret love child.'"

Beth grimaced. *"Puhleeze."*

"They've stopped, haven't they?"

"Yeah."

"Bigger fish to fry." He took her hand and laid it flat against one of his. With his other hand, he traced each of her fingers, slowly, almost meditatively, watching the movement of his finger. "I'm sorry you were put in that mess because of me."

"It wasn't your fault. All you did was be a Good Samaritan."

"Yeah, but it certainly wasn't your fault, either. I'm even sorrier that I doubted you." He looked back into her face in the dim light cast by the moon and stars. "I'm too cynical."

"It's easy to understand, if you have to deal with that kind of stuff all the time."

"The tabloids usually aren't that bad about me. I'm not a real celebrity, a star. I think they jumped on it because they've never been able to pin any sort of scandal on me before. When they got the chance, they went at it full blast."

"So you've always been a good boy?" Beth could hear the hint of flirtation in her voice, and it surprised her a little.

He grinned. "More like a dull one." There was an undercurrent of seduction in *his* voice, as well, a certain husky quality that did strange things to Beth's insides.

"I doubt that." She swayed forward slightly.

He did the same. "Trust me. I'm Old Reliable."

"And what should I rely on you for?" she asked lightly.

Jackson's only answer was to bring his hands up to cup her face. He gazed at her for a long moment, and his hands slid down her neck and onto her shoulders. The touch of his skin on her bare flesh sent a shiver through her, and Beth was reminded suddenly of how long it had been since she had been with a man.

She told herself that Jackson was slick and sophisticated, and that in any situation with him she would probably be in over her head. Joseph's father had been like that— wealthy, worldly—and look what had happened with him. She had to be more careful this time.

But then Jackson's mouth was on hers, and Beth stopped thinking at all.

She wrapped her arms around his neck and gave in to the sweet pleasure of his kiss. His arms went around her, and he pulled her in tightly against him. They kissed for a long time, oblivious to the world around them. Finally Jackson raised his head. His eyes glittered, and his face was flushed and slack with desire.

Beth drew a shaky breath. "Well…" she said. "I…uh…"

"Yeah." Reluctantly his arms fell away from her. "This is probably not a very good thing to start."

Beth shook her head. "Yeah." She realized that her verbal and physical signals were confused, which, when she thought about it, pretty much reflected what she felt inside—confusion. This was not what she needed at the moment. All her energies should be concentrated on the baby and on getting back to work. She did not need romantic feelings mixing up her insides.

"I better get back inside," she murmured.

"Okay. Will you come to the set?"

She nodded. "Tomorrow, if I can get someone to baby-sit Joey."

Baby-sitting, of course, was the least of her problems. There was always someone around who was happy to take care of the baby. It had, after all, been sixteen years since there had been a baby in the family. She had said it only to have an excuse for not showing up.

However, after a night of tossing and turning, going over all the reasons why a man was the last thing she needed in her life right now, Beth did not even think of using her ready-made excuse. Instead she called Daniel's son, James, who quickly agreed to come over and take care of Joseph for two or three hours—provided that Beth would introduce him to Jackson Prescott.

"I'm the only one who hasn't met him," he said plaintively. "And I'm the only one who would like to."

Beth chuckled. "Well, he said he would come over again, and when—if—he does, I'll introduce you."

So the next morning, at ten, she drove to the spot where they were filming. A guard stopped Beth long before she reached the trailers and the huddle of people in the distance. He checked his list, talked to someone on a walkie-talkie and a moment later a young woman showed up, looking harried, and escorted Beth along the dirt road to the center of the activity.

The trailers stood to one side. Stretching in front of them was a barren patch of ground, then a battered car in front of the facade of a wooden shack. There was a small truck on a set of tracks leading away from the car, and atop the truck were a seat and a camera. There was various other equipment scattered around, none of which Beth could identify except for banks of lights and a long boom with a dangling microphone. Several people stood or sat under a canopy, protected from the blazing August sun. A number of other people scurried around moving equipment and measuring things, talking into headsets. It looked like utter chaos.

Off to one side, apparently oblivious to the hubbub around him, stood Jackson, dressed in shorts and a T-shirt, with an old ball cap on his head to ward off some of the sun. He was talking to an older man with a long, graying ponytail and a backward-turned hat. Jackson was talking and gesturing, and the older man was nodding. The girl who had escorted Beth edged toward the men and caught Jackson's attention. He asked her a question, and she answered, pointing toward Beth.

Jackson turned and saw Beth, and a smile broke across his face. "Beth!"

He left the other two and came over to her. "Hi. You came. I wasn't sure."

"Yeah. Here I am."

He stopped just short of her and stood a little awkwardly. "I told Jackie to get you a chair in the shade. It's the most comfortable seat in the house. I have to work." He nodded toward where the other man stood waiting for him.

"Sure. I understand."

She didn't talk to him again until they broke for lunch, but she found it interesting to watch the filming. After a long time the chaos died down into stillness. An actress came out of one trailer, and an actor out of another, and two more people came forward from under the canopy. They took up their positions on the porch of the "shack" and beside the car, and then there was another round of waiting while more things were checked and people hurried out to fix the actors' hair and makeup for a final time.

There were a few minutes of filming, then several more takes, involving more checking of hair and makeup, and finally everyone broke away. The actors returned to their trailers and the canopy, and the chaos began all over again. Beth noticed that throughout the morning, which included several apparent crises, including an argument with the head cameraman and a tantrum by one of the actors, Jackson retained his calm. It was no wonder, she thought, that she had instinctively realized that he could handle a race to the hospital and a frantic birth. He was used to handling problems every day of his life.

Lunch was a catered buffet under the canopy, and Beth ate it with Jackson, sitting at a table in one corner of the little pavilion. Everyone left them alone, but Beth could feel the curious glances from the cast and crew.

"Don't you have one of the trailers?" Beth asked curiously.

Jackson grinned. "No. Just the two stars. The other trailer's the makeup and costume rooms. One corner of it is a little office, which my assistant works out of. Directors always seem to be in the middle of the fray. It's the way I like it. I want to keep my eye on everything. The last thing I need is to be shut away from it in a trailer."

"At least you would be out of the heat," Beth commented, sitting back and fanning herself with an empty paper plate.

He looked concerned. "Are you too hot? You want to go into the makeup trailer for a while?"

Beth laughed. "No. I'm fine. You forget, I grew up in this heat."

"I'm glad you came out."

"Me too."

"You want to have dinner tonight?"

"I thought you were going to be too busy."

"I have to eat. We could meet in Hammond. What do you say?"

"Okay." She knew it was foolish. She had given herself a thorough talking-to last night. There was no future in an affair with a director from L.A. To begin with, they lived thousands of miles apart, or at least they would once he returned to Los Angeles after the filming. With a new baby, there was no room in her life for a man, period, much less for one who would breeze into it for a few weeks and then breeze right back out, leaving her no doubt sadder, but probably not a whit wiser.

Besides, they lived such utterly different lives. Though she lived in a city, she was used to a quiet, serene life. She spent most of her days alone in her studio, painting. She didn't go to glittering parties. She didn't spend her days under the high pressure of deadlines. She worked and lived at her own pace, answering to no one, and that was the way she liked it. She was no more likely to give up her life than Jackson was to dump his career among the movers and shakers of Hollywood.

It was, obviously, a romance that was doomed from the start. Yet Beth could not bring herself to administer the deathblow cleanly and early. She liked being with him too much. So she agreed to have supper with him that evening. And when they found that everyone stared and whispered when they went into a restaurant in Hammond, Beth smiled and suggested that perhaps it would be easier if the next time they had dinner at her house.

She saw him frequently after that, despite his earlier

statement that he would have little time on location. Somehow he seemed to make time, coming out almost every day to the ranch for an hour or two before he went back to watch the dailies. Beth noticed her family was getting used to having him around. James, who had been overawed to meet him, soon was chatting away with him about old films as if they had known each other all their lives, and even Daniel and her father allowed that he was "all right."

The baby, it was clear, soon recognized Jackson, who could always make Joey gurgle and coo and smile. Beth began sketching scenes of the two of them together, and when she found the pose that she liked the best, she decided to start an oil portrait, her first since she'd moved back to the ranch. If it turned out well, she thought, she would give it to him. Jackson had admired the large portrait of her mother that she had done a few years ago for her father and which hung over the mantel in the living room.

Jackson spent most of Saturday evening with her at the ranch house, and after she had put Joseph down to bed for the night, with the monitor beside her father's chair as Marshall watched an exhibition game in the den, she took Jackson outside, promising to show him the delights of an evening out in West Texas.

"We going dancing?" he asked in some amusement. "I better go back and put on my boots."

"Nope. Nearest dance hall's an hour away. I was thinking of someplace closer. Here, take this." She shoved a cooler at him and grabbed some quilts, waving him out the door. They put the quilts and cooler in the back of her father's pickup and climbed in the front.

Beth set out from the house, driving a way Jackson had never gone before, following a track that led deeper onto the land instead of out to the road. After a while the track disappeared, and Jackson realized that they were simply driving cross-country, dodging mesquite bushes and sagebrush and cows.

"Where are we going?" he asked as they bounced and rattled along. "By the way, can you bruise a spleen?"

Beth chuckled. "We are going to look at something I'll bet you've never seen, city slicker."

"Coyotes?" he hedged.

She smiled. "This looks like a good spot."

Beth pulled to a stop. Jackson glanced around. He couldn't see anything about this place that was different from any of the rest of the land. It was all dark, with darker lumps of bushes here and there.

"Come on." Beth jumped out and walked around to open the gate of the pickup. Jackson obediently followed.

Beth hopped up into the bed of the truck and laid out the blankets, then gestured for Jackson to join her. She opened the cooler and pulled out two beers, handing one of them to him. Then she lay down on the truck bed, patting the blanket beside her. Jackson lay down where she'd indicated.

"Is this it?" he asked.

Beth chuckled. "Yep. This is it. Lying out looking at the stars." She pointed straight up. "But look at them! You never see anything like that in the city. I know."

He had to agree. The night sky was enormous and velvet black, darker than it ever was in any city, and it was filled with a multitude of coldly glittering stars, the moon a silver-white crescent among them. It was relaxing, soothing, to lie out here in the cooling evening, surrounded by utter quiet and the vast reach of the empty land below and the starry sky above. Jackson could feel the strains of the last few stressful days oozing out of him.

He took another swig of his beer and set it beside him, then crossed his arms behind his head and gave himself up to contemplating the vastness of the universe for a while. Beth, who had seen the same view thousands of times, still gazed at it in admiration. In her career, she dealt with beauty—recreated it, brought it out in rich textures and glowing colors, struggled to add it where it was not. But nothing she could ever do could compare to the beauty of nature, the perfect blend of color, texture and space. It was a fact that she had realized anew time after time, always with a pang that was part ache and part joy.

They started to talk, first about how the filming had been going and when he and the others would be returning to Austin to finish filming there, then drifting to her work and her house in Dallas, and finally to what it had been like growing up in Angel Eye, Texas.

"I always wanted to get out," Beth remembered with a smile. "Now I find it rather peaceful and beautiful in its own stark way. But back then, all I could see was the dullness and the gossip and the never-ending emptiness. I felt like if I stayed here I would smother to death."

"Me too. Where I grew up was a little bigger, different landscape—magnolias instead of mesquite—but stagnant. Choking. I couldn't wait to get out."

"Course it didn't help having three older brothers who were the biggest guys in town. I hardly ever went out the first two years I was in high school because all the boys were so scared of Quinn. Thank God he graduated and went off to college, so at least I managed to have a few dates my junior and senior years."

"You have an interesting family—an artist, a rancher, a novelist, a cop—that's a mixed bag."

"Well, we never believed in being ordinary." Beth smiled. "And the boys aren't as different as it sounds. Quinn's a cop, and Cater writes mysteries. When they were young, all three of the boys had the biggest collection of *Hardy Boys* mysteries you've ever seen. That's what I read, too. I'm probably the only girl in the world who didn't read Nancy Drew. Probably the only reason Daniel didn't do something similar was because he got married right out of high school, and they had Jimmy pretty quickly. So he stayed here and got work in Hammond, and Dad gave them some land. And ranching's in all the boys' blood. Whenever Dad or Daniel needs extra workers, Quinn and Cater come to help."

"Which way do you suppose Cory is going to go?"

"I'm not sure. He's still at that stage where he's interested in half a dozen things. But I think at heart he's a rancher. Now, Jimmy, Daniel's son—"

Jackson laughed. "I don't think that boy's interested in working the land." Jimmy had bent Jackson's ear about movies and directing every time he had found Jackson at the house, and he had been ecstatic when Jackson had told him he was welcome to watch the filming. Jimmy had been on location every day since and was quite annoyed that school was starting next week, so he wouldn't be able to see the last few days of filming.

"Mama was artistic," Beth went on. "I guess that's where we get it. She drew and painted when she had the time, which wasn't often. And she used to tell the most wonderful stories. I remember she always said that when we kids were older, she wanted to write and illustrate children's books. But then, about the time the rest of us were getting big enough we didn't need so much seeing after, along came Cory. Then she died."

"That must have been hard for you. How old were you?"

"Thirteen. Yeah, it was hard. She was my friend and ally, as well as my mother. You know, us girls against the guys. And being a teenager, too—there are just some things a father and brothers can't help you with. My friend Sylvie and her mother always went shopping together, and sometimes they fought over what Sylvie could buy, but they had *fun*. Her mom would stay up when Sylvie was on a date, and when Sylvie came in, they would talk about it. Sometimes, when I went on a date, I would go over to Sylvie's to dress and do my makeup and hair so that when I said, 'How do I look?' I'd get a response like, 'Oh, I like that color eye shadow,' or 'Hey, your hair is different,' instead of 'Fine, honey.' Dad wouldn't have noticed my hair unless I dyed it green."

Jackson chuckled. "Your dad's great. We walked around the yard the other night—looked in the barn, looked in the corral, checked out the row of trees he planted. I'll bet he didn't say more than two sentences—and both those times were when I asked him a question. Then, when we came in, he nodded at me and said, 'You're good company, son.'"

"That's Dad. The less you talk, the better company you are. He said he got used to not talking, being out on the land by himself so much, you know. But he was a good father. He tried really hard to make up to Cory and me for Mama dying. He went to all our school plays and parent-teacher conferences. He was in the stands at all the boys' games. He even went to my dance recitals." Beth giggled. "I can still remember looking out in the audience and seeing him sitting there with this look of grim resignation on his face. Poor man. I think he felt guilty because he never remarried after Mama died. He told me once that he thought he should have given us another mother, but he couldn't bring himself to put some other woman in Mama's place. He loved her so much."

They were silent for a moment, then Jackson asked softly, "What about Joseph's father?"

He could feel Beth's body go rigid beside him. "What about him?"

"Well, he seems conspicuously absent," he said cautiously.

"He *is* conspicuously absent. And he is going to remain so."

"Does he even know that Joseph was born?"

"No. He doesn't even know about the *possibility* of his being born."

"You didn't tell him you were pregnant?"

"No."

"Don't you think he at least has the right to know he has a son?"

"He has *no* rights." Beth sat up, her jaw clenched. Why did Jackson have to bring *him* up?

"I'm sorry." Jackson laid a hand on her back.

She flinched, but when his hand remained, warm and undemanding, she relaxed a little. "No. *I'm* sorry." She let out a long sigh and lay back down. "I get a little…antagonistic on that subject."

"So I see. I didn't mean to upset you. I was just thinking about it from the male perspective. I would think he would want to know, to be a father to Joey." He turned on his side and lay propped up on his elbow, looking down at her.

"You don't know Robert. I don't think he would give a flip about knowing about Joey. It's my guess that he would tell me that he already has two sons and, besides, how does he know that Joseph is really his? That's the sort of man Robert Waring is."

"I see."

"He's cold, calculating, deceitful—" Beth drew a breath and forced herself to relax. "Oh, I'm not being fair to him. He's also charming—extremely charming *and* handsome, *and* sophisticated, *and* intelligent. I met him at a party at a bank opening. I had painted the portrait of the chairman of the board that hung in the lobby, so I got an invitation to the grand opening. Robert did business with them. He was urbane and witty, and after the opening, he asked if he could take me out to a late supper. Well, it went on from there. I would see him every few weeks. He lived in Chicago, and he came to Dallas often on business. I suppose that's why it took me so long to figure it out. I didn't know that back in Chicago, he lived with his wife and two teenage boys."

"Ah."

"Yeah. Ah." Beth grimaced. "I was hopelessly naive. It never even struck me as odd that the only numbers I had for him were business numbers—his office phone, his pager, his cellular phone. He frequently worked late, and usually if we talked in the evenings, he was at his office. I assumed he was a bachelor who wasn't home much—if I thought at all. Looking back on it, I'm not sure I did."

"No need to kick yourself about it. People don't expect someone to lie to them at every turn, particularly someone they're close to. If a person sets out to fool you, they will— unless they're really *bad* at it."

"He wasn't bad at it. Not at all. I found out by accident. I was doing a portrait of the bank president's wife—a very nice and very chatty woman. We talked a lot while she was sitting for me, and sometime in there, I mentioned Robert and having met him at the opening of their new building. She said, 'Oh, yes, Robert, I've met him several times. Such a charming man, and his wife is so elegant.' You can imagine how I reacted."

"Mmm-hmm."

"I'm sure I turned completely white, but I hid behind my easel and managed to say, 'Oh? I didn't realize he was married.' She told me that he very much was and had two sons. Then she said that I mustn't get mixed up with him, of course not knowing it was a trifle late for that. He was, she said, a terrible ladies' man. So after she left, I called him up and asked him if it was true, and he told me yes and not to be hysterical. He made it quite clear where I ranked on his list of priorities, which was somewhere down below his golf game, I think."

"I'm sorry. I know that's terribly inadequate, but…"

"Well, live and learn, Dad always says."

"Some lessons are harder than others, though."

"Yeah. About a month after that, I figured out that I was pregnant." Beth smiled a little to herself. "It was hard at the time. But I can't really say I regret it. Otherwise I wouldn't have Joey."

"That's true. He is worth a lot of pain."

"Yeah."

Jackson gazed down at her for a long moment. He brushed his knuckles down her cheek. "I am not married," he said. "Never have been."

Beth looked back at him, wondering where this was going. She could not read his expression, for his head was backlit by the light of the stars and moon. "What are you telling me?"

He smiled. "I'm not sure. I guess…that I'm not the same sort of man as Robert Waring."

He paused. It was on the tip of his tongue to blurt out that he loved her, that he wanted to have much more than a few evenings with her. But he stopped himself. *That was crazy.* He barely knew Beth Sutton. He was an adult, not some crazy teenager who fell in love on the basis of an intense meeting and a few hours spent in her company. He had a movie to shoot. In a few more days he would return to Austin to resume filming there, and after that he would go back to Los Angeles.

Jackson wanted to kiss her. He wanted to make love to her out here under the stars. But something held him back. Making love did not necessarily mean making promises for the future. But, somehow, he felt that with this woman, for him, it would be a promise.

He bent down and kissed her lightly on the lips. "We had better be getting back."

"Right now?" Beth asked, her eyebrows rising. She had seen the hesitation on his face, the desire that had flickered in his eyes and been squelched. "But you haven't gotten to the best part of one of these Angel Eye evenings."

"Oh? And what is that?"

"This," she replied, hooking her hand behind his neck and pulling him down for a kiss.

Chapter Six

HER LIPS WERE SOFT AND MELTING, and Jackson could not keep from responding to them. A kiss, after all, was not making love, and he would stop long before they reached that point.

Their lips clung, their tongues twining around one another, seeking, exploring. It seemed to Jackson that the more he tasted her, the more he wanted. They kissed again and again, their desire escalating.

Beth shivered and pressed up against him, her arms wrapping around him. It had been so long since she had felt this kind of passion, this roaring, rushing ocean of desire that swept her along almost mindlessly. *Had she ever felt it?* She couldn't remember it—not like this. She had meant only to kiss him as she had the other night. She had, she admitted, felt a trifle annoyed at his ability to turn away from her so easily, and she had wanted to prove that she could make him desire her. But now she found herself at the mercy of her own passion, her body, its desires dormant for so many months, reawakening to its own needs.

His mouth was urgent and hungry, every kiss a demand and a delight all in one. His hand moved down her body, setting up a wild tingling wherever it touched. He cupped her breast, his thumb circling her nipple through her blouse. Beth let out a little moan, and she felt a tremor run through Jackson's body in response.

They broke off their kiss, and Jackson rained kisses down her throat and onto her chest. Completely forgotten were his plans for restraint and control. His fingers went to her blouse, unbuttoning it and delving beneath her lacy brassiere to touch the soft orb of her breast. His touch felt so right, so good, that Beth unconsciously moved her hips. She realized that she had been wanting this for days—maybe even weeks. She just had not acknowledged it, had not wanted to accept the fact that she could again be this hungry for a man…if, indeed, she ever had been. She could not remember feeling such a volatile storm of sensations and emotions before. It was, frankly, a little frightening.

"No, wait." Beth edged away, putting her hands up to his chest.

Jackson stopped, his breath rasping in his throat. For a long moment he struggled for control. Then, with a groan, he rolled away onto his back and flung one arm across his eyes.

"I'm sorry," Beth said, sitting up. "I know I'm the one who started that, but…I don't know, it was all moving too fast. I'm not ready for—" *For what? Commitment? Sex? Loss of control?* "I don't know. I don't want to make another mistake."

He nodded. "You're right. This probably isn't the time or place." He had known that before they kissed—*now if he could just convince his raging libido of that fact.*

"No. You were the one who was right. We should have gone home when you suggested it." Beth began to scoot toward the gate of the truck.

Jackson reached out a hand and grabbed her arm, stopping her. She glanced at him. He smiled. "Maybe so. But I'm glad we didn't."

Heat rose in Beth's cheeks, but she flashed back a grin. "Me, too."

THE NEXT DAY, BETH WAS STANDING in line at the grocery store in Angel Eye, a basketful of diapers, baby food and food in front of her, when she glanced over at the magazine rack. There, on the front of the tabloid, right next to a picture of a car trunk lid on which an image of Jesus had supposedly formed, was a picture of her and Jackson walking out of some door. They were talking, their heads turned toward each other, and they were holding hands. Across the top of the photograph, the headline blazoned: Prescott's Secret Love Nest!

Beth groaned, then glanced quickly around to see if anyone had heard. She wondered if anyone else had seen it, if they had recognized her. After another furtive look around, she snatched the top issue of *Scandal* off the rack and looked at the picture up close. The door they were exiting, she decided, was the front door of the ranch house. She couldn't stop a little smile at the thought of how her father would react to having his home labeled a "secret love nest."

How had they gotten this shot? She decided that it must have been taken with a telephoto lens, with the photographer sitting somewhere out of sight. She certainly hadn't caught a glimpse of anyone taking their picture at any point. *But how had they known to send a photographer out to take it?*

It boggled her mind the way the tabloids were able to jump so quickly on a story. She supposed that someone on the movie crew had tipped them off—or any of the townspeople of Hammond or Angel Eye who had happened to see them together. She and Jackson hadn't been very secretive about their relationship.

Beth read through the story, a mishmash of truth, speculation and downright lies. But it sounded convincing, even to her. They even mentioned in the story that her child was named after Jackson's father. Beth shook her head. She had never thought that *that* decision would come back to haunt her.

For a brief moment, she thought about calling Julie McCall at *Scandal* and setting the record straight. But even a moment's immediate reflection made her change her mind. For one thing, it would be hard to convince the woman that there had been nothing between her and Jackson, not when they had a picture of the two of them holding hands. For another thing, she rather doubted that the tabloid cared about publishing the truth. They just wanted a good story, and no doubt a "secret love child" and "secret love nest" were more appealing. What was it about secret love that was so intriguing to people, anyway?

Maybe no one would notice, she thought desperately, but that hope was dashed when the cashier looked up and saw her. "Why, hi, Beth! How are you? See you got your picture in the papers."

Beth smiled weakly. "Yeah. Hi, Maggie Lee."

"What will your daddy say about all that?" the checker went on, snapping her gum and dragging Beth's groceries over the scanner.

"He won't like it. I imagine you can guess that."

Maggie Lee chuckled. "Sure can. Marshall never was one who liked attention." She paused for a moment, then asked, "So what's going on with you and that movie fella? You all going to tie the knot or what?"

"We're just friends. You can't believe all that stuff in the tabloids."

"Aren't they a hoot? I just love those things. But, you know, I figure some of that stuff has got to be true. They couldn't just publish those things if they were bald-faced lies. There has to be some kernel of truth there, that's what I always say."

Beth suppressed a sigh. She wondered how many people reasoned as Maggie Lee did. Probably a lot, she decided in despair. She endured the rest of Maggie Lee's conversation, paid her bill and got out of the grocery store as fast as she could.

"DON'T LET IT BOTHER YOU," Jackson counseled when he came over that evening and she showed him the copy of *Scandal*, which Peg Richards from up the road had thoughtfully dropped by. "Just shrug it off."

"Doesn't it bother you?"

"Some. But there are worse things. At least they aren't accusing us of killing somebody or being unfaithful to our spouses or something. They've done worse than this to people before."

"I suppose." Beth leaned over his chair, looking down at the cover again. "It's just—oh, I hate having people know stuff about me. Even worse, having them think they know stuff that isn't true. I even thought about calling the magazine and telling them what really happened."

"Uh-uh," Jackson said quickly, shaking his head. "Trust

me. You do *not* want to talk to them. I've known people who have made that mistake. They would turn your words around, and you would come out looking like a fool or someone wicked. Remember how they ran with that one thing you said to them last time?"

"Yeah, I know." Beth sighed and went to pick up the baby, who was beginning to make fussy noises in his playpen. He wriggled his arms and legs, fighting to go to Jackson, and she obligingly plopped him down in Jackson's lap.

"Don't worry," he reassured her. "You get used to it."

"I'm not sure I would." Beth sat down beside him, distracted from her irritation with the article by the sight of Jackson with the baby.

She had been working on the portrait of him with Joey off and on for several days. She had gotten to where she worked on it every day during the baby's nap and often in the evenings after Jackson left and she put Joey to bed. At the moment she was suffering from her usual midwork doubts and was afraid that the finished product would turn out all wrong. Well, she consoled herself, if it did, she didn't have to show it to Jackson.

She continued to look at him, wondering how a man playing with a baby could be so sweet and so sexy all at the same time. She hadn't been able to stop thinking about the other night in the bed of the pickup truck. There were times when she wished that she hadn't stopped. She looked at Jackson's fingers, long and thin, big-knuckled, with a light sprinkling of hair across the backs of his hands. He had beautiful hands, she thought, and remembered them roaming her body through her clothes. She found herself wishing that she could feel them against her bare skin.

"We're going back to Austin in a couple of days," Jackson said and shot her a sideways glance.

Beth's heart dropped. She wondered if he had seen the disappointment in her face. "Oh. Well…"

"It's not that far to Austin," he went on. "I was thinking that I could take a weekend off soon and come to visit…if you'd like."

"Sure."

"Or maybe you could come to see me there." He was still looking at her in that cautious way, and Beth realized that he was feeling his way along, unsure of how she would react.

It made her smile to think that this world-famous director was not entirely confident of her interest in him. "I'd like that," she told him honestly. "But I can't leave the baby."

"Bring him with you. I rented a house for the time we're in Austin. You could both stay there. I could rent a crib. And I can set my assistant to finding a nanny to take care of him for a while if you wanted to go out and do anything. You could stay a few days…if you'd like, of course."

"Yeah," she answered, smiling. "I'd like. Very much."

BETH WAS EXCITED THE WHOLE drive up to Austin. She told herself that it was because it was the first time she had taken off with the baby on her own for any length of time. But she knew that was not the reason for the quivery anticipation in her stomach—or at least not for most of it. She was excited about seeing Jackson again. It had been over a week since he'd left Angel Eye. She wondered if he had missed her, if he had thought about her every day as she had been thinking about him. She wondered if his nerves, too, were jangling with anticipation. *Would he be happy to see her? Or would he think that she wasn't as pretty, as funny—as anything—as he remembered her?*

Many of her questions were answered when she pulled into the driveway of the house to which he had directed her and, before she had even gotten out of her car, the front door of the house opened and Jackson came out, grinning. An answering smile broke across Beth's face, and she quickly opened the door and jumped out. Jackson was down the steps and across to the circular driveway in about three steps, and he pulled her into his arms, lifting her off her feet.

"It feels like it's been forever," he said and kissed her thoroughly. Beth was rosy and laughing by the time they stepped apart. "Has it only been a week?"

She nodded. "And a few days."

"Every day seemed about thirty-six hours long." He pulled her into his arms again for another hug. Behind them, the baby set up a wail.

"Oops. I'd better get Joey out of his car seat." Beth slipped out of Jackson's arms and got into the back seat to unstrap the baby. Jackson was already reaching to take him when she turned around.

"Wow, look at this fella!" Jackson exclaimed. "Hey, slugger, you've grown since I saw you last. Same baby blues, though." He kissed the baby on the forehead, then cuddled him against his shoulder. "Do you think he remembers me?" he asked with a tinge of anxiety.

Beth had to chuckle. "I'm sure he does. He's crazy about you. In fact, I think he missed you. He was a little cranky at the beginning of the week."

He shot her a look. "Oh, right. I'm not *that* gullible about him."

"I'm serious! I really think he was wondering where you were."

Jackson gave the baby another pat and handed him back to Beth so that he could carry their bags into the house. "I thought we would have dinner here tonight," he said. "I guessed that you might be tired from traveling. We can go out tomorrow, if you want."

"You cooked?" Beth asked, surprised, as she followed him into the Mediterranean-style stucco house.

"Do I detect a note of chauvinism in your voice?" he responded tartly, then grinned. "Actually I had it catered. Believe me, you'll like it better."

He carried her bags through a spacious entryway and down a hall. On one side of the hall were rooms. On the other side were rows of windows, looking out at a spectacular view of Town Lake.

"Wow!" Beth stopped and looked down. Right below them was a sparkling aqua swimming pool with a miniature waterfall, and beyond it the bluff dropped straight down to a small inlet. In the distance the lake shimmered in the late-afternoon sun, the sails of boats bright triangles of color against the dark water.

"Yeah. Beautiful, isn't it? The family that lives here is on vacation in Europe. Fortunately they were willing to extend it for an extra month." He turned into the next door. "Here's your room."

It was a modernistic room with stark white furniture, accentuated by a neon bright bedcover and drapes. Beth stepped into the room behind him, relaxing at his words.

Jackson saw her expression. "What? Did you think I was going to plop your things down in the master bedroom? I told you—no strings attached."

"I know." She smiled. "It's just nice to have my opinion of you confirmed."

He opened a door and stepped through into a small sitting room. "I put the crib in here. I thought this would be a nice place for him."

"It's great," Beth answered honestly. "We might just move in with you."

"Is that a promise?" He smiled, then turned serious, pulling her into his arms loosely, the baby between them. "I'll tell you the truth—I've been lonely as hell this week. Every evening when we stopped, for an instant I would feel this anticipation, but then I would remember that I wouldn't be going out to the ranch to see you and Joey. I would have given a lot to have come home and heard just one little gurgle or coo—or that crazy wind-up swing that plays faster the tighter you wind it."

Beth laughed. "Maybe I should have brought the swing with me."

Jackson left to set out their dinner, giving Beth a chance to change and feed the baby. When she came out, Jackson had the table set in the breakfast room, where they could look out over the water as they ate. Beth put Joseph down on a blanket in the middle of the wide, empty floor, accompanied by a few of his toys. Replete and dry, he amused himself while they ate a leisurely dinner and talked.

They stayed up late, long after Beth had put Joseph down in his bed, enjoying being together too much to go to bed. Beth knew she would regret it the next morning, but she did not retire until she was yawning so hugely that Jackson pulled her to her feet and turned her in the direction of her bedroom. She gave in, and he walked her to her door. There he kissed her good-night, and though the kiss turned into several kisses, at last he pulled away and went back down the hall and up the stairs to the aerie of a master bedroom on the floor above.

THEY SPENT A LAZY SATURDAY, lounging by the pool or playing with the baby. That evening a smiling gray-haired woman, whom Jackson characterized as "bonded and certified and thoroughly checked-out," came to sit with the baby while Jackson and Beth went out to eat. Beth went a little reluctantly; it was the first time she had left Joseph with anyone but a member of the family. However, with a mental squaring of her shoulders, she walked out the door. And only twice during the evening did she give in to the urge to phone the sitter to see how Joseph was doing.

However, she could not bring herself to stay out after midnight, and the first thing she did when they got back to Jackson's house was to go to the baby's room and peer over the side of the crib at him. Joey was sound asleep, of course, his chubby-cheeked face a study in relaxation. Beth smiled down at him, swallowing the lump in her throat.

She heard a noise and turned her head. Jackson had walked quietly into the room, and he came up now to stand behind her. He encircled her waist with his arms and leaned his head against hers, and for a long moment they simply stood, watching the baby sleep.

Then, softly, they slipped out of the room and back down the hall to the modernistic living room. The large sectional sofa was a buttery soft dark green leather, a lovely contrast to the immaculate white carpet, which Beth shuddered to even think of keeping clean. They sat down together on the sofa and stretched their legs out in front of them. He slid his arm around her shoulders, and Beth leaned against him, letting her head rest on his shoulder. It was a natural and very pleasant feeling, being with him this way, almost as if they were an old married couple relaxing together with the baby asleep down the hall.

They talked desultorily as they sat. After a moment's silence, Jackson said, "I wanted to tell you why I asked you about Joey's father."

"It's all right. You don't need to explain. It was a natural question. I just overreacted."

"I don't know about that. But I don't think it was really an idle question on my part. You see, I found out last year that I have an eighteen-year-old daughter that I never knew about."

"What?" Beth sat up, jolted, and turned to look into his face. "Are you serious?"

"Very," he replied grimly. "When I was sixteen, I was very much in love with a girl. Jessica Walls. She was a year younger than I was. We had all these plans, how we were going to go to college together and get married when we were juniors and—well, you know how kids are. We were serious and intense. The summer before my senior year, right about the time I turned seventeen, she moved away. It took me completely by surprise. She came over one evening and told me she and her mother were going to Atlanta for the summer. The summer turned into my whole senior year. She wrote me the next August, after we'd been exchanging letters all summer, and told me she wouldn't be coming back at all. I was heartbroken and furious. I felt that she had betrayed me. I didn't do well in school. I dropped out of sports. It was a bad year. Anyway, when I graduated, I had no desire to go to college, and I hadn't exactly been a stellar student anyway, so I decided to go far away. The

West Coast seemed as far as I could get. I wound up in L.A. and sort of lucked into that first movie. I got interested in directing and, well, after a while, I forgot all about Jessica."

He sighed and stood up, beginning to pace in front of the couch. "Until last year, that is. She wrote me a letter, and in it she told me that the reason she had left town all those years ago was because she was pregnant. Her family was very religious, and she said it broke her parents' hearts. She felt guilty and bad, and when her parents insisted that I know nothing about it, she agreed, to please them. She and her mother went to live with her aunt in Atlanta. Her aunt was several years younger than her mother, and she had never been able to have children. So she took the baby and raised it as her own. It was a little girl. The aunt named her Amy."

"Why did she tell you after all this time?"

"Because Amy needed money. Her aunt has been very sick for the last few years, and they've had big medical bills. They don't have enough money to send Amy to college. So Jessica decided to break her vow to her parents in the hopes that I would give her the money for Amy to go to school. She sent me a picture of her, I guess to convince me that Amy really was mine. It's pretty obvious that she's a Prescott."

"So what did you do?"

"Gave her the money, of course, and I paid off the medical bills, as well. I would do more, except that it would make Amy wonder. She thinks the college thing is some kind of scholarship that Jessica got for her from her employer, and she doesn't know about the medical bills. But if I gave them more money to live on, she would have to wonder."

"She still doesn't know that you're her father?"

He shook his head and sat back down beside Beth. "No. I wanted to see her, but Jessica was dead set against it. She says Amy has no reason to believe that she's anything but the aunt's daughter. She doesn't have any of those yearnings that adopted children have to know their real parents, and they don't want her to be disturbed." He shrugged. "Hell, I can hardly insist on it, knowing how it would shatter her life. I mean, Jessica has been living there close to her all those years, and she never let on."

"Oh, Jackson..." Beth reached out and put her hand on his arm. "I'm so sorry. It must be hard for you."

"Yeah. It's weird. I mean, I never even knew she existed, and now, even though she's really a stranger to me, I feel a connection, a *longing* to know her. My life would probably have been completely different if Jessica had told me. Hell, Jessie and I might have gotten married, and I'd be back home in Alabama being a roofer or something."

"A loss for the movie world."

"I guess. I suspect her parents were right and it would have been a bad decision. Both of us would probably have wound up miserable. Still, it's hard knowing you have a child and you've never even seen her. That you've missed all those special times, that if she saw me, she would look right past me and not have a clue who I was."

"It's her loss, too," Beth told him, putting her arms around him and leaning her head against his shoulder. "You would have been a great dad. I can see it with Joey. You're wonderful with him."

"I love him," he said simply. He smiled sheepishly. "Does that sound silly?"

"No, not at all. I think it's wonderful." Beth could feel her throat swelling with emotion.

He stroked his hand across her hair. "I'm glad you think so." He hooked his forefinger beneath her chin and tilted it so that she was looking into his face. He looked at her for a moment, then said softly, "Because, you know, I think I love the little guy's mother, too."

Chapter Seven

BETH STARED AT HIM IN SHOCK. Jackson chuckled. "Caught you off guard, huh?"

"But—but you couldn't."

"Why not?"

"I mean—well, it's too soon. You're probably mistaking your feelings because of our sharing Joey's birth and—"

"Elizabeth Sutton, are you trying to tell me that I don't know my own mind—or my own heart? I am thirty-six years old, you know, and have been functioning on my own for some time." His eyes twinkled with amusement.

Beth had the grace to blush. "Of course I don't mean that you don't know what you think or feel. It's just—well—" She faltered to a halt as she realized that, of course, that was exactly what she *had* meant.

Jackson was a grown man and obviously not the sort to fall in love every few weeks with a new woman. After all, he had gone this long without getting married even once, which in Hollywood was no mean feat. Warmth spread throughout Beth as she accepted that he *did* know what he meant; he *did* love her.

Jackson smiled. "I'm not asking you to reciprocate. I know it's sudden. But I wanted to tell you how I feel."

"Jackson, I…"

He shook his head, placing his forefinger against her lips. "You don't need to say anything. I don't expect it."

He bent and kissed her lips lightly, tenderly, then raised his head and gazed down into her eyes. Whatever he saw there must have pleased him, for his face softened with feeling, and he bent to kiss her again, this time more deeply. Beth let out a sigh of pleasure, and her arms went around his neck.

Their lips moved against each other with ever-increasing passion, until Beth's blood was racing hotly through her veins. Desire pooled between her legs, setting up a throbbing ache. She moved her legs, unable to keep still, and delighted in the immediate and unmistakable response of his body. They had shifted and moved as they kissed, until now they were lying pressed together full-length on the sofa. Their arms were tight around each other, and their legs intertwined. His hand roamed down Beth's back and onto her hips, cupping and caressing, then finally down onto her legs.

She had taken off her hose and shoes earlier, when she had gone to check on Joseph, so his hand slid over bare flesh. He moved upward, beneath her dress, caressing her thigh. His fingertips reached the lacy edge of her panties, and he hesitated, then edged beneath the lace. Beth shivered at the intimate touch.

She was on fire, aching for him. She didn't want to think about the future or the consequences. She wanted only to feel, to give herself up to the fire roaring through her. His mouth left hers and trailed hot kisses down her throat while his hand roamed over her buttocks, squeezing and caressing. Beth murmured his name, and Jackson groaned in response.

"You're beautiful," he whispered. "So beautiful."

He rose up on his elbow and looked down at her. "I want you."

For answer, Beth merely smiled. It seemed to be enough, for he stood up, reaching down to pull her up, too. They started up the circular stairs to the master bedroom, pausing every few feet along the way to kiss and caress each other again, all the while peeling off various articles of clothing. Their progress was slow, and by the time they reached the bed, they were naked, with a trail of clothes behind them.

They fell on the bed and rolled across it, kissing and touching each other in a frenzy of desire. Finally, when they could stand the teasing no longer, he moved between her legs. She opened to him, arching up to meet his thrust. He went deep inside her, and Beth let out a long sigh of satisfaction as he filled her. He moved slowly, afraid that he might hurt her in this, her first lovemaking since the baby, but after the first brief twinge of pain, Beth felt only pleasure. She wrapped her legs around him, urging him on, and he began to move faster, pounding into her with all the force of his passion.

He let out a hoarse cry as his seed poured into her, and Beth clung to him tightly, her own tidal wave of pleasure rushing through her.

Afterward, lying awake in the darkness, Jackson's arm around Beth, he said softly, "Don't go tomorrow."

"What?" Beth murmured sleepily, floating on a hazy wave of contentment.

"I don't want you to go back to Angel Eye tomorrow. Stay for a few more days. You could do that, couldn't you?"

"Sure." Beth smiled. "I could do that."

SHE WOUND UP STAYING FOR the rest of the week. She hadn't intended to. She was afraid that they would grow tired of each other, that their budding relationship would start to bend under the stresses of togetherness. She worried that Jackson would press her to reveal her feelings for him, now that he had told her that he loved her, and she wasn't prepared for that. She wasn't even sure how she felt about his loving her, let alone how she felt about him.

But, to her amazement, none of her forebodings materialized. He did not mention again that he loved her. She could feel it in his caresses and see it in the way he looked at her sometimes, but those moments only created a feeling a warmth inside her, not anxiety or pressure. Nor did he ask how she felt about him or even try to work the conversation in that direction.

They did not grow tired of each other. Jackson was gone most of every day, working, leaving Beth to putter around the house, taking care of the baby and doing whatever she wished. She visited Cory and Cater a few times. Cater lived in a restored turn-of-the-century house, and he let Cory have the garage apartment out back while he was going to U.T. Cater, who was plotting his newest book, was stuck and was happy to avoid the problem for a few hours of talking or playing with the baby or going to a movie. Of all her brothers, Cater's personality was the most suited to Beth's, and though he was not the closest to her in age, they got along the best. Cory, as always, was thrilled to have an opportunity to see Joseph. It had surprised everyone the way he had fallen for Joey, for Cory had been the most sports-oriented of the boys, the most likely to return to the ranch, not someone interested in children. Now he was talking about changing his major to elementary education.

Beth told herself that this week was not a real indicator of what life with Jackson would be like, that it did not show that he was the perfect man for her. After all, she wasn't working and had nothing to do but take care of the baby in a beautiful home and putter around doing whatever she felt like. When she and Jackson were together, it was special, not something that was going to continue to happen for the rest of their lives. It was fun because it was temporary, and at the end of the week they would return to their lives.

Beth drove home on Sunday. Jackson asked her to stay a few extra days. He had to return to L.A. Thursday, he told her, so they wouldn't be able to see each other on the weekend. But much as Beth did not want to leave, her mind kept telling her that she should. She was with Jackson too much, she thought; it was coloring her thinking. She was drifting into thinking that she was in love with him, that they might have a life together, and she told herself that such thinking was dangerous. They were very different; they led different lives and expected different things. She needed to be by herself, she thought, to see things from another perspective.

The other perspective, she quickly found, was loneliness. She had hardly driven out of Austin before she began to miss Jackson. She told herself that it was silly, that it was only temporary.

Unfortunately the temporary condition went on far too

long. Beth found herself wanting to turn and say something to him. She stored up little anecdotes about the baby or Angel Eye or her father to tell him. She missed his laugh. She missed his smile. She missed his warm arms around her. At night in bed, she woke up and reached for him, then realized with a dropping heart that he was not there. Sometimes she cried, even as she told herself that she was being ridiculous.

To occupy herself, she worked on her portrait of Jackson and Joey with renewed zeal. It was coming to life beneath her hands, and there were moments when she was sure it was going to turn out to be one of the best things she had ever done. She thought about Jackson's face when she gave it to him, and the thought made her smile.

Jackson called her every night, even during the time when he was in Los Angeles. He sounded tired, and Beth was aware of an urge to be with him, to make him smile with a quip or a story, to smooth the frown from his brow and massage the knots of tension out of his neck and shoulders. He told her that he missed her, too, and they made plans for her to drive up to Austin again as soon as he returned.

Then Joseph got a cold. It was the first time he had ever been sick, and Beth nearly panicked. His nose started running, and he had the sniffles. His skin was hot to her touch. He got worse as the evening went by, and her father's assertion that it was only a cold did nothing to ease her fears. The doctor's office was closed when she called, but one of the other pediatricians in the practice soon returned her call. He, too, did not seem overly impressed by Joseph's symptoms, and he suggested that she bring him into the office the next morning, meanwhile giving him liquid acetaminophen to reduce the fever. But Joseph was cranky and wouldn't go to sleep. He continued to cry, no matter how much she rocked him or patted him. He would fall asleep for a few minutes, then wake up and cry again.

About nine o'clock she called Jackson. "Joey's sick."

"What's the matter with him?" Jackson sounded alarmed.

"It's a cold. The doctor says it's not an emergency, and so does Dad, but he sounds so awful and chuggy, and he won't sleep." To her surprise, her voice hovered near tears. "I'm sorry to bother you."

"No. Don't be sorry. Listen, I'll drive down there."

That did make tears start in her eyes. "No, that's okay. It's not anything, really. I know I'm being a worrywart. I'm sure the doctor's right."

"But you shouldn't be worrying alone."

He made it to the ranch in less than three hours, setting a speed record for time from Austin, Beth was sure. When he rang the doorbell and Beth opened the door, her heart lifted. Joey was just the same, but suddenly she *felt* better. Jackson enfolded her and the baby in his arms, and Beth leaned her head against his shoulder, feeling comforted.

Insisting that Beth go to bed and get some rest, Jackson stayed up with the baby, rocking and walking with him. Finally he lay down on the bed with Beth, the baby between them, and the three of them slept.

About five o'clock, the baby woke up, crying, and Beth fed him. Jackson sat up, sleepy-eyed, and rubbed his head, looking around him vaguely. "How's he doing?"

"Okay, I think." Beth grinned sheepishly. "I feel like an idiot for getting you down here. Kids have colds all the time."

"Yeah. But it's a first for this one. And for you," Jackson replied, smiling. "I better get back to Austin. Why don't you and Joey come with me? We could take him to a pediatrician there."

She shook her head. "No. I'm sure he'll be fine. I probably ought to take him to his regular doctor. They have his records."

"Okay. Will you come up when he's feeling better?"

Beth nodded. "This weekend, probably."

"And you'll call me if he gets worse—or you'll come to Austin?"

"I promise."

He reached out and cupped her cheek tenderly. "I love you."

"I love you, too," Beth replied automatically.

Jackson froze, staring at her intently. "Really?"

Beth smiled self-consciously. She hadn't even known she was going to say it until she did, but she knew that it was the truth. "Yes. Really."

He grinned. "Beth…" He reached out and took her hand. "When you come to Austin this time, stay with me. I mean, for longer than a week or even two. I—I want you stay with me forever."

Beth stared at him, astonished. "What are you saying?"

He paused, considering, looking a little amazed himself. "I think I'm asking you to marry me."

"What!" Beth jumped to her feet, fear clutching her stomach. "But, Jackson…this is so—"

"So sudden?" he ventured, his eyes lighting with amusement. "So unexpected? Isn't that what they say in old novels?"

Beth giggled. "I guess so. But I'm serious. I don't think you've taken the time to think about this."

"I don't have to think. What matters is how I feel. I

know that I love you. I know that I've been miserable for a week without you. I know that I was happier that week when you and the baby were with me than I have been at any other time in my life."

"But, Jackson…"

"But what? You just said that you loved me."

"Yes, I do. But that's a big step—from loving someone to marrying them. People do fall out of love."

"I'm not going to fall out of love with you. And I won't stop loving Joey, either. We're a family, Beth, and we have been since the day Joey was born. I knew it then, but I was too embarrassed and disbelieving to say so. From the day I met you, I haven't been happy apart from you."

Pleasure flushed Beth's cheeks, but she stepped back, shaking her head. "I don't know. I—I'd have to think about it. There are things to consider. I mean, you have to live in Los Angeles. And I live in Dallas."

"You could do what you do anywhere in the country. There are just as many—no, I'm sure there are *more* people in L.A. who want to have portraits painted than there are in Dallas. If nothing else, it's bigger—and think of the egos. I have a room in my house that would be perfect for a studio—great sun, a beautiful view. But we don't have to live in Los Angeles, either. We could live wherever we wanted. There are lots of movie people who don't reside there. Between computers and faxes and phones and planes, you can communicate all you want with the studios. Hell, you can't get away from those people anywhere in the world. I know—I've tried."

Beth smiled faintly. "It's not just that. It's the idea of Joey having to grow up the child of a famous person, of his always being thrust into the spotlight. Those tabloids mess-ing in our lives. Having people intrude on me and my family like that—following us and taking pictures of us and popping up everywhere, printing wild stories all the time."

"They *are* a fact of life. But you'll learn to deal with them. I promise. I have. And, really, this is the most exposure I've had in them except for when I dated Melanie Hanson. Even then, it was because they wanted stuff on her, not me. Once this blows over, they'll hardly ever have stories about us. Directors and producers just aren't the fodder that actors and singers and models are. And I promise you that I will put everything I've got into making sure that you and Joseph are shielded from them. It's possible. Other people have kept their kids out of the limelight."

Looking at him, Beth wanted to say yes. Her love for him welled up in her, but still she held back. She had to be practical, she thought. She had to think for both herself and Joseph. She could not afford to make a wrong decision again just because she was in love with a man. She had to make sure that there was a solid basis for their relationship, that they could make it work.

Seeing her hesitation, Jackson reached out and took her arms reassuringly. "Hey. You don't have to give me an answer right now. I'm not trying to rush you. I love you, and I'm willing to live with your decision. If you don't want to marry me, I'll accept it. If you want to wait for a while, that's fine, too. This isn't a now or never proposition. I told you—I plan on loving you for the rest of your life."

Beth smiled gratefully at him. "Thank you. I do need time to think about it. I just don't…want to make a mistake."

"Sure." He bent and kissed her on the forehead, then stepped back. "You're coming up this weekend, if Joey's feeling better?"

She nodded, and he left. Beth followed him to the door and stood watching until his car disappeared in a cloud of dust down their road. *What was she going to do?*

BETH SPENT THE REST OF THE WEEK nursing Joey through his first cold. As her father and the doctor had indicated, it was a rather minor ailment, and he was feeling better by the end of the day, his fever gone. Within two days, his runny nose was drying up, and he could breathe more easily.

Beth found that her own problem, however, was not as easy to deal with. She kept thinking about Jackson and his proposal, in a quandary about what to do. She thought of how much she loved him and how happy they had been together. But she reminded herself that she had to be logical, that one week of getting along beautifully did not mean that their whole lifetime would follow the same pattern. *What would their life be like when they had to deal with problems? How would they get along when things were rocky instead of smooth?* And no matter how much she loved him, she just was not sure that she could handle the fame. She had hated the way the tabloids had intruded on her life. *Wouldn't it be much worse once they were married?*

When she wasn't worrying over her decision to marry or not marry Jackson, she thought about Robert Waring. Ever since Jackson had told Beth about his daughter, she had been wondering if she had been wrong not to tell her former lover that she was pregnant. Maybe his reaction wouldn't have been what she expected. Even if he was a creep, maybe he would have been interested in Joseph; maybe Joseph would benefit from having a father.

Wouldn't Joey wonder about his father when he grew up? And what was Beth to say about the man? That she had decided without even asking Robert that he would not be interested in knowing whether he had a son? That she had decided for both of them that Joseph should have no father? Perhaps things *had* turned out better because Jackson's girlfriend had not told him that she was pregnant. But perhaps they hadn't. At least Jessica had had the excuse of being a teenage girl who had listened to her parents' advice. Beth had made the decision all on her own, as a grown woman. *What if she had just been punitive toward the man because he had hurt her?*

That thought cut Beth like a knife. She couldn't bear to think that she might have made a decision that was unfair or even harmful to her child simply because she wanted to get back at the man who had deceived her. And how could she ever really be free of the man if she knew that she had deceived him in turn?

Finally, on the morning when she was to drive to Austin again, still debating what she was going to tell Jackson, Beth decided to end one of her worries. She picked up the phone and dialed a Chicago number, a little surprised to find that it took her a moment to recall it. Once it had been indelibly etched on her brain. It was Robert's private line, and his secretary did not pick it up.

After three rings, Robert's familiar low voice answered, crisp and efficient. For an instant, Beth's throat closed and she could not answer.

She cleared her throat. "Hello, Robert."

There was a stunned silence on the other end of the line.

"This is Beth Sutton," she went on.

"Yes. I recognized your voice," he replied coolly. "I just could not believe that you had had the nerve to call."

"What?" Anger bubbled inside Beth. *He* was upset with *her?*

"After that righteous indignation of yours, now I find out that you were seeing that Hollywood director all the time. My secretary showed me a copy of that tabloid and said, 'Elizabeth Sutton? Isn't that the name of the woman in Texas who used to call you?' Of course, she just thought it was a curiosity. She didn't realize you had been telling me you were in love with me all the while you were having an affair with him."

"I can't believe this. *You* are accusing *me* of infidelity? After what you did? To begin with, those stories are untrue, and even if they were, at least I wasn't married with two children. I wasn't cheating on my spouse!"

"You were lying," he retorted evenly. "I find it hypocritical of you to berate me because I lied to you."

"I didn't lie to you. Honestly, Robert, I wouldn't have thought you naive enough to believe the tabloids. Or is it just a convenient excuse for you? Makes you feel less in the wrong?"

"My God, Beth, I saw the picture of you with him on the front of one of them." For the first time there was the faintest thread of emotion in his cool voice.

Beth had to smother a giggle at the thought of Robert, handsome and dignified in his Italian suit, picking up a tabloid and devouring it. "Well, believe what you want, Robert. I called you because over the months I have realized that I—acted unfairly."

"Stop right there." There was an irritating smugness in his voice. "Please don't humiliate yourself, Beth. I can assure you that there is no chance of our resuming our affair."

Beth let out an inelegant snort. "That is *not* why I called.

What I *am* trying to tell you is that when I found out that I was pregnant, I made a unilateral decision to keep the baby and raise it as a single parent. I decided not to even tell you. I've thought about it a lot recently, and I realize that I may have been unfair. You probably had the right to know that I was pregnant with your child. I shouldn't have kept it from you."

There was another long silence. Then Robert's glacial voice said, "If you think that you are going to get a dime out of me for that baby, you are dead wrong. The whole world knows that it's Prescott's."

"It is *not* Jackson's child," Beth snapped back, fury rising in her. "How dare you accuse me of something like that!"

"Don't be absurd. It's obvious that you're hoping to get money out of me in return for not bringing a paternity suit. And I'm telling you right now that you won't win. That child is not mine, and I will not let you extort me into paying child support."

For the first time in her life, Beth was so furious that she literally saw red. It took her a moment before she was in control of herself enough to speak evenly. She thought of this man, who would not even acknowledge Joseph, and she thought of Jackson, driving three hours to see Joey when he caught a cold. "You are absolutely right, Robert. You are not his father and you never could be. Jackson Prescott is his father."

She hung up the phone with a sharp click. Then she threw her things into the car, wrapped up the portrait of Jackson and the baby and stuck it in, too. At last, after strapping the baby in his car seat, she set out for Austin.

Her confrontation with Robert Waring had left her feeling free, not only of him, but of the fears that her relationship with him had engendered in her. She wanted to race to Jackson, to tell him that suddenly, from an unexpected source, she had been shown the path she should take. Maybe her heart had played her false with Robert. She had fallen impetuously in love with him without really knowing him. But her affair with Robert Waring was a far different thing from the love that had developed between her and Jackson, just as Jackson was a far different man than Robert.

Even though she had spent only a brief time with Jackson, as she had with Robert, she knew Jackson as she had never known Robert. She had seen him in a crisis; she had felt his support and strength. They had weathered some bad times; she had just been fooled by the fact that they had done so with laughter and warmth. The race to the hospital, childbirth, even the ridiculous confrontation between Jackson and her brothers, had all been problems, as had the stories splashed all over the tabloids. It was simply because they had gotten through them so well that she had thought they had never faced anything but happy times.

She had seen Robert for only brief stretches of time, moments that had been consumed with the physical fire between them. But she and Jackson had been together day and night. They had been together making love and changing Joey's diaper. She knew him—knew how he acted, what he thought, how he handled things. Perhaps she did not know every detail about him, but she knew the essentials, the things that really mattered, as she had never known with Robert Waring. It didn't take a lifetime to figure out that she loved Jackson or that he was the right man for her. It only took letting go of her fears and listening to her heart.

She zipped along the roads leading to Austin, listening

to music and singing along. She hoped Jackson would be home when she got there, as he had been the last time.

He was. But this time when he came out to greet her, there was an oddly wary look in his eyes. Beth hopped out of the car, smiling, and ran to leap into his arms and hug him fiercely. She began to rain kisses all over his face, and he laughed with delight, finally seizing her face between his hands and holding her still long enough for a thorough welcome kiss.

They got the baby out of the car and carried the bags inside. Jackson carried the baby, talking to him and checking him out for any lingering signs of his illness. Beth walked into the open living area and whirled around to face him. She beamed across the room at Jackson.

"I've got something to tell you."

"Wait." Jackson sighed. "You'd probably better see this first. You're going to come across it sooner or later. We might as well get it over with."

Beth frowned, his grim expression sending tendrils of fear creeping through her. "See what?" She had the awful feeling that all her plans and hopes had just come to naught.

He crossed to the coffee table in front of the sofa and picked up a thin magazine. Beth let out a groan, recognizing a tabloid even at that distance. "Not another article."

Jackson nodded. "It's a beaut."

He handed it to her. Across the top, above the name *Scandal*, ran a headline about the mummy of an alien baby, thousands of years old, that had been found in Egypt. The rest of the paper was filled with a picture of Jackson with his arm around a beautiful blond woman. Both of them were smiling broadly and obviously happy. The caption read: Prescott Dumps Texas Cutie, Returns to His First Love.

The woman was Melanie Hanson, one of the most beautiful and popular actresses in Hollywood.

Beth's heart felt as if it had dropped to her toes. For a moment she couldn't speak. She simply stared at the picture as though, if she looked long enough, it would somehow change into something more acceptable. She looked up bleakly. "Jackson?"

"God, Beth, don't look at me like that. It's not true. I swear to you that it isn't."

"But that's you. That's her. It doesn't look spliced."

"It's not. That is us. We had dinner together when I was in Los Angeles last weekend. And we were happy to see each other. But it isn't what they say. Melanie and I are friends. That's it. We are very good friends. It doesn't mean any more than a picture of you and one of your brothers with your arms around each other."

"But you said the other day that you and she were once an item. Didn't you?"

"Yes. And we were. We dated some when she first starred in one of my movies. But we quickly realized that we weren't interested in each other romantically. We liked each other, but as friends. We've been good friends ever since. She and I have gone out like this a hundred times, and they've never made a big deal of it before. It's just because of the stories about you and Joseph. They're trying to keep the story going. To sell papers."

"Oh." Beth had been watching his face, and now she looked back down at the paper in her hand. It seemed bizarre that any man would not be madly in love with a woman as beautiful as this one.

"It's you I love, Beth. You are the only one." He looked

at her anxiously, his muscles so taut with tension that the baby picked up on it and began to whimper in his arms.

"Okay. I believe you."

Jackson let out an enormous sigh of relief. "Thank God." He started toward her. "I was afraid that I was going to lose you."

"No. I've learned to have faith in you. Not the tabloids." She grinned. "Besides, I'm making a vow. I am going to learn to deal with them."

"I promise you, I will put a stop to these stories somehow. I won't let it happen again."

"That's going to be a pretty tall order. You know how the tabloids are about Hollywood weddings."

He stopped again, staring. "What? Are you saying that—"

"I mean, when we get married, they'll be flying over with helicopters and trying to sneak into the church and all that, won't they?"

Jackson's face lit up. "Yes, they will. And you know what, at this moment I don't really care."

He crossed the remaining stretch of floor in two long steps and pulled her against him with his free arm. The baby, in his other arm, cooed, watching them intently, as Jackson bent and kissed Beth.

Jackson raised his head, grinning. "Hell, we just might invite them to the wedding."

* * * * *

Turn the page for a preview of
Bestselling author

Candace Camp's

newest historical romance

AN UNEXPECTED PLEASURE

Available this July at your favorite book outlet
from HQN Books.

Prologue

New York, 1879

THE SHRIEK CUT through the night.

In her bed, Megan Mulcahey sat straight up, instantly awake, her heart pounding. It took her a moment to realize what had awakened her. Then she heard her sister's voice again.

"No. No!"

Megan was out of her bed in a flash and running through the door. Theirs was not a large home—a narrow brownstone row house with three bedrooms upstairs—and it took only a moment to reach Deirdre's door and fling it open.

Deirdre was sitting up in bed, her eyes wide and staring, horrified. Her arms stretched out in front of her toward something only she could see, and tears pooled in her eyes before rolling down her cheeks.

"Deirdre!" Megan crossed the room and sat down on her sister's bed, taking Deirdre's shoulders firmly in her hands. "What is it? Wake up! Deirdre!"

She gave the girl a shake, and something changed in her sister's face, the frightening blankness slipping away, replaced by a dawning consciousness.

"Megan!" Deirdre let out a sob and threw her arms around her older sister. "Oh, Megan. It was terrible. Terrible!"

"Saints preserve us!" Their father's voice sounded from the doorway. "What in the name of all that's holy is going on?"

"Deirdre had a bad dream, that's all," Megan replied, keeping her voice calm and soothing, as she stroked her sister's hair. "Isn't that right, Dee? It was nothing but a nightmare."

"No." Deirdre gulped and pulled back from Megan a little, wiping the tears from her cheeks and looking first at Megan, then at their father. Her eyes were still wide and shadowed. "Megan. Da. I saw Dennis!"

"You dreamed about Dennis?" Megan asked.

"It wasn't a dream," Deirdre responded. "Dennis was here. He spoke to me."

A shiver ran down Megan's spine. "But, Dee, you couldn't have seen him. Dennis has been dead for ten years."

"It was him," Deirdre insisted. "I saw him, plain as day. He spoke to me."

Their father crossed the room eagerly and went down on one knee before his daughter, looking into her face. "Are you sure, then, Deirdre? It was really Denny?"

"Yes. Oh, yes. He looked like he did the day he sailed away."

Megan stared at her sister, stunned. Deirdre had a reputation in the family for having the second sight. She was given to forebodings and premonitions—too many of which had turned out to be true for Megan to completely dismiss her sister's "ability." However, her predictions usually ran more to having a feeling that a certain friend or relative was having problems or was likely to drop in on them that day. The more pragmatic side of Megan believed that her sister simply possessed a certain sensitivity that enabled her to pick up on a number of small clues about people and situations that most others ignored. It was an admirable talent, Megan agreed, but she had her doubts whether it was the otherworldly gift that many deemed it.

Deirdre's looks, she thought, contributed a great deal to the common perception of her. Small and fragile in build, with large, gentle blue eyes, pale skin and light strawberry-blond hair, there was a fey quality to her, a sense of other-worldliness, that aroused most people's feelings of protectiveness, including Megan's, and made it easy to believe that the girl was in tune with the other world.

But never before had Deirdre claimed to have seen someone who was dead. Megan was not sure what to think. On the one hand, her practical mind had trouble accepting that her brother's spirit was walking about, talking to her sister. It seemed much more likely that Deirdre had had a nightmare that her sleep-befuddled mind had imagined was real. On the other hand, there was a small superstitious something deep inside her that wondered if this could possibly be true. The truth was, she knew, that like her father, she wanted it to be true—she hoped that her beloved brother was still around in some form, not lost to her forever.

"What did he say?" Frank Mulcahey asked. "Why did he come to you?"

Deirdre's eyes filled with tears. "Oh, Da, it was awful! Dennis was scared and desperate. 'Help me,' he said, and held out his hands to me. 'Please help me.'"

Frank Mulcahey sucked in his breath sharply and made a rapid sign of the cross. "Jesus, Mary and Joseph! What did he mean?"

"He didn't mean anything," Megan put in quickly. "She was dreaming. Deirdre, it was just a nightmare. It must have been."

"But it wasn't!" Deirdre insisted, gazing at her sister with wide, guileless eyes. "Dennis was here. He was as clear to me as you are. He stood right there and looked at me with such pain and despair. I couldn't be mistaken."

"But, darling…"

Her younger sister gave her a look of mingled reproach and pity. "Don't you think I know the difference between a nightmare and a vision? I've had both of them often enough."

"Of course you have," their father responded, and turned to glower at Megan. "Just because there are things you cannot see or hear, it doesn't mean they don't exist. Why, I could tell you tales that would make your hair stand on end."

"Yes, and you have on many occasions," Megan responded, her tart tone of voice softened by the smile she directed at her father.

"Clearly you did not listen to the tales well enough," Frank told Megan. "Or you did not keep an open mind."

Megan knew she would never convince her father of the unlikelihood of her brother returning from the grave, so she tried a different tack. "Why would Dennis come back now? How could he need our help?"

"Why, that's clear as a bell," her father responded. "He's asking us to avenge his death."

"After ten years?"

"Sure, and he's waited long enough, don't you think?" Frank retorted, his Irish brogue thickening in his agitation. "It's me own fault. I should have gone over there and taken care of that filthy murderin' English lord as soon as we learned what happened to Dennis. It's no wonder he's come back to nudge us. The sin is that he had to. I've shirked me duty as a father."

"Da, don't." Megan laid a comforting hand on her father's arm. "You did nothing wrong. You couldn't have gone to England when Dennis died. You had children to raise. Deirdre was but ten, and the boys only a little older. You had to stay here and work, and see after us."

Frank sighed and nodded. "I know. But there's nothing holding me back now. You're all grown now. Even the store could get by without me, with your brother Sean helping me run it. There's nothing to stop me from going to England and taking care of the matter. Hasn't been for years. It's remiss I've been, and that's a fact. No wonder Denny had to come and give me a poke."

"Da, I'm sure that's not why Dennis came back," Megan said quickly, casting a look of appeal at her sister. The last thing she wanted was for her father to go running off to England and do God-knew-what in his thirst to avenge his son's death. He could wind up in jail—or worse—if his temper led him to attack the English lord who had killed Dennis. "Is it, Deirdre?"

To Megan's dismay, her sister wrinkled her brow and said, "I'm not sure. Dennis didn't say anything about his death. But he was so distraught, so desperate. It was clear he needs our help."

"Of course he does." Frank nodded. "He wants me to avenge his murder."

"How?" Megan protested, alarmed. "You can't go over there and take the law into your own hands."

Her father looked at her. "I didna say I was going to kill the lyin' bastard—not that I wouldn't like to, you understand. But I'll not have a man's blood on my conscience. I intend to bring him to justice."

"After all this time? But, Da—"

"Are you suggesting that we stand by and do nothing?" Frank thundered, his brows rising incredulously. "Let the man get away with murdering your brother? I would not have thought it of you."

"Of course I don't think he should get away with it," Megan retorted heatedly, her eyes flashing. "I want him to pay for what he did to Dennis just as much as you do."

Her brother had been only two years older than she, and they had been very close all their lives, united not only by blood, but also by their similar personalities and their quick, impish wit. Curious, energetic and determined, each of them had wanted to make a mark upon the world. Dennis had yearned to see that world, to explore uncharted territories. Megan had her sights set on becoming a newspaper reporter.

She had achieved her dream, after much persistence landing an assignment on a small New York City rag, writing for the Society section. Through skill, determination and hard work, she had eventually made her way onto the news pages and then to a larger paper. But it had been a bittersweet accomplishment, for Dennis had not been there to share in her joy. He had died on his first journey up the Amazon.

"Aye, I know," Frank admitted, taking his daughter's hand and squeezing it. "I spoke in heat. I know you want him punished. We all do."

"I just don't know what proof can be found, after all this time," Megan pointed out.

"There was something more," Deirdre spoke up. "Dennis was—I think he was searching for something."

Megan stared at her sister. "Searching for what?"

"I'm not sure. But it was very precious to him. He cannot rest until he has it back."

"He said that?" Again Megan felt a chill creep up her back. She did not believe that the dead came back to speak with the living. Still…

"He said something about having to find them—or it. I'm not sure," Deirdre explained. "But I could feel how desperate he was, how much it meant to him."

"The man killed Dennis for some reason," their father pointed out, his voice tinged with excitement. "We never knew the why of it, but there must have been one. It would make sense, don't you think, that it was over some object, something Dennis had that he wanted?"

"And he killed Dennis to get it?" Megan asked. "But what would Dennis have had that the man couldn't have bought? He is wealthy."

"Something they found on their trip," Frank answered. "Something Dennis found."

"In the jungle?" Megan quirked an eyebrow in disbelief, but even as she said it, her mind went to the history of South America. "Wait. Of course. What did the Spanish find there? Gold. Emeralds. Dennis could have stumbled on an old mine—or wherever it is you get jewels."

"Of course." Frank's eyes gleamed with fervor. "It's something like that. And if I can find whatever it is that he found and that murderer stole, it could prove that he killed Dennis. I have to go to England."

Megan stood up. Her father's excitement had ignited her own. For ten years she had lived with the sorrow of her brother's death, as well as the bitter knowledge that his murderer had gotten away. Part of her passion as a journalist had come from her thwarted desire for justice for her brother. She had known she could not help him, but she could help others whose lives had been shattered or whose rights as human beings had been trampled. Among her peers, she was known as a crusader, and she was at her best in ferreting out a story of corruption or injustice.

She could not entirely believe that her sister had seen their brother. But her father's words made sense. The man who had killed Dennis must have had a motive…and greed had always been a prime motive for murder.

"You're right," she said. "But I should be the one to go." She began to pace, her words tumbling out excitedly. "I don't know why I never thought of this before. I could investigate Dennis's death, just like I do a story. I mean, that's what I do every day—look into things, talk to people, check facts, hunt down witnesses. I should have done this long ago. Maybe I can figure out what really happened. Even after all these years, there must be something I can find. Even if it's something that wouldn't stand up in a court of law, at least we'd have the satisfaction of knowing."

"But, Megan, it's dangerous," her sister protested. "I mean, the man has murdered already. If you show up there asking questions…"

"I'm not going to just walk up to him and say, 'Why did you kill my brother?'" Megan retorted. "He won't know who I am. I'll think of some other reason to talk to him. Don't worry, I'm good at that."

"She's right," their father said and his daughters turned to him in astonishment. He shrugged. "I'm a man of reason. Megan has experience in this sort of matter. But," he added with a stern look at Megan, "if you think I'm going to let you run off and track down a murderer alone, then you haven't the brains I credit you with. I'm going, too."

"But, Da—"

He shook his head. "I mean it, Megan. We're all going. We'll track down Theo Moreland and make him pay for killing your brother."

A DADDY FOR
HER DAUGHTERS

Elizabeth Bevarly

Chapter One

SLOAN SULLIVAN KNEW IT was going to be a bad day the minute his boss told him he was going to have to lend a hand. And not just for today. But for a whole month.

It wasn't that Sloan already felt as if he lent a hand— several hands, in fact—at the Atlanta, Georgia law firm where he had been a partner for years. But, too, this month simply wasn't looking to be a good month to schedule in something like lending a hand. He had back-to-back appointments and professional functions out the proverbial wazoo throughout February. And March was pretty booked, too.

In fact, as he sat at the big table bisecting the boardroom of Parmentier, Barnaby, Shepperton and Ganz, flipping frantically through his organizer, Sloan couldn't find a single opening for lending a hand until spring. And even then, he was going to have to pencil in lending a hand, because that was coming up on the Masters Tournament, and he always went over to Augusta for a few days, because there were always parties to attend, so he might very realistically have to make an erasure and postpone lending a hand until sometime during the summer instead.

To be perfectly honest, Sloan just didn't have *time* to lend a hand, regardless of the season. He was much too busy with other things—mostly work. An estate attorney's work just never seemed to be done.

He ran restless fingers through his dark hair and glanced up from his organizer, only to find his silver-haired boss gazing expectantly back at him from the other end of the massive, smoked glass table. "I'm sorry, Edgar," he said to Edgar Parmentier, the senior partner of Parmentier, Barnaby, Shepperton and Ganz. "But this really isn't a good time for me. Normally, I'd jump at the chance to lend a hand. You know that. But I just can't find the time right now. Surely, you understand."

But Edgar only glared at him with that gimlet-eyed stare that always made Sloan want to run for the nearest, well gimlet—shaken, not stirred. "What I know and understand, Sloan," he said, "is that you'd just as soon pretend that everyone in the world lives the same way you do—pampered, privileged and prosperous. You don't want to lend a hand, because then you'll have to admit that not everyone's life is as cushy as yours is."

"That isn't it at all," Sloan objected. Even if, maybe, he couldn't quite disagree with his boss. He really didn't like to think about things like poverty and indigence and disadvantage and people who needed a hand. Hey, who did?

"That's exactly it," Edgar insisted. "You Sullivans have lived in your ivory tower—or, at the very least, in your stately manor—for too long. It's time at least one of you saw how the real world lives. Come on, man," he further jeered. "Show some backbone. This will be good for you."

Sloan told himself to object to his employer's assessment of his family—of himself—then realized that, in all honesty, he couldn't. He *was* pampered, privileged and prosperous. He'd grown up being pampered, privileged and prosperous. And he *liked* being pampered, privileged and prosperous, too. The Sullivans were one of Atlanta's most illustrious families and had been for generations. And Sloan had no intention of giving up his pampered, privileged and prosperous lifestyle anytime soon.

So, in fact, there was no reason for him to object to Edgar's words. Somehow, though, he wasn't comfortable with his boss's evaluation of him. It made him sound so shallow. And hey, there must be *some* depth to his character. Right? He'd come this far, after all.

Sloan shook the thought off. "But, Edgar—" he began again.

"It's *always* a good time for doing good deeds, Sloan," his boss cut him off. "And the Lend a Hand Month council has scores of excellent causes lined up this year. Pick one."

The older man dipped his head toward a brown felt fedora turned upside down at the center of the table. Inside were more than two dozen folded slips of paper, each recorded with some kind of month-long good deed that needed doing, and for which Edgar Parmentier had volunteered one of his employees—with or without that employee's go-ahead. So far, four of the eight partners at PBS and G had chosen from the hat. Whatever good deeds were left after the partners' meeting would be divvied up among the associates and office workers of the law firm. Come February, five days hence, PBS and G would be well represented among the do-gooders. Whether its employees liked it or not.

Of course, the vast majority of employees didn't mind lending a hand at all. And Sloan wouldn't, either, if it just came at a better time. But he had things to *do* next month. Lots of things. Lots of really important things. Tennis dates with Bambi Winston. The Farringdons' annual open house. Babs and Leonard Bayard's cocktail party. It was a never-ending series of social obligations. And work, too, he reminded himself. Why, setting up the Maury and Antoinette MacCorkindale estate alone was going to take weeks.

"But, Edgar—" he tried again.

"Choose," Edgar commanded, jabbing a stubby finger at the fedora.

With a frustrated sigh, Sloan reached into the hat and drew out a slip of paper. So far, the good deeds chosen had been anything but appealing. Dennis Robertson was going to be spending each of his February weekends painting the interior of a nursing home. Fred Schwartz would be serving baloney and beans at a local food shelter during half of his lunch hours. Lauren Riordan would be reading books to preschoolers at a nearby women's shelter during her lunch hours. And Anita Spinelli was going to spend her next four weekends putting together food baskets for the underprivileged.

Sloan held his breath as he unfolded his piece of paper to see what inconvenient blow fate had dealt him. Would he be singing rondos to a group of Cub Scouts? Baking cookies for a church bazaar? Walking dogs for the elderly? What? He unfolded the scrap of paper…and was surprised to see that he was actually halfway suited to the job he would be required to do—and only two evenings a week, at that.

Halfway being the operative word here. Because although the *basketball coach* part was familiar enough, the *rural Georgia high school* part was not.

Still, it appeared that the Fighting Razorbacks of Stonewall Jackson High School in Wisteria, Georgia—roughly forty-five minutes from Atlanta—needed an assistant coach for the next month, because their regular one had been laid up by a hunting accident. Sloan, of course, had never actually coached basketball before, but he'd had the honor of warming the bench for Vanderbilt. And, of course, he'd played basketball in high school—very well, too. In fact, as starting center, he'd taken the Fighting Ptarmigans of Penrose Academy right to the state championship twenty years ago. Well, the state championship for tony private schools, at any rate. Still, if he'd won one for the Ptarmigans, he could certainly do the same for the Razorbacks.

Then, for some reason, the image of a razorback having a ptarmigan for lunch erupted in his brain. How strange…

Immediately, Sloan shook off that thought, too. They were high school students he'd be coaching, he reminded himself. It would only be two nights a week. And only for a month. How tough could this assignment be?

IT WASN'T UNTIL SLOAN PARKED his Jaguar roadster outside the gymnasium at Jackson High School that he began to regret his final words after drawing this assignment from a hat. He'd never visited rural Wisteria before, and hadn't realized just how *rural* Wisteria was. Jackson High School, for instance, was one of only two in the entire town. And this one, he couldn't help but notice as he'd driven over them, was definitely on the wrong side of the tracks.

He knew it was the wrong side of the tracks, because on the *other* side, Wisteria had been very picturesque, filled with white frame houses and tidy yards and old-fashioned mom-and-pop type shops. There had even been an ice-cream parlor on one corner of the downtown—and how quaint to think of the business district as "downtown," Sloan thought again—not to mention a town square which was really a square, and which, during the warmer months, was no doubt green and lush and landscaped to perfection. This side of Wisteria, on the other hand, was…

Not.

Not picturesque. Not filled with white frame houses and tidy yards and old-fashioned mom-and-pop type shops. Not quaint. There were no ice-cream parlors, and nothing that had the potential to be green or lush or landscaped in any way. What he *had* seen lots of on this side of Wisteria were auto parts stores—which were more part than auto, truth be told—junkyards, trailer parks and what appeared to be illegal dumping grounds. Oh, and of course, Stonewall Jackson High School, whose gym was a massive, looming, bleak structure that couldn't possibly keep out the rain, or last beyond the next big gust of wind.

It stood apart from the school, which seemed to be in no better shape than the gym, truth be told, all of it squatting amidst the biggest gravel parking lot Sloan had ever seen in his life. Then again, much of the gravel didn't appear to be parking lot. It just appeared to be…gravel.

The small gray stones crunched beneath his two-hundred-dollar sneakers when he stepped out of the car, and the damp February breeze brought with it the oily stink of a paper mill that must lie on the outskirts of town. Strangely, he hadn't noticed the smell on the *other* side of the tracks. But here…

Sloan did his best to breathe shallowly.

A sign above the main entrance to the gym hung a bit listlessly on one side, and many of its plastic letters were missing. Still, Sloan was able to get the gist of *ad Razo ba ks Eat Their Y ung! Go Te m!* Not that he necessarily wanted to get the gist of it. But he did anyway.

Evidently, the Razorbacks meant business, he thought as he zipped his hooded sweatshirt over his sweatpants and Vanderbilt T-shirt to ward off the chill. Then again, Sloan had been brought up to date on the team by the Jackson High principal before coming to Wisteria. The kids were indeed poised for the regional championship, and they were definitely kicking butt. Even this late in the season, they were still undefeated, and had royally trounced a couple of schools everyone had considered shoo-ins for the regional, perhaps even the state, title.

Then again, according to the sign, they did eat their young, Sloan reflected wryly. That showed a real flair for offense. He began to suspect that he had grossly underestimated just how demanding this volunteer position was going to be.

His suspicions were only reinforced when he pushed open the gymnasium doors and strode through the decrepit lobby to the cavernous—and likewise decrepit—gym itself. The bleachers were empty, which surprised him, even if the team was only practicing right now. Generally, when a team was doing as well as the Razorbacks were, there were always fans in the stands to encourage them and cheer them on, even at practice. Parents, too, often showed up to watch.

Yet the Razorbacks didn't seem to have any visible means of support.

Oh, wait, yes they did, Sloan realized belatedly. Because a large group of girls stood on the other side of the gym, chatting. Cheerleaders, probably, he thought, seeing as how most of them were wearing shorts, and a few were in sweats. Or they may be girlfriends of the team members. It was nice that so many of them to be here, showing support for their menfolk.

And just where were the menfolk? Sloan wondered, scanning the gym again. There wasn't a single team member in sight.

Then the shrill cry of a whistle alerted him to the fact that the team was indeed, as kids said nowadays, "In da house." At least, Sloan thought that was what kids said nowadays. He did have VH-1, after all. Even if he didn't watch anything except "House of Style." At any rate, even after that long, piercing shriek came to an end, no team appeared. Only the girls on the other side of the gym ran to the center of the room, presumably, he thought, to create some kind of pyramid for the boys to run through.

But no boys appeared. No, the only thing Sloan saw with the scattering of the girls that he hadn't noticed before was what turned out to be the source of the whistle—a woman who was striding toward the middle of the group of girls. Who, incidentally, he also noted, had yet to climb atop each other and form a pyramid for the boys. The woman caught sight of Sloan just as he caught sight of her, and after saying something to a couple of the girls he couldn't hear, she smiled, lifted a hand in greeting, and began to jog toward him.

She was tall, he noticed, easily five-ten or -eleven, slim,

but curvy, with small, round breasts and short, dark hair. She had a basketball tucked under one arm and was dressed almost identically to Sloan, though where his sweats were navy blue, hers were gray. And the T-shirt she wore indicated she'd attended Clemson.

As she drew nearer to him, Sloan noticed that she was about his age—late thirties—with clear gray eyes, touches of silver and auburn in her hair, and a spray of freckles over her nose and cheekbones. Her mouth was good, full and smiling, and her smile was good, too, broad and uninhibited. She wore not a bit of makeup, but somehow, she didn't really need it. She was wholesome and healthy-looking, and Sloan was surprised to discover that he found her attractive. Usually, he didn't go for wholesome and healthy-looking. Usually, he went for flashy and luscious-looking.

"You must be Mr. Sullivan," she said as she halted before him, extending her hand.

He nodded and accepted her hand automatically, and he noticed right away that it wasn't like most women's hands. No, this one was large and raw-boned and callused, with fingernails clipped short, and completely devoid of jewelry.

"Yes, I'm here for the Lend a Hand thing," he said as he let her hand drop. "I'm looking for Coach Carmichael. Do you know where he is?"

Her smile fell some, and she eyed him curiously for a moment. Then she fisted the hand that wasn't holding the basketball on her—surprisingly curvy—hip and smiled again, her gaze never once veering from his. "I'm Naomi Carmichael," she told him. "*Coach* Carmichael. And I can't thank you enough for taking time out of your busy schedule to help us out this month."

Sloan narrowed his eyes at her. "*You're* Coach Carmichael?" he asked, confused. *"Us?"* he asked further, even more confused.

"Yeah, us," she said. Then she gestured over one shoulder with her thumb, toward the group of girls who were eyeing him with open curiosity. "The Lady Razorbacks," she said further. "Thanks for volunteering to be our assistant coach for the next month. We really do appreciate it."

Chapter Two

"THE LADY RAZORBACKS?" Sloan Sullivan cried as he gazed passed Naomi, over her shoulder, and out at the gym floor.

Naomi narrowed her eyes at him and wondered at his flabbergasted reaction. Surely he'd known he would be coaching girls, she thought. And even if he hadn't, what was the big deal? Why would the gender of the team be significant? Their regular assistant coach was a man.

"Ye-es," she replied slowly, "the Lady Razorbacks. Will that be a problem, Mr. Sullivan?"

He glanced back at Naomi's face, then at the girls on the floor again, then back at Naomi once more. "But—but—but—I mean… It's just… How could… This isn't…"

Honestly, Naomi thought. For an educated man, he sure didn't have much of a vocabulary. Then again, a man who looked like he did probably didn't have to talk very much to get ahead, even if he was an attorney in his real life.

He was tall—several inches taller than Naomi, and that

was saying something. At five-eleven, she didn't have to look up to very many men, a fact of her physique that she enjoyed *a lot*. Still, Sloan Sullivan was easily five or six inches taller than she. And he probably outweighed her by a good sixty or seventy pounds, too—but not because he was overweight by any means. No, she could see, even through layers of clothing, that every ounce of this man was pure muscle. She'd been told by Phil Leatherman, Jackson High's principal, that Mr. Sullivan had played basketball in high school and college. Obviously, the athlete in him was still alive and kicking. He may be a workaholic attorney these days—which she'd also learned from Phil—but he clearly took time out of his busy schedule to keep himself in shape.

She guessed his age to be close to her own thirty-eight, thanks to the faint lines fanning out from his eyes and bracketing his full lips, and the few threads of silver winding through his black hair. The razor-straight tresses were conservatively and expertly cut, and somehow Naomi knew—she just *knew*—he paid more for one haircut than she spent in a week feeding herself and her four kids. Of course, she did buy store brands and use coupons—lots and lots of coupons—but still. His hands were big and masculine, but she'd noticed when she shook with him that they weren't callused or overworked. And his eyes were…oh… So blue. A dark, rich, velvety blue, like the morning glories that climbed up the back trellis in the summertime. Oh, yes. The epitome of tall, dark and handsome. Quite the dreamboat was Mr. Sloan Sullivan.

Now, now, Naomi, she cautioned herself. She knew better than to have thoughts like that. Just because it had been more than four years since she'd been intimate with any—

But she didn't allow herself to think about things like

that. It was tough enough getting through life as a single woman—a single woman who'd been dumped by her husband, no less—and raising four daughters on a teacher's salary, and trying to keep them, and herself, out of trouble. Naomi didn't need to go looking for more. And this Sloan Sullivan, with his hundred-and-fifty-dollar haircut and his Vandy sweats, was Trouble with a capital *T*. Because only a few minutes after meeting him, Naomi was already yearning for things she hadn't had for a very long time, things she wasn't likely to have again for even longer.

She hadn't met too many men who were inclined to ask out a woman who had four kids. Especially not in a town like Wisteria, where the only single men were widowers in their eighties. And, judging by the looks of him, Sloan Sullivan was a man whose taste ran more toward young, petite, dainty little blondes in slinky dresses, and not towering, butch brunettes who didn't know the meaning of the word *foundation*—either for face or body support.

Still, Wisteria was Naomi's home, and had been for the bulk of her adult life. And Wisteria was, for the most part, a good place to raise kids. It was quiet, the pace was slow and crime was pretty much nonexistent, save the occasional adolescent prank. But, hey. Naomi had been an adolescent, too, once upon a time. Even if she couldn't find a single thing about herself these days that reminded her of that carefree kid.

She pushed the thought away and focused her attention on Mr. Sloan Sullivan again, realizing he hadn't yet answered her question.

"*Will* it be a problem, Mr. Sullivan?" she asked again. "*Do* you have some objection to coaching girls?" And if he did, Naomi thought further, would he mind if she smacked him around a bit, until she'd knocked a little sense into his thick head?

He returned his attention to her face, and she marveled again at how handsome he was. Damn. This was going to make the next month even more difficult to get through than it had already promised to be. It would be hard enough for the team to maintain their fevered momentum with a new—and temporary—coach whom none of them knew. But with their new—and temporary—coach looking like... like... like...*that,* the Lady Razorbacks were going to be totally distracted.

And worse, so would their coach.

"But...but...they're girls," Sloan Sullivan said, his voice tinted with petulance and something akin to distaste.

Naomi nodded and tried very hard—really, she did—not to be too sarcastic when she replied, "Whoa, good call, Mr. Sullivan. You're absolutely right. They are, in fact, girls."

"But girls can't play basketball," he said, still sounding like he'd ingested something that didn't agree with them.

"Oh?" Naomi asked crisply. "Why not, pray tell?"

"Well, because they're *girls*," he said. "They don't have the—"

"Your next word may be your last, Mr. Sullivan," Naomi interjected as diplomatically as she could. "If I were you, I'd think good and hard before I chose it."

Immediately, he snapped his mouth shut. But she could tell he wasn't quite ready to concede the battle. Maybe what he needed was a little push in the right direction, she thought.

"Let me tell you something about girls who play sports, Mr. Sullivan," she said coolly. "Statistically speaking, girls who are involved in sports during their school years grow up to be stronger, healthier women. They have a lower incidence of breast cancer and depression and heart disease, and they have higher self-esteem and self-confidence. They're less likely to become pregnant before they're ready, and they're more likely to leave an abusive relationship. Not to mention, they just have a helluva lot of fun.

"Now then," she continued, her tone a *tad* less brittle than before, "you were saying, Mr. Sullivan? About girls playing basketball? They can't because they don't have the *what?*"

And with that, Sloan Sullivan finally did back down. Sort of. As much as a man of his accelerated height could back down, anyway, Naomi supposed.

"Well, they just play like girls, that's all," he finished a bit more tactfully.

Naomi smiled. "Damn straight they do," she retorted. "Watch this."

Without warning him any further, she spun around and hurled the basketball toward her center—her daughter Evelyn—who caught it effortlessly and began to dribble, rocketing down the length of the court with staggering velocity and equilibrium, weaving in and out of the girls who tried to interfere, until she vaulted toward the opposite hoop and, with a sweet-sounding *swish*, stuffed it for two points.

"In your face, Mom!" she shouted with a smile as she landed gracefully on the floor beneath the goal.

"Mom?" Sloan Sullivan echoed.

Naomi nodded and smiled. "That's my girl!" she yelled. Though whether she was congratulating her daughter or overstating to her new assistant coach, volume-wise, her relationship to the team's center, Naomi wasn't entirely sure. "Katie's mine, too," she added indicating the shorter version of Evelyn, who was, at that moment, high-fiving her sister.

"You have two daughters on the team?" Sloan asked.

"Yep," Naomi told him. "Evy's my center, a junior, and Katie's a guard, a freshman."

"They resemble you," he said, nodding. "And you teach English, as well, I understand?" he asked further, something he'd obviously gleaned from his own chat with the Jackson High principal.

"Yep," she said again.

"You must be a busy woman, Mrs. Carmichael," he observed as he watched the team reconvening at the center of the floor.

"Yeah, I am," Naomi agreed with a smile. "Especially when you include the two other daughters I have at home."

He said nothing in response to that, but turned briskly to look at her, his expression both startled and inquisitive. And there was something about the way he looked at her in that moment that made Naomi feel…funny. Not funny ha-ha, but funny strange, because what she felt seemed kind of familiar somehow, even if she hadn't felt it for a very long time. He seemed to be appraising her, she realized. And she realized that, somewhere deep down inside herself, a little part of her wanted him to like what he saw. Unfortunately, another not-so-little part of her was worrying that she didn't measure up.

But measure up to what? she wondered. She hadn't cared what any man thought of her for a long time. She didn't care now, she assured herself. She was a thirty-eight-year-old woman with four children, a woman whose husband had hit the road the minute he found out about the impending arrival of number four. She didn't have time to worry about what other people—what men—thought of her. And she didn't have the inclination, either.

But that didn't stop her from caring just then what Sloan Sullivan thought of her. And Naomi didn't like it that she cared as much as she did.

Somehow, she stopped herself from running a hand through her short, dark hair, to smooth out the unruly tresses that she hadn't brushed since that morning. And somehow, she kept herself from biting her lips, hard, in an effort to put a little color in them. Instead, she spun around and shouted out a few instructions to her team, and then watched her girls go to work.

The moment she blew her whistle, they broke off into two camps and began to practice. Where normally, Naomi would have joined them, shouting out more instructions and pointers, this time, she didn't say a word. But she did turn to gauge Sloan Sullivan's reaction as he watched the Lady Razorbacks work out. At first, he had a little trouble keeping up with them, so swiftly and deftly did the girls move. Eventually, though, he got into the spirit of things. His gaze ricocheted from one player to another, darting up and down the length of the court as the girls did. And with every passing moment, Naomi could see the admiration in his eyes grow.

"Wow," he finally said with much understatement. "They're, uh… They're pretty good."

Naomi smiled proudly. "Yes, they are. They're extremely good. They're going to the state championship, Mr. Sullivan. And they're going to win it. The question now is, are you going to help us get there? Or are you just going to be dead weight?"

He glanced at the rapidly moving girls again, then back at Naomi. "I'm in," he said with a smile. "Let's go all the way."

Naomi reminded herself that he was talking about team sports, and not sexual escapades. Still, she couldn't quite squelch the itinerant heat that wound through her at hearing his words. She would *not* be going all the way with Sloan Sullivan, she hastened to remind herself. She had just met the man, and she would only have contact with him two nights a week for one month.

She wouldn't be going all the way with anyone, she told herself further, forcing herself to be brutally honest, because she figured she needed the reminder just then. Not until she'd finished raising four daughters and sent them all off to live their own lives, at any rate. Of course, seeing as how her youngest, Sophie, was only four, by the time all the girls were out of the house, Naomi would be so old and dried up, no man would want her. And even if, by some wild miracle, she found a man who did want her, by then, she would have forgotten what it was that a man and a woman were supposed to do together.

So, for now, she'd have to settle for "going all the way" with her team. And she told herself, as she always did, that that would be enough. Funny, though, where before, Naomi had always believed herself when she told herself that, suddenly, as she looked at Sloan Sullivan, she wasn't so sure she did anymore.

"Practice ends at seven," she told him, shoving her troubling thoughts away for now. "You busy afterward?"

He seemed surprised by the question, but slowly shook his head. "No, not really."

"I don't live far from here. Of course, nothing is far from anything in Wisteria," she added with a halfhearted smile. "But if you want to follow me home after practice, I'll fix us some supper. And then, after the girls clean up and head to their rooms, you and I can talk strategy for the team."

When she'd first started voicing her offer, Naomi had noted that Sloan Sullivan suddenly began to look terrified. But by the time she finished talking, he seemed much relieved, as if, initially, he'd been afraid she had something else in mind. She smiled sadly at the realization. Poor guy. He'd been scared that she was making plans for just the two of them. Plans that didn't revolve around basketball, even if they'd maybe focused on a little fun and games.

And as much fun as games might be with him, Naomi thought further, there would be little point. Men like him, although they were certainly good at games and running around, never stayed long enough for the main event. It was just as well he'd only be coaching the girls for a month, until Lou Melton, their usual assistant coach, would be back at work. Because by the time March Madness rolled around, Naomi would need a guy in her court who would be there for the girls and for her. And Sloan Sullivan simply was not that kind of man. He was far more suited to big business boardrooms and high-society cocktail parties, draped with ornamental women who wouldn't know a rebound from a double dribble.

"Planning a strategy for the team sounds like a good idea," he said. And then, for a second time, he assured her, "I'm in."

Oh, that he was, Naomi thought. That he definitely was. Even after knowing him for a matter of moments, Sloan Sullivan was already, definitely, *in*. And all she could do now was hope it wouldn't be hard to get him *out* again, once their month of working together was over.

Chapter Three

SURPRISINGLY, NAOMI AND her daughters didn't live on the same side of town where they worked and attended school, Sloan noted as he pulled his roadster to a stop in the Carmichael driveway behind the aged, tired-looking Carmichael minivan. In fact, Naomi's was very much like one of the charming white frame houses he had passed on his way through Wisteria earlier that evening, situated only a couple of blocks from the town square. The yard was tidy, if small, a good bit of it arranged in such a way as to suggest that, in the greener months, it was a fairly extravagant garden. And although the place really didn't seem large enough to accommodate a family of six—presuming there was a Mr. Carmichael to go with the rest of the Carmichaels, something Sloan found himself feeling apprehensive about for some reason—he supposed the homestead would qualify as "cozy."

Not that coziness was anything he wanted to invite into

his *own* life, mind you, but, looking at Naomi Carmichael's house, he could certainly see why something like coziness might appeal to other people.

The inside was as charming as the outside, he noted further as he followed the three Carmichael women of his acquaintance inside. The furnishings were old but comfortable, not quite antiques, but sturdy and full of personality nonetheless—overstuffed chairs covered in chintz florals, curio cabinets filled with mementos, large, well-worn, wool-hooked rugs spanning most of the hardwood floors. The living room was painted a dark, rich green, which flowed surprisingly well into the terra-cotta-colored dining room beyond. Built-in shelves in both rooms were crammed full of books and family photographs and an assortment of mismatched knickknacks. More photographs and watercolor paintings of flowers and gardens filled the walls, and plants tumbled from every other available surface. All in all, the Carmichael home looked like a place where a lot of living—and a lot of color—went on.

Briefly, Sloan compared the house to his own downtown Atlanta condo, which was sparsely furnished in what he liked to think of as "clean contemporary." White walls, minimalist white furnishings, white carpeting, and splashes of primary colors in abstract, geometric artwork and accent pieces. It was by no means child-friendly. And it was, to put it mildly, not much like the home into which he had just wandered.

And strangely, for the first time since moving into his place, Sloan wondered if maybe the condo could stand a little improvement in the interior decoration department. This in spite of the fact that he'd paid a small fortune to one of Atlanta's premier interior design firms to do the place for him, exactly the way he had asked for it to be done. Somehow, he suspected Naomi Carmichael had achieved her look without any outside input, and without paying thousands of dollars to someone named Serge.

"Ginny! Sophie! We're home!" she called as she closed the front door behind Sloan, and strode past him toward the dining room, into which her other daughters had strolled and then disappeared.

Assuming he was supposed to follow the women, Sloan did so, and eventually he found himself in the kitchen—which was as old-fashioned, colorful and lived-in looking as the rest of the house, right down to the floral wallpaper, the glass-doored, natural pinewood cabinets, the braided rag rug and the ladder-back chairs surrounding a heavy, pinewood table. Once again, Sloan found himself responding to his surroundings in a way that was totally uncharacteristic, feeling oddly contented in an atmosphere that should have been alien and uncomfortable.

In response to their mother's summons, two more girls scurried into the room to join the rest of the family. The oldest of the newcomers, Sloan saw immediately, was the identical twin of the ninth-grade point guard, Katie. The fourth Carmichael girl, though, was considerably younger than her sisters. Even to his untrained eye, Sloan could see that she wasn't yet school age.

"Hi," the smallest one said when she saw their guest. She smiled, her mouth full of perfect little teeth. Sloan had no choice but to smile back. "Who're you?" she asked further.

Naomi intervened before Sloan had a chance to, telling her daughter, "This is Mr. Sullivan, Sophie. Mr. Sullivan, this is my youngest daughter, Sophie."

"How do you do, Sophie?" Sloan asked, his smile growing broader. Automatically, he extended his hand toward the little girl, the way he would have done had he just been introduced to a new law partner or associate.

Much to his surprise, Sophie took his hand and shook it soundly, three times, before releasing it. "It's nice to meet you," she said with practiced courtesy.

Sloan stifled a chuckle at her formality. Like the other Carmichael women, Sophie had dark hair and a smattering of freckles, but where her sisters all had dark-brown eyes, this one had her mother's clear gray. In fact, she was a miniature of her mother, right down to the short haircut. The other girls, though they did resemble Naomi, probably favored their father more. Which reminded Sloan that there must be a father of the girls, somewhere, and he wondered just how he might find out where the man was without seeming forward or, worse, interested.

Because he *wasn't* interested, he assured himself. Not in Naomi Carmichael. No way. Even if he did find her attractive—very attractive, actually—he was in no way interested in her. Not in any kind of a—he shuddered to even think the word—*romantic* sense, at any rate. For one thing, Naomi Carmichael was probably married. Though, he had noticed during practice that she wasn't wearing a wedding ring. Not that that was an indication of anything—the absence of the wedding ring *or* the noticing, he assured himself— because sometimes married people didn't wear rings, especially if they were physically active. For another thing, Naomi Carmichael had children. And for another thing, Naomi Carmichael wasn't his type—not by any stretch of the imagination.

Sloan was just…curious. Yeah, that was it. Curious. He was curious about her because she was so much different from the women he usually met. Over the course of the evening, he'd watched her with the Lady Razorbacks, noting her skillful coaching, her graceful motion, how she nurtured the girls without being motherly, and drilled them without being harassing. And he had quickly come to the conclu- sion that she was one of those women he normally avoided—strong, self-confident, self-sufficient, no-nonsense. Not that he liked weak-willed, small-minded clinging vines, he hastened to amend. Au contraire. But a man liked to think he was needed. And Naomi Carmichael gave him the impression that she lived her life very nicely, thanks, without needing any intervention from anyone.

So that was another reason he wasn't interested. Just curious.

"And this is another of my daughters," she said, bringing him out of his troubling thoughts, "Ginny. Katie's twin, obviously."

"Only in looks," Ginny was quick to point out.

"Yeah," Katie readily agreed. "Ginny's a total girlie-girl."

Which, of course, Sloan could have discerned all by himself, seeing as how the girl was dressed like Sorority Barbie, her perfectly coifed hair swept back with a glittery headband, and wearing a pink T-shirt and lavender miniskirt and pink tights, and having apparently just knocked over a department store cosmetic counter in a clean sweep of goods. Compared to her sister's bedraggled—sweaty—ponytail, ragged—sweaty—practice clothes, and cosmetic-free—sweaty—face, she was clearly a twin in looks only.

"Beats being a jock," Ginny easily countered her sister. "At least I get dates."

"Oh, no you don't," Naomi was quick to cut in. "You don't date until you're sixteen."

"But, Mo-om," Ginny began to object. "I went out with Stuart Benson just last weekend."

"Yeah, and six other kids," Katie said. "That's not dating. It's mobbing."

"Is not."

"Is, too."

"Is not."

"Is, too."

"Is not, jockstrap."

"Is too, girlie-girl."

"Enough!" Naomi interrupted.

Immediately, the girls quit their bickering, but they shot each other enough ugly looks that Sloan figured the argument was by no means over. No, it would probably be a while—say the year 2020—before those two settled anything.

"We have a guest," Naomi reminded her daughters. "I know it's hard, but try to act like human beings. You can start by washing up," she told the two who were athletically inclined. Then, taking her own advice, tugging at the damp fabric of her T-shirt, she turned to Sloan. "I'll just be a second. Dinner will be ready in less than twenty minutes."

"That's fast," he said, surprised.

"Listen, if it has to be boiled for more than fifteen minutes or microwaved for more than ten, you won't find it in my kitchen," Naomi told him.

And, oh, how palate-pleasing that sounded, Sloan thought wryly. He made a mental note to stop by his favorite deli for carryout before driving to Wisteria next time.

And then Naomi was gone, abandoning him to her other two daughters. Which, at first, didn't seem like it was going to be a problem, because Ginny immediately cited an intense need to make a phone call and left the room. Sloan waited to see if Sophie would likewise have some kind of pressing social obligation—what did nonschoolage children do with their time, anyway? he wondered—but she remained in the kitchen, eyeing him quizzically.

This was a first for Sloan. He had absolutely no idea what to say that might start a conversation. Normally, he was totally at home with strangers, could make chitchat effortlessly and for hours on end. It was a necessary talent for someone who attended as many social functions as he did. Unfortunately, none of those social functions he had attended before now had prepared him for how to make small talk with someone so, well, small.

So, going for broke, he said, "Hey, what about that Barney, huh? Is he cool or what?"

"I don't like Barney," Sophie told him matter-of-factly. "He's for babies."

"Ah," Sloan replied eloquently. "I see. Yes. Well."

"I'm too big for Barney. I like Thomas."

"Jefferson?" Sloan asked before he realized how ridiculous the question would be.

"Tank Engine," Sophie told him, smiling. "He's a train. And he has lots of train friends."

"Ah. I see. Yes. Well."

"Wanna see my track?" she asked.

And there was something so earnest in the way she posed the question, something so genuinely pleading in her little face, that Sloan found he couldn't say no. He supposed it wasn't easy being so much younger than everyone else in the house. Not that he understood why she was responding to him, when he was just as old or older than the others. Still, he could see that she craved the attention of someone new, so how could he turn her down? Besides, he'd had a train set when he was a boy, and it might be kind of fun to revisit that sort of thing.

"Sure," he said, smiling at the little girl. "I'd love to see your track. And Thomas. And all of his train friends."

Chapter Four

NAOMI LEFT THE UPSTAIRS bathroom five minutes later, after cleaning up as best she could, and changing into a pair of clean blue jeans and a nondescript, wash-faded, once-red sweatshirt. And also after trying to forget about how horrific her mirror reflection had looked after two hours of practice, and how Sloan Sullivan had seen her that way.

She hesitated in the hallway when she heard voices—Ginny's husky, I'm-on-the-phone-with-a-boy voice coming from the room she shared with Katie, where she had evidently taken the extension, and Sophie's British-tinted, Ringo-the-Thomas-narrator voice coming from her room next door. Silently, Naomi crept in that direction, peering through the open door to find her youngest introducing Sloan Sullivan to all the friendly, cheerful inhabitants of the Island of Sodor.

She couldn't help but smile at the scene. Sophie lay in the middle of the floor on her stomach, knees bent, feet tracing random semicircles in the air above her, one of them missing a sock. She dragged a long line of colorful engines along one of her more sophisticated track designs, one that wound in and out on itself, under her bed and back again. Sloan sat pretzel-fashion on the floor on the other side of the track, one elbow braced on his thigh, his chin cupped in his hand, looking genuinely rapt with attention. If Naomi hadn't known better, she would have sworn he was actually enjoying himself.

"The troublesome brake van," Sophie was saying, "came around the curve much too quickly. 'Stop! Stop!' cried Edward, who barely had time to move out of the way."

"Uh-oh, looks like that troublesome brake van is being a problem again," Sloan said.

"He's always a problem," Sophie told him, using her regular voice now. "That's why he's the *troublesome* brake van."

"That makes sense." Sloan bent forward, reaching for one of the red engines, pushing it along the length of wooden track before him. "Who did you say this was?" he asked. "James?"

Sophie nodded. "James the red engine. He's very useful."

"Well, he's about to make himself even more useful," Sloan told her. "Because just between you and me, I think James could take the troublesome break van any day."

Naomi bit back her laughter but was helpless to stop the smile that curled her lips. Poor Mr. Sullivan. Once Sophie corralled a willing subject—or even an unwilling one—she didn't let go easily. She could potentially keep the guy up here for hours. Then again, from the looks of things, it didn't seem as if Mr. Sullivan would much mind being kept up here.

And it would keep him *out* of Naomi's hair while she prepared their dinner, she thought further, as would, no doubt, the presence of her other daughters. So with Sloan Sullivan's happily offered, "You're in trouble now, Mr. Brake Van!" echoing in her ears, she tiptoed past Sophie's room toward the stairs and made her way back down to the kitchen. True to her word, within twenty minutes, she had the table set for six—the first time she could remember it being set for that number since her husband Sam had taken a powder more than four years ago—with stir-fry chicken and oriental salad ready for immediate consumption.

She called her brood to order and, with a series of heavy *thump-thump-thumps* down the stairs, they rapidly arrived, all four girls plunking down in their usual spots and reaching haphazardly for food as they chattered amiably—and nonstop. Only when each of them had filled a plate did Naomi look up to find Sloan Sullivan standing in the kitchen doorway, looking very much like the proverbial deer in the headlights.

She smiled. "We don't stand on ceremony here, Mr. Sullivan," she told him. "If you want to eat, you have to jump right in. But I apologize if we ran over you."

He shook his head and smiled, but there was something decidedly flummoxed in the gesture. "No, it's not that. It's just… It's just been a long time since I've dined in, that's all," he told her. Then he smiled. "I guess I'm waiting for a hostess to show up and seat me."

Naomi nodded. He did seem more of the dining-out type, she thought. "We had to let our hostess go," she told him, smiling back. "So have a seat," she added, gesturing toward the only chair left vacant.

Belatedly, she realized she had assigned to Sloan Sullivan the place her ex-husband used to occupy when he lived with them, and something about the realization bothered her. A lot. So, not sure why she did it, Naomi jumped up and moved herself to that spot instead, indicating that their guest should take the seat she'd just vacated. He did so without question, and she passed him the food—or what was left of it, once her daughters had finished filling their plates.

As was the Carmichael tradition around the dinner table—and, unlike many families, Naomi made sure they all sat down to a meal together at least five nights a week, even if it sometimes meant eating late—the girls launched into rapid-fire discussions of their respective days. Naomi asked the usual questions about school and homework and extracurricular activities, the girls gave the usual answers, and all in all, everything was exactly as it should be, exactly as it always was.

Well, except for the drop-dead gorgeous man sitting in their midsts. But other than that…

Not once did Mr. Sullivan interject a word into the dinner conversation, but Naomi wasn't sure if that was because he didn't find the subject matter interesting, or he simply felt too intimidated by the tight-knit Carmichael crew to wade in among them. Somehow, she suspected it was the latter, though, because he did smile several times during the course of the conversation at something one of them said. And once or twice, she caught him looking as if he wanted to say something, but stopping himself before he did, as if he were unsure of his reception.

After dinner, Naomi assigned the girls their usual cleanup tasks, asked Evelyn to put Sophie down for the night, then, with coffee cups in hand, she and Mr. Sullivan retreated to the living room to discuss roundball strategy. Funnily enough, though, what they ended up talking about was something else entirely. After a moment or two of idle chit-chat—thanks again for your help this month, Mr. Sullivan, and how do you take your coffee?—the conversation turned abruptly to the personal, though that was thanks to Mr. Sullivan himself.

"I couldn't help noticing as we drove here," he said, "that you and your family live much closer to a different high school from the one where you teach and they attend class. How come the three of you don't take advantage of the closer one?"

Thinking the question a legitimate one, Naomi shrugged and offered her standard answer. "Jackson High is where I happened to find a job four years ago, when I returned to teaching. And I like teaching at Jackson," she hastened to add, because people tended not to believe her on that score, even though she was being perfectly honest when she made the assertion. "When the girls were old enough to go to junior high and high school, it just made sense to enroll them at Jackson with me. Sophie attends preschool near the house, and after we drop her off in the morning, the rest of the girls and I all ride to school together. And, of course, we can ride home together, too. It works very well, especially since I have such a hectic schedule."

"And Mr. Carmichael?" her guest asked. "Is his work not convenient to the school nearer your home?"

The question sounded perfectly innocent—and was perfectly understandable—coming on the heels of her response to his first question. For some reason, though, Naomi got the feeling that there was something more Mr. Sullivan wanted to know about than her ex-husband's contribution, if any, to their family life.

Nevertheless, she replied, likewise honestly, "I have no idea where Mr. Carmichael works these days, or if he works at all. I haven't heard from him in years."

Naomi must not have been as good at keeping the bitterness out of her voice as she'd hoped to be, because her guest had been lifting his cup to his mouth as she spoke, but halted the movement abruptly enough when she concluded that some of the coffee sloshed over and into his lap. His blue eyes widened in response to the coffee's temperature—because surely that wasn't incredulity she saw there—and, with his free hand, he hastily began to brush at the small stain that dampened his sweats.

"I, uh, I see," he said, clearly uncomfortable with this new turn of conversation. "So, then, I, uh… I mean, I guess he's not, um… He isn't, ah… He's not, uh…"

"Here," Naomi finished eloquently, taking pity on Mr. Sullivan for the second time in one night. How strange, taking pity on someone whose lifestyle was, she was certain, infinitely easier than her own. "No. He's not," she added. "Here, I mean."

Her guest nodded, but said nothing.

Naomi expelled a soft sound of resignation. "I'm divorced, Mr. Sullivan. I haven't seen or spoken to my ex-husband for over four years now. He even pays his child support through his attorney."

"But Sophie—" he said, cutting himself off immediately when he must have realized he was prying. "I'm sorry," he immediately apologized. "It's none of my business."

Naomi sighed again. "Look, it's not a big deal. Evelyn, Katie and Ginny, obviously, were old enough to know what was going on. Or, at the very least, to know something was wrong between me and Sam. I don't like to talk about it in front of Sophie, though. Her father left right after I discovered I was pregnant with her. She never knew him."

Naomi inhaled a deep breath and released it slowly, wondering how much she should say about her past to this man she had just met, this man she would only know temporarily, even if they would be working closely together over the next four weeks. Finally, though, she heard herself telling him, "Our marriage had been rocky for a while. Then, one night, Sam decided not to come home. He served me with divorce papers shortly thereafter. I signed them without hesitation, because I knew it was pointless to try to get him back. Frankly, at that point, I didn't want him back. Evelyn, Katie and Ginny helped me a lot with Sophie after she was born, and the five of us have been a very tight-knit group ever since. The last I heard, Sam was living in Atlanta, where he had been doing most of his work, anyway. I don't hear from him. Ever. End of story."

Sloan Sullivan seemed not to know what to say in response to so matter-of-fact a tale about the decline of an American family. Finally, though, he smiled halfheartedly and told her, "You don't have to call me Mr. Sullivan, you know. Call me Sloan. We are going to be working together, after all."

Naomi smiled sadly, but with heartfelt gratitude. "Thanks," she said, hoping he knew her appreciation was for a lot more than just the first-name basis thing. Then her smile grew happier. "And you," she added, "can call me Coach."

He laughed at that. "Will do. Coach."

The tension seemed to ebb after that, but they still didn't talk all that much about basketball. Instead, Naomi found herself answering questions. About how long she had been coaching—four years. About what had brought her to coaching in the first place—she had loved playing center for her high school and college teams. And about how she managed to juggle coaching, teaching and raising four daughters—not especially well, quite frankly, seeing as how she was organizationally challenged.

What was even stranger, though, was that Naomi didn't mind answering all of Sloan's questions. Normally, she was wary around men. Not just because of the difficult years with her ex-husband, but because, growing up, she'd always been taller than the rest of the boys, lanky and not particularly feminine. As a result, she'd intimidated most of the boys she'd known, and none had ever been interested in her. She hadn't dated much, hadn't had a real boyfriend until college. She had been a virgin on her wedding night, and she hadn't been with anyone since her ex-husband.

She just wasn't comfortable around men, unless they were talking about sports with her. Which, of course, she and Sloan were. But they were also touching on the personal, and that was something Naomi always strove to avoid with the opposite sex.

With Sloan, though… For some reason, she just didn't mind speaking frankly about such things. She didn't mind talking about herself or her past. Maybe because she knew that, with him being the kind of man he was, there was no way he'd ever be interested in her. So, in a sense, she was simply making friends with him. And hey, who couldn't use a friend now and then, right?

"What about you?" she finally said, when she began to grow tired of talking about herself.

He seemed surprised by the change of subject. "What about me?" he echoed.

"Are you married?" she asked bluntly. "Have any kids?"

He shook his head vehemently. "No. I've never been married. Never had the time," he added with an embarrassed smile. "And I can't honestly see myself with children. I'm not good with kids. Especially young ones."

Naomi found his response strange. Not only had Sloan interacted surprisingly well with all the girls at practice that evening, but she'd also seen how good he'd been with Sophie earlier. He'd seemed very comfortable in his association with her, had been in no way condescending or anxious or reserved, the way people without children so frequently were around kids—preschoolers especially. Still, she didn't call him on it. He must have his reasons for feeling the way he did. However erroneous those feelings might be.

"My work takes up a good part of my life," he told her. "I really don't have time for a family."

"You might be surprised how much time you could take from your work and still get things done," she said pointedly. "You just have to choose your priorities and put those first."

He nodded. "I agree completely. And I've made my work my first priority."

"Fair enough," she said. "At least you're honest with yourself. And others. A lot of men…" She stopped herself before saying anything more. She really didn't want to sound bitter. She wasn't bitter, she assured herself. Just…wary. That was all.

"A lot of men what?" Sloan asked.

She shrugged, but there was nothing casual in the gesture. "A lot of men make their work their first priority, but swear that it's really their family that comes first," she finally said. "Then they delude themselves into thinking that, because they're good providers in the financial arena, then they must be good fathers, and that's all that's important, and everything is fine, and it doesn't matter that they're never home, and never have anything to do with their families at all, and that they've actually assigned their family to last place instead of first."

Sloan said nothing for a moment, then, very softly, he asked, "Is that what happened in your marriage?"

Naomi told herself to change the subject again, that this was something that was not only none of his business, but also something she had no desire to discuss—with Sloan or anyone. Then she realized she was the one who'd started it, the one who'd brought it up in the first place, and that, too, seemed very unlike her.

In spite of all of her misgivings, though, and for some strange reason she didn't want to ponder at the moment, she heard herself telling him, "Maybe. My husband was a general contractor, and that meant he worked long hours, late hours, weekend hours. Even when he was home, he always seemed to be holed up in the office on the phone. We hardly ever saw him. He was never here—physically or emotionally. There were times when I found myself thinking he took on more work specifically because he didn't *want* to come home."

Sloan seemed to be genuinely puzzled by the comment. "Why wouldn't he want to come home to such a beautiful family?"

Naomi smiled indulgently at his remark. She and the girls weren't unattractive, she knew. But neither were any of them, save perhaps Katie, anything remotely resembling "beautiful." Her daughters were handsome. Striking. Had classic good looks. But even Naomi knew better than to consider them "beautiful." Beautiful suggested flowing blond locks, lush, womanly curves, and dainty, fragile dispositions. Her daughters, to a girl, were tall, dark, slender and strong. And as for Naomi, well... There were days when she didn't even feel strong anymore.

Still, she felt obligated to respond to Sloan's question. "If you must know," she began, "I don't think Sam was ever comfortable in the company of so many females."

"What?" Sloan asked, sounding honestly incredulous. "How can a man feel uncomfortable around women? That makes no sense."

Oh, he would feel that way, she thought. A man like Sloan could no doubt charm the socks—and more—off of any woman he chose. He seemed the epitome of the term *ladies' man.*

"Sam was a real man's man," Naomi said. "Very athletic, very car-oriented, fascinated with heavy machinery, that kind of thing. If the girls and I ever needed to go shopping, we'd drop him in the Sears tool department and know we could come back three hours later, and he'd still be happily browsing, or buying, or just talking metal shop with the guys."

Although Naomi didn't tell Sloan, she also knew that Sam's manly manliness was what had caused him to marry her in the first place. She was, in essence, one of the guys—therefore, he could always be comfortable with her, when he considered the majority of women to be alien creatures. But as the years went by, and he gradually found himself saddled with three daughters in addition to a wife, he'd begun to feel as if he were drowning in estrogen. He'd simply stopped feeling comfortable in his own home. And then, when Naomi had gotten pregnant that fourth time—unexpectedly—Sam had begun to fear that another pair of X chromosomes would be invading his turf. So he had left. All of them.

"He just wasn't comfortable around so many women," Naomi abbreviated. "And he spent as little time at home as possible as a result."

"But Sophie," Sloan objected again. "Surely, if he'd known you were pregnant with her, he wouldn't have—"

"Sam knew about Sophie," Naomi said quietly. "When I told him I was expecting again—it came as something of a surprise to both of us—he asked me to terminate the pregnancy. I refused. But the possibility of having another daughter, to him, was—" Naomi inhaled deeply and released it slowly, hoping the bitterness would leave with it "—unacceptable," she finally finished. "So he took off."

Sloan studied her in silence for a moment, then, "Oh," he said, very softly.

Naomi nodded. "Yeah. Oh," she agreed. "Now you know why I really don't like to talk about Sam in front of Sophie."

An awkward moment of silence ensued, until the clock on the mantelpiece began to chime. *One, two, three*, Naomi counted mentally. *Four, five six…* On and on it went, until twelve chimes had sounded.

"Good God, is that the time?" Sloan asked, glancing first at the clock, then down at his watch. "Midnight? But how can it already be midnight? I feel like I just got here."

Chapter Five

NAOMI WAS NO LESS SURPRISED by the hour than he, though she didn't feel as if Sloan had just gotten there. No, in many ways, it seemed as if eons had passed since she'd said hello to him earlier that evening, because it had felt so comfortable having him here in her home. She felt as if she'd had him here on a number of occasions already, and that the two of them were simply indulging in a regular, weekly ritual.

Funny, that, she couldn't help thinking. Normally, she didn't warm up to people so quickly. And she couldn't remember the last time she'd entertained anyone in her home with whom she had felt such an immediate sense of kinship. Certainly she'd never discussed the details of her marriage with someone she'd known such a short time. With Sloan, however, talking about her past—talking about so many things—hadn't felt awkward at all.

"Gosh, I am really sorry," she said, rising from the chair where she had parked herself for what she now realized had been hours. They'd finished their coffee long ago, and neither had expressed a desire for more. Their conversation, however, had obviously flowed quite freely. "I didn't mean to keep you so late."

"It isn't your fault," he replied, mimicking her gesture, pushing himself to standing. "I had no idea it was nearing midnight. When did that happen?"

Although it was true that the girls had all come in to say their good-nights a while ago, Naomi hadn't noted the time then, nor had she marked its passage since. And neither, evidently, had Sloan. Honestly, she couldn't remember the last time she'd lost track of the hour this way, but they'd been talking so companionably—and it had been so nice to talk to someone her own age for a change, she couldn't help thinking further—that she just hadn't been paying attention.

"You have a long drive back to Atlanta," she observed. Not that she was willing to offer him an alternative, mind you. She was just making an observation, that was all.

"It's not a problem," he assured her mildly. "I've had late drives home before."

Oh, she'd just bet he had—much later than this one, no doubt. She'd wager Sloan had women all over the metro Atlanta area, and that most of his women kept him in their homes well past midnight. Not that she considered herself one of Sloan's women, of course. But she'd bet good money that most of the women he spent the evening with turned out to be women he spent the night with. And probably not a single one of them was sharing her roof with four other females besides. Not unless there was some pret-ty kinky stuff going on. Stuff that Naomi would just as soon not ponder, thank you very much.

"Can I help you clean up?" he asked, surprising her. First

of all, men didn't usually offer to do something like that, and second, he had a long drive home. Why would he want to make his departure later than it already was?

She shook her head. "There's not much left. The girls took care of most of it. You go on."

For one scant, strange moment, neither of them moved or spoke, as if they weren't quite sure what they were supposed to say or do. Sloan just stood in front of the couch, where he'd been sitting, and Naomi just stood in front of the chair she'd occupied herself. And in that scant, strange moment, she was overcome by the oddest sensation that something was supposed to happen, that one of them was supposed to do something very specific—she had no idea what. And then the moment was gone, and she was extending her hand toward the front door, in a silent indication that he should use it.

"Well, I guess I'll see you again on Thursday," she said, suddenly feeling awkward and nervous for no reason she could name. "Maybe next time we can get to that strategizing we somehow never got to tonight."

"We didn't, did we?" he said, seeming as perplexed by the realization as she. "Thursday then, for sure."

"You can stay for dinner again, if you'd like," Naomi heard herself offer, even though she'd never formed the invitation consciously in her head.

"I would like that," he said, surprising her yet again. "I'd like it a lot."

Naomi nodded once. "Fine. I promise not to keep you as late next time."

He started to say something else, went so far as to open his mouth to form the words. But he must have had second thoughts, because he closed it again before uttering a sound.

He took a few steps toward the front door, then stopped and turned around to look at her. Naomi had started to follow him, but had been looking down at her feet instead of at him, and therefore wasn't paying attention when he came to a halt. Not until she ran right into him, anyway. Not until she felt his hands on her upper arms, steadying her to keep her from stumbling backward.

Hastily, she glanced up, only to find him gazing down at her, and she was overcome by the realization that never in her life had any man ever looked down at her this way. Never had she had to actually tip her head backward to meet a man's eye. But Sloan Sullivan was a large enough specimen that he made Naomi feel almost pint-size in relation. It was an unsettling feeling, acknowledging that a man was so much bigger than she was. But, strangely, it wasn't an altogether unpleasant one.

No, not unpleasant at all.

"I—I—I…I'm sorry," she stammered, confused by the keen heat that spilled through her midsection at the way he towered over her. "I, ah, I guess I wasn't looking where I was going."

She thought he would release her then, but he didn't right away. Instead, he only hesitated a little, loosening his grip on her some, but not quite letting go. "Are you okay?" he asked.

Naomi nodded, not sure she trusted herself to say anything more. By now, the heat that had spread through her abdomen was moving outward, seeping into every extremity, pooling deep in her belly, warming parts of her that hadn't felt warm for a very long time. Too long a time. Way too long a time.

"I'm fine," she finally managed to reply. And she hoped

he didn't notice how weak and quiet her voice suddenly sounded.

For another brief moment, he continued to hold her, and then—almost reluctantly, it seemed—he released her. He took another few steps toward the front door—moving backward this time, so that he could continue to look at her—and said, "Let's definitely talk basketball Thursday night. You could fill me in on the year thus far, the girls' strengths and weaknesses, that kind of thing. I feel like I'm coming in to this thing so cold."

That's funny, Naomi thought. *I'm feeling kind of warm myself.*

Aloud, though, she only said, "Um, fine. That would be, ah, fine. You're right. There's a lot we need to go over."

He nodded, but said nothing more, only kept walking backward until his backside hit the front door. Still looking at Naomi, he reached behind himself for the doorknob, turned it, and opened the door. But he seemed reluctant to step through it, seemed as if there were still something very important he wanted to tell her.

But all he did was lift a hand in farewell and then tell her, "Good night. See you Thursday."

"Good night," Naomi replied automatically. And before she could stop herself, she added, "Be careful driving home."

She had no idea why she tagged that final admonition onto her goodbye the way she did. It was the kind of thing she usually would have said to her daughters. Be careful. Because she cared about what happened to them, obviously.

But, then, why wouldn't she care about Sloan, too? she asked herself. It was only natural. He was a nice man. Not to mention her temporary assistant coach. She needed him. At least for the next month. Of course she cared.

Nevertheless, as she, too, raised her hand in farewell and watched Sloan smile, repeat his good-night, and pass through the front door, closing it behind himself, Naomi knew her caring stemmed from a lot more than anything basketball related. And that, she decided, couldn't possibly be a good thing.

Could it?

That, Sloan thought as he backed his car out of Naomi Carmichael's driveway and into the street, *was a very odd encounter.* And for a variety of reasons, too, he couldn't help thinking further as he maneuvered his way back through her neighborhood and "downtown"—oh, that really was a quaint way to think of it—Wisteria, toward the state road that had brought him here to begin with. Once he left the outskirts of town completely, he was swallowed by the darkness, the black ribbon of two-lane highway bisecting the even blacker night. Clouds obscured whatever light might have shone from the moon and stars, and the headlights of his roadster illuminated nothing but more darkness up ahead.

Sloan felt almost as if he were the last man on earth. A little more than forty-five minutes lay between him and his Buckhead town house, but he was reluctant to turn on the car stereo. Somehow, the silence was much more welcome. And certainly more conducive to thinking, of which, Sloan figured, he had a lot to do. So he drove on in silence and thought about the evening he had just spent with Naomi and her daughters, and how very odd the whole occasion had been.

The first reason why it had been odd was because he didn't normally visit anyone who had children. Especially four of them. Especially ranging in age from four to sixteen. Few members of Sloan's social circle were even married, let alone procreating. He wasn't ever around children, ergo he wasn't ever comfortable with them. Ergo, he should have felt wholly *un*comfortable in the Carmichael home, surrounded as he had been, by such utterly alien creatures. But he hadn't felt uncomfortable at all. On the contrary, all of the Carmichaels had made him feel quite welcome. And it hadn't just been the children who were alien, he thought further. Because Naomi, too, was unlike any other woman he had ever met.

Which brought him to the second reason why his encounter had been so odd. Simply put, Sloan didn't generally spend hours talking to women. Certainly he'd never *lost track* of those hours by talking. No, he spent hours doing other things with women—he'd even lost track of hours doing those other things with women—but never talking. He only talked extensively to women who were his coworkers—though he *didn't* lose track of the time in those cases. And with his women co-workers, he had no desire whatever to do those other things he might spend hours—and losing track of the time—doing with another woman. With Naomi Carmichael, however, who was, in a sense a co-worker...

Well, suffice it to say that, at some point during the evening—Sloan wasn't sure when, exactly—he'd realized that talking wasn't the only thing he wouldn't mind doing with her.

Enter odd reason number three. Sloan just didn't go for women like Naomi. Ever. He dated women who were ultrafeminine, ultra-attentive to their physical appearance, ultrasuccessful in their chosen fields, and ultra-aware of him as a man. He did not go for women who were nearly as tall—and every bit as athletic—as he was, or women who favored a wardrobe of sweats—even when entertaining guests in their homes—or women who worked in less-than-desirable surroundings—like Jackson High School—or women who seemed no more aware of him as a man than they were aware of the living room carpet as a man.

Not once had Naomi Carmichael offered Sloan any sort of come-hither come-on this evening, yet in spite of that, he'd been more than a little aware of her as a woman. In fact, he'd been very aware of her as a woman. Too aware. Even though she didn't seem to be aware of her own womanhood at all herself. Even though she'd been dressed almost identically to him. Even though she pulled in an income that was only a fraction of his own. Even though she was someone's mom. *Four* someones' mom. The realization of such things hadn't swayed him at all in finding her very attractive.

Stranger still was the fact that she had revealed to him such personal things about herself and her past—and that Sloan had *encouraged* her to reveal such personal things—and he hadn't once felt uncomfortable during the exchange. Which, he thought, pretty much amounted to odd reason number four.

Comfort, he reflected again. That was what it all seemed to come back to. He had just been comfortable in a place, and with people, and in a situation, where he *should* have felt remarkably *un*comfortable. But he hadn't felt uncomfortable at all. What was likewise curious was that now that Sloan had felt the comfort of the Carmichael home, he realized how much comfort had been missing in his own. Even his own home, after years in residence there, hadn't ever felt as comfortable to him as one evening spent in the home occupied by Naomi and her daughters.

Wherein lay odd reason number five.

Even after knowing her a matter of hours, Sloan realized that, simply put, he liked Naomi. He liked her a lot. He also liked her daughters. He couldn't imagine what kind of an idiot her husband must have been to have left such a family behind. Ah, well, he thought further. Who was he to try to understand the mysterious behavior of others, when his own was nothing short of bizarre?

It was going to be an interesting month, he couldn't help thinking further. And for some reason, he suddenly found himself looking forward to lending a hand to the Lady Razorbacks. He only hoped he could stop at a hand. Especially when so many of his other body parts seemed to be so interested in their coach.

Oh, yes. An interesting month indeed.

Chapter Six

THURSDAY EVENING WAS AN almost identical repeat of the previous Tuesday, right down to little Sophie's wanting to introduce Sloan to more very useful engines—which, he had to admit, he enjoyed immensely. He hadn't played with trains—or any other toy, for that matter—since he was a boy, and he'd forgotten how much fun it could be to just lose a little time, a little reality, playing make-believe. Games of pretend were such a big part of little lives, he reminded himself. And it was just too bad that, when their lives got "big," people tended to forget about the importance of things like that. Sophie, though, was remarkably adept at reminding Sloan of a lot of the things he should remember.

All of the Carmichael girls were, really, he realized very quickly. Evy and Katie's single-minded focus on basketball reminded Sloan of what it was like to choose a goal and pursue it relentlessly until it was achieved. He hadn't done anything like that himself since college. His goals always seemed to change from one day to the next, and he often abandoned one goal before achieving it because another came along that seemed more important. Then he'd abandon that goal, too, for something else that took his fancy. In fact, he couldn't recall the last time one thing had been more important to him than anything else in the world. And Ginny's breathless preoccupation with boys reminded Sloan what it was like to fall in love for the very first time. And the second time. And the third time. And how every single time seemed to be more passionate and unbearable than the time before.

Even by that second night, the Carmichael women were already getting under his skin, he thought, as he watched them all abandon their places at the dinner table to move into what looked like a well-orchestrated evening tradition of cleanup and homework rituals. And as the younger Carmichaels retreated to their respective roles, Sloan and Naomi once more retreated to the living room to enjoy coffee and conversation. In fact, the only difference tonight over Tuesday night was that when Sloan once more found himself seated in Naomi's very comfortable living room with a very comfortable Naomi, *he* was the one who ended up imparting bits of himself and his past to *her*. As the evening wore on and the coffee ran out, they once again forgot about talking basketball strategy and the conversation instead took a turn for the personal. Sloan's personal.

He told her about growing up in Atlanta, but he found himself skirting the subject of his family. It wasn't that he was ashamed of them—on the contrary, he was proud of his parents' and his younger brother's accomplishments and status, and his own, in the community. But somehow, Sloan wasn't comfortable—there was that word again—discussing his family's wealth and prominence with Naomi, who seemed to be struggling, though succeeding fairly well, just to get by. Too, he honestly didn't think his own background and family made for conversation that was all that interesting. So instead he focused vaguely on his childhood and education, less generally on his decision to go into law, and more specifically on the job he performed now.

And, much to his delight, he did uncover a few more things about Naomi, too—but only because he had to consciously turn the topic of conversation to her whenever she seemed intent on steering it back to him. He learned about her own upbringing in a small town in South Carolina, about her three older brothers—no sisters—about how she'd lost her mother to cancer when she was six, and about how she couldn't deny that much of her athleticism had come about not just because she was so surrounded by males while growing up, but also because she wanted to keep herself as healthy as possible—especially now, so that her girls wouldn't experience a loss as deep as her own.

And as Sloan listened to her talk, he realized something very important about Naomi Carmichael. She was a doer. A doer and a get-doner. And she relied on no one—no one but herself—to do and get done. And although he couldn't help but admire the quality, something about it being so present in Naomi bothered him more than he wanted to admit. Because suddenly, he kind of liked the idea of lending a hand, and not just to the Lady Razorbacks.

Which was crazy, he told himself. Not only did Naomi clearly not welcome such things into her personal life, but she wasn't a woman suited to him. And even if she had been a woman suited to him, she had four—*four*—children. No

matter which way a man looked at it, there was just no getting around that. Whatever strange attraction he might be
feeling for her—and the attraction was, most definitely,
strange—it was totally out of character for him, and, he
knew, utterly temporary.

He reminded himself that in a month's time, his obligation to Naomi and the Lady Razorbacks would be over. He
would have no reason to come to Wisteria, and over time,
this strange attraction would go away. If he acted on it, it
would only make things more difficult when the time came
to tell Naomi goodbye. And it would distract them both
from the matter which had brought them together in the
first place—coaching a basketball team that was poised for
the state championship.

Not that Naomi had offered any strong indication that
she would welcome any acting on his part, anyway, Sloan
reminded himself further. Still, he couldn't deny that there
was *something* buzzing in the air between them. He had no
idea what, precisely, it was. But he could tell from the way
he caught her looking at him sometimes that Naomi felt it,
too. Even if she was as unwilling to act upon it as he was.

Which, of course, was good, he told himself. Because he
was unwilling to act on it, too. And that was why, in the days
and evenings and weeks that followed, Sloan made damned
sure he kept his attraction to Naomi to himself. Nevertheless, in the days and evenings and weeks that followed, it
somehow became a custom for Sloan to have dinner at the
Carmichael home after each Tuesday and Thursday night
practice. And also, in the days and evenings and weeks that
followed, somehow—and Sloan honestly had no idea
how—his attraction to Naomi only multiplied.

He told himself after each of their encounters that he

only imagined the magnitude of his fascination with her. And then, just about the time he started believing himself in that regard, he would see Naomi again. And the fascination would be there once more, stronger than ever, mocking him.

It made no sense. Here was a woman he saw primarily during athletic encounters, during which time they were both dressed in ragged workout clothes, and during which time they both did a lot of yelling and sweating, yet every time he saw her, the pull Sloan felt for her grew a little bit stronger, a little bit tighter, a little bit more urgent. She was just so strong, so commanding, so admirable. There was no way a man could ever *not* find her fascinating. But there was no way—no way—Sloan could allow himself to act on that fascination.

No matter how badly he might want to.

Finally, though, on their last night coaching together—the Lady Razorbacks' regular assistant coach would return to his duties the following week, just in time for the start of the state tournament—Sloan felt like he had to do *some*thing. His time with Naomi was almost over, he reminded himself. There would be no reason for him to come back to Wisteria, though he did have every intention of attending the tournament games to see how the girls fared. He had to. Not just because he had a vested interest in their performance, but because he'd become rather attached to several of them. Especially, he couldn't help thinking, the Carmichael girls.

So, as had happened on every previous Tuesday or Thursday night over the past four weeks, on the final Thursday night of Sloan's coaching duties, four weeks after that first Tuesday night, he ended up staying much too late at Naomi's house. Because, as had been the case on all the evenings that had come before it, the conversation and the surroundings—and the company—were just too appealing for him to conjure the desire to leave. Finally, though, reluctantly, he did make himself get up off of the sofa and head for the front door. But not before finalizing plans he felt it necessary for both of them to make.

"So, what are you doing this weekend?" he asked as he pulled open the front door, preparing to leave.

Obviously perplexed by the question, Naomi arrowed her dark eyebrows downward and studied him with much confusion. "This weekend?" she echoed.

He nodded. "Yeah, I thought maybe the two of us could get together this weekend and talk about the team and the tournament," he reminded her. "I mean, I know your regular assistant coach is coming back next week for the tourney, but until then, I still feel like I need to contribute something."

"Oh," she replied, still sounding a little puzzled. Then, before Sloan could suggest a place for them to meet, she hurried on, "I, ah, I—I can't do this weekend. I, um, I have a…uh, a…um, a thing. A thing that I, um…that I need to go to."

Sloan eyed her warily, wondering at her sudden attack of nerves. Over the last four weeks, he'd never seen her anything except cool, calm and collected—except, of course, for those few unguarded moments when he'd caught her gazing at him in a way that was warm, wanton and wistful. Why, suddenly, was she blushing and stammering and looking at everything in the room except him?

"A thing?" he repeated dubiously.

She nodded quickly, and, he couldn't help thinking, not

a little anxiously. "Yeah. A, ah...a thing. This weekend. I have a definite, um, thing. To go to, I mean. A really important thing. A thing I can't get out of." Seemingly as an afterthought, she added, "I'm sorry."

Sloan told himself not to take it to heart, the fact that she was so obviously giving him the brush-off. Clearly, she had no *thing*. Clearly, what she *did* have was a reluctance to see him in any capacity other than the one she'd seen him in for the last month. She was trying to tell him politely that she didn't want to see him outside the realm of coaching, even if, ostensibly, the whole point to getting together would be to discuss coaching. He told himself to be big about it and let her off the hook. For some reason, though, he couldn't let it go that easily.

Feeling playful—and boy, before making Naomi's acquaintance, had it been a long time since Sloan had felt playful—he asked, "What kind of thing?"

Her eyes widened in panic at the question. "Um, you know, a...a thing."

"An important thing," he said, recalling her earlier, if vague description, and trying not to smile at how easily he'd cornered her, and at how uncomfortable she became when she was cornered. This could potentially be a lot of fun. And man, it had been a long, long time since Sloan had had a lot of fun. Then again, he reflected, he'd had a lot of fun over this last month, hadn't he? With all the Carmichael women, come to think of it. But before that, he couldn't remember the last time he'd had any *real* fun.

"Right," she told him. "An important thing. A really important thing."

"And where, exactly, is this important thing to be held?" he asked. "Here in Wisteria?"

She seemed to give the question some thought—for a full two or three seconds, at least, Sloan noted—then shook her head quickly. "No, not here in town. Somewhere else."

"Where?" he persisted.

Looking more panicked with every passing second, she told him, "It's, um, it's much too far. It's in, uh… It's in, um… It's ah…Atlanta," she finally told him. "I have a thing in Atlanta."

Immediately after saying it, she must have realized her faux pas, because she squeezed her eyes shut tight in obvious distress. Sloan smiled devilishly, knowing her reaction came about because she realized she had just played right into his hands. And it was with no small effort that he kept himself from laughing outright.

"Really?" he said with much interest. "Atlanta? Well, you'll be right in my backyard. This is perfect. We can meet for dinner with no problem. In fact," he added, hoping he wasn't laying it on too thick, "I just remembered I have a thing this weekend, too. Maybe it's close to where your thing is."

She eyed him *very* suspiciously at that.

"Really," he said. "I have a thing this weekend." And in that moment, he made definite plans to have a thing that very weekend, just so he wouldn't be lying to her. Unlike *some* people he knew. "What day is your thing?"

She narrowed her eyes some more. "Saturday?" she said.

He expelled a sound of utter incredulity. "Mine, too," he told her, doing his absolute best not to do or say anything that might spoil his total solemnity. "Wow. That really is a coincidence. So where exactly in Atlanta is your thing going to be?" he asked further.

She parted her lips fractionally, as if she wanted to say

something, but had no idea what. "Well, where's *your* thing?" she asked, turning the tables.

Sloan pulled a site out of thin air. "At the Four Seasons Hotel," he told her.

She nodded with—dare he say it?—relief. "Oh, see, that'll be a problem, because my thing is on the other side of town, at the San Moritz."

Hoping he *really* wasn't pouring it on too thick now, Sloan opened his hand and smacked his palm resolutely against his forehead. "That's what I meant to say. The San Moritz. I always get that mixed up with the Four Seasons. But what I meant to say was the San Moritz. That's where my thing is, too." He smiled. "We must be going to the same thing."

Naomi continued to eye him with much suspicion, but she didn't say a word. Oh, she opened her mouth to do so— several times, in fact—but no words ever actually emerged.

"So what's your thing?" Sloan asked mischievously.

She smiled—devilishly, if he wasn't mistaken, something that made his own smile fall a bit. "It's a meeting of the Clemson University Alumni, Georgia chapter," she told him smugly. "Guess we're not going to the same thing after all, since you went to Vanderbilt."

Oh, he wasn't going to let her off that easily. "Still," he said, "since we're both going to be at the San Moritz on Saturday, we might as well get together. Do they give you dinner at those things? The San Moritz has a great restaurant. I'll make us a reservation for seven, how will that be?"

Instead of replying to his question or suggestion, Naomi asked, "So what's your thing in Atlanta this weekend? You never did say."

This time it was Sloan's turn to open his mouth and have

no words come to his aid. He struggled for several tense seconds, then smiled. "It's a reunion of sorts, too. I'm getting together with some old friends from high school. Future Estate Planners of America. FEPA." Then, before she had a chance to say a word, he hurriedly added, "The San Moritz Hotel, seven o'clock Saturday night. I'll see you then."

And as quickly as he could, Sloan hurried out the door and down the front walk to his car. Before she had a chance to call him on his ruse. Before she had a chance to say no. Before she had a chance to back out.

And before *he* had a chance to change his mind. Not that he would, he quickly realized. Because suddenly, he couldn't wait to see Naomi Carmichael again. Especially since, *this* time, it would be on *his* turf.

Chapter Seven

"YOU LOOK AWESOME, MOM."

Naomi gazed into the full-length cheval mirror tucked into the corner of her bedroom and wondered what on earth had possessed her to do this ridiculous thing. But when she saw her reflection, she immediately had her answer. Obviously, it wasn't *her* doing this ridiculous thing. No, the woman doing this ridiculous thing was a total stranger. Because the woman in the mirror, although she bore a vague resemblance to Naomi, clearly was *not* Naomi.

Instead of her usual sweats and or blue jeans, she was dressed in a plain, long-sleeved, knee-length cocktail dress with a modestly scooped neck, a garment she hadn't removed from her closet for years. Smoky stockings hugged her legs, and her feet were tucked into low-heeled black pumps. The only jewelry she wore were the pearl earrings her aunt Margery had given her for her high school graduation.

And it didn't stop there. Ginny had insisted that her

mother *had* to wear makeup if she was going to be going someplace so nice, so she had given her mother a complete makeover which, instead of making Naomi look as if she'd just been hit by a Lancôme bomb, made her look as if the beauty fairies had visited her in the night and had smoothed out and perfected each of her facial features without cosmetic enhancement. Her eyes seemed larger and darker, her lashes longer, her mouth fuller, her cheekbones more prominent. Yet somehow Ginny had done it all without making Naomi look like a streetwalker.

Ginny had also acted as her fashion consultant, *tsk-tsk-tsk*ing at every article of clothing Naomi possessed until stumbling on the black dress at the very back of the closet. She'd had to dig for the earrings, too, but had been delighted once she'd discovered them—and not just because she intended to borrow them for the upcoming ninth-grade mixer.

Evelyn, however, was the daughter who had *insisted* that Naomi absolutely *had* to go to Atlanta tonight. She'd overheard the conversation between her mother and Sloan the Thursday before, and the moment the door had closed behind him, she had hurried into the living room to start making plans. Naomi had quickly cut her oldest daughter off, had insisted she was going to call Sloan the next morning and cancel their date, that she never should have agreed to see him in the first place, that he had caught her unawares, and she simply hadn't known what to say. She *had* known, though—and she still did—that going out socially with Sloan Sullivan would be a very bad idea. Because over the course of the last four weeks, she had begun to care about him way too much.

Every Tuesday and Thursday afternoon for the last

month, she had found herself feeling as nervous with anticipation as a girl going out on her first date with a boy she'd had a crush on for years. She'd found herself wishing she could wear something other than sweats for their encounter, knowing full well that a little black cocktail dress like the one she wore now simply was not appropriate apparel for basketball practice. And as she'd watched him during practice, noting the fluid movement of his body and the rapt center of his concentration, she had grown more and more attracted to him physically.

Worse, as she'd watched him interact with her family, she'd grown more and more attracted to him emotionally. With every meal he'd shared with her and her daughters, she'd noted an easiness and camaraderie of spirit in him that few people—few men—would be able to manage when confronted by so many women. And she'd seen, too, how attached her daughters were becoming to Sloan. Especially Sophie, who craved attention and so seldom got enough. All of them, she thought now, craved attention from him in one way or another, attention that had been missing in all their lives for much too long.

Naomi also told herself now, as she had told herself all along, that she couldn't allow Sloan into her life—into their lives—any more than she already had. Because he was only a temporary addition. Very temporary. And she didn't want the void he would doubtless leave behind when he went to be any bigger than it already would be.

And although Naomi hadn't been able to tell Evy all of those things, she had assured her daughter that she couldn't—wouldn't—see Sloan socially. Evy, though, had made her promise that she would keep their appointment.

"You need this, Mom," she had told her mother. "You never get to go anywhere. And you and Mr. Sullivan get along so well together."

"But, Evy," Naomi had objected, "I can't drive all the way to Atlanta just to have dinner with a man."

"Why not?" her daughter had demanded. "This is perfect. You'll be in your own car, and you can leave whenever you want to. He's a nice man, Mom. A total hottie. I know you like him. And I can tell he likes you. And you never get to have any fun."

And that, Naomi had thought then, was the kicker. She really didn't ever get to have any fun. And Sloan was a nice man. Not to mention a total hottie. She did like him. And she knew he liked her. She just wasn't sure it was a healthy—or productive—kind of liking. Because it was only a temporary liking. Wasn't it?

Still, Atlanta wasn't that far away, she reminded herself. It might be fun to go out to eat with him, someplace nice. It was only dinner. And she would pay for her share so that she wouldn't feel indebted to him. And she and Sloan did get along well. And this could be a nice kind of conclusion to their—working—relationship.

Of course, there was that other relationship, she reminded herself. The one-sided one she'd created in her besotted brain. The one that had been generated by one fantasy after another over the last month, not all of them sexual in nature, though, certainly, there had been a few where she and Sloan had been—

Well. Involved in something other than coaching.

Oh, for heaven's sake, what was the harm? she asked herself, pushing her annoying thoughts away. There was little chance that Sloan was going to try anything funny. Although there had been one or two times over the last month when she'd looked up to find him watching her in ways that were…question- able…he'd really offered no indication that he was interested in her in any way other than a friendly one. As long as she could keep *herself* from jumping *his* bones and ravishing him shamelessly and doing something she'd regret later—and she was *pretty* sure she could keep herself from doing all those things—then what was the harm?

"Beat it, you guys," Evelyn said now to her sisters, scattering Naomi's thoughts once and for all. "Mom and I need to have a woman-to-woman talk before she goes out."

Well, that certainly sounded ominous, Naomi thought as she gathered up the few things that would fit into the little beaded purse Ginny had loaned her, an accessory that was roughly the size of a carpet fiber.

The other girls protested, but Evy stood firm. "Out, runts," she insisted, pointing at the bedroom door. "Now."

Grumbling, each of her three sisters obeyed. Evy closed the door behind them and leaned back against it, gazing at her mother as if she were about to lay down the law. If it hadn't been for her accelerated height, in her faded blue jeans and massive flannel shirt, her tattered ponytail caught high on the crown of her head, Evy could have passed for a girl much younger than sixteen. However, when she opened her mouth to speak, she sounded every one of her years. And then some.

Meeting her mother's gaze levelly, Evy said, "I hope you've left enough room in that purse for a condom."

Naomi gaped at her. It was, to say the least, not what she had expected to hear from her daughter. "*What?*" she said.

Evy pushed herself away from the door and crossed the room to stand in front of her mother, crossing her arms over her midsection as if she meant business. "Look, Mom," she said gravely, "things have changed a lot since you were dating before. You have to practice safe sex now. And I also want you to know that if you don't want to come home tonight—"

"Evelyn!" Naomi gasped, jumping up off the bed and straightening to her full height, which was still a couple of inches taller than her daughter. "Of *course* I'll be coming home tonight. And I do *not* need to save room in my purse for a condom."

Boy, had times changed. Naomi remembered her aunt Margery telling her to always save room in her purse for a dime, in case a boy got fresh with her, and she needed to make a phone call for her father to come and get her. Now her daughter—her *daughter*—was telling her to be sure and pack a condom.

In response to Naomi's exclamation, Evy only smiled and shrugged. "Well, if, at some point in the evening, you decide that you *don't* want to come home tonight," she insisted, "just remember that I'll be here to keep an eye on things. Really, Mom. It's *so* not a big deal."

Spoken like a true sixteen-year-old, Naomi thought. A sixteen-year-old who had yet to even date a boy, let alone dabble in anything even remotely resembling sex. Basketball was Evy's passion, Evy's life, right now, and had been for years. She had no interest in dating. Which, of course, was just fine with Naomi. Still, her daughter's lack of socializing with the opposite sex hadn't exactly broadened Evy's horizons. Not that Naomi necessarily wanted them broadened, mind you, but she did worry sometimes that her daughter just didn't have a realistic view of the whole male-female dynamic.

Then again, that might not be such a bad thing, she couldn't help thinking.

"Oh, and just in case," Evy added. She reached behind herself, into her back pocket, and withdrew a small plastic packet, extending it toward her mother. "I really do think you should take a condom with you. You never know. Like I said, it's not a big deal."

Naomi gaped at her daughter again. "Where did you get that?" she demanded.

Evelyn lifted one shoulder and let it drop. "One of the girls at school."

Naomi bit her lower lip thoughtfully. She had known for some time now that this conversation would eventually take place. She'd just been hoping she could put it off for a bit longer, until Evelyn was, say…fifty or so.

"You have friends who are sexually active?" she asked, hoping she kept her voice casual, when in fact she felt like grabbing her daughter and locking her in the closet until she could have her fitted for a reasonably comfortable chastity belt.

"One or two," Evy said.

Well, at least she was being honest, Naomi thought. "And how do you feel about that?" she asked her daughter.

Evy gave her another one of those one-shouldered shrugs and said, "Personally, I think it's kind of gross."

Oh, thank God, Naomi thought.

"But there is this guy in my chemistry class who's kinda hot," she continued.

Oh, dear…

"And I think he's interested in me," Evy continued.

Oh, no…

"But I don't think I'm near ready for anything physical, you know?" her daughter finished.

Naomi felt some measure of relief, but couldn't quite keep herself from pointing out, "A minute ago, you told me it's not a big deal."

"I meant for you," Evy said with a smile. "You do have four daughters, Mom. I figure you've done it at least four times. Probably more."

Naomi smiled back, then cupped her daughter's face gently in her hand. "It never stops being a big deal, Evy," she said softly. "Remember that. It is *always* a big deal. That's why you want to be in love when it happens. Because it *is* a big deal. Always."

Her daughter smiled back. "I'll remember that."

"I hope you do."

Evy glanced down at the condom she still held in her hand, and Naomi told herself not to panic that her daughter seemed so comfortable with the thing. "Guess you won't be needing this then, huh?" Evy asked.

Naomi smiled at her daughter again, but for some reason, she couldn't quite bring herself to say no. Still, her lack of a response must have told Evy something, because she tucked the condom into her back pocket again.

"Are you going to give that back to the girl you got it from?" Naomi asked hopefully.

"Maybe I'll keep it as a reminder," Evy said. "I'll hang on to it for a while."

"A long while, I hope," Naomi said pointedly.

Evy laughed. "Yeah. I imagine it'll be a long while. I got basketball to think about."

So she did, Naomi thought. Would that Naomi had been able to keep her own thoughts on basketball for the last month, she wouldn't be in the strange position she was in now—a position she still couldn't believe she'd let herself be talked into.

Because she *had* let herself be talked into it—there was no way she could deny that. *Let* was the operative word here. She could have come clean with Sloan Thursday night and just told him he'd caught her in a lie, and that she'd just wanted to avoid seeing him socially, because it wasn't a good idea. He'd known she was lying anyway—any fool could tell that. And he'd deliberately maneuvered and manipulated the conversation until he had her right where he wanted her. Worse, Naomi had allowed him to maneuver and manipulate, fully knowing what he was trying to do. He'd finagled a way for them to be together, and she'd done nothing to stop him.

Why?

It was a question that had circled through her head for two days, and she was no closer to an answer now than she had been the first time she'd asked herself. She didn't know why she wanted to drive all the way to Atlanta, just to have dinner with Sloan. Even if he was nice and charming and interesting. Even if she did find him profoundly physically attractive. Even if he did make her feel things she hadn't felt for a very long time, things she had begun to think she would never feel again. Even if she hadn't been able to stop thinking about him since their first encounter.

Okay, so maybe she knew why she wanted to drive to Atlanta to have dinner with Sloan. Because she was lonely, and she found him attractive, and it had been a long, long time since she'd felt so comfortable with another human being. She still didn't think it was a very good idea. Because in spite of their attraction to each other, anything the two of them might undertake wasn't going to go anywhere. Sloan was a workaholic who lived in another town, a man who had infinitely more interest in taking on the stock market than he did in taking on a family. He was a man who could commit to nothing except his job. He'd made that totally clear to her that very first night.

But in spite of her little pep talk to herself, Naomi scooped up the little black beaded purse, smoothed a hand over the elegant black dress, and took one final look at herself in the mirror. Because, even knowing everything she did, she wanted to have dinner with Sloan Sullivan. It was only dinner, she promised herself. That was all. Dinner and a little conversation. It would be just like all those Tuesday nights and Thursday nights had been, except that the two of them would be in different surroundings. More romantic surroundings. More intimate surroundings. And they wouldn't be sharing the surroundings with four other people. No, the two of them would be *aaalll alooone*.

Dinner, Naomi reminded herself forcefully. It was only dinner. And conversation. And then, for sure, she would come home. And then she would never see Sloan again. And then…

She sighed heavily. And then, she had no idea what she would do. She'd just have to take it one step at a time.

Chapter Eight

WHEN SLOAN FIRST CAUGHT SIGHT of Naomi, he almost let his gaze wander right over her, so unexpected was her appearance. And it wasn't unexpected just because he had been fairly certain she would chicken out at the last minute and not come tonight. No, it was also unexpected because, when he finally did register her appearance, he at first didn't think the woman he was looking at was Naomi, because she just didn't look like herself tonight. No, tonight, she looked... She looked... She looked...

Wow. She looked...*wow.* In fact, she looked very, *very* wow.

He couldn't quite say what she had done to herself that made her look so different from the way she usually did, because, in truth, she didn't really look any different from the way she usually did. Except that, somehow, she looked totally different from the way she usually did.

Or something like that.

Her short, dark hair was the same as always—except different, in that she had tucked the curly tresses behind her ears, something that showed off her facial features more prominently than before. And her facial features looked the same as always—except different, in that her sooty eyes seemed larger, darker, sexier, somehow, and her full, lush mouth looked even tastier than it had before. Although she wasn't wearing her standard sweats, what she did have on was by no means revealing or provocative—well, not provocative in the traditional sense of the word, anyway— which shouldn't have made her look all that different from the way she usually looked. Except she did look different. Because the black dress hugged her curves with *much* affection, and due to its lack of decoration, it focused Sloan's attention back on her face, a face he hadn't realized, until this moment, was so beautiful.

Everything about Naomi tonight just seemed to have jumped up and yelled, "Hey, look at me! Do I look fabulous or what?" Because she did look fabulous. Extremely fabulous. In fact, she looked much too fabulous for Sloan's comfort and peace of mind.

But then, that was good, right? he asked himself. Because not only was it going to be a joy to gaze at her from the other side of the table, but now he could finally understand his attraction to her. Underneath all the sweat and sweat suit he'd seen of her so far, there was a woman. A womanly woman. Obviously, somehow, he'd known that all along, and that was why he hadn't been able to stop thinking about her since their initial meeting.

Because he *hadn't* been able to stop thinking about her since their initial meeting. No, she had pretty much consumed his thoughts—both conscious and unconscious—for the last month. And now he understood that that was because Naomi Carmichael was, quite clearly, a womanly—unforgettable—woman. A womanly woman who, he had to admit, seemed all the more feminine now because, over the past four weeks, he had seen her looking, well, not particularly feminine. Not especially womanly.

Tonight, though, she was most definitely womanly. And then some. Before now, he would have considered her a handsome woman with classic, elegant features. But tonight, through God alone knew what magic, she had become a raven-haired beauty. To put it mildly. And, tonight, he had her all to himself, on his own turf, where anything might happen. Anything at all.

Well, well, well.

When he realized how long he had been gazing at her without making an effort to attract her attention, Sloan rose from the table where the hostess had seated him and began to approach the front entrance where Naomi stood. But she must have sensed his motion—or perhaps she had just sensed *him*—because, immediately, she turned her head toward him. She smiled when she saw him, but he could tell right away that she was nervous. Maybe even as nervous as he was himself.

And then he wondered why *he* was nervous. Sloan Sullivan was never nervous. Never. Especially around women. And Naomi, in particular, was a woman he shouldn't be nervous around. Because, hey, they were only friends, right? And they were only here to talk basketball. And they were only going to have dinner. Dinner and a little conversation. To discuss the strategy for the Lady Razorbacks in their upcoming tournament. Why should that make him feel nervous?

Oh, sure, Sullivan. Basketball. Strategy. Riiight.

That was why he had gone to such lengths to ensure that she would meet him here tonight, he told himself. That was why he had taken two hours to get ready beforehand. That was why he had insisted to the hostess that she seat them at a table well away from the main traffic area, where the lighting was low and romantic. And that was why, before he'd left home tonight, he had impulsively tucked a condom into his wallet.

That last action still had him wondering at himself. How on earth could he be anticipating—even subconsciously—that things between himself and Naomi would go anywhere beyond the dinner and conversation stage tonight? Or any other night, for that matter? She had four children, he reminded himself. She wasn't his type. Nor was she the type to go for some casual sexual encounter. Therefore that last little accessory he had added to his person tonight would be in no way necessary. In spite of that, he had packed it, anyway.

Just in case.

Wishful thinking? he wondered now. And if so, just what was he wishing for? Because he wasn't the kind of man to take advantage of a woman just to quell some physical urge. And even if he was, he wouldn't take advantage of a nice woman like Naomi Carmichael. And that, he reminded himself, was precisely what she was. A nice woman. She was what his grandfather Sullivan had always termed, "The other kind of girl. The kind you marry."

So just what, exactly, was Sloan thinking?

He pushed his troubling thoughts away for now, promised himself he *wouldn't* think, and focused instead on the vision of loveliness who approached him. She seemed to grow more nervous with every step she took toward him, which was only fair, Sloan had to conclude, because he grew more nervous with every step she took toward him, too.

"You look absolutely edible…uh, incredible," he quickly corrected himself as she came to a halt in front of him.

He saw right away that his slip of the tongue—or slip of the libido…whatever—made her even more nervous than she already was. Of course, it made him more nervous, too, among other things, so they were still on equal footing— or some other body part—there. She ran her gaze over him from head to toe, silently evaluating his dark suit and white dress shirt, and the discreetly patterned Hermés silk he'd taken a full fifteen minutes to select from his eclectic—and ample—assortment of neckties. Then she nodded her head approvingly and grinned again.

"You look pretty edible…uh, incredible, yourself," she mimicked, smiling. "Is this the real you?"

He narrowed his eyes in puzzlement. "The real me?" he echoed. "What do you mean?"

"I mean is this the way you usually look?" she clarified. "Is this the type of thing you usually wear? For work and— and the rest of your life, I mean."

"Oh. Yes," he said. "I guess it is. Certainly I'm dressed like this more often than I'm dressed the way I have been for practices. This is closer to the real me than the other person you've seen."

She nodded, seeming to give his response much thought. Then she gestured to her own clothing and said, "This *isn't* the real me. I *never* dress like this. I'm far more often dressed the way I am at practices. *That's* the real me," she reiterated. "The one you've seen up till now. This—" with a sweeping hand, she indicated her apparel again "—is a total aberration."

Somehow Sloan got the impression that she really, really, *really* wanted to emphasize that point very, very, *very* strongly. So he nodded back and said, "I see. Well, *both* versions of you are very nice to my way of thinking."

The conversation stalled a bit there, and he found himself wondering what she was thinking, what *she* might be anticipating—even subconsciously—from the evening ahead. Had *she* tucked a condom into her purse, for instance? he wondered. Somehow, he thought not. Still, dressed as she was—and nervous as she was—he didn't think she was especially focused on basketball and tournament strategies, either.

It was going to be an interesting evening.

He gestured toward their table, mumbled a few meaningless words, and then turned and led her in that direction. Ever the gentleman, he pulled out the chair beside the one he had been occupying himself—suddenly, he didn't want to be sitting *across* from Naomi, but much rather preferred to sit *beside* her—then, when she was comfortable, he scooted her in. He resumed his seat, as well, then turned to her and realized he had no idea what to say. Fortunately, he was rescued from having to perform a thought process by the prompt appearance of their server, who inquired as to their drink preferences.

When he glanced over at Naomi, he noted that she appeared to be... Hmmm... Well, the word *flummoxed* came to mind most readily. Because she seemed to have no idea what she was supposed to say, in spite of the straightforwardness of the question. She opened her mouth, as if she intended to order, but no words emerged, as if she couldn't conjure what, exactly, it was that she wanted.

So, valiantly, Sloan stepped in and told their server, "Why don't you bring the lady a champagne cocktail?" There. That should do it. He hadn't met a woman yet who didn't like a champagne cocktail. "And I'll have a JWB and water with a twist."

The young man made a mental note of the order, nodded obsequiously and, like a good little waitron, promptly disappeared.

"Thank you," Naomi said when he was gone. "It's been so long since I've eaten in a nice restaurant, I couldn't remember what I like to have. Usually, when I go somewhere with friends, or even with the girls, I have a margarita, or an ice-cold bottle of Rolling Rock." She smiled, and something inside Sloan grew warm at seeing it. "Somehow, though, that just doesn't feel right in a place like this."

He smiled back, that warm something inside him spreading now to his every extremity. Wow. That felt really, really good. "Then you're long overdue for a night like this," he said. And somehow, as he said it, even he got the impression that he meant something other than dinner in a nice restaurant.

Naomi seemed to think so, too, because she reacted to the statement by blushing becomingly. She didn't seem offended, though, Sloan noted. So maybe the two of them weren't on *exactly* the same wavelength. Still, he could practically feel that little foil packet in his wallet starting to heat and hum against his chest.

"So," he said suddenly, hoping to quell that heating and humming—at least for now, "should I ask you how your alumni reunion is going, or do you just want to come clean and tell me you were lying about that?"

She expelled an anxious, though good-humored, little sound. "Gee, you didn't believe me?" she asked.

"Should I have?" he countered easily.

She eyed him thoughtfully. "I don't suppose it would do any good to insist I was telling the truth, would it?"

He shook his head. "No. It wouldn't. No more good than me telling you that *I* was being honest about *my* engagement."

She gaped comically. "You mean you weren't? How shocking."

He grinned back. "Yes, isn't it?"

She expelled a soft sigh of resignation, then folded her arms in front of her on the table and leaned forward a bit, as if she were about to impart a kernel of great wisdom. "I'm sorry I wasn't honest with you about that," she said softly.

Sloan mirrored her gesture, leaning in, as well, something that brought their foreheads almost to touching. And he took heart in the fact that she didn't pull back even the slightest bit when he crowded into her space that way. He also noticed that she smelled wonderful, of some faint, floral fragrance that was utterly tantalizing.

"Why weren't you honest?" he asked, just as softly.

She shrugged a little halfheartedly. "I don't know. I guess I just didn't think this was a good idea."

"This?" he echoed. "You don't think it's a good idea for us to get together this way and talk strategy for the team and the upcoming tournament? What kind of coach are you anyway?"

She met his gaze levelly, her dark lashes lowering just the slightest bit, something that lent an air of sultriness to her already seductive appearance. "Gosh, color me presumptuous," she said, "but I just can't quite convince myself that the reason we're here tonight is to talk Lady Razorbacks basketball."

He met her gaze unflinchingly, but felt as if he were being pulled down into dangerous depths the longer he looked at her this way. "Isn't that the reason we're here?" he asked.

She hesitated a moment before replying, "Is it?"

"I don't know," he said, still focusing on her eyes. And as he did, he felt the dangerous depths rising higher around him, virtually enveloping him, making him think how he really wouldn't mind so much drowning, as long as Naomi Carmichael was the one who was flooding him. "Why did *you* come tonight?" he asked further, his voice growing quiet as he posed the question.

She hesitated only a moment before countering deftly, "Why did you?"

He smiled. "I asked you first."

She smiled back. "And I asked you second."

Sloan studied her in silence for a moment more, then, when he heard the soft strains of one of his favorite Gershwin tunes coming from the next room, he told her, "I came to dance."

Her smile fell some, and she arched her dark brows in surprise. "You what?"

"Dance," he repeated. He tilted his head toward the

music, to draw her attention to it, too. "They're playing our song," he said with a playful grin.

"Our song?" she repeated. "I didn't realize we had a song."

"We do now," he told her.

She listened intently for a moment. "'A Foggy Day' is our song?" she asked skeptically.

"Well, it's as good as any," he said. "Come on," he cajoled good-naturedly. "Dance with me, Naomi."

She looked faintly panicked in response. "But… but…but…" she began. Unfortunately, no other words except for that one—rather inelegant one—came to her aid.

Unhampered by her unwillingness, Sloan stood with much purpose. But the moment he did, their waiter returned with their drinks, and Naomi seized on their arrival to negate his intention.

"Our drinks," she said with much relief. Before their server had even settled hers on the tabletop, she snatched it up, grasping it as if it were a lifeline someone had just tossed to her over the side of the *Titanic*. "We just got our drinks. We have to have our drinks." She lifted her lifeline, smiled jarringly and said, "Cheers!"

For a moment, Sloan thought about challenging her, insisting that they enjoy one dance before dinner, to whet their appetites, if nothing else. But Naomi looked so distressed, so frightened, by the prospect of even dancing, that he took pity on her.

For now.

Reluctantly, he seated himself again, and reached for his own drink. "Cheers," he concurred, though with a bit less enthusiasm. Before drinking, however, he vowed, "We'll have that dance after dinner, then, shall we?"

And before Naomi had a chance to reply one way or the other, he lifted his drink to his mouth and sipped. Done deal, he decided. They would dance—or something—after dinner.

Chapter Nine

NAOMI COULDN'T REMEMBER the last time she'd had such a wonderful meal, in such a wonderful place, with such a wonderful man. Of course, she decided as she watched Sloan surreptitiously from beneath lowered lashes—which was the way she had watched him throughout the evening—that was probably because she'd never had such a wonderful meal, in such a wonderful place, with such a wonderful man. Not until tonight, anyway.

She sighed with much feeling as she spooned sugar into her coffee and shifted her attention to the remnants of the chocolate torte she and Sloan had shared for dessert. She really, really, really wished she could finish it. She so hated to see chocolate—especially rich, expensive chocolate—go to waste. But she was so full, she simply could not touch another bite. Between the champagne cocktail, the four—count 'em, *four*—dinner courses, the bottle of, very nice, Pinot Grigio and the very generous serving of torte, she feared that if she consumed one more bite of anything, she would, quite simply, explode. As it was, coffee was probably pushing it.

But she was having such a good time, she wanted to prolong it in any way she could. The evening had been utterly magical, the kind of occasion she'd normally only fantasize about. No, actually, that wasn't quite true. Because Naomi couldn't have even fantasized something as nice as this. Her fantasies over the last few years had run more toward things like, oh, say…going fifteen full minutes without having to hear, "Mom! She's looking at me again!" or "Ms. Carmichael, I just don't understand this whole gerund thing," or "Coach, I can't work out today 'cause I got my period." Yeah, fifteen minutes of uninterrupted silence, fifteen minutes totally lacking in turmoil would definitely be a fantasy in Naomi's normal life. This evening, on the other hand…

This evening had transcended fantasy.

Sloan was just so… She bit back another sigh as she turned her gaze upon him again. So handsome. So sweet. So witty. So kind. So successful. So charming. So… So everything. All month long, she'd been insisting to herself that he wasn't her type, that he was too smooth, too polished, too rich, too successful, too… Too everything. He was a prosperous big-city attorney who'd gone this long without having married, so obviously, he enjoyed his successful, metropolitan, single lifestyle. He was the kind of man who, she had gathered from their numerous conversations, was used to a string of high-profile, late-night, social commitments, someone who would never be satisfied with the quiet, predictable, home-and-hearth routine that Naomi so dearly embraced.

Nevertheless, after tonight, and thinking back on the

previous evenings they had spent together, coaching the girls and sharing dinner and indulging in conversation afterward, all Naomi could think was that Sloan Sullivan was really very…

Perfect. He was perfect. Which, of course, meant he wouldn't be around for long. Certainly no longer than his month-long commitment to the Lady Razorbacks. Which ended, she reminded herself, tonight.

"You owe me a dance," he said suddenly.

And just like that, Naomi's warm contentment exploded into hot confusion. "Uh…what?" she said eloquently.

He smiled. "You owe me a dance," he repeated. "The one we didn't get to have before dinner. We can have it now."

"But…but…but…"

"Come on," he coaxed, standing. "It'll shake off the dinner lethargy before we have to go home."

Naomi stopped herself before she allowed herself to think about other ways to shake off the dinner lethargy— talk about fantasizing. Oh, sure, over the last month, she'd had one or two—hundred—instances of fleeting— or prolonged—fantasies of a questionable nature where Sloan Sullivan was concerned. Fantasies in which the two of them were…strategizing. Naked. But she'd assured herself that such fantasies were perfectly normal for a woman her age who had a healthy sex drive—even if that drive hadn't been driven for a looong time. It was just fantasizing, that was all. Perfectly understandable, considering the circumstances and situation. As long as she didn't insert the key—so to speak—in the ignition of her sex drive, she'd be totally and completely—

"You know you want to," Sloan said, jarring her back to reality. And, man, she hated it when that happened.

"Uh," she began again, as eloquently as before. "I, um, I, uh… What?"

"Dance," he said again, grinning indulgently. "With me."

"Oh. I, um, I'm not sure I can dance after that big meal," she hedged.

"Sure you can," he insisted. "That'll just make it even more enjoyable, because we'll have more energy."

Hmm, Naomi thought. For some reason, he seemed to be talking about something other than dancing when he said that…

"C'mon," he wheedled one last time, extending his hand toward her.

And, God help her, Naomi found that she simply could not resist the promise—or the temptation—that lit his blue, blue eyes. So, without questioning why she did it—or speculating upon what the ultimate outcome might be—she, too, stood and placed her hand gingerly in his.

The moment she touched him, a warm, wistful sensation suffused her entire body, wandering indolently through her limbs before pooling heavily deep in the pit of her stomach. Wow, she thought. She would have sworn there wasn't room for anything else in there, but somehow, Sloan just slipped right in.

He had already signed the credit card voucher—laughing her off when she'd insisted on paying for her half of the meal—so Naomi looped her little purse over her wrist and allowed him to lead her into the next room, where a small ensemble was playing something languid and lusty and low. A half-dozen or so couples were swaying languorously on the floor, and, without comment, Sloan led her to the center of them all. Then he drew her into the circle of his arms, pulled her *very* close, and tucked her head comfortably against his shoulder.

Never in her life had Naomi been able to lean her head comfortably against a man's shoulder. At best, she had always looked eye to eye with one. At worst, she'd had to keep a straight face while one nestled his head against her breasts—what little she'd had to nestle against when she was in high school, anyway. She'd always felt like such a great, hulking ogre around the boys at school and at college. Even her ex-husband had only been a scant half-inch taller than she. With Sloan, though, she felt almost petite.

She smiled at the thought. Talk about a fantasy…

But he was a fantasy, she reminded herself. Because in many ways, he really was too good to be true. Men like him simply did not come along very often. And for women like her—women who were busy being moms and going gray and driving minivans and pushing forty—men like him never stayed long.

She tried to remind herself of that again as she gingerly urged her hands over his shoulders and folded her arms loosely together behind his neck. Really. She did try to remind herself of that. But as he looped his arms around her waist and urged her against his long, hard body, Naomi realized she wasn't really listening to herself—mainly because she was too busy nestling herself more resolutely against him. And as she filled her lungs with the spicy, masculine scent of him, as she registered the heat of his body seeping into her own, as she felt the gentle, rhythmic thumping of his heart beating in time with hers, she realized that she wanted to think about the fantasy instead.

And then somehow, as Naomi was nestling herself against Sloan, he was suddenly nestling himself against her, too. As a result, the two of them ended up with their bodies rubbing flush against each other, and it felt almost as if he were wrapping himself around her, enveloping her in all that was him. And Naomi let herself be absorbed willingly, because she'd found herself in a place that was just too sweet to retreat from.

As the music shifted, so did their bodies and their rhythm, fluidly, as if each were completely in tune with the other. Without planning any of it, they moved gracefully as one, and without ever speaking a word, they expressed quite eloquently their wants and needs and desires. Vaguely, Naomi reminded herself that she was going to have to be going home soon. But every time the realization drifted into her head, she halted it by promising herself, *Just one more song…*

But as one song folded into another, each of the other couples began to leave the floor, leave the room. Eventually, even the band took a break, replacing their live music with taped. Naomi and Sloan scarcely noticed, however. They'd left the real world behind some time ago. They didn't need live music or other couples to enjoy what they'd discovered. They simply needed to draw each other close.

For long moments, they danced without speaking, their bodies swaying gently to and fro, to and fro, to…and…fro… One song segued into another. And then another. And then another. And with each passing tune, they grew more comfortable with each other, moving their hands from shoulder to neck to back to arm and around and about again. Bit by bit, Naomi investigated every polite inch of Sloan she was able to reach, her discovery making her fingers itch to explore those other, less accessible, parts of him, as well. He, in turn, explored her body at his leisure, with deceptively harmless little touches that struck flames wherever they fell.

And the more he touched her, the more Naomi wanted to be touched. And with every caress he stole of her body, the next was a little bolder, a little more curious. Tiny fires erupted along her arms and shoulders and back, then wandered inward, imploding in her midsection with an incandescent heat. For the first time in years, she wanted a man—really *wanted* him. And for the first time in years, she allowed herself to think about what it might be like to have him.

And then suddenly, before she realized what was happening, Sloan was kissing her. Or perhaps, she thought hazily, she had kissed him. In either event, it wasn't a soft, uncertain, solicitous kind of kiss she might have expected for a first-time kiss, but a confident, almost commanding kind of kiss that scorched her from her mouth to her belly. It was the kind of kiss that demanded a response. So what else could she do but respond?

And the moment she did… Oh. Sloan swept her away into a tempest. Their bodies, which had swayed so sublimely for… How long was it now? she wondered hazily. She couldn't quite remember…. But their rhythmic to and fro halted abruptly the moment she returned his kiss, with a fierceness and fire to mirror his own. And then the two of them only stood still in the center of the deserted room, hands tangled in hair, fingers bunching in fabric, mouths locked in heated exploration, bodies on fire with need.

Naomi couldn't think, couldn't form a single, coherent idea in her brain. All she could do was feel—the way her blood was humming in her veins, the way her heart was hammering in her chest, the way heat pooled deep in her pelvis, demanding satisfaction. And heavens, how she never wanted those sensations to stop. Heavens, how she wanted to cling to Sloan Sullivan forever.

"Oh, Naomi, I've wanted to do this for so long," he gasped against her jaw before covering her mouth with his again.

Naomi nodded, not sure she trusted her voice, hoping she conveyed to him her total agreement on that score. She had wanted it, too. For so long. Probably from that first night the two of them had spent chatting in her living room. As he'd left that night, she'd felt as if something were missing, as if there were something she wanted, needed, to do before he left. Kiss him, that was what it had been, she realized now. Kiss him and hold him and maybe even—

"I want you, Naomi," he murmured as he pulled away again. He gazed down into her face, his eyes dark with his wanting, his cheeks flushed with his passion. "I know it sounds crazy, but I want to make love to you. I think I've wanted to make love to you since that first night I met you. Over the past month… Watching you… Talking to you… Spending time with you…"

He seemed incapable of finishing a single thought, and Naomi was completely sympathetic. She couldn't begin *or* finish one herself. She let her eyes flutter closed, hoping that by blocking out the sight of his face, she might retrieve her senses and say the things she knew she should say. But by blocking him out visually, she only sensed him more powerfully in other ways—through his heat, his scent, his touch. And she realized that even though she knew what she *should* say, she doubted very much she could get the words past her throat. Because, to be honest, she didn't want to get them past her throat. She wanted to keep them buried inside.

Sloan dipped his head to hers again, but this time, instead of pressing his lips to hers, he dragged his open mouth along the sensitive column of her throat. "I can get us a room," he rasped as he went. But even through his rough passion, Naomi could sense his uncertainty. "It would only take a minute," he hurried on. "Please, Naomi. Let me get us a room."

Oh, God, she thought. Heaven help her, she wanted to say yes. She wanted to say yes very badly.

"It doesn't have to go any farther than you want it to," he promised her before kissing her hastily again. "Just…we need to be alone. At least for a little while. Now. Please."

Before she could think about what she was doing, and before she could second-guess herself, Naomi nodded quickly.

Sloan, evidently as uncertain about his own reaction as she was of hers, didn't wait around long enough for her to change her mind—or for him to change his mind, either. With another quick, passionate kiss, he murmured, "Stay right here. I'll be right back."

And after what seemed like seconds, but must have been much longer, he *was* back. Brandishing a plastic key card.

Naomi swallowed with much difficulty as she looked at it, but when her gaze flew to his, and she saw that he was as confused and consumed as she was, she nodded silently. He took her hand in his, and with surprising calmness, led her to a bank of elevators off the lobby. She watched the illuminated numbers as they rode up in silence, then let him lead her, their fingers still linked, to a room at the end of a hall. He opened the door for her and bid her enter first, and she preceded him in. Her gaze went immediately to the big king-size bed at the center of the room, already turned down, chocolates on the pillow, as if someone had been expecting them.

And then she heard the door click softly closed behind her.

Chapter Ten

WHEN NAOMI TURNED AROUND, she saw Sloan standing with his back pressed against the door, his gaze fixed on her face, as if he couldn't quite believe that they had done what they had done. And he looked at her with some uncertainty, too, as if he couldn't tell for sure if she would stay or she would go.

A thrill of something hot and urgent rocketed through her, and she suddenly felt as if she were a teenager, poised to experience her very first sexual encounter with a boy she'd dreamed about for years. She wasn't sure what to expect, but she couldn't wait to get started. Here was mystery and the unexplored and the promise of something electrifying.

Middle-class, single, working moms didn't do this kind of thing, she told herself. They didn't go to luxury hotel rooms with incredibly handsome, charming men, with nothing but the clothes on their backs. They didn't indulge in passionate, impromptu sexual encounters. They didn't dare.

Did they?

As she argued with herself mentally, Sloan continued to gaze at her in silence, as if he were waiting to take his cue from her. So, banning any and all second thoughts, and without blinking an eye, Naomi tossed her little black beaded purse onto a nearby chair. She was staying, dammit. She did dare.

This was just so exciting, she thought. So thrilling. So fantastic. So unreal. So unlike her. She didn't want to think about the repercussions, didn't want to think about anything at all, except for how she felt in that moment. Good. She felt *good*. Better than she had felt for a long, long time. For so many years, she had been doing for other people, and neglecting herself. For so many years, she had been a mother to her daughters, a teacher to her students, a coach to her team. But she'd never seemed to find the time or opportunity to be just a woman. She'd never done anything for herself.

Tonight, she would do something for herself, she vowed. Tonight, she would be just a woman.

Evidently taking the tossed purse as a positive sign, Sloan reached for his necktie and began to untie it. Naomi watched with fascination—and a dry mouth—as he unlooped the length of silk and tugged it from beneath his collar. He tossed it to the chair beside her purse, then shrugged off his jacket and discarded it, too. Then he went to work on the buttons of his shirt. With each one he freed, he took a step forward, until the garment hung open and he stood mere inches away from Naomi.

Oh, my, she thought. When she saw the rich scattering

of dark hair that spanned his broad chest, her throat parched up like paper. Which was strange, seeing as how other parts of her body grew damp in response to the sight. Before she even realized what she was doing, she lifted her hands and tucked them under his shirt, skimming the garment open wide before nudging it over his shoulders and down his arms. He smiled as she performed the gesture, then cupped his hands over her shoulders and pulled her close, covering her mouth with his. Naomi buried her fingers in the soft hair of his chest, marveling at the density of the muscles she encountered beneath her fingertips.

He growled something soft and contented as she pressed her palms more resolutely into his warm flesh, then he shot a hand behind her, to the zipper of her dress. Naomi, too, murmured a low, feral sound as he dragged the zipper down, down, down, past her waist and over her bottom, until the dress gaped open and she felt the cool kiss of air on her bare back. She moved her arms so that he could skim the garment down over them, then the dress pooled in a heap of black at her feet. She stepped out of her shoes, hooked her thumbs into her panty hose, and pushed those down over her legs, as well. And then she stood before Sloan in nothing but a pair of plain white panties and a perfectly functional white bra.

Mom underwear, she couldn't help thinking. Immediately, she wished she'd had the foresight to don a pair of sexy black lace panties and demicup bra instead. Then she remembered she didn't own a pair of sexy black lace panties or a demicup bra. She only owned plain, functional white cotton. She wasn't the sexy black lace type. At least, she hadn't thought she was. Not until now. Sloan, however, seemed not to notice or care. No, he was much too busy unhooking that functional white bra and tossing it, too, to the floor.

Naomi was amazed that she didn't feel one scrap of self-consciousness in being undressed with this exciting, thrilling, passionate man. Instead, she felt emboldened. Because Sloan had ceased kissing her as he undressed her, and now he gazed at her half-naked body with much reverence.

She knew she was in good shape for a woman her age who had borne four children. But she knew wasn't a teenager anymore, either. And for one brief, terrifying moment, she knew that was as obvious to Sloan as it was to her. Then he smiled, an utterly lascivious, salacious smile, and she realized that maybe, just maybe, he didn't want a teenager. Maybe, just maybe, he wanted a woman instead.

He opened his mouth to say something, but for some reason, Naomi didn't want him to talk. She didn't want to talk, either. She only wanted to touch and feel and experience. So before he could speak, she pressed her lips to his, slipping her tongue into his mouth as she moved her hand to his belt.

But she gasped and pulled back some when she felt his hands on her breasts, his fingers closing over her possessively. He palmed her and squeezed her and rolled his thumbs over the swollen peaks, then he bent and filled his mouth with one of them. First he raked her nipple with the tip of his tongue, and then he laved her with the flat of his tongue, and then he sucked her deeply into his mouth. She gasped again at the wantonness of the sensations that shot through her, tangling her fingers in his dark hair. She wasn't sure if she was trying to stop him from doing what he wanted to do, or ensure that he continued forever and ever. She only knew a heat and a passion and a hunger that fired through her body, through her soul, through every last part of her. And she only knew that she wanted more.

"More," she murmured aloud before she even realized she meant to speak. "Oh, Sloan. More. Please. More."

She wasn't sure, but she thought he chuckled seductively against her damp flesh in response to her command. Then, for a moment, she wondered if he had heard her at all. Because he didn't alter what he was doing, only continued to lave her as he filled his hand with her other breast, capturing the tender peak between thumb and forefinger, rolling the stiff bud gently as he suckled its twin. Clearly, he intended to do this at his own pace. And, lucky for her, his pace seemed to be very, *very* leisurely.

Gradually, though, he began to urge her backward, toward the bed. Naomi went willingly, pulling him along, even though she knew he would follow enthusiastically. When her legs bumped against the mattress, they buckled beneath her, and she landed on her fanny. Sloan didn't even break stride as he joined her on the bed, fairly crawling over her as he pressed her backward onto the mattress. At some point she had freed his belt and unfastened his fly, and she felt him pressing hot and urgent against her thigh as he lay down beside her. Immediately, her hand flew to that part of his anatomy, her fingers dipping into his open trousers to curl around his solid length.

"Oh," he said softly in response to her exploration. "Oh, Naomi. Oh, boy…"

She grinned at her command over him, then urged him over onto his back. He lifted his hips long enough for her to tug down his pants and boxers, then kicked them off completely. But her command of him ended there, because he rolled her onto her back then, insinuating one strong thigh between her legs. The pressure of him there was an exquisite torture, and, instinctively, she thrust her hips upward. The rubbing of their bodies struck a spark of heat against that most sensitive part of her, and she moaned softly at the keen pleasure the gesture brought with it. Then she lowered her hips to the bed again, an action that generated yet another scintillating friction of heat, one that shot an erotic shudder of delight coursing through her. Again and again, Naomi bucked against his thigh, her body growing warm and fluid with every movement she made, until she finally groaned aloud her frustration at being unable to satisfy herself that way.

Sloan seemed to understand her distress, because she suddenly felt his hand at the waistband of her panties, shoving them down over her hips and legs without ceremony. And then his hand was there, where his thigh had been before, his fingers moving deliberately, unhurried, between the damp folds of her sensitive flesh. She cried out at the invasion, but thrust her body upward again, and he buried a finger deep inside her. She bucked again, and he inserted two. Again, and he penetrated her with three.

Over and over he pleasured her that way, widening his fingers, driving them deeper, until Naomi cried out her ecstasy, and her physical response flowed hotly over his hand. For a moment, she could only lie there, reveling in the ripples of delight that echoed through her. Never in her life had she experienced such an exquisite pleasure. Never before had she been taken to such heights. Before she returned to earth entirely, however, Sloan lifted her from the mattress and, seating himself on the edge of the mattress, he straddled her over his lap.

Still feeling drugged and dazed by her release, Naomi

lifted her hands instinctively to his shoulders, curling her fingers into his hot, silky flesh. Instinctively, she knew she would have to hold on tight for this ride. When she glanced down between their bodies, she saw that, at some point, Sloan had sheathed his heavy, stiff shaft in a condom. Vaguely, she wondered if she should be concerned about his preparedness, as if he'd been planning what she told herself she'd never seen coming. Then he was situating her over his long member, his hands gripping her hips firmly as he guided her down onto his teeming length.

And then he was inside her—*deep* inside her—penetrating her so fully, so completely, she halfway feared he would split her in two. Soon, though, Naomi ceased to think at all. Because she realized then that, on the contrary, instead of being split in two, she was forged into one—with Sloan. Throwing back her head, she cupped her hands over his shoulders, digging her knees into the mattress and spreading herself wider, so that he could fill her entirely.

And he did fill her entirely. So entirely, she knew in that moment that she would never feel empty again. As he buried himself inside her as deeply as he could, she wove her fingers through his silky hair and pulled him close. He nuzzled her breasts as he drew closer, then opened his mouth over one and drew her inside again. Now she was in him, and he was in her, she thought. There was no way the two of them would ever be separate again after this.

She wasn't sure how long they coupled that way, only knew that with every motion of their bodies, she gave more of herself to Sloan, and took more of him for herself. Eventually, he changed their positions again, so that she lay on her back on the bed with him kneeling before her, circling her ankles with strong fingers as he opened her legs wider, lifted her hips from the bed as he hooked her ankles behind his neck. And then, just when she thought she was about to come apart, he changed their positions again, and she was bent over on the bed, and he was behind her, his hands on her waist as he thrust himself into her again and again and again. Finally, though, they lay side by side, facing each other, and as Sloan kissed her again, he draped her thigh over his, cupped his hands over her bottom, and drove himself into her. Deep.

Gradually, his pace increased, and Naomi met every plunge and every lunge. And then, with one final forward thrust, his body went absolutely still, and he roared his completion, spilled his fulfillment. Naomi was no more able to keep her own joy inside, and she, too, cried out in both anguish and ecstasy.

Then he moved their bodies again, so that she was on her back once more. He kissed her hungrily, ravenously, thoroughly, almost as if this would be the last time he allowed himself the pleasure to do so. She returned his kiss with equal fire, equal furor, until he finally broke the contact. For a moment they only gazed into each others' eyes, gasping for breath, groping for coherent thought, both of them more than a little dazed by what had happened.

Then Sloan smiled a small smile and, very softly, he said, "I'll be right back."

And then Naomi was alone in bed, wondering where he had gone. The condom, she recalled immediately. He'd had to dispose of that. That modern safety measure that had prevented the mingling of their physical essences and protected them from both unwanted pregnancy and sexually transmitted dangers.

Would that it had prevented the mingling of their emotional essences, too, she couldn't help thinking. Would that it could protect her, at least, from other, more insidious dangers, too.

Because now, as the warm rosy afterglow of their lovemaking turned into a crisp, stark light of reality, Naomi realized the enormity of what she had just done. She had just made love with a man who had entered her life only temporarily. She, a woman of nearly forty, a woman with four daughters, a woman who had prided herself on being sane and solid, had just done something completely stupid. She, a woman who, until now had only had one lover in her entire life, had just made love with a man who, she was quite certain, had taken infinitely more lovers than that. A man who, she was likewise certain, would have no idea of the significance she attached to what they had just done. A man who did this sort of thing as a pastime. A man who'd had a condom at the ready, and no second thoughts.

Which was just as well, Naomi decided. Because she was having more than enough second thoughts for both of them.

It never stops being a big deal, Evy. It is always a big deal.

The words she had spoken to her daughter only a few short hours ago came back to haunt her like a bad dream, and only then did Naomi realize her fatal mistake. Sex *was* a big deal. To her, at least. It had always been a big deal. That was why she had been a virgin when she'd met the man she ultimately married. And it was why she hadn't been with anyone since her husband had left. So why, suddenly, had she abandoned her conviction and done something like this?

Naomi decided immediately that she didn't want to explore the answer to that question. Not here. Not now. Not until she was alone someplace where she could make sense of everything that had happened tonight. Of everything that had happened over the last month. Because she was fairly certain that once she did make sense of it—if indeed such a thing were even possible—she wasn't going to like what she discovered.

As quickly as she could, she located her discarded clothing and got dressed. She finger-combed her hair, knowing the gesture was futile. She knew she must look exactly like what she was—a woman who had just engaged in a night of hot, unbridled—if casual—sex. Except that it hadn't been a whole night. And it certainly hadn't been casual. Not to Naomi, anyway.

Alone. She needed to be alone right now. Alone and far away from this place where she had just made a gross error in judgment. Perhaps the grossest error—in more ways than one—that she had ever made in her life. Sloan was still in the bathroom, even though he'd had plenty of time to take care of what he'd needed to take care of, and she could only conclude that he hadn't yet emerged because he had no more idea of how to react to what had just happened than she did. He probably wanted to be alone, too, she couldn't help thinking. Alone and far away.

But, hey, he was the one who had gotten the room, so she should be the one to get lost, right? Right. It would be the polite thing to do, right? Right. At least, Naomi thought that would be the polite thing to do. She had no idea how one was supposed to act after having casual sex. She'd never had casual sex before. Not even tonight. Intuitively, though, she suspected that leaving was the way to go here. Because the longer she lingered, the more in danger she became of doing something really stupid. Like crying, maybe. Or worse, like asking Sloan to make love to her again.

Quickly, she snagged her purse and ran a hand through her hair again. Part of her screamed at her that she should stay and see this thing through, that running away would only compound the mistake she had already made. But another part of her—the scared part—told her to flee. And as much as Naomi hated being scared, as much as she told herself to be strong, she couldn't help herself. She didn't know what to do. And in times of distress, she thought, there was just one foolproof method of survival.

Run away.

So Naomi did.

WITH NO SMALL PANIC COURSING through him, Sloan gripped the sink in the hotel bathroom, gazed at the man in the mirror, and wondered who the hell the interloper was. He didn't recognize himself. How could he? He'd just done something totally out of character, something he'd sworn to himself he would never do. He'd just lost control with a woman. Completely and utterly lost control. He'd become so intoxicated with wanting her, needing her, *having* her, that he'd ceased to think, had only acted, and oh… What those actions had made him feel. Feel for the woman with whom he'd been acting. And she wasn't just any woman. No, Naomi was a *nice* woman. A nice woman who deserved infinitely better than a casual one-night stand with a man who lost control.

But had it been casual? Sloan asked himself. And had it only been for one night? It sure hadn't felt casual. It had felt… Incredible. Never in his life had he enjoyed an experience like the one he's just shared with Naomi. From the moment she had stepped into his arms on the dance floor, he'd felt as if the two of them had wandered into some kind of alternate reality. And then, when he'd kissed her—or had she kissed him? he wondered; he couldn't really recall now—when he'd tasted her sweetness and felt her warmth suffusing with his own, he'd simply been swept away.

He grinned wryly at the idea that he, Sloan Sullivan, pragmatic workaholic and confirmed bachelor, could be *swept away* by anything—especially a woman. Especially a woman who had four children, and who lived in a white frame house, and who drove a minivan. Especially a woman who could bring home the bacon and fry it up in the pan. Then again, he thought further, recalling the hot and heavy sensations that had plagued him for the last four weeks, she was also a woman who'd never let him forget he was a man. 'Cause she was most definitely a wo-man, w-o-m-a-n.

Good God, he thought. She'd even moved him to song.

He gazed at his reflection in the mirror again, marveling at how he even seemed to have changed physically since the last time he looked at himself. Maybe it was just good lighting, but his eyes seemed brighter all of a sudden, and the lines bracketing his mouth seemed to have eased. Even his skin appeared to be glowing. Somehow, making love to Naomi made him look and feel as if he had shaved years off of his life. He certainly hadn't felt this good, this vital, this *alive*, in a long, long time.

God, what was he supposed to do now? Unfortunately, no answer was forthcoming from the man in the mirror. Because Sloan had no idea what to do now.

But there was a woman waiting for him on the other side of that door, he reminded himself, and she was most assuredly expecting some kind of a response. Sloan just wished he had a response to give her. One that made sense, anyway. Because all he knew at the moment was that he wanted

Naomi again. Badly. And he suspected it was a reaction that wouldn't be subsiding anytime soon. Because right now, in this moment, he couldn't imagine a time in his life when he would stop wanting her. And that pretty much scared the hell out of him.

Afterglow, he told himself quickly. What he was feeling now was simply the result of that uncertain, unreal afterglow that came in the moments after making love. *Of course* he was going to be feeling this way after incredible sex. *Of course* he was going to want to do it again. Lots of times. For the rest of his life. After a day or two, such feelings would subside. After a day or two, his desires and needs would go away. After a day or two, his hunger for Naomi would be nonexistent. Oh, sure, he'd miss her now that their…association…had come to an end. But in a day or two, he'd be fine. Of course, that didn't help him with the right now….

He inhaled a deep breath and told himself to stop being ridiculous. He'd had lots of afterglows to deal with over the years. There had been lots of women with whom he'd dealt—for lack of a better word—after making love. In many ways, Naomi was no different from any of them. Even if, he couldn't help thinking further, she was totally different from all of them.

He shook the thought off and opened the bathroom door, then strode through it as casually as he could manage. Which was no easy feat, seeing as how he was stark naked and utterly confused. But he realized even before looking around that the room was empty. Empty of a lot more than Naomi, too.

But mostly, he noticed that she was gone. Almost as if she'd never been there at all. And she was probably gone in a lot more ways than one, he couldn't help thinking further. And somehow, the realization of that came as no surprise to him at all. And for some reason, too, it settled deep in the pit of his stomach, like a cold, congealed lump of clay, a sensation, he suspected, that wasn't going to go away anytime soon.

Great, he thought. This was just great. What was he supposed to do now?

Chapter Eleven

THE GYMNASIUM OF East Central High School in suburban Atlanta was a complete one-eighty from the Jackson High gym to which Naomi and the Lady Razorbacks were so accustomed. This school clearly didn't suffer from underfunding, as evidenced by the bright lights—not a single one of which was broken or burnt out—splashing illumination down over vivid red bleachers that looked as if they'd just been purchased, and a state-of-the-art scoreboard that was flashing in time to the Jackson High School pep band's rendition of "Rock Around the Clock."

And the Razorbacks' opposing team, the Lady Falcons of Dorman High School of Augusta, appeared to be no less well equipped than the school hosting the state finals. The Falcons sported crisp-looking red-and-gold uniforms that could very well have been designed by a professional, a sharp contrast to the Razorbacks' tattered and faded blue-and-white jerseys and shorts.

The Falcons seemed to be better equipped with school spirit, too, Naomi couldn't help noticing. The bleachers were packed with students and parents and sports writers, the vast majority of whom waved red-and-gold banners for Dorman High. Only a few splashes of blue and white here and there offered any indication that the Lady Razorbacks of Jackson High School weren't—quite—alone, even though their school was much closer to Atlanta than Dorman was. All Naomi could hope was that her Razorbacks would outdo the Falcons in terms of strategy, scrappiness and heart.

Then again, she already knew those superior qualities were pretty much givens. In two weeks' time, the Jackson High team, with the help of Naomi and their returning assistant coach, Lou Melton, had outstrategized, outscrapped and outhearted every school they'd played, until, finally, they had made it to this, the state championship game. If they could just maintain their momentum and their determination—and Naomi was certain that they could—then they'd be taking home the state trophy to Jackson High School in Wisteria for the first time in the town's history.

Naomi braved another glance into the stands, where one particular splash of blue and white had alerted her earlier to the presence of what might very well be the Lady Razorbacks' number one fan. Sloan Sullivan had attended each of the tournament games as a spectator, had shouted louder and longer than even most of the parents had. He'd always managed to work his way down to the bench at some point during the game, to say hello to the girls and offer some unofficial coaching. He'd greeted Naomi with a formal nod or a softly uttered "Hello" each time, but he hadn't approached her to talk. Which was just as well, she always told herself on those occasions. Because she had no idea what to say to him.

There had been times over the last two weeks when she'd assured herself she had only dreamed—or fantasized—the evening she'd spent with him here in Atlanta before. Invariably, though, she'd recall with too much clarity the way they had been when they were together, the ways he had touched her, the ways he had kissed her, the ways he had set her entire body on fire. And she would be forced to remember that what the two of them had done together that night had been all too real. And all too extraordinary. And all too temporary. And much too big a mistake for her to ever repeat it again.

Her face flamed now just to remember that night. The things they'd done to and with each other, the errant, erotic words he'd whispered in her ear at the height of their passion, the way he'd made her feel...

She squeezed her eyes shut tight and spun back around again, before Sloan caught her looking at him. He hadn't called her once since that night. Of course, she reminded herself, she hadn't called him, either. And she was the one who had run out on him that night, she reminded herself further. There was no reason for Sloan to think she really wanted to have any further contact with him. Maybe he was as confused and embarrassed by what had happened as she was. Maybe he found it as difficult to approach her as she found it to approach him.

In which case, both of them were doubtless thinking the same thing: that what had happened was a mistake and an aberration, something that should never, ever have happened in the first place, something that should never, ever happen again.

Naomi told herself she should be relieved that they were on the same wavelength. She told herself she should be happy that they'd come to an unspoken agreement, because it prevented them from having to experience any further awkwardness. So why didn't she feel happy? Why wasn't she relieved? Why, even two weeks after the fact, did she still want Sloan every bit as much as she had wanted him that night? More, even? Worse, why did she miss even more than making love to him those quiet evenings the two of them had spent alone just talking?

Because as breathtaking and incredible as sex with him had been, those nights spent talking over coffee had commanded just as many of her wistful memories and melancholy regrets over the last two weeks. Since Sloan had departed from her life, Naomi's house felt so empty now somehow. Funny, that, seeing as how it had always felt so crowded before.

Or maybe it wasn't so funny, after all, she thought further. Because she knew that the girls, too, felt Sloan's absence rather keenly. Sophie, especially, asked when he would be coming to visit them again. And Naomi, heaven help her, hadn't had any idea what to tell her youngest daughter. Nor had she known what to say to her oldest daughters, even though she suspected that Evy, at least, understood the situation pretty well. Oh, her oldest daughter might not know *exactly* how far things had gone between Naomi and Sloan that night, but Evy was a big girl. She'd known Naomi and Sloan were attracted to each other, had witnessed her mother's apprehension and excitement before going out with him that night. She hadn't pressed Naomi for details when she'd come home so late, but she knew something was up. And Naomi hadn't had any more idea what to tell Evy than she had known what to tell Sophie about why Sloan had so abruptly severed personal ties to all of them.

For now, though, she pushed all those errant thoughts of Sloan away. She had a team to coach, a team that was going to take home a championship trophy tonight. After that…

Well, Naomi wouldn't think about that right now, either. Another nice thing about being in the tournament was that it had given her something to focus on besides Sloan. But once this game was over, and she no longer had game plans and practices on the brain, she knew her mind was going to fill with thoughts of him.

Later, she told herself again. She'd think about all that later. Right now, she—and her girls—had a game to win.

AFTER MUCH SWEATING, shouting, and nail biting—and after two agonizing overtimes—the Lady Razorbacks squeaked by the Lady Falcons, thanks to Evy's three-pointer in the last two seconds of the game. Like the rest of the team, Naomi was hoarse from yelling and cheering by then, but she didn't care. They'd all worked so hard for so long, and now—finally—they could celebrate. They were the best in the state. And they had a big ol' trophy to prove it.

She was so caught up in the celebration, in fact, that she didn't even notice the visitor to the locker room until Evy walked up with him in tow.

"Hey, Mom, look who I found," she said as she tapped her mother on the shoulder.

Naomi spun around to find her daughter standing beside a very reluctant-looking Sloan, and, just like that, a hot flame ignited in her belly and spread a rapid wildfire throughout her entire system. Although she'd seen him from a distance often enough over the last couple of weeks, she wasn't prepared now for this up close version. Especially since he didn't appear to be either of the Sloans she had come to know and—dare she admit it?—love. Neither sweats nor business suit adorned his form right now. Instead, he wore lovingly faded blue jeans and a tight, long-sleeved, navy polo that strained over his broad chest and shoulders and doubled the intensity of his blue velvet eyes.

Naomi opened her mouth to say something—though heaven only knew what, because her brain felt as empty as a pocket—when Evy saved her the trouble. Sort of.

"I made him promise to join us for the victory celebration," she said. "He hasn't said yes yet, but maybe if you asked him, Mom, coach to coach, I mean…"

She smiled as she let her voice trail off over that last part, as if she knew perfectly well that coaching had nothing to do with it, then she nudged Sloan discreetly forward. And then, pretending she saw something over Naomi's shoulder, she shouted at one of her teammates and abandoned them both.

At first, Naomi couldn't say anything, because she was much too busy reveling in the joy of just being close to Sloan again, at feeling giddy and light-headed with his simple nearness. His eyes really were as blue as she'd recalled them being, she noted. And he really was as tall and as broad as she had remembered. She had thought maybe she was embellishing him in her memories, making him more of a man than he actually was. Now, however, she saw he was every inch the man she had thought him. And then some. And she was nearly overcome by having him close enough to touch again. She just wished she had the nerve to reach out and touch him.

"Of course you should join us for the victory celebration," she finally managed to say, trying not to stammer, doing her best not to blush, but unable to halt the way her heart hammered hard in her chest. Heavens, just looking at him made her dizzy. "You're part of this team, too," she added.

"Not really," he denied good-naturedly. "I was only around for a month."

"Hey, you made quite an impression during that month," she said. "You made a huge difference during that month." Too late, she realized how he might misconstrue the statements. Then again, she thought, maybe, deep down, she hadn't been thinking about the team when she'd uttered them.

His dark brows arched up slightly at her comment, and he offered her a halfhearted smile. "Did I?" he asked.

She hesitated only a moment, then nodded. "Yeah. You did."

He eyed her thoughtfully in return, then, softly, he said, "With the team, you mean."

Naomi hesitated once more, then thought, what the hell? She might as well come clean. "Yeah, with them, too, I guess."

His smiled kicked up a few notches. "I wanted to call you," he said, his voice even softer now. "After that last night, when we…" He gazed past her at the celebrating girls, and even though the members of the team clearly had their minds on something other than their coach and her former, temporary, assistant, he dropped his voice a little more. "After that night, I couldn't stop thinking about you. About how much I wanted to make love to you again. About how much I just wanted to see you, spend time with you." He took a step closer, started to reach for her, then checked himself and dropped his hand back to his side. "I've missed you, Naomi. So much. For the last couple of weeks, I've felt like a part of me has been gone."

Naomi's heart pounded harder with every word he spoke, rushing blood through her veins at a frenzied pace. She told herself not to hope, not to put too much into what he was saying. But when she looked into his eyes and saw the flicker of heat burning there, she knew—she *knew*—his feelings mirrored her own.

"Why didn't you call me?" she asked him.

"Why didn't you call me?" he countered.

She closed her eyes. "If you knew how many times I wanted to…" But she couldn't quite make herself finish the statement.

"Why did you leave that night?" he asked her.

She opened her eyes again, then shook her head slowly. "I panicked. I didn't know what to do. I'd never done anything like that before with anyone, Sloan. And I realized you probably did stuff like that all the time, and—"

"I'd never done anything like that, either, Naomi," he assured her fiercely. "That was most definitely a first for me."

She grinned. "You didn't seem like a virgin to me."

"You know what I mean."

"But you're still a lot more experienced than me," she pointed out.

"Am I?"

"I've only been with one man besides you," she confessed.

"And I've *never* been with a woman like you," he assured her. "Never."

She swallowed hard at that. "Then why didn't you call me?" she asked again.

He expelled a soft, frustrated sound. "I wanted to. So badly. But I figured you had too many other things to worry about right now," he said. "I didn't want to distract you from the tournament by making you wade through... stuff...with me."

"Are you kidding?" she replied, feeling a bit bolder now after all of his revelations. "You've been nothing but a distraction to me since the day I met you."

He grinned hopefully. "You mean you won the championship in spite of me?" he asked.

She shook her head. "No. Not in spite of you. We couldn't have made it without you. It's amazing the way you showed up right when we needed you the most."

"We?" he echoed.

"Me," she corrected herself. "You showed up right when *I* needed you most. And *I* couldn't have made it without you." She inhaled a deep, fortifying breath and decided to go for broke. "I still don't think I can make it without you. I know I don't *want* to."

He considered her with much speculation for a moment, then asked, "About this victory celebration...?"

"Ah, yeah," Naomi said. "Lou and I promised the girls we'd go for pizza or burgers or whatever they wanted before we take the bus back to Wisteria tonight."

Sloan nodded thoughtfully. "You're going back to Wisteria tonight, too?" he asked.

"Well, originally, I had planned to, yeah."

"I couldn't maybe talk you into, oh...staying the night?"

Naomi smiled, then turned to look over her shoulder at Evy, who was currently enjoying a traditional, after-championship baptism. "Well, gee, I *guess* I could depend on my oldest to take care of things at home for a night. She's normally very responsible. When she's *not* getting a Gatorade shower, I mean."

"My place?" Sloan said when she turned back around to gaze at him again. "It's not quite as homey as yours, but—" he smiled devilishly "—it's closer."

Naomi smiled back, feeling every bit as devilish as he looked. "You know, maybe that's something we can rectify," she told him.

He looked faintly puzzled. "What do you mean?"

"I mean maybe we can meet halfway on that home thing eventually. Surely we could find *some*thing between Atlanta and Wisteria that has some promise."

His smile grew wider by a mile. "Maybe we can meet halfway," he agreed. "Eventually. So what do you say, Naomi? Tonight? Your place or mine?"

She felt her own smile growing wider as she said, "I have an even better idea. How about *our* place instead?"

AS AFTERGLOWS WENT, Sloan thought, this was one of his better ones. He pulled Naomi closer and snuggled her damp, warm, naked body against his, tugging the sheet up over them in the king-size bed in the room they had taken at the San Moritz Hotel. *Our place*, he remembered her calling it only a few hours ago. He liked the sound of that. Maybe they should make it a tradition to come here every year, on their wedding anniversary or something, to commemorate the first time they—

He halted himself before finishing the thought. *Every year?* he asked himself. *On their* wedding *anniversary?*

He waited for a shudder of terror to rock him at the very thought of being married to someone. And waited. And waited. And waited. Strangely, though, there was no shudder of terror that even trickled through him. No, all he felt was a warm, wistful sensation of being exactly where he belonged wandering through him instead. The thought of being married to Naomi, instead of horrifying him, only made him feel wonderfully complete.

"Hey, Naomi," he said absently, letting his fingertips glide slowly over her upper arm and shoulder, then back again.

"Hmmm?" she murmured, nestling her head beneath his chin, draping her thigh over his.

"I've been thinking," he continued.

"Thinking?" she echoed softly. "How could you think during that? My brains were totally scrambled."

He smiled. Good. That was what a man liked to hear after making love to a special woman. And Naomi, he had learned over the last several weeks, was most assuredly special. Among other things.

"I wasn't thinking during *that*," he told her. "You had me way too worked up to do anything as mundane as think."

"Good," she murmured. "That's what a woman likes to hear after making love to a special man."

Sloan narrowed his eyes suspiciously as he gazed down at the dark head snuggling against his chest. Jeez, they weren't even married yet, and already she was reading his mind.

"So what were you thinking about?" she asked him, her voice a quiet purr and warm caress against his throat.

"I was thinking that, you know, the two of us made a good team when we were coaching," he said.

"Well, we *are* responsible for the current state champs," she reminded him unnecessarily.

He nodded. "Yeah, and it made me wonder if we'd be as good doing other things together."

She turned her head to look up at him then, her smile wicked, wanton and wild.

"I mean at something besides what we just did together," he qualified.

She batted her eyelashes at him. "Oh."

"Though, mind you, we are awfully good at that, too," he agreed. "But I had something else in mind. Another game we might play together that we'd be good at."

"What's that?" she asked.

"House," he told her. "I thought me might be good at playing house."

Her dark brows furrowed downward in confusion. "House?" she repeated. "But…I never even played house when I was a little girl. Why would you want to—"

"Okay, then we won't play it," he said. "We'll just do it."

Now her dark brows arched upward in surprise. "What do you mean?"

"I mean I want to live with you, Naomi. With you and your daughters. I want us all to be together. As a family. Because I love you. All of you." When she only continued to gaze at him in massive befuddlement, he hastily added, "As long as that's what you want, too, I mean."

"You want us all to live together?" she said. "You love us? All of us?"

He nodded, feeling nervous for the first time since the two of them had started talking again. Surely this didn't come as a surprise to her, he thought. Surely she saw this coming. Then again, a few hours ago, he'd been worried he would never speak to her again, and she hadn't looked any too certain about the future, herself.

"Gee, I don't know, Sloan," she said gravely. "I don't think I could live with a man unless I was married to him." She punctuated the remark with a dazzling smile, and he knew then that she was only stringing him along. "Of course, seeing as how I love you, too, maybe that won't be a problem?"

"Fine," he said. "Then I'll marry you. I need to make an honest woman out of you, anyway." He hesitated only a moment before reminding her, "We did rather neglect something very important this evening, after all."

She studied him in confusion for a moment, then, suddenly, her eyes widened in obvious concern. "A condom," she said. "We didn't use one."

"No, we didn't," he confirmed. "You, my darling wife-to-be, could, as we speak, also be a mother-to-be."

She shook her head quickly. "Oh, no. No, no, no, no, no."

He smiled and nodded. "Oh, yes. Yes, yes, yes, yes, yes."

She nibbled her lower lip anxiously. "Well, Sophie *did* ask Santa for a baby brother last Christmas...."

Sloan grinned again. "Would she be just as happy with a baby sister?"

"Another girl?" Naomi asked. "Are you serious? Could you handle living in a house with that much estrogen?"

"Are you kidding?" he replied, mimicking her shocked tone. "When Evy and Katie can kick my butt at roundball and Sophie has a train setup like the one I always wanted when I was a kid? Piece of cake."

Naomi smiled, too, then snuggled closer still to Sloan. "As long as you don't mind the family plan, Mr. Sullivan, then yes, I think we could play house very nicely together."

Sloan sighed heavily and with much contentment, then scooted both their bodies down deeper onto the bed. "Then let's get started," he told her. "You be the mommy, and I'll be the daddy. Naomi and Sloan and their daughters." He grinned as he heard her laughter bubble up, then gathered her as close as he could. "You know," he said softly, "I just don't think it can get any better than that.

* * * * *

Turn the page for a preview of
Bestselling author

Elizabeth Bevarly's

first title for HQN Books

YOU'VE GOT MALE

Available this October at your favorite book outlet.

Chapter One

AVERY NESBITT WAS IN LOVE. Madly, passionately, fabulously in love. She was besotted. She was bedazzled. She was befuddled. She was in love like she'd never been in love before.

And it was with the sort of man she would have thought simply could not exist outside of dreams. He was smart and witty. He was creative and articulate. He was handsome and sexy. He always said what she needed to hear, right when she needed to hear it. He knew her backward and forward, just as she knew him inside and out-. And he loved her exactly the way she was. That, more than anything else, had sealed her love for him and ensured it would last forever. Andrew Paddington just made Avery feel as if she was walking on clouds, as if all was harmonious in the universe, as if nothing in her life would ever go wrong again. He was just perfect in every way.

The bastard.

Theirs had been a whirlwind courtship, one that had

come at Avery out of nowhere, caught her completely unaware, and swept her into a fantasy worthy of an epic romance. Andrew had become entangled in her thoughts and
her dreams, in her consciousness and her subconsciousness,
in her ego and her emotions. He packed her days with delight and her nights with pleasure, filled her with joy until
she was buoyant and giddy. And that was no small feat for
a woman who was normally pragmatic, cynical, and down-
to-earth. And even though Avery had only met him a
month ago, she'd decided immediately after that first encounter that their relationship must have been destiny. It
had been pre-ordained. It was simply Meant To Be.

Bastard.

What difference did it make if they'd never actually met
in person? Physical trappings weren't what love was about.
Love was a meeting of minds, a melding of souls, a blend-
ing of hearts. Besides, they'd exchanged photos, and the
ones he'd sent to her depicted him as a sandy-haired twenty-
something with the eyes of a poet, the mouth of a trouba-
dour, the hands of an artist, and truly phenomenal pecs. He
was an utter, unmitigated masterpiece.

Bastard, bastard, bastard.

Who cared if they'd never actually spoken to each other?
Vocal avowals of devotion were as nebulous and incon-
stant as the wind. Avery had Andrew's love for her in writing. In the loveliest prose she'd ever read, words—
feelings—wrought so tenderly, they would move even the
vilest of despots to tears. After only four weeks with him,
she had a huge file filled with his e-mails to her, and she'd
logged every chat room exchange they'd shared in a special
folder titled "Snookypie." For the exchanges that had been
especially poignant, she'd printed them up on special paper,

and on those nights when she was feeling dreamy and lovey-dovey about Andrew—and couldn't find him on-line for one reason or another—she lit candles and opened a bottle of wine, then took the notes out to read and caress them, and pretend he was right there in her Central Park West condo with her.

Bastard squared.

But now, the unthinkable was happening. Andrew was cheating on her with another woman. And Avery was finding out about it just like women did on those bad Lifetime movies. She'd walked in on him and found him in bed with another woman.

Well, okay, figuratively speaking. What she'd actually done was go on-line to look for him and found him blabbing away with some cheap bit of cyberfluff. And it was in, of all places, a "Survivor: Mall of America" chat room. This after Andrew had assured her that he loathed and detested popular culture as much as Avery did. But what really toasted her melbas was that the cyberfluff he was chatting with, who went by the screen name of—she'd had to bite back her nausea when she saw it—Tinky Belle, was clearly an idiot. But Andrew was agreeing with her that the music of Clay Aiken could, if people would just open their eyes and ears and hearts to it, bring peace and harmony to the entire planet.

Bastard *cubed*.

Unable to believe her eyes, Avery felt around until she located the chair in front of her desk and clumsily pulled it out. Then she nearly missed the surface of her desk entirely when she went to set her bowl of Cajun popcorn and the bottle of Wild Cherry Pepsi on top of it. She tugged at her electric blue pajama pants spattered with images of French landmarks and numbly sat down, adjusting the oversized purple sweatshirt boasting Wellesley College as she did. Then she wiggled her toes in her fuzzy pink slippers to warm them—her blood flow seemed to have stopped entirely— adjusted her little black-framed glasses on the bridge of her nose, pushed one of two long, thick black braids over her shoulder, and studied the screen more closely.

Maybe she was wrong, she told herself as she watched the rapid-fire exchange scroll by. She shouldn't jump to conclusions. Surely Andrew wasn't the only guy out there in cyberspace who used the handle Mad2Live. It was a phrase from *On the Road*, after all. And there were probably lots of Kerouac fans on-line. Andrew loved Avery. He'd told her so. He wouldn't cheat on her like this. Especially not with some brainless ninny who said things like, "ur 2 kewl mad."

Please, people! she wanted to shout at the screen whenever she saw message board shorthand. *Speak English! Or Spanish! Or French! Or German! Or some legitimate language that indicates you're at least halfway literate! And capitalize where necessary! And for God's sake, punctuate!*

Even though she was a computer geek in the most extreme sense of the word, Avery couldn't bring herself to type in anything other than the language she'd learned growing up in the Hamptons. Tony private schools could mess with you in a lot of ways, she knew, but at least they taught you to be well-spoken. That shouldn't change just because your language of choice was cyberspeak.

She watched Mad2Live and Tinky Belle—gag—swap warm fuzzies for as long as she could stomach it, and ultimately decided there was no way that this Mad2Live could be Andrew. Andrew would never, ever, concede that the

"Survivor" series was, as Tinky Belle claimed, "qualty educatnl programing u cn wach w/ the hole famly."

Oh, yes, Avery thought. *It was definitely mus c tv.*

She was about to leave the chat room to visit another—she was, after all, supposed to be working tonight—when Mad2Live posted something that made her fingers convulse on the mouse: "You, Tinky Belle, are a dazzling blossom of hope burgeoning at the center of an unforgiving cultural wasteland."

Acid heat splashed through Avery's belly when she read that. Because those were the exact words Andrew had used to describe her that first night they met in a Henry James chat room. Except for the Tinky Belle part, since Avery's screen name—at least, that night—had been Daisy Miller. There was no way there could be two Mad2Lives on the Internet flirting with women by calling them dazzling blossoms of hope who burgeoned in cultural wastelands. That was Andrew—her Andrew—through and through.

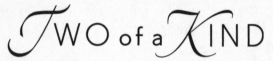

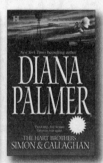
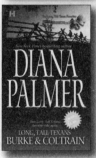

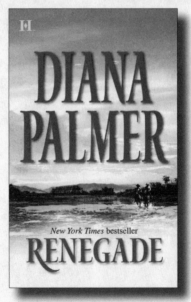

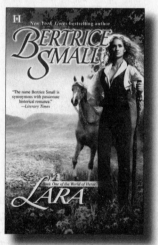

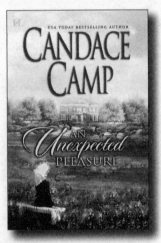